STRANDS OF EXISTENCE 4: CLOUDLESS HORIZON

Aino Lahteva

To the ones that are a little different.

CONTENTS

I

Rime's presence felt like a field of black ice on the other side as I leaned on the door of my room in the White Needle. After my arrival home, I sensed him sitting on the last step of the stairway as he had been every day for all the days I had been gone. The nexus, now partly intertwined in my form, had told me of Rime's visits, of his sorrow for finding an empty room for weeks, of his regret for keeping me in the dark. Was the remorse enough to warrant forgiveness?

This silence could turn into an argument the moment he realized I had returned, or maybe he would embrace me, and all would be as it had been for a moment. Neither option felt comfortable or likely.

The door handle was heavy and unyielding, then it clicked, and the door opened. Rime stood up and turned to face me so slowly that I wondered whether he wanted to see me or feared to see me. He looked emotionless, apart from the first moment when his countenance relaxed and his eyes hinted of a smile that could have been. Then he averted his gaze as if he decided what to do about us at that very moment.

"Good. You have returned. I was worried," he stated, only quickly looking me in the eyes while taking a more official-looking pose.

"I'm sorry I left as I did. It was just too much. I needed to breathe."

"No need. Everything is fine," Rime replied with a false light, forced tone. "We will continue our work for the city and the world when you are ready. I will be in my office once you have need of me." He turned away.

"Will you not chastise me?" I asked. "You should. I was reckless and selfish, leaving all of you behind without a word. A person of my position should never do that."

"If I admonish you for being selfish and leaving me behind, what should I expect from you after what I did? Let us carry on as we always should have remained. I am always here," Rime promised and began to descend the stairs. His words made me mute at a time when everything should have been said. It felt like he was referring to a time before we became "us." We should have never been.

My stomach sank as I watched him disappear into the winding staircase and out of sight. I wanted to shout after him, to run after him, but something stayed me. I couldn't even ask him about the other child. The one made into an emptied soul his mother was raising somewhere in this city. Not that I would have wanted to suddenly claim the task for myself, but I felt I ought to at least know of him. Maybe my conflicting feelings for Riestel were to blame, or maybe the fact that Rime had broken us. I needed him to be the one to fix us if he wanted to. I truly wished he would. My entire body urged me to act, but I only closed the door. Maybe this was the gentle option, to let him leave of his own accord. Our future was hanging so very delicately in the balance either way.

The Needle's room was exactly as I had left it. Except for a fresh flower Rime had left on the table and the dried-out petals from previous ones. A mixture of all sorts of early-blooming flowers. It was hard to understand that he had climbed the Needle's stairs each day to bring a flower to me and then just turned to leave when I arrived home. A penance suffered but not completed. For both or just one of us? I had no answer to that.

I turned the fasting bracelet on my wrist. There hadn't been one day since our wedding that I had not worn it. Would there be a day I wouldn't feel its weight? I pressed it to my skin to the point it left a mark. He had changed me in so many ways that he would always be a part of me. It wasn't an ending I liked to imagine, but it was a progression I had to consider.

The nexus, at least, seemed happy to have me close again, and it was pleased with my progress. Well, as much as one could discern or claim it had any emotions. I had come to the conclusion that it at least could mimic feelings, even if it were more of a tool to use. Even if it didn't always immediately offer me what I wanted, I could see it responding to my actions to improve our connection.

I shifted through various paths and strands to find a connection to Arid.

"Safe?" Arid asked as on our return we had not had them as escorts.

"Yes, thank you. We are both fine. The journey was much harder but educational. I wanted to thank you for everything once more."

"No need. But call out when you wish. We begin preparations to come there."

"I look forward to welcoming you and the others," I told her. The thought of Arid and the arochs who were ordained as greater spirits among them being here for us when the Witch would show herself brought much comfort. They would be our living shield.

It would be a chore to convince everyone in this city we should open the gates and let our enemies in. They had lived and fought with us for years. First, on Istrata's request, as they had thought she also served the Source, and the Source hadn't yet seen the betrayal coming. After they realized Istrata wasn't going to become what they sought and asked for, they fought two never-ending wars. A circle of protection enclosing us in a world where there was life and a larger one, keeping her taint away with them in the middle as a great dividing river.

They had been protecting us all these years in a twisted way. Acting out fights and dying to keep us from pushing further into the barren lands and beyond them where the Queen was draining the world to fill her dark heart. If we had ventured to the lands she had already poisoned, we would have only fed her quicker to satiety before even having the chance to rescue ourselves.

Any permanent losses the arochs had were due to the war on the outer ring, not from our blades. The attitude they had toward us was unbearably forgiving. We were the chosen people for this world. They were the guardians. They would yield each life a thousand times for our survival. Even if it would, in the end, diminish them to nought.

"Arid?"

"Yes?"

"I wanted to ask earlier, do your kind bear any ill will against us for your duty?"

Arid laughed. I could hear here hair chime all the way here.

"No. We are created for it," she answered and explained that as we loved our children, they loved us—even if we were infuriatingly slow and destructive.

Arid explained with pictures through the lighter world that they acted as a wall between us and parts of the world that were plagued and diminishing. There were quite a few of their kind strewn out over the world trying to protect the important, powerful sites. Sites where the great spirits had taken root and life was still strong and where they wanted neither Istrata nor us to go and cause trouble with our lack of understanding. Places where we might still live after all of this. Kerth was one but almost lost. We had not warmed to their attempts to make peace or accepted their tries to communicate once they decided to try a different approach; the decades of war had made us deaf to them.

"We have protected you long already," she said. "We do not waiver. We waited too long, our fault as well. But there is hope."

Arid showed me that they could have stopped after they realized what Istrata had done and how she had fooled them into fighting us, but at that time, they had thought that if they kept on the pressure, we would surely be more prepared for the battle with her. So, they continued to fight in order to refine us until recent times when they had thought to attempt peaceful means due to the worsening situation.

"Could you have done something then? While the Queen slept for decades slowly poisoning the world? Why not seek her out and try to destroy her before all this happened? The Source did not explain much on our visit."

I could feel Arid's entire being flinch. A wave of frustration pulsed from her.

"We could not find her. We failed," Arid admitted, bitterly and explained that as they were partly creatures of the lighter world, and try as they might, they were not able to handle, utilize, or even reach the heavier plane. They could sense it and touch the surface of it. If they tried to enter her realm, they ceased to exist. The only possibility after the discovery had been to wait for the Queen to return to this reality.

"I'm sorry for making you upset."

"At me. Not you," she said as her tone softened. "Must go now, get started. Be well."

"I will see you soon."

After my journey to the arochs, I knew the Source needed to be set free. It was tied to this world until all of its knowledge and power was transferred to those who would become the Keepers. Those who will give themselves fully to a task. It wasn't an easy choice and one that I had not consented to yet. To be a god was to serve. I now understood the Queen well. Why become something that will eternally dance to destroy if there might be a way around it? A way to not become a tool, a force of nature, and forget your earthly interests, to detach from the world, to love it from a far, and scar it, killing its inhabitants whenever the balance was skewed. Of course, taking up the Source's offer meant one would still be a god, which was a pretty inviting counter argument for accepting that destiny.

After my time with the arochs, I felt burdened. They would help as much as they could, but ultimately, a lot rested on us. At least, I was now almost ready to start poking about the strands of the Queen's existence. But I wasn't yet sure what route was worth the risk. What would be the most unlikely little connection to take to get inside her memories? Hopefully, I will figure it out soon.

I picked up the dried petals from the floor and the table and released them to the wind from the window. Elona was jumping for joy around Riestel far below. She must have missed him terribly. She waved at me. It warmed me much more than I would have thought just a few months ago. A broken family of broken people, happy nonetheless. I watched them sprint about for a moment. Her giggles rang across the whole Peak.

The road the Source offered would take me away from all of these people. It was a sullen, melancholy thought. I, who had always felt isolated, had found a family and friends. If the world had been in a better way, I may have turned away from this road. However, we adults were things to sacrifice for her future. Our mission would not be to seek happiness for us but for the world. Hopefully, we could still steal a few morsels of joy amidst all this to sustain us.

Despite the surprising and aloof welcome, I knew I should talk to Rime soon about all I now knew, all that had happened, and what I had learned. He would probably have many new things to tell me as well from their research. If only our resident genius, Moras, would have some good news.

I left the Needle, as being alone was too anxiety-inducing at the moment. I had expected to be greeted with an uncomfortable but warm welcome or a huge fight, not merely nothing.

Outside, Riestel was making spheres from water, which Elona chased and burst as fast as she could. I sat next to Arvida on the yellow-painted iron bench among the lace-like shadows created by the branches of nearby trees. The summer sun was brutally hot, and a thick curtain of moist air draped over our skins.

"Welcome back," Arvida said, smiling as she covered her eyes with her hand to try to look at me. "Elona missed you horribly. I did a little too.

Life is so boringly uneventful without you. Did you meet Rime? He's been wandering about the Peak like a homeless person ever since you up and puffed away."

"Kind of. He just noted that I was back and walked away. Hard to imagine he's been pining after me with that welcome."

"Don't be such a melodramatic halfwit," Arvida scolded me. "Obviously, he missed you. How would you feel if you had driven away the person you love and then just have to sit and wait to see if they come back? He probably just got flustered finding you there."

"Rime? Flustered? That would be something entirely new. Do you think that it is even possible?"

"Well, I cannot be completely certain. I didn't read his feelings if that is what you are asking. It is merely an observation of how he has acted. You have much to talk and think about. The fate of this city might be the death of us all, so don't waste time if you want to be with him for whatever time we have left."

"Good cloudless skies, when did you become such a dispenser of wisdoms?"

"Happens to the silliest of us with enough life lived. Obviously, it makes it simpler when you are so easy to read." Arvida smiled and nudged me. "Give him a chance and then decide."

"He doesn't need to explain it. I already know it was his trump card to get Frazil to bend the knee if nothing else worked. And I know very well that if he would have told me, I would have meddled and perhaps caused unwanted chaos. Still…he and his mother planned it out from beginning to end without me. Without trusting me. I was used just like anyone else. Rime will admit to that in a heartbeat. The annoying thing is, I can't be mad. It would be easier if I could be. It hurts because he did it for the benefit of everyone if we consider the circumstances. For everyone. How can I accuse him of choosing that path when the entire city is very likely better off? It cut deeply, but he reigns now. We can force through any reformations needed and wanted and organize all as we wish, so it also makes my future better and easier."

Arvida nodded, biting her lower lip a little. Her meticulously curled, spiraling locks bounced with each small movement.

"Yes, right. I can sort of understand. It hurts as you feel you have no right to those feelings. I will not press the issue then. You do as you will… Well then, how was traveling with Riestel? He is so relaxed now. He even called me by my name. Correctly. Imagine that."

"We have achieved a balance of sorts." I chuckled and glanced at Riestel and Elona. "He has made it abundantly clear that I will be forever stuck with him. There is no escape."

"And you? Are you glad about it?"

"I've accepted that. Whatever path I will travel, I will never be alone again. We are the two sides of the same coin. We will never be free of each other. It makes me feel...tranquil. Happy even."

"Meager gossip. Are you truly telling me nothing juicier happened between you? You were gone for weeks together!"

"And what should you want to know, oh ye town-crier of gossip?" I asked, tilting my head back as I heard someone approach from behind. Heelis's beautifully peach-colored face shone above mine as she stood behind us. She looked invigorated, not all gaunt and sickly, like after she had been incarcerated. She scrunched her nose and flicked me on the temple. I rubbed my head a moment as she cheerfully plopped herself between us without waiting for us to make room.

"Well?" Heelis insisted. "Did something happen between you two?"

"Much, but nothing of the kind you'd like to know or I'd tell." I sighed. These two were relentless.

"Humbug. And you, any progress?" Heelis inquired, turning to Arvida. "I need something to perk me up. Juone is so cheerfully engrossed in being a daddy that I could scream for some romance. Merrie is of no help either when I try to pry about her relationship. Her feelings are so pure and sweet that there is no guilty joy in listening to her stories."

Arvida grinned like a cat.

"Maybe something," she whispered.

Heelis and I perked up. Arvida snickered a little into her sleeve.

"Thanks to my new, highly influential friends, I am finally a notorious divorcee...so I spent a night at Tammaran's a few days past," Arvida revealed, trying not to look too pleased.

"And? Worth the wait?" Heelis pressed with gleaming eyes and pressed her palms together in prayer.

"Well, he is a pretty tall man, but now I can safely say the length is not limited to just some body parts."

Heelis giggled like a teenager, which spread to all of us like the plague, no matter how hard we fought it. Riestel stared at us a little way off and raised his left eyebrow. I shook my head and pressed my hands to my cheeks as they were getting tired from laughing. Just like that, returning here felt a little better, despite the inevitable dark times ahead.

II

The light summer day was soon spent even though we did naught but laugh and talk. I ascended the Needle's stairs back to solitude, humming. The room was like a beautiful calm pond, though something disturbed the surface. There were more flowers on the table. And on the floor and balcony. Small white, cloud-like flowers and big, bright trumpet-looking ones. Fabrics, gift parcels, and jewelry.

There were also dozens of letters, each very similar to the other. They welcomed me back and requested favors. Some wished me to admit their children to the Temple; others wanted some office they thought I might grant them. After opening all that I could bear to read, I piled them high and burned them. I wasn't here to grant favors and wishes. Certainly not by letter. If they truly held their desires important, they should at least seek an audience and make some effort instead of sending generic bribes.

The same continued the next day. A constant flow of gifts and requests. I told the servants bringing them to me to just keep them or sell them. The only half-interesting message was from the Good Queen Friti. Her awkward and stiff attempt at mending fences was amusing and incredibly futile. I admired her a little for humbling herself. I might not have been able to do so. Their life was in Rime's hands. I would not meddle anymore.

Arvida had told me yesterday that the royals had retreated to their previous manor in the Temple District to wait for the new palace to be built in the center of the city. Apparently, they had chosen this course of action out of sheer desire to show the people that the new ruler was a man of the people and would not hide in the Peak.

Because of this mightily selfless move, the halls of the Needle and the palace attached to it were almost empty. There were certainly servants about, but they didn't form a constant, steady stream of food and linens and drinks that the upkeep of different nobles and visitors had required.

The main kitchen was still bustling with people. The yellow-brick room's ovens and stoves produced so much heat that just stepping into the room made one sweat. Even the scorching summer day outside paled in comparison.

"Wait in the hall!" the head-cook snapped as he laid eyes on me. "We have made it clear enough that we do not accept requests. I make what I make, and that will be served."

"I'm not here to make any wishes." I smiled. "I'll just take a tray and some bits and pieces."

"Listen here!" he said, lifting his spatula at me menacingly. One servant hurried to whisper something to him. He quickly lowered the utensil and scratched his head with the handle.

"Apologies, I don't get out much, so I didn't recognize you, Consecratoress," he said, a little flustered, but I sensed that even with that knowledge, he would deny me if I happened to push my luck.

"You do as you wish in your domain. I'm simply here to gather some available supplies. I'd like to take the War Council his breakfast. I assume he hasn't had it yet."

"No, he always wishes it delivered to his room at an exact time. We should plate up."

"Good. Let me help. I'll just add my breakfast to the tray as well."

"Yes, Derra. Help her gather everything. And give her an apron."

Derra was a nervous young man. He brought me all sorts of small dishes. He just appeared from different directions, handing me things while mumbling, and then disappeared to get the next necessary thing. Once the tray was filled, I found myself nervously twirling my hair. It would have been easier for me to just wait until Rime came to me, but considering all things, I wanted to establish where we stood as soon as possible. We had to be able to work together for Kerth, no matter our relationship. I was probably the weaker link in the equation, so if I did this on my own terms, I might be less moody and annoying.

The heavy, old-fashioned flower-painted tray was tricky to carry. I still made it to the light taupe colored the hall in front of Rime's office without spilling most of the hot water. I laid the tray on the ornamental side table by the door for a moment. My hair was still damp and messy from the humidity of the kitchen. When I was weaving my locks into a loose braid, the office door swung open. Rime stepped out and turned to lock the door. When he noticed me, he straightened stiffly into a polite stance.

"I'm heading to my chambers for breakfast," he said.

"I brought it to you," I told him and pointed at the tray. "We should talk." I realized I still had the apron on. It made me embarrassed. The plan hadn't been for him to see me all disheveled and in a wrinkled attire when he was immaculately dressed, hair and beard combed and oiled.

"Right...come in." Rime avoided my gaze and made room at the door. As I passed him, the familiar scent of mint wafted in the air. I could remember its notes even in my sleep. He never used any other herb for his hair, and he always used it in the same amount each day. Once I was in, I cleared some room on his desk. I lifted the plates and the teapot off the tray and quickly wiped away the spilled water. Rime poured the tea as he was more particular of the two of us in how long it should brew. Then he gestured for me to sit and took his place at his desk after opening the curtains. The morning sun dotted the room through the thin day curtains.

"I should probably say..."

"I should probably say..."

We fell silent.

"Sorry."

"Sorry."

We fell silent again. I had expected many problems from this conversation, but timing hadn't been an issue that had even crossed my mind. The stray tea leaves at the bottom of our cups were all of a sudden quite interesting to both of us. This wasn't going to work if I hesitated. I glanced at Rime. He waved his hand to signal that I could speak first.

"I know what you want to apologize for," I said. "You don't need to. I understand the situation and your calculations. You even asked my permission for it. At least, I assume that was what you were referring to when you asked if you could take the road with the highest stakes. It was still a shock, and had I known what you meant... I don't know. I had thought that I would not be affected by such things...by your dedication to the city's wellbeing when it trampled on my interests. I know you've never placed anyone above it. Not even yourself. Some part of me just wanted to believe I was the exception.

"As for me, I want to say I'm sorry that I left so abruptly that night. It was a childish thing to do. I was just so full of it all: the constant plots and stepping on eggshells, the insecurity. I should have told you, nonetheless. I was just afraid that if I came to see you, I would accuse you of things unfairly."

Rime cleared his throat, looking uncomfortable, and shook his head. He leaned his elbows on the table and crossed his fingers under his jaw. A habit he had acquired from his father.

"I had an entire speech rehearsed for this moment, and now you made it entirely void. If I have nothing to apologize for, why do I feel guilty? I could plea my case with a dozen alleviating facts...but they were all my decisions in the end, and I cannot deny that I did place you second that time," Rime admitted carefully. "But that doesn't mean..."

"I understand that. I don't want you to feel that you did wrong when you chose all of them. You've made many harsh decisions during your career. Sometimes, they won't spare you either. If you never needed to pay a price for your doings, you'd be corrupt like the people you ousted. You need to make decisions against your own wellbeing at times for the country's benefit. I don't know if I could, so I am glad that you can. And a little sad at the same time."

"I..." he began but then frowned. "Thank you."

"We can seal our own problems away if talking about them is too much. I mainly wanted to tell you what I have learned and to plan for the future. One cannot avoid it anyway." I secretly hoped he would not allow me to change the subject. Being alone with him without having a connection to him was painful.

"Yes, that has to take priority." Rime leaned back in his chair. His gesture hinted at annoyance. "Where did you actually go? I presume you left with the arochs...and Riestel as the haughty annoyance of a man was nowhere to be found either."

"We went to their home. Riestel came to keep me safe and to meet an old acquaintance. We went to one of the holy sites our lore had forgotten. They are the centers that life once sprung from and where the membrane between this and the lighter world is at its thinnest. The arochs protect them. They live within them; they are a part of them. They are born and die to be born again directly into a similar body they had. Like a never-ending circle. Unless they voluntarily give their lives to save a part of the land. Then they forego their souls and unite with the land."

"So, they can help mend the earth?"

"At the expense of their own kind. They become local guardian spirits when such happens."

Rime looked amused for a moment.

"We did joke at the Borders that they all looked the same, but none of us thought they actually were the same, over and over again. Why are they coming to you for help? Do they want to stop the wars, or is there more to it?"

"Yes. Give me a map and a pen. A map you don't mind me drawing on, then a sheet that is larger than the map."

Rime rummaged through his draws for a copy he didn't need and handed it over with a pen. I placed the small map in the middle of the paper. I marked the borders of the aroch land and the road to it. Then, I noted down what the Source had shown me: all known holy places outside our kingdom, the ones that were lost and the ones that still held on. Istrata's envoys had emerged in many places, trying to destroy all the lighter souls and locations of importance.

"Look," I urged.

Rime walked behind me, bowing closer, leaning on the table with one hand. Just like he had done in that small brown kitchen long ago when he told me about the city, I would have traded this insecurity with that wonderful, tingly "what if" of the beginning anytime. His official coat brushed the skin of my arm. I wanted to rest my head on his shoulder for a moment, but I didn't dare to.

"What am I looking at?" he asked when I had been quiet for a moment.

"Right, I marked all the centers I know on this. If Kerth should ever fall, these are the places where life can still be resuscitated and may be able to carry a civilization and be farmed. Unless she will get to them first. The Source also told me of its deal with Istrata..."

"The Source?"

"That's who or what created this world."

Rime stared at me, a little suspicious. "Are you saying you met an actual god?"

"No, kind of, she or he...it...is a builder of sorts. The Source makes worlds but isn't the beginning; it isn't the end all and be all of creation or consciousness. Whatever that might be," I mused. "When the Source finishes its work, it chooses guardians, keepers, gods, for that specific world who are responsible for developing it and keeping it safe. The Source cannot penetrate into our world anymore. It lives in the weave of it, in the structures of the lighter world, among ideas and potentials. Once the world is planned and made, the laws are set, and it has no means of changing them. That can only be done by a creature that is part of both worlds."

"Istrata was supposed to be that creature, I suspect if they had a deal like you said."

"Correct."

"And now it wants you."

"Yes, me…and Riestel. Anyone whose powers manifest in a certain way and strong enough," I answered, trying to play down the strong hint of destiny.

"But right now, it is just you two that will do," Rime insisted.

"As far as I know, yes." I sighed. "Istrata agreed to the role as the guardian or god, whatever word you wish to use, but something changed her mind. Something made her rebel. Partly, I'd imagine, it has to do with the way she hated her gift of fire. Partly her child's fate. There could be much more to it or not. I'm struggling to understand how a woman who, according to Riestel, was so kind and caring changed so much she wants the world to become twisted and stalled."

"The future she is after will bring nothing good. I feel the heavy world in me, and it affects my mind. It distorts. It makes you fall into this stasis of strangely mesmerizing depression. It has changed me, and not for the better. Without it, I might have played things differently…"

It was horrible to hear Rime talk this way. There had to be a way to heal him.

"Have you been well enough?" I asked. "That doesn't exactly sound good." I wished he would have come to me for comfort. It was so hard to try to cross this chasm between us. Maybe it could be done one step at a time.

"I'm reasonably well. All that can be done for me has been done. Physically, I'm better than ever."

"Physically…but mentally?"

Rime gave a pressed smile and brushed his forehead. He straightened up and walked to crack open the window. He looked back at me. The soft sunlight pouring in cast a heavy shadow on his face.

"For most, living a long life and continuing quietly after death in one form or another is a longing and a silent promise. For us, whose blood has been tainted by the ritual to create emptied souls, the only granted thing is the knowledge that this is all we have. I'm not going to pretend that doesn't make me bitter," Rime sighed as the warm summer wind blew hot, fresh air in.

"Moras hasn't found any way to restore or make a soul, then?"

"Most research is focused on the exact opposite. They have seen no hints that it would be possible. If I had some semblance of a soul left, it would have been in the heavy world since my birth. Would you wish to have that within you? Also, Moras theorized that it would have merged and slowly disintegrated in that world. The substance seems to slowly eat whatever it touches. Unless it is countered by your fire and returned to a healthier state and guided back to the cycle."

"I don't have any better news. The Source cannot assist as it is outside the world. The arochs don't have her abilities," I told him quietly and walked to him by the window.

Rime stood steadily, and his breathing was calm. Now that he faced the window more, the morning sun softened his features. He nodded and lifted his gaze toward the sky. Then he smiled briefly.

"That's fine. It was a long shot. If I can spend a few more years as myself...I can call it a triumph."

"We might still find something," I said hastily. I felt a little uneasy saying it when neither of us nor anyone else had any clue where to even begin. A soul could be exchanged from one body to another, but the other way around just seemed unnatural. A soul couldn't be claimed and changed to belong to another. The only person left to turn to was Istrata. My soul had become mine through time because Istrata had severed her connection to it and sewn it to me. But I had been a clean slate and a copy of her in the beginning. In a way, I was still her but just molded to a different outcome by my experiences. A version of her she could have never become.

"We might, but there are more important things than one man's life. Are there not?" Rime asked and drew a deep breath. "All of this knowledge and your new skills should be put to use. You said Istrata had relinquished her fiery powers. By all reason and likelihood, that means she has traded those powers for similar ones to mine or that she uses the consecrator's talents with a machine, like Irinda and all other knights.

"You are her cut-up and transferred soul, so she must live like one of us through the heavy material. Because I had no machines or contraptions to help stabilize me when I grew up, my connection to the black tar is different from Irinda's, more organic. I can use the ichor itself. There is no need to feed it through a machine or use souls. Certainly, I can, but there is no point. I can, therefore, be your practice target. We can see what works and what doesn't if I fight you and the other consecrators. Then we will be a little more prepared to meet Istrata."

Rime's determined words and his readiness to take on even more to carry for the world's sake forced me to turn my head. Once I regained my composure, I felt anger.

"I cannot understand you," I said.

"Now, you sound more like yourself." Rime laughed. "You have been so very calm. Is it now time to tell me what a fool I am for having this fatal attitude and that I should be more selfish?"

"Possibly." I frowned. He smiled. He was too at peace with all this. "Don't you have any feelings left? Don't you want a soul or a new life? Why don't you ever want anything just for yourself? Be a little selfish!"

"But I was, once," Rime said, looking right at me. "I tied you to myself. It was the most selfish thing I have ever done. Mother had already plotted my rise and how to get me into my father's path so I could guide the city toward a better future. Then... You happened. You happened and...I..."

"And?" I pressed.

"And I saw a better opportunity."

"That's all?" I asked, my heart spiraling down.

Rime stepped right in front of me. "I also saw a chance to be happy while doing all that I was meant to do. I'm sorry my actions allowed it only to last for a few sweet years. But I wouldn't change anything about the time I spent with you. I understand and bear the consequences of the deeds."

We were so close to each other that I could feel his body warmth through the air. Kiss me, I prayed. Touch me. Break this wall. I begged him in my thoughts, but he took a step back and walked to the door.

"I have a meeting set up. Thank you for not hating me," he said.

"And the child? The one with your mother?" I asked quickly before he could leave.

"What of him? He is my kind. I will not bring him here. He is loved and doted on by my mother and will be so until the fate of this world is decided."

"What if I want to see him?"

"You will not see him. You need to purge the world, and he is a thing to be purged, like I am, in the worst-case scenario. I will not allow you to feel even more pain than you will already just from doing your duty. I am deeply sorry, but I will never relent on this. I will see you later."

III

The meeting with Rime had gone in many ways better than I had feared and worse at the same time. Better, because we could talk and get along. Worse, because of the same thing. It was as if we had never been lovers, the way he acted. But I still had these emotions within me, and I missed him to comfort me and talk with me in the wee hours of the night about all the ways this world could be improved.

I kept telling myself it was for the better, knowing I was considering the Source's offer. It would be wrong to give into these feelings again and to tempt him along for the ride. If I accepted the role offered to me, there was no place for me to build a family in this world, and there was no way for Rime to follow me unless he could be healed. The same applied to the other child. It seemed like such a cold thing to do, to not try to seek him out. To not see him even once. However, there was a truth to Rime's words, which hurt but made enough sense for me to try to accept his decision.

I looked through the nexus, trying to sort out all the threads connected to me. It was easy to distinguish and follow those woven from powerful emotions and memories, but the strands formed from quiet, secret desires you didn't want to admit even to yourself existed. Those were tricky to find and even more difficult to follow. I feared Istrata might catch me immediately if I tried it. There had to be a way to soothe her suspicions.

Riestel arrived to help me with my practice by volunteering his memories. He sat down opposite to me, with the nexus between us. "Let's begin. I promised to take Elona swimming today."

"Just a moment," I replied and refocused myself. I chose a strong, light, shining thread that passed from me to Riestel. Touching it made me feel weightless. Suddenly, we were face to face at the Northern Shrine, where I had for the first time realized his connection to the Witch Queen and, by that, to me. My head laid in his lap among the firtrees and the lit hanging braziers, and I listened to his clear and tender humming. Riestel opened his eyes and stopped.

"I found you," he whispered.

"Already?"

"I told you it would be easy when you choose a moment that is deeply shared."

"And now, do I just jump to the next one?"

"Not yet. Get a feel of how to function here. You can move in and see only what you or I remember. And you can change things accidentally or on purpose. Of course, you should avoid it at all costs. Do you remember how I broke the memory when you dreamed of kissing me at the bathhouse, and a new connection was made?"

"I might," I muttered and looked away. Dream or not, even my skin remembered it, and by the look on his face, he knew it.

"Well, this space is different," he mercifully continued. "It is based on what truly happened; you are not creating this as it already exists. Get up and look around."

I did as he recommended. An image of my body and his were left as they were. When I stood there, I could see what he meant. A part of the memory was exactly as the Shrine, but the parts I had not especially paid attention to or were not as familiar with were obscure, dimly lit, and hard to make out—foggy even. Some sharpened a little when I tried to remember the situation and the location. Some parts I had never really looked at with intent simply remained distorted and empty.

"Can I leave the Shrine?" I asked.

"You may try. If this moment connects to other memories seamlessly, you may be able to move within their bounds. Should you have forgotten something, it will block you unless you can retrieve it from general memory. Do not force it. If you force it, you may corrupt the memory and end up patching it with something that never was."

"Have you done so?"

"A few times. I tried to keep some memories as vivid as possible, but I was so determined to remember them right that I can't be sure if they are genuine anymore as I might have added things that only felt real but did not exist."

"Why does that matter?"

"On the grand scale, not a lot, but on a personal level, it is a sad thing. That knowledge is lost to me or untrue. You should actually learn how to twist a memory," Riestel said. "It is almost impossible that any living creature has fully intact memories. If you go diving into her head, you should know what cannot be trusted."

"How do the changes manifest?"

"I'll show you one. Turn back to the nexus and choose a crimson thread that goes from me to the past."

As I touched the dark red strand, the Northern Shrine faded, and I was in Elona's chamber. I was bent over the crib. The body I was in felt odd. It was me, but it wasn't me. There was enough of the same that I could control it if I wanted to. The connections and the memories a person was not a part of would be forever locked away from outsiders unless one had this gift of the nexus. I studied the room and Elona but saw nothing odd.

"What should I see?" I asked as Riestel appeared next to me.

"This was the moment when I felt Istrata was no longer the person I knew. I couldn't say why, and I've tried countless times to remember what in her expression worried me as she stared at Elona, but I just couldn't get a hold of it. I can't recall if it was an eerie smile or a lack of emotion. There is a mirror on the wall. Look into it while you are still in her."

I glanced at the mirror and flinched. My face had two hazy mouths overlapping each other; one was smiling in an unsettling way, and the other was pressed shut tightly. The sight made me feel a little ill, and it made me lose concentration. I opened my eyes in the Needle's room.

"Why couldn't you pick something less horrid?" I scolded Riestel.

"It was the clearest example I have to offer. If I showed you some minor change, how could you spot it? I'm sorry if it upset you, but if you are going to rustle around in Istrata's memories, you must be prepared to see many such things. I have no idea of the extent of her actions, but I unfortunately presume that some things we will wish we had not known of."

"You could have warned me."

"Now, that you can purely blame on my character." Riestel laughed and inched closer. "But I'm glad I remember your face perfectly." He brushed my cheek.

"Stop," I said. "You know what we agreed."

"Yes, yes, and that's why I'm behaving, mostly," he answered softly. "Will you come?"

"To the beach? I have much too much to do."

"You won't concentrate on anything but daydreaming of me, I'm sure. Might as well come."

"I will shove this shoe into any orifice that will shut you up."

Riestel got up, chuckling.

"Sounds intriguing. Didn't figure you were that kind of girl." He grinned. "Come on then. Use whatever respite we still have to your benefit."

The water in the reservoir was already lovely as the late spring and early summer had been warmer than usual. Elona was splashing about with sheer determination to make the whole lake ripple. I sat in the shade on a rock by the water, staring at the glimmering surface as Riestel emerged from his dive. His light skin, combined with the water droplets running down his body, almost burned my eyes as the evening sun caressed him. But his smile, as he picked up Elona and threw her into the water a little way away, was by far the brightest.

Would Riestel really give her up and follow me if I chose to walk the suggested path? Or would I be giving up both Rime and Riestel and all whom I considered family? And for what? Power, control? An eternity in the service of this world. It was a servant's position. I had come to realize that some time ago. To be a guide, a guardian, a harsh mother to this world. To nurture it and to destroy it in proper measure. I would not be a good god or an evil one. I would simply be a servant to the whole of it. I had never wanted such a position. It felt like an unnecessary burden. Maybe that was something I shared with Istrata. The higher one climbed, the less freedom one seemed to have.

"Why you!" I yelped when Riestel splashed me.

"Daddy, noughty!" Elona laughed and started to chuck water at her father. "Help me!"

I slid into the lake and splashed water at Riestel as well. He laughed and grabbed Elona, twirled the girl for a few moments, and sent her flying into the water as she giggled. Then he looked at me.

"Don't you think about it."

"Oh, but I am," he said with a smirk.

I felt the water flow increase by my feet. The wave spun me around and nudged me right into the water near him. I grabbed his hand and pulled him under with me. After a moment, we both crawled on the sandy shore, laying partly in the water, coughing and snickering. The small, glass-liked beads of smooth, round sand were like small multi-colored jewels stuck on his skin.

"Stop looking at me like that," Riestel whispered.

"Like what?"

"Like you might want to beg," he said and rolled on me. "We both know your heart isn't available yet, no matter how in-between it is. I will not be a crutch. You two need to resolve your issues before I will be a consort of any kind. Not that I would mind being used. Look at the time. He must be here already." Riestel grinned devilishly, got up, and waved. "Look, it's your husband. I hear he comes here daily for a swim."

I staggered up from the sand like a startled bunny. Rime was on the left side shore.

"How long has he been here? Did you know he would be here?"

"I knew. He's been here for quite a while. Lurking, looking, trying to decide whether to come to punch my face in, I'd assume."

"Hardly," I scoffed. "He doesn't seem to mind that we are drifting apart."

"He doesn't mind? The man who brought you flowers every day you were gone is refusing to wave back to me, trying to ignore the fact that we CAN SEE YOU!" Riestel yelled, entirely amused.

"Shut up! Good skies, are you trying to make me faint of shame?" I scolded him, trying to keep myself from turning beet red and making more of a scene.

"Not really. I'm simply trying to get you two to figure out what you are doing. I can live with having to wait, but I can't stand watching you two waste time. Maybe a bit of jealousy is just what the patient needs."

I took a step away.

Riestel blocked me. "Don't do that. Don't go running to him now. Let him simmer for a while. Test his determination."

I stared at Riestel. "Why are you trying to mend this mess?"

"Like I said, I don't want you before you are ready to give your heart to me —and only me. I trust it will happen, eventually. In the meantime, I might as well try to see that Elona's mother is happy. She likes that, you know," Riestel remarked and then huffed, becoming more serious. "Look. I already know you

22

love me. Admit it to yourself or not. Now, we just need the time to be right for us. And it is not as long as you are holding him here tightly." Riestel pressed his palm on my heart. He was right. Annoyingly so. I still loved Rime. Deeply. I needed him. But there was no doubt that similar feelings had appeared for Riestel.

"You're a better person than I," I finally noted.

"Not really. I did torture you for a year... Or a few lifetimes. Killed you more than a few times. I don't mind paying penance for that. If it means helping you find your way back to him, it won't break me. I'll even aid your search for a cure and live with the results. If the mut can have a few more lives to live after this one, I shouldn't complain. Helping him is the correct thing to do."

I could not believe my ears. I hated Riestel for being so understanding. He should have berated me for having these feelings. He should do something obnoxious like he usually did. That way, these emotions would diminish. Instead, each compassionate word made them deeper, no matter how thickly veiled in insults or innuendo they were.

"Let's go. I'm hungry!" Elona exclaimed.

As we walked side by side, Elona zoomed around us, appearing before us and after us and sometimes to the side of the road. She was taking every opportunity to move after being so long in her decayed state and a prisoner of her body. I could feel Rime following us, but resisted the urge to try to spot him. A dark, creeping yearning reached for me. His presence was so wrong in the world, and yet, I wanted it to stay with me for a bit longer.

Riestel seemed absentminded and delighted with his thoughts. Looking at him, I knew where I belonged. I knew why I was here. I knew what was expected of me. It was like having taken a wrong turn down an intriguing, dark path with dangers and thorns ripping at my skin and suddenly seeing an even smaller path deviating from the wrong path toward the correct one. The trouble was I wasn't done exploring the shadows, even if they were also trying to cast me back to the light and the correct path.

As Elona munched on bread on the Peak's left bow and Riestel had gone to fetch something for her to drink, I tried to settle on a course of action.

"You two are getting along," Rime said in a monotone voice, walking to me below the Needle.

"Yes, daddy likes her a lot," Elona remarked with a muffled voice from having taken a large bite. I could see Rime's jaw tense up a little, but nothing else.

"I'm sure he does," Rime responded and turned to me. "I need to talk to both of you. Can Arvida take her for a few hours?"

"Right now? I'm not sure. I can go and ask."

"Tomorrow will do. Let's not waste time if she isn't here. I'll be at the field close to the lake all day tomorrow as I'm overseeing a joint exercise of the consecrators and some of the army units. I would like both of you to come there. Anytime you feel like it. But I'd prefer the evening once we are finished."

"Yes, I'm sure I can come."

"Both of you."

"I'll drag him along if you insist," I agreed and tried to look annoyed at the thought of having to bring Riestel along.

"Good," Rime said laconically. He had apparently decided to pretend he had no emotions about anything. Fine. Should we both play this senseless game as Riestel suggested or should I just tell him I still loved him and perhaps wanted to make things work?

"Can I ask why you want us there?" I pondered instead.

"I think it is about time we tested what works the best against what I can do. And to test the limits of what I can do so we have some idea of what Istrata may have up her sleeve," Rime explained. "That's all."

"That is a sound idea," Riestel said as he handed Elona a glass of bright pink springberry juice. "There's no way to tell how long we have until she comes, so we should begin soon. See, I told you to relax while you still had the chance. Now it's back to the grind," Riestel groaned.

"Wonderful." I sighed. "I guess we need a proper night's sleep. I should get some practice in with the nexus still today, so I'll head to the Needle."

"Good. Walk this nuisance home for me," Riestel said and shoved me closer to Rime.

"I..." Rime hesitated but wasn't quick enough to figure out how to decline politely.

"Byeee," Elona bid us, yawning.

We stood awkwardly for a moment. I had many things I wanted to say, but they were all jumbled up inside my mind, and none were making it out coherently. Finally, Rime just gestured for us to walk toward the Needle's entrance.

Walking slowly and exchanging glances would have, at one point, been a dream come true. Now, it was simply an odd exercise. We knew each other so well, and yet neither of us was the same person anymore. We reached the door all too soon. Rime nodded his head to leave me for the night. I pinched his sleeve with my thumb and two other fingers. Rime froze.

"I have a long day ahead tomorrow. I need to return to my office to have time to rest," he said without looking at me. The abrupt refusal to play this scene out threw me off balance.

"There was just some lint on your coat," I told him and pretended to flick it into the evening air. If he had adamantly decided to distance himself, there wasn't much to do. I had once turned his head by force, but that was a simple cure for a simpler rift. Chasing him might work against me as he would try harder to keep me at arm's length. It truly irked me when Riestel gave advice that made sense. That, at least, was a familiar feeling.

IV

Memory walking was now a part of my everyday routine. Riestel was a compliant victim when it came to sharing his privacy. He was so comfortable with the idea of me rummaging through his thoughts that it made me uncomfortable doing it. How could he not dread what I might find? I did.

I needed to learn to contain my emotions when in these pockets of the past. If I became angry or sad, it was more likely to alert the owner to my presence. I needed to move like a passing whisper, leaving no trace, touching nothing but still gaining information. It was exhausting.

I visited the same scenes over and over again. I saw myself tortured through Riestel's eyes. I saw him crying alone, loathing himself after having to keep his emotions in check all those times. Especially after he had realized I wasn't breaking and that there was a chance he had finally found what he had been waiting for all these centuries. I had vexed myself with these scenes many times already. I needed something that I wasn't prepared for and knew exactly what I should look for, though I did not wish to.

Picking through the threads available to me, I wound my way to a much earlier time. A time when Riestel had lived in the Harbor. The first life after the Queen's death. The first time I surfaced. As a small white mouse, I followed Riestel as he waded through the deep blue night in his brown boots by the sea. The wooden piers creaked as he passed one vessel after another. His step had a light, speedy bounce to it. I knew that feeling. The feeling of having your future right in the palm of your hand and being so sure it will be the one you always wanted and dreamed of. I inhaled as deeply as a tiny mouse could.

Further away from the piers, in the Harbor's very western end, where the wooden structures slowly disappeared, and the harbor became a mere wharf with dodgy dinghies instead of stalwart vessels, shone an oil lamp. A man whose face was lost to time held it. His voice was distorted, and I could barely make out the words. Riestel nodded and told him to leave his presence. Riestel waited impatiently for the man to disappear into the city. Once Riestel was sure he was alone, he ran onto the sandy shoreline. Kneeling by something that was still half in the water.

I could see I lay there, on my side, on the silt. Riestel called to me, turned me over, and let me go with a look of pure horror on his face. My features were partly recognizable, but mostly, it looked as if I had melted like a vax figurine someone had forgotten to properly finish and then left too close to the heat. There, at that moment, died all of his dreams and most of his hopes. I kept breathing to regulate my emotions. I felt every ounce of his pain, but I kept breathing, pushing it down, forcing it to wait until I was done.

Once I emerged into the regular world, I lay on the floor, exhausted, with tears running down my face. Seeing me like that wasn't as horrible as I had thought, but seeing the look on Riestel's face, feeling his excitement and anticipation of a life with his love shatter, was overwhelming. He had waited so long by now. It was amazing he wasn't more bitter.

"I see you simply had to do that by yourself," Riestel noted and leaned over me, standing. "I asked you to allow me to accompany you. Or at least to just sit here and make sure you have someone around when you come out."

"I'm not crying for me," I uttered and tried to control my sobbing. "But my heart breaks for you."

Riestel's face went pale, and he sat down on the floor next to my head.

"You silly, soft creature."

I sat up and hugged him. At first, he seemed tense and unwilling to accept any sympathy, but then he laid his hands around me and held me.

"You're a silly, soft creature." He sighed. "You have so many sorrows inside, you could accidentally extinguish yourself."

"Shut up," I told him and started laughing. It was strange. Riestel was the only one I felt comfortable showing my weakness to. With Rime, I wanted to prove I had what it took, that I could be relied on, and was worth taking along for the ride. I knew Rime had always been supportive; he had always listened to my worries and counseled me. He had never looked down on me, but I wouldn't have felt this free to just let go of all pretense. He had that effect on most people, the feeling of wanting to become something more, something better, so he would not be disappointed.

We let go of each other.

"I'm relieved," Riestel said quietly.

"Why?"

"Because now there is nothing left for me to fear. I have fulfilled my promise to her, you, and Elona too. I have done all I set out to do, and after it all, you forgave me. I can feel all you feel, and I cannot feel even the slightest bit of resentment or anger anymore. I can't say there wouldn't be regrets if I die in the battle against her, but now, I can go peacefully if that should happen. I do hope it won't, though, as I would like to heal this sorry world."

"We will heal it. Whatever the cost."

"Will we? Together?" he asked with a smirk.

"That's what I said. Stop emphasizing it."

"Fine. We should get less friendly anyway, as we should head to the rehearsal area as Rime will be there to meet us."

"Do we have to? I do not want to fight him."

"You must. There is no one better to test against in preparation. His skills are the strongest an emptied soul has possessed, as far as I know. If Istrata has truly made herself into something akin to them, we will not have any other way to find out what she can do and what we can do about her."

"I know. I just don't know if I have it in me today."

"All the more reason to go. She will not appear when you are ready; she will appear when she is," Riestel urged.

"Slave driver."

"Is that an invitation to whip you?" He pressed his lips together so that they flushed with red as he relaxed them.

"For the love of… Just…choke already," I groaned as he pulled me up off the floor.

The gentle summer night was filled with sounds of fighting and metallic clashes. It seemed like a ceremony to welcome more troubles. So much ruckus in her beloved city, close to the Needle. It was almost blasphemous while she slept.

As we arrived at the field itself, most were leaving. It delighted me as I wasn't in the mood to battle and even less to battle as a crowd watched. The fires around the oval area illuminated the traces of feet and weapons in the sand. Some of the temple folk bowed as they walked past.

I was surprised to catch a glimpse of the fair Merrie in the audience. She was not a fighter and had adamantly exclaimed against any participation in these activities. Her skills as a Maidan's worshipper were for beauty and delight only. I was happy to grant her that privileged as her smile promised all who saw it a brighter future. Besides, without her reaching out to me and easing my way to convince the Temple to fight for us, we might be in a very different place now.

Then, I noticed why Merrie was here. She was rocking from heel to toe, waiting for Veitso to finish his duties. He was always the last one to leave Rime's side. This evening was no different as the two talked and planned. The idea of Merrie and Veitso made me smile. It was, by all accounts, a very unlikely match, but in its very absurdity, it made all the sense in the world.

"Good, you came," Rime noted and sent the last unit with Veitso away. "This is working well. We have more cooperation and skill than ever to work in unison with the Temple. There is much value in these exercises."

"That's reassuring to hear," I answered. "Are there many units with consecrators now?"

"Around fifty that have both protective and offensive members. There are a few hundred consecrators properly integrated into the army at the moment. There aren't any other qualified enough that would like to use their skills in this manner. I would not force a healer or a performer to practice attacks just because it would suit my purposes unless it were the only option."

"So, how do you want us to teach you a lesson?" Riestel inquired, almost humming.

"If it was just you, I'm confident it would be an even match," Rime replied and frowned slightly. "Although, I'm sure you have some tricks I haven't yet seen. Let's see if I can bring them out into the open one of these nights."

"I have tricks, alright." Riestel smiled. "But you will regret asking to see them."

I stood and listened to them trade insults for a few moments more and then walked off to the side. I didn't want to do this. It felt wrong. I had never come across this kind of resistance from myself to learn new things and see what I could do. It was like I was going to be exposed as a fraud. What if my power couldn't match his? What if I simply failed? It had never occurred to me this viscerally. There was a chance I could fail. And then all of them would know I wasn't enough.

A warm hand touched my neck. Rime crouched down beside me.

"It's tough. I know. I need you to do this. If you do not, we might as well shout surrender from the top of the Needle and embrace the stagnant world she will bring," Rime admonished me with a tender ring to his voice. I could feel his hunger picking my worries off one by one and consuming them. I felt less weighted down and cleaner.

"I will be here to back you up," Riestel promised and offered his hand.

Rime withdrew his fingers from my skin and got up. He walked to the other side of the field. I took Riestel's hand.

"How can he expect me to fight him?" I whispered.

"Do you think he wouldn't fight you if you became a threat at any point?" Riestel asked with a somber sadness about him.

"He would. I know that."

"Then do him the same courtesy. Are you afraid that he will be more than you can handle, or are you afraid that we will actually find a way to defeat him? And yes, I know, I will shut up now."

"You know me frighteningly well. Better than I sometimes know myself. I'm...grateful for that."

"He will merely showcase his skills first. You can see and study him. We won't do much tonight, but we need to begin."

"I already saw what he can do in the court that day when he impaled all those soldiers."

"You did not spend one moment trying to figure out how he can manifest such things, so don't try to weasel your way out of this with that excuse."

Riestel lifted his hand and gave a nonchalant wave. Rime bowed his head, and a dark shroud enveloped him. It was thick and viscous, sprawling out from beyond the artificial membrane created by force when Istrata had begun her experiments.

"Is he pulling it out from the heavier world?" I asked.

"I believe so," Riestel said with a shudder. "I wonder if he could also pull it out from the lighter layers? That would clean them faster than those taps Moras uses."

The ground gave an inaudible cry as Rime disappeared into it, being pulled under by the sludge. I could feel the pain of the structures of the created world with all my cells as he tore through them. Rime appeared from behind us and then to the side. Dozens of copies of him made from the darkest flowing mass emerged. They obeyed his command, and it was impossible to say which was him. It hadn't occurred to me in the slightest that his powers could be this developed.

"Time to experiment," Riestel urged me. He flicked his fingers, and the slowly advancing wave of dark figures froze in an instant. For a moment, nothing happened. Then the ice simply got devoured and turned black.

Riestel hummed and drew crystalline groundwater to the surface through the sand. It washed and diluted the dark figures away. It healed the stone and roots the substance had torn and scarred on its way to this world. But soon enough, the ichor was back. Next, Riestel conjured thousands of sharp ice discs. He shredded the figures into pieces. The figures began pulling back together.

"I will be nothing but a hindrance," Riestel noted. "I cannot destroy them or the substance permanently. No matter what form I will take, it will not help in that. I can buy time, and I can heal what has been hurt, that is all, as it has been for the last centuries. But I suppose we already knew that. I think Rime merely asked me here as an emotional crutch."

"Storms and high seas! Do you both think I am an absolute baby? I do not need either of you constantly hovering over me like I'm some delicate little porcelain doll! My gods, marry each other, will you!" I exclaimed, getting a little tired of them both being so incredibly supportive and almost getting along.

The fire burst out to the entire field out of sheer annoyance. The flames engulfed the creatures. They burned, but very slowly. They limped forward until they lost their limbs. I had to constantly force the fire to bite into them, to grab hold of them. When I did, we could all see the black tar burn away and release a small amount of lighter energy into the surroundings, just as the soul sand would.

"Happy now?" I huffed.

"Not really," Riestel answered. "I mean, it was always going to work to some extent, but you cannot fight an entire army of those. The fire just doesn't transform them effectively enough. We need to figure out something that will make them easier to burn."

"Like what?" Rime asked, stepping out from his black shield.

"What if there isn't anything that can do that?" I asked.

"Then we will have to figure out how long I and the others can handle and stall them as you dispose of them before the mass can overrun the city. It will be a long, arduous war," Riestel said. "It will be like having to climb the Needle a hundred thousand times."

"We will have to test that scenario," Rime said. "We will need all the other battle-capable consecrators to test how long they can hold and how much of the mass they can hold in comparison to how much she can burn through and in what time."

"How will that help?" I asked. "We can't know how much we'd need to fight off."

Rime stood still for a moment and lowered his gaze. Then, he wiped his forehead and looked at me. I wasn't going to like the news.

"I've been to that world. I can see an ocean's worth of it, at least. You know it too. From your dreams. It is exactly like that."

"I can't burn a whole sea."

"Slowly, you can. Either we conquer this or die," Riestel said. "I should hope you have no trouble choosing which is the preferable outcome."

"I don't want this world to perish any more than the next person. I was just hoping you would have had something up your sleeve with all that talk before we did this."

"I know when and where to expend my energy. This was just a small exercise to ease you into it. We will have to do much more soon," Riestel answered, clearly unamused. "I will do anything and everything required. You *should* know that."

"He is right. We will have to train more methodically. I merely wanted to get us off to a proper start, to break the ice. We will continue tomorrow."

"Tomorrow?" I groaned.

"Tomorrow, the day after that, and the day after that. Every day until we figure this out," Rime replied. "I will request all battle-capable consecrators to go through measured tests."

"But…" I started and froze when I realized something. "All of them will have to expend the soul sand or directly draw from the life force that is already waning. Where can we get enough to transform for our uses and not destroy the world just from our consumption if we need to fight a whole ocean?"

"You can use the distorted souls we need to clean anyway to make some reserves," Riestel said. "Then there are the suffering who were taken from the Spring pox house. I'm sure Frazil simply transferred them somewhere. However..."

"However, what?" I pressed.

"However, if we need more and we cannot take any from the land or the lighter realm to preserve any chance of healing after the battle... you must call on the nobles. There is an ancient degree that dictates that their families are given luxury and special status in exchange for their lives."

"You cannot be serious," I protested. "How would that look? I beg your pardon, good citizens, can I just slaughter a couple of hundred of your kin to save the rest?"

"That is the oath they made to rise to such riches," Riestel said, unaffected. "I'm not saying they will hold their end of the bargain. I'm just saying there is such an agreement."

"Is there an actual contract?" Rime asked, frowning.

"In the time I lived my first life, we didn't believe in papers and seals. We believed that the promises we make are etched into our very essence. A person's word was their character and destiny."

"So, there is no way to truly enforce it," Rime concluded. "Unless it was put on paper later."

"I would not want to enforce it," I muttered and got two angry glances. "Fine, I know you aren't keen to do so either and are just figuring out the possibilities in case worse comes to worse. I understand that. It just seems to me someone has to object." I felt a little ill at the discussion.

"I think we all can agree such an option is extreme," Riestel concurred.

"Indeed." Rime nodded. "Still, I would have you think about it, not in a spectrum of good and evil but purely of survival. If cornered, we can choose to perish heroically and lose this world to her, or we can fight with everything we have, no matter the cost. Whatever you decide, I will abide by. You are the person the Source wishes to appoint to this world to usher it and grow it. If you see there is no chance for it or that the price is too high for you to accept, then we will yield."

As Rime spoke, I felt an unfathomable sadness well in me. Yielding wasn't something I did. Yielding wasn't something that I even could do. I hated the idea alone. I already knew I would do anything and everything to clean this world and restore it. I just really didn't want to know the horrible decisions I might need to face down the line. The mere thought of talking about this option to the nobles brought me anxiety. I could never force them to lay their lives down because of a contract made long ago… Actually, that was likely a lie. Beyond the morality of it, why had such a contract been made? The person who had thought of it must have known about the potential destructiveness of the excessive use of our skills.

"We will not yield," I finally said. "No matter the cost, we need to stand alive at the other end. For Elona and all others that carry our future."

Rime took a deep breath and nodded. He looked relieved despite a melancholy smile. Riestel was looking at Rime. Then averted his gaze down as if he felt sympathy for him.

"Good. Then we will find out all the options, everything and anything we can use," Rime decided. "I will call the Noble's current governor to visit. There is no harm in talking to Usko. Of course, I can't see them jumping eagerly at the chance, but we should still speak to him. He has always supported us. Even against his peers."

V

Moras's apprentices had been busy testing all sorts of aspects of our world and life itself. The walls were filled with lists of preferable animals and plants. There was even the beginning of a unified theory of our reality forming and how and why the heavy reality seemed to be so corruptive and destructive. With what I knew from the Source, I was able to verify some of their assumptions. Some things I held back as those weren't necessary for anyone but me to know.

Their tests and test subjects, although some cruelty was inevitable, didn't have the same repulsive aura as Istrara's attempts to stitch together features of different species and to form them to her liking. The rabbits had given birth to the next generation after the fully tainted ones. The improvement wasn't anything to cheer about, but there was a slight shift toward healing in those who had been purely fed with healthy hay and vegetables.

"Lovely to have you back, Consecratoress," Moras welcomed me, seeming slightly nervous, likely due to our past. He still seemed to assume that Tammaran was with me when I came to visit.

"I would like you to catch me up on things. I know you and Rime must have talked long and hard about all, but I would rather not speak with him of this because he will shield me from learning whatever there is to learn if it is something that might unnerve me."

"You place me in an unfair position." Moras shook his head. "Both of you demand to keep the other feeling hopeful."

"Should we not feel hopeful, then?"

"I did not say that, merely that both of you want to know everything and that only you should know such things. I feel torn over my allegiance, and I do not wish a repeat of what happened with Frazil and you."

"I know. It is unfortunate, but due to the betrayal having been directed at me, I must insist that you choose to trust me with everything. I cannot help him if you don't. Rime wishes to carry the worries of the world because he thinks it will ease my pains too. It doesn't; it merely delays all. I have to be strong enough on my own."

"Well, then… You already know the black tar is made from suffering spirits and souls who cannot just let go of their pain and have not been dismantled properly in time. They simply become more and more putrid until they become a mindless, bitter, yearning mass. We can alleviate it if we recycle it through cleaner creatures, but the time needed for it… Simply put, it is decades and centuries. We can do it; we can heal it, but it will be a task for generations. Of course, your fire will help, but there is so much to purify that we need all methods we can muster. Unless you become more capable, the closer to ascending you get."

"And Rime? How does all this affect him? Have you a cure for him? Anything at all?"

"No," Moras admitted with a strained voice. "Only a sealed fate. We must drain the entire heavier world with force into this one and retain the tainted matter here so it does not return to the heavier world. We have been letting out the ichor from the lighter world to stop it from stagnating. We have to do so to destroy it all, to prevent this from happening again. So that there won't be any, if you allow the metaphor, infected pockets left that may in the future lead others down the same path as the Queen."

"The cure for the world will kill him? I gather that is what you mean." My heart sank.

"His consciousness is tied to the heavier world like ours is to this and the lighter. He exists in that plane the way our souls exist in the lighter. If we empty all into this world, he will be robbed of whatever life the heavier side gave him at birth. It may not mean he will die immediately; he might be able to live this life to the end. What I certainly know is that he will not have another life after we do so."

"He might be able to build a soul, might he not? We all have that possibility. Or could we fashion one?"

"Not to my knowledge. We have a natural connection to the lighter realm.

His was severed and destroyed. I do not know how to force a new one or how to build one. Those connections are above me. They are so fundamental to this world; I highly doubt a mere mortal such as I could ever triumph over those laws."

"A mortal might not," I whispered. A goddess in the making might. Istrata might have come upon the knowledge. I had to begin taking risks with my memory hopping. I needed to look to her past. Or should I contact her? Should I have her guide me in the past as she had once promised to show me her world? If she became accustomed to my presence that way, she might not be so easily disturbed when I would try to infiltrate the memories she might want to hide.

"Thank you. Please—"

"Do not tell him what I told you. I get it." Moras grunted and rolled his eyes instinctively and tried to mask doing so by suddenly stretching and yawning. Tammaran had done a fine job harassing him to submission and loyalty.

After my talk with Moras, I began practicing my memory traveling. For the next weeks, I would only leave the Needle when needed to practice against Rime. Everything else took second place. I needed to know. I needed to save him.

The rehearsal battles grew larger and larger. Riestel and the other consecrators would direct, hinder, and cut down Rime's dark figures to allow me time to burn them. Regular fire, if they stood it in long enough, also helped. We made fire pits and ushered them in. The biggest discovery was that all of the masses needed Rime's consciousness to advance. If his attention could be drawn to one particular area or his concentration broken, it would allow us to break his creations down more efficiently.

As most others were leaving to get some rest after Rime drove them hard, I began to gather the soul sand resembling residue from the field. Every bit was valuable. We already had a few barrels of it, just from these matches.

"You were preoccupied tonight," Rime remarked as he was passing by.

"I can't always help it. I'm training to use the nexus all morning and day, and then I do this for evenings on end."

"I don't want excuses. You need to be focused every time we step on this field. Otherwise, we are wasting time."

"Could you not tonight?" I sighed as he walked further away. "You lecture me every time we do this. I'm allowed to be tired. I'm not a machine. I realize we have issues, but you are being wholly unfair. If you don't love me anymore, that's fine, but you don't need to begin hating me for your decisions," I told him bitterly.

Rime halted, and his posture improved. He turned back to me, enough for me to notice the shadow over his eyes cleared for a moment.

"I... I think I am too tired as well. I'm sorry. The fighting always leaves me in a foul mood. I will attempt to be more considerate."

"Good," I answered and returned to my task. He would do what he needed to, and I would do what I needed to.

Apparently, Rime felt more than a little guilty as the next day, he sent word that we could all have a rest day. It was a welcome gift to most. For me, it was simply more time to practice other things as I began to feel ready to access Istrata's memories. It was a gamble, of course. A horrifically costly one if it should fail. We weren't ready to face her, but I felt confident enough in my skills to begin snooping around and getting her used to my presence without alerting her to it.

Before I would begin my attempt, I took to my new routine of going through one space in any of the Needle's rooms at a time and trying to bleed out any small residues of the heavy goo tainting the lighter realms. I would look for areas that made me unnerved or anxious. Once I found one, I would poke a small hole in the membrane between the realities and let it into this one in order to burn it. Slowly, I became able to touch an object and draw it out from the fabric of it.

After my daily cleaning, I inserted my hand into the nexus. Several threads bit into my skin and deeper into my flesh. The connection between me and it became more solid every time I used it. The Source had told me that one day, the nexus would become like a second heart or mind to me, a natural part of me should I continue using it. It would allow me to see and feel all and everyone in this world, should I wish. With its help, I would be able to weave the fates of any I chose. Well, not quite that dramatically. I would be able to offer them paths to travel, but I wouldn't be able to force them to step on them —just as she and Istrata had done for me.

In the form of the white mouse, I followed a small, almost see-through strand. These nearly invisible memories would offer small, faded glimpses of Istrata. They were memories she rarely thought of, suppressed, or was forgetting.

One I particularly liked to watch again and again in silence was her simply practicing hand movements and singing. Her tresses flowed down to her shoulders freely, and their tips fluttered in the air a little as her hands spread about warm air. She looked serene, completely in tune with her fiery talent. It was one of the few moments I could find she seemed to enjoy her skills. It seemed almost impossible that this person would become so full of vitriol for her gift that she wanted to shun it and damage the entire world in the process.

There were small moments that hinted at her patience wearing thin. Endless meetings that all seemed to mash into one long, boring dream of people constantly demanding things, wanting things from her, wanting to dictate how she should behave as a ruler and who should be granted benefits and who not for the most ridiculous transgressions of etiquette. Then came a succession of funeral pyres after funeral pyres, with weeping families looking for support from her at all hours.

I could feel Istrata's frustration and fatigue as her suggestions fell on deaf ears, and every improvement took months of arguing with lawmakers and others in the ruling class. Despite her growing discontentment with those around her, when she walked outside her kingdom, I could easily sense the pride she had in it. And it was glorious during her reign. I couldn't deny that. It was a paradise, and yet none seemed content or happy. Everyone complained about the smallest issues and transgressions.

The Needle shone like a beacon above the city. Even at night, it was lit with so many ornamental lights that it competed with the Moon herself as they both cast their image on the dark, deep waters of the port. The wide, sparkling river ran on the surface of the mountain; orchards bore fruit so big I had never seen the like. No walls separated the city areas. I couldn't find huts or slums in her memories. Just beautiful artwork and fine craftmanship wherever I peered. She had been right to be so certain I would be impressed and would likely prefer what I saw to the city's current state.

I wondered what Istrata would show me once I asked for her to do so. How would this beauty make me see that her current path was the righteous one? Would it not end all of this forever? Would it not prevent us from reaching this level of sophistication and art ever again? Why, then, would showing me this make me think her choice was the right one?

VI

The scenes that unfolded in Istrata's memories had me convinced that it was time to take the next step. I sat down close to the nexus and focused. I called to her, consciously drawing her attention. She had always been able to connect to me when I needed guidance or wished to speak to her. However, that had mostly been through the energy of the statues. I hoped that I could still reach her now that I had destroyed all of them.

After a while of mentally shouting into nothingness, I could feel the connection beginning to form.

"Child, you have kept me waiting a long time and laid waste to my statues."

Her tone was raspier than before, though it still had the element of the honeyed whisper I had gotten used to. A soft invite to follow. The shift in the voice told me I was finally in contact with the real Witch Queen, not just one of her theatrical messengers. Not a puppet to play a never-changing part.

"Apologies, but you must have anticipated I'd rebel. You made me."

"I did," she replied in a hushed, amused voice. *"Why now?"*

"I don't know how much you have followed me or know of my life through other means… I've seen much good and bad in the world. We overthrew one ruler and replaced her with another, yet nothing truly changed. I know the statues must have meant much to you. I feel remorseful for breaking them." I slipped in a small lie as a test.

"They took much of me to make."

"I have your soul now. I have the Needle. I have the city."

"Has it approached you?" Istrata asked with a tenseness in her voice.

"It has. The Source." I volunteered the information. "And that is why I'm calling out to you."

An eerie silence fell like a blanket covering the room. The temperature dropped a little. I swore I could see a shadow slide quickly across the wall. Was it her or just my nerves?

"You are not fully connected to it yet. Good. Then you will finally listen to the latter part of my proposition...?"

"Show me your world, the one you ruled and the one you wish to create."

"Can you travel the strands?"

"A little. Riestel has taught me what he can."

"I am pleased. He has served well then. Child, I will illuminate some for you to follow and meet me. I will guide you to my world."

I did not appreciate her calling me "child" constantly. Though, I did understand the purpose: it was done to stress my lack of knowledge and understanding as much as to assert dominance. There was no love or caring associated with that word for her.

The strand that I could see was gleaming and strong. Clearly important for her or rehearsed for this occasion. As I stepped into the memory, a shudder went through me. Her figure loomed on the opposite side of the golden field of wheat dotted with blue starlets. It was bizarre looking at my old form. A mirror, and yet, not the same at all. As she turned to the light, her figure illuminated like a dove's wing in front of the sun. She smiled warmly, and all the forgiveness in the world emanated from her being.

The wind around us was like a warm embrace, carrying the scent of ripening wheat. The sky and the sun were brighter than I had seen in this life. Glancing around, I couldn't see any clues that she would have tampered with the memory. She gestured around us. The lush autumn lands bore so much bounty it would have fed the entire city, reaching all the way to the horizon and likely beyond.

Another strand appeared close to me. Though it would have been lovely to remain here in this picturesque landscape, I touched it. The wind pushed me gently, and I was flooded with scenes of her good deeds. A winding path of memories from helping orphans to fighting threats, signing laws for the betterment of her people, and working to achieve a lovelier future. A charming, soft-spoken, eloquent coating that covered her exhaustion and growing resentment. Not one scene was altered. All in her kingdom was many times better off than in the Kerth I knew. Then why had all this happened? Where did everything go wrong? Or was it just a creeping progression of small errors and disappointments?

"Do you see, child? Do you see that I only wish and bring good?" she asked. Was that her plan? To simply convince me that I should trust her motives? It seemed like a very weak hand to play.

"I see that you have the best of intentions," I replied, faking to seem a little out of breath with moving from one memory to another.

"You are not yet convinced. I hope you will take from this that I have never done anything to harm my people or my lands. Understand it, and you might look at my actions from a different perspective. One of belief. Belief that my goal is nothing but good."

"No, not yet. Can I visit these places as I think of your offer?"

The Queen stared at me with her eyes narrowing. The radiant figure acquired a grayness to it as if she was leaking color.

"It's just... I would like to understand better. Why create me? If the people loved you and all was well, why the need for me?" I questioned. It couldn't hurt to ask directly; she would think it was only natural for a child to be curious about her origin.

Her eyes grew a dark veil, much like Rime's.

"Because they did not see it. They were not grateful. In the end, I hesitated. I gave them time to see that my ideas and ways were better. They failed me by constantly hindering, questioning, and delaying. I could have made them all ascend beyond humanity," she replied, and her lips twitched. *"Let your mind study what you saw here and rest. Call me again, and I will show you the other side. You may explore the memories should you wish. Do not pry. You need not know my personal life."*

"Oh, don't worry. I have no interest in seeing you and Riestel all entangled."

"I did not create you to be so crude. You are my kin of a sort. Speak softer and more eloquently. Not like a commoner."

"I...well, this is how most talk. Even Riestel nowadays."

"Truly? Then, take it as another piece of evidence that things are not improving. Language is the key to our thoughts and a way to master them, and should it be sloppy and disjointed, so will you be on the inside."

And then she was gone. I felt relieved. She had not noted that I was pretending the traveling was more difficult than it was. She had no reason not to call me out as a liar if she had noticed. Not one that I could think of anyway.

Now, I had her permission and the ability to travel to her memories in the strands. I would need to do it so often that she would lose interest in tracking me each time. Until she would grow accustomed to me. I would also need to sneak in and out as the mouse. That way, she would slowly get desensitized to me poking about.

Hopefully, anyway.

I ran out of the Needle once I felt sure she was completely detached from me. Rime would not have time, nor did I wish to make him uncomfortable again or start another argument, so I found myself at Riestel's door once more. I took a few deep breaths and knocked. He opened the door to a very quiet apartment.

"Where's Elona?" I asked.

"She is sleeping at Arvida's tonight. What do you want, barging in on my wonderful plans to get some well-earned rest?" he asked as if he wasn't happy to see me.

"I did it. I talked to her."

"Her?"

"Istrata," I whispered, very pleased with myself. "I traveled with her to the past. I saw it all. The glory and the bloom of the country."

Riestel pulled me in and sat me down on a chair.

"You did what?" he asked, a little taken aback.

"You heard me just fine, or are you getting so old your ears are failing?"

Riestel stared at me, tilted his head, and let out an amused cough. "You are mad as a rabid rat. That was an enormous risk to take."

"What else should I have done then? And you thought it a good option earlier."

"I meant it as a compliment, you dolt."

"Didn't sound like one, you ass."

Riestel grabbed my hands, kneeling before me. His face beamed. "I have a thing to tell you now that I know you will not waver from this path."

"What is it?" I asked as a strange glow covered the world. Everything felt so light with him. Like we had our own little reality, and all those things around us were just something to get to eventually.

"He will hate it," Riestel warned.

"Then he will. I can't save anyone unless I use all the means I can. Just tell me."

"Sit on the floor then. I'll get you some wine first."

"Why would I need wine?"

"You can't slap me as fast as you normally can if you have a few glasses in you."

"Can I back out?" I asked, suddenly feeling like this was going to be a colossally bad idea.

"Absolutely not."

Riestel pulled the cork out of the bottle with his teeth and spat it toward the table. It rolled off lazily over the edge. He shrugged.

"Someone will clean it eventually," he noted. "Drink."

"You are so spoiled," I groaned and picked the cork up. "See, not that difficult." I put it back on the table, sipping from my glass.

"Shall I get you an apron? Just to add to the atmosphere if you insist on cleaning."

I gave him an annoyed glance, which he seemed very pleased with.

"Get to it already," I ordered.

"You might have noticed it before. It's something we can create when we combine our talents."

"What do you mean before? We haven't combined our skills. I mean, we've fought together, but I can't remember any effects that would have happened from it."

"You are thinking of the wrong kind of together." Riestel smirked. "Do you remember when we performed the fasting ceremony for your friends? Those little flashes or the tingling feeling when we cracked the seal?"

"I'm just amazed you do. You didn't exactly relish having to bless their union."

"Silly creature. I loved it. Every moment I could steal with you. I felt I was slowly coming back to life, looking at you. It didn't matter that you hated me."

I coughed the wine from my windpipe and had to cover my mouth not to spit it out.

He sneered. "Charming as always."

"Don't just suddenly try to be all heartfelt; the shock alone will kill me," I scolded him as the wine began to spread within and make the world all lovely and fuzzy. Truth be told, a part of me felt guilty sitting here, feeling happy. However, the other part wanted to play with fire. Just a little, just to alleviate some of the stress and disappointments over the last months.

"Oh, I'll do much worse," Riestel promised. "Spread your legs."

"That's really not going to happen," I declined, a little taken aback.

"You have such a one-track mind. I meant sit like this." He laughed and straightened his legs to a wide "V," smiling ever so wickedly.

"Fine," I mumbled, a little disappointed. The moment I sat as he asked, he pulled my legs over his and me right to him, so there wasn't even an inch between us. Then, he took my glass and put it down before I managed to spill the rest on his floor.

"Stay put," he ordered as I tried to squirm away. "Mirror my hands."

Riestel laid his hands on my shoulders and moved them up to the bare skin of my neck. I hesitated to do the same, but he wasn't letting me go. I finally placed them similarly, trying to avoid his gaze, as it made me highly uncomfortable.

"Look at me," he told me. "I know it's difficult, but do it. You need to let yourself feel the tension. The more, the better."

I lifted my eyes to his and felt like my face was hotter than after a hundred bee stings. The blood in my veins quickened, as did the energy in my channels. My body heated, and the air between us became a swirl of thick, humid heat and cold. A shiver rose within my spine. The air crackled as time ceased to exist in the moment.

"This is our natural way. Don't fight it, let it gather," Riestel whispered and closed his legs behind me, encircling me. Our breath mixed. I felt an immense urge to melt into him. As his chest rose, mine gave way. Over and over again. There was an intense pleasure in being so close and yet not doing anything. A strong wave of pure bliss washed through me. A loud crack jolted me to my senses as bolts of lightning rushed out from us. The bolts shattered the glass and left a burn mark on the wall.

"I can see that was rather good for you," Riestel whispered. "How about returning the favor?"

My hand rose instinctively to slap him, but he caught it.

"See," he exclaimed, triumphant.

I felt mortified, staring into his eyes with so much desire. I knew better than to give into temptation even if I was exactly where my desire to tempt the fates for a moment had led me. I hurried to my feet and ran out. The amount of shame from letting this go that far was nearly eclipsed by the realization that being there felt so right and exciting. It filled me with a sense of ageless love. Being alone with him made me feel intoxicated. The pull clouded my mind. It was so difficult to fight it. At this rate, I'd betray my promise. I had kissed him before, but I hadn't been myself. It had been Istrara's consciousness more than mine. This time, there would be no excuse.

There was a small pond just between two statues of white peacocks. Kneeling beside the water, I tried to steady my breath. Just a moment later, Riestel's face reflected from the water.

"Could you stop running?" he asked quietly.

"I can't."

"Why?"

"Why? Why do you insist on torturing me? You know I'm his wife. You know I don't want to let him down. Without him, I would have perished in your tests. I was so close to losing myself, and he was all that kept me sane."

"I know...but I just can't help it. I had been missing a piece of myself for so long, for what felt like forever. When I'm near you, I feel as if everything is the way it should be. I know it pains you and him. I'm selfish, not blind. And I'm sorry for not feeling the slightest bit of remorse for it. I waited centuries, and in a world that might perish at any moment, I will take my pleasures when and where I find them," Riestel explained almost absentmindedly, without breaking eye contact.

"We don't have to do it like that every time, right?" I asked and got up to face him.

"Of course not. It was purely for my amusement," he confessed.

The air between us was gathering charge again. We both felt it. The desire to reach out and just forget everything for a sweet moment.

"However," he noted with an impish look. "It was definitely the fastest way for you to learn it."

"Fine," I responded, almost not hearing my own words. The world beyond his face seemed to fade away. All I could think of was his touch.

"Do it then," I dared.

"No," Riestel said with a smile. "I will not make you regret tonight. But I will make you long for another outcome." He pulled me into his arms. He tilted my head gently so that our lips were an eyelash's width apart. Exchanging breaths again, we made the air move in hot and cold swirls. The thick, humid air enveloped us in a gentle fog. All the hairs on my body stood up. A tingle crept up from one cell to another. I yielded fully to the feeling.

Riestel twirled me around with his left hand, sliding below my breasts and taking my right hand into his right hand and pointing it away from us. The charge gathered and shot out from our joined hands. The other peacock statue blew up into a million stone splinters and dust particles.

I laughed, elated.

"Let's try this on the black tar!" I decided. "My fire can't rip it apart fast enough. This might."

"We should," Riestel agreed. "But perhaps we need to practice alone first if you don't want him to see us evoke it like this. I would not mind an audience, but I know you might."

VII

O ver the next training battles, things progressed well, even though Riestel and I kept our private rehearsals a secret for now. All three of us panted, sweaty and weary, as we finished for the day. A few of Rime's guard members nodded approvingly by the field. Rime did not fault us for our lack of trying, which was almost a miracle.

There had been a small breakthrough today as when I was forcing the black tar to burn, I noticed the faster I could force it to purify, the more sand was left. The sand from the suffering was anything but pretty with its jagged and irregular shapes. It was painful to use as fuel, but it was perhaps possible with practice to further refine the grains. I could use them in their coarse form, but the others could not.

Rime was physically the least tired of us, though not at all unaffected. The more we rehearsed, the more often we would notice that as we stopped, he would remove himself from our vicinity for a few moments to cool off. He had made it clear; no one was to approach him before he had regained his wits and composure. We could see how much each bout took out of him, and every time, recovery took a little longer. Once he shook it off, he was back to his polite but stern self.

The ichor Rime drew and controlled took its toll. He became less and less social, giving orders by written memoranda and commandments. One could see how vexed the members of his guard were. He had always had a dark side, but now the lighter moments were truly far and few in between.

"I'm pleased," Rime told us as he returned. The veins in his eyes were still black. "You two are making good headway. You keep the ichor under control better, and your fire bites into the figures better. It's still not great but a clear improvement, especially together with the other consecrators."

"I'm glad you think so. But should we not have at least a few days of rest soon? This is draining us all," I said. "The others are almost getting hurt trying to force through the exercises. And I feel we are using more of the life forces than we should…"

"No, we shouldn't rest," Rime replied.

"I think Isa might be right," Riestel said. "And she means you. You are the one who needs the break more than us. We are simply tired. You are in need of a whole retreat."

"I'm perfectly capable of continuing," Rime said, dismissing the concerns.

"You are not. I dislike you more than any other man here, and even I can see you are pushing too hard," Riestel admonished. "Tomorrow, we rest. How will you help your city or Isa if you lose control permanently?"

To my amazement, Rime nodded. The two men had developed some sort of mutual understanding that I wasn't a part of at all. I was pleased that their animosity decreased, but it was odd to watch them being almost cordial.

As nice as a rest would have been, I couldn't help myself and headed for the nexus first thing in the morning. Then, crawling in my furry disguise ever so quietly and slowly, I crossed the floor in one of Istrata's memories. Reaching into the air, I could see her notebooks piled on the table in the Needle. She turned from her tasks and, with a simple reaching of her hand, made the pen dance and write what she wished.

My heart thumped and skipped as I clawed my way up onto the table. I hid behind the books to calm down. As she returned to her work, I peeked hurriedly at the notes. Most words were unintelligible or faded from her memory. The lines she just added, however, could be read. "A possible solution. A curious black substance left over from the creation of the knights. Like a discharge from a wound. The Enforcer does not know of it. Perhaps I can shape this world without submitting to her. For truly, not one person will ever again dictate my destiny. I will not be a servant to these ungrateful people. I will be their benefactor whether they like it or not."

The scene faded, and I returned to my body. I visited the memory again and again to ensure I had read the sentences correctly and to memorize the appearance of the notebook in case I could find it among her belongings. We had focused on the actual treaties and left her more personal and obscure ramblings alone, as they had been of no direct help with the resuscitation efforts.

If I understood her writing correctly, she had not taken well at all to the Source's offer. That was easy to see from the name she called it. This memory had to have been from after she had been driven to think people would never appreciate her and listen to her. Could she have concluded that as long as they had free will, they would always choose wrong in her mind?

The thought hurt a little, maybe because I recognized the way of thinking in me. Many times, I felt I knew better but had to watch things be done another way. That feeling had been dangerously validated by being a sort of chosen. Despite the fact that I was chosen because there was no one else to choose from, as there was no one else with this connection to the world. Istrata had made sure they had all been lost.

The Source had told me of the limitations of the powers and their development. Without temples to guide us, people were still always drawn to one element or type of power due to their natural connection to the world. A quality ordained at birth, just as height and dimples. Some might possess the capability for more than one, but choosing to focus on the strongest yielded the best results as the channels would get accustomed to just one type of flow.

The easiest way to get people to follow their strongest path had been to introduce the idea of following the will of some stronger being. Thus, the gods as we knew them were implemented. The tradition was old and one that Istrata had attacked in order to show people what the world was really like. Perhaps, just to spite the Source.

Istrata had had an eagerness to do away with all old, false beliefs. I felt closer to her for it, but at the same time, I had already dismissed it as a course of action. People here needed faith, and better to have faith in things that make you aspire to be better and fulfill your life with the pursuit of improvement than to surrender fully to the idea of everything just being the way it is, without any higher goal and no reason to become more than you are.

Having been a shut-in all day, I became aware of my stomach rumbling, but I wanted to try to find the notebook. It might yield some more insights into her. Moras didn't recognize it when I described it to him, but he did admit that he couldn't possibly remember all of them anyway. He also told me that the ones they were not using for study had been arranged in an empty room on the floor just above us.

The floor contained four rooms used for storage. One just for her books, notes, and equipment. I went through each shelf, but there was nothing that looked like the one I had seen. Strange. She had kept them all in such good order. Could there still be another place we didn't know about? The pockets between the plains. Could there be some I hadn't yet noticed? It seemed unlikely as I had combed the entire Needle for such places after learning of them. But…those were places between this world and the lighter one. Could there be others between this and the heavy world? What if there were, and I simply couldn't sense them or reach them? Maybe Rime could, being more her kind.

"Do you know where Rime is?" I asked Moras, passing his floor again.

"He was in for his daily check-up but left. He might have gone for a walk. He usually does that afterward."

"Thank you."

Rime didn't seem to enjoy spending time around people anymore, so he would have probably sought a peaceful route. I looked around outside. What seemed like the best location to go to avoid most servants and residents? The mountain. He might have gone up.

I walked along the edge of the mountain that held the entire city at its base and slopes. There were some small paths, but nothing that looked like it would lead anywhere. Then, I noticed him sitting at the Needle's height on a ledge. He looked so small and lonely, leaning on his knees and staring off into the distance.

The upward slope wasn't at an extremely steep angle, but the stone was hard and smooth in many places, making the ascend slow. It was almost more like stone that had been polished by the sea than rock you would expect to see at these heights. The climbing made me feel a little lightheaded. I should have eaten before running out to look for him.

"What are you doing here?" Rime asked and looked over the ledge as he heard me approach. He looked a little annoyed, but I got the feeling it was more of an attempt to keep me at bay than actual irritation.

"I could ask you the same thing," I muttered. "Help me up. I'm not going away whether you like it or not."

"It's not a question of like. I just—"

"Exactly."

"Hold on, I'll come down. This isn't big enough for two to sit on comfortably," Rime told me. "There is a path that leads here, you know. You didn't need to go through all that."

"And how should I have known about it?"

"Follow me."

"I usually have."

"I can't tell if you are angry at me or playing," Rime noted, his mood seeming to improve a little.

"I can definitely say both."

"I thought we talked things over."

"That doesn't mean I feel fine about all of it," I answered, a little too honestly for my liking.

Rime stopped on the path and glanced at me, frowning. "I don't want to give you false ideas anymore. I don't think I can offer you a future in the state I'm in."

"Don't, not now. I'm not here to talk about us. We can settle things later. But I do need your help finding the rest of Istrata's hiding spots."

"Her what?"

"Well," I started as we reached ground level. "I have a theory…" I continued as I slipped on the very last smooth stone. Rime grabbed me, and before I knew it, I was held tightly in his embrace. I closed my eyes and rested my head on his shoulder just for one stolen moment. Tentatively, he did the same. It fulfilled a longing but also stirred up another emotion I had not expected. The ichor in him was so strong it made my skin crawl. We both stepped back.

"Are you alright?" he asked.

"Yes, thank you. A bit dizzy as I skipped eating today. I wasn't paying attention," I answered. "Anyway, I got to thinking about pocket planes and that there could be more than just the ones I can sense. I don't have a connection to the heavier world as you do. I can only sense it in this plane and the lighter, as it doesn't belong in those."

"I don't have any training for a task like that."

"You don't need any. You just need to feel them out and then travel to them."

"Sounds simple enough."

"Well, there might be a little more to it. I know you are busy with many things. I would still request your help. I don't have anyone else to turn to."

"What about Riestel? Wouldn't he know of them?"

"I don't think he would. Istrata kept many secrets from him concerning her experiments. There is no way for him to feel them out, either. I merely thought that you might be the answer as you force similar pathways into existence when you jump from one location to another. At least, I think the mechanic is the same. Though, if you don't want to help, I suppose I can try with Riestel."

Rime's expression went from irritated to hesitant. "I will try. I can't promise it'll be of use."

"That's enough for me."

"When do you want to start?"

"Now."

"Now? That's a bit..."

"Look, I'm not going to give you time to weasel your way out of this. You can avoid me all you want after we check the Needle. That's fine."

"I'm not trying to avoid you."

"You absolutely are. You are trying to find an excuse to bolt even now."

"I do not run from conflict," Rime answered and scowled. I had rarely known him to lie to me. He never ran from disputes. That was true.

"Then you are running from me," I called out his attempt to misdirect my thoughts.

"Isa, I—"

"I, I, I. Stop. I'm trying to save you. I will be here until I do or until you die. You can push me away all you want, and I will accept that if it makes you feel better. But you cannot make me give up on your existence. Whether we are together or not, you matter."

Rime looked away. I felt how desperately he was trying to keep everything together. Pushing him to break now would a cruel deed that would only serve my vanity.

"I need to eat. Meet me in the Needle a little later," I said, as I didn't want to force my presence on him. "Please come. It must be done soon."

VIII

T he night came, but Rime did not.

The early morning found me alone and in an annoyed mood. Maybe I shouldn't have asked for his help after all. If the matter weren't so important, I would just leave him to his foolishness. The idea of going to look for him and making the same plea again made me feel ill. I didn't want to have to chase him like a needy puppy.

A knock on the door interrupted my agonizing.

Rime stepped in, looking a little like a hungry wolf. I could feel the bite of his darker side from many steps away. Seeing him having to fill himself with that tarry ichor almost daily made me endlessly sad.

"This is a surprise," I noted, trying not to sound too harsh.

"I did mean to come yesterday, but I felt I needed to be alone for a while longer."

"And you couldn't send word? You aren't the only one who has things to do."

"Apologies. For being late and for being an idiot. I know you will always care for me as I do for you. I'm just so tired. I try to sleep, but my eyes just don't close. Even if I do fall asleep, it allows me no rest." Rime sighed, leaning a little on the wall next to the door.

"Is it from the connection to the heavier world? The machines aren't helping to control it well enough, then?" I asked, concerned.

"They help. Without the metallic structures Moras planted in me, I might not have made it back to my old self after that outburst at my father's coronation festivities."

"Do you have nightmares, or why can't you get rest?"

"When I close my eyes...I see nothing. Just a vast, dark ocean that swallows me. Like a cold hand that pulls me in deeper until..." He shuddered.

"You don't need to tell me the details if it pains you," I said, stopping him, as it was uncomfortable for him. "The more you use the skills, the faster you sink into the heavier world."

"Yes. I feel it all the time now."

"I could...maybe... I could try burning some away from within you. It will feel like you'd be boiling inside. And there is no way for me to clean you completely. I can't remove it from any of the main channels. It could kill you. Still, maybe I can get out enough so you can sleep and dream. To a state more like you were in when we met. It will leave you weaker, of course, less able to use your powers."

Rime lifted his hands and held them palms up to the skies at shoulder height, moving them up and down like a scale.

"Pain or agony?" he asked with a grim smile. "I'd rather have my legs broken a thousand times than lose myself to this nightmare. I think we have rehearsed enough to plan. I do not need to be in full form at the moment."

"Do you want me to try it now?"

"No. You need me to find the pockets. It might lessen my ability to do so. But I would request that it be done tonight. Especially if I find what you need."

"Of course. Anytime you want."

"What should I search for, then?" Rime asked, looking a little less anxious. "How should I look?"

"That's the tricky part. I don't know," I said and smiled nervously.

Rime looked at me in disbelief. His practical mind would need more than "a feeling."

"There are no rules for it. I found the ones in the lighter world just by feeling them out. Not much help, I know. Let me explain. The lighter world, to me, feels pure. It fills me with hope and excitement, like the first moments of an infatuation. Think of what the heavier world makes you feel and then of places where that seems to permeate the world. If you manage to breach one, this is what you are looking for," I told him and showed him a sketch of the notebook. "Well, any notes will do, really. This is just the journal I know about."

"This is not going to be a fun task." Rime sighed. "Alright. I will go and walk around the Needle. I will let you know if I find something."

"Do you want company?"

"Not for something like this. How do I enter them?"

"You know how to enter the heavier world, and you know how to move between this and it. That's instinctive for you at this point, yes?"

"It is."

"Do it very slowly. If you charge through, you will miss it. Just push into the separating membrane ever so softly, and if there is something in its structures, you will have time to notice it and direct yourself into it. The doorways are small and thin, but they exist."

"Right. I'll see you later."

"Alright," I agreed, feeling rather strange after the discussion.

I did not like it one bit that he went to look for them alone, though it was understandable. It would be easier for him to concentrate without me lurking over his shoulder and waiting. Learning new skills was less embarrassing alone. For me, anyway.

As the day waned, I began to worry. There was something in the air that made me nervous. Like the Needle itself was darker. He must have found some of the spaces. Darkness and shadows hardly ever made me feel skittish. Now, the hair on my arms was standing up. The door to the room began to slide into the shades, like in an eclipse.

Rime came through the blackened door. His face was covered in a dark veil. The outside evening sun had a hard time illuminating the room. Rime said nothing. He walked to the small table and placed a few notebooks there. One was very likely the one I was after.

"A gift for you," Rime told me in a cold voice. "I feel as if I've been gnawed to the bone. It was like jumping head first into mud, and it gets everywhere." He leaned on the table. "Please get it out." He fell to his knees and then to the floor.

I helped Rime to a seated position.

"Take me to the balcony. I'd rather suffer amidst beauty."

"I'm not pretty enough scenery for you?" I asked, trying to alleviate his worries and give him enough support to get him outside to the sun.

Rime grinned, tired.

"You know you are."

"I like hearing it."

He gave a short laugh that turned into a cough as we sat down.

"You should have declined me," I scolded him. "If I would have known it would make you sicker, I wouldn't have asked."

"Exactly why I didn't tell you. So, you did not need to ask knowing it."

"There is no point in you sacrificing yourself for everyone else."

"If someone has to..."

"Hush, take a breath. This will hurt." I sat straddled on his lap and placed my hands on his chest.

I could feel how full he was of the ichor. All his channels, his blood, his eyes. It was everywhere. I felt his channels as carefully as I could and began to burn the mass away. His eyes flashed as dark as the mouth of a cave, but he stayed his reaction to defend. His breath became labored, and his hands squeezed the fabric of his trousers.

His pain reminded me sharply of Launea's fate when I had nearly killed her in a very similar manner. Her facial scars, though greatly diminished now, were a constant taunting reminder of the inadequacy of my skills. Rime knew everything that had happened then, and yet, he trusted himself to my care.

"Hang on," I whispered. "I'm working as carefully and as fast as I dare."

The metal contraptions in and around Rime's spine and the artificial channels Moras had created within him heated to the point of burning him from within. His body started to tremble, then shake and jolt, as I forced more of the substance to burn. I had to allow for areas to cool before continuing, which only prolonged the suffering. Rime's breaths became more like growls of pain. They were sharp and unevenly spaced apart.

The veins on his neck pulsated. I begun to ease off. I would never forgive myself if I hurt him irreparably. I had to stop the thought before it went further. If I focused on the stakes and allowed my feelings to surface, the possibility of errors would by manyfold.

Rime grabbed my wrist and kept my hand of his chest. "Keep going. I trust you. Be quick."

Taking a deep breath, I readied myself. I knew his channels almost as well as my own. This was Rime's will, I had to allow it to him.

I pushed the fire in, further, deeper, and faster than I had ever done without an intent to kill. Rime's body tensed as he convulsed with his back arching and his fingers curling into fists. Then he went limp. His eyes closed and his head tilted to the left. All color seemed drain from him.

"Rime?" I called him and pressed my ear to his chest. His heart was quiet. As mine was about to burst from panic, I felt the beat return. I shook my hands to chase away the nervous tremors and try and calm myself. Rime did not need to know how close he had come to death.

Rime opened his eyes, weary and sweaty.

"I will not do more. I would damage you beyond repair," I told him as calmly as I could.

Rime smiled and took my hand. His eyes were again green with amber flecks shining almost bright orange as the sun's last rays landed on him. The ichor that did remain in him began to heal him right away.

"I feel clean, more like myself." He sighed and breathed in heavily, like someone stepping out to fresh sea air from a musty cave.

And suddenly, everything about Rime was as it had been when we had been happy. His manners, voice, touch. I hadn't even noticed how much he had changed, as it had been so gradual.

"You know… I have nothing but love for you, but I cannot be with you, not the way I am. And there is no point in saying that maybe we will meet in another life. I will not have one, and you will be a being far different after all this if we win." Rime softly wiped some sweat off his brow. It was slightly grayish as the destroyed ichor mixed with it.

"Don't say such things."

"But I have to, just in case. I miss you next to me. I know something is growing between you and…him. And…that's alright. I'm too late in my apology, but I need you." Rime kissed me ever so gently. He looked at me as if to ask if he was still allowed to feel what he felt.

"No one has taken your place," I replied and held him tightly. Both of us were almost at the edge of our strength, so each movement was filled with a slow, lazy tenderness. Looking into his eyes, I smiled and nodded. Just once more. His warm body pressed on mine. I closed my eyes as he clasped my hands above my head against the warm stone. Once he came, we stayed in the embrace for a small eternity. He kissed me again and let me go.

Neither of us knew what to say, so we just sat in the rays of the setting sun as its golden warmth made us lean on the wall to enjoy its heat. I squeezed Rime's hand, and he mine. His head slowly nodded to my shoulder as he fell asleep. I remained awake to guard his dreams and watched the sun disappear.

When the dim late evening brought safety, I felt hot tears running down my face. I laid his head on my lap to make it more comfortable for him. If there was nothing else I could do yet, at least I could let him dream. His breathing was deep and quiet as I stroked his hair. If I could have given him a piece of my soul, I would have.

Morning came, and Rime slept. He twitched a little from being in an awkward position and then opened his eyes. His hair was all slanted.

"Did you sit there all night?" he asked and looked up at me. "You should have woken me; it must have been uncomfortable."

"Nothing I couldn't handle. How are you feeling?"

"Better than in a long time."

"I can treat you now and then, but I don't think it is safe to do it very often as it does leave burns inside you no matter how delicately I do it."

"Understood. Still... I had a dream. I haven't seen a dream in months." Rime smiled as he got up.

"What did you dream of?"

"A different life. A different time. A simple profession and a family. A house I had actually built. I felt so... I felt so unimaginably free and happy."

"I guess I wasn't there," I noted, feeling a little jealous.

"No, you were not," Rime said and lowered his head. "But I won't be either."

IX

Seeing Rime the way he used to be was conflicting. I felt such relief that I could do something for him, that he could rest and find life bearable. There was an attraction between us still when the ichor did not fill him. One that he was doing everything in his power to fight. He missed me as I missed him. That wasn't enough to keep going. But it wouldn't stop me from trying to save him, giving him every ounce of support that I could. As much as I wanted to hold on, I felt like that night had been a goodbye.

I didn't tell Riestel what had happened between me and Rime. I needed a proper mourning period if this had been it. There was still a slight spark of hope within me, an annoying, persistent nagging that kept telling me that he would change his mind once I found a cure. It might very well happen; the trouble was, it truly might be too late then because of my feelings for Riestel, and if I waited until such a time, hoping and pining, I might have wasted what little life I had left.

The notebooks Rime had retrieved proved to be interesting. They didn't provide answers within themselves but hints at moments of her life that might give some glimpses of a solution. I felt too nervous to just jump in them to have a look. If she had placed these books in pockets to which only she had had access, it wasn't likely the memories linked to them were not somewhat fresh in her mind. She might even be guarding them. Any misstep could alert her. Perhaps I should talk to her again before trying. If I were to get caught, it was unlikely she would agree to a friendly chat afterward.

The night I had spent with Rime and the morning after it had left me drained emotionally, which might benefit me when talking to Istrata. It was hard to read someone utterly exhausted for subtle clues. I didn't wish to invite her to the Needle again. This was my sanctuary now. Her presence seemed like an offense.

The finest summer day I had seen in my time in the city cast its shimmer on the Peak. The wind rustled through the fresh leaves. A small turquoise butterfly, either a pheasant's eye blue or an eastern peak blue, glided past. The wings gleamed. Then it occurred to me I hadn't seen one all summer before this moment. Where had it come from when all others were missing or dead? Following the butterfly, I wound my way to a small abandoned hut on a slope past the reservoir. Behind it was a tiny blooming meadow with buzzing bees and several butterflies. The green of the flower stems was healthy and strong —beautiful and alarming.

Cautiously, I touched the leaves of a delicate purple and blue riverbellflower. Next to it, blazing orange, was a cranestarlet. The ground itself oozed life. It was abundant and overflowing. The revival efforts were starting to show. This was what we were fighting for. It gave me a sudden burst of determination.

I looked for a good out-of-the-way spot outside and concentrated on the Queen's name.

"Child, I hear you. No need to for such a deafening call," Istrata answered, and her shadow was cast on the earth, no longer merely an ethereal voice. *"I feel I've almost rested long enough."* She sighed. *"How are your thoughts on this auspicious day?"*

"I've been visiting those memories... And I am convinced that you do what you see would be best for the world."

"I've noticed you come and go frequently."

"I hope that hasn't been a bother."

"It has not, merely amusing. You have seen my endeavors to make this world into a good place for all. If you believe now that I only mean well, what have you to tell me?"

"I have no answer yet. There is one thing that eats at me. That is... In the beginning, Riestel always talked about you as this wonderful benefactor who would do all for her people and was a gentle soul... Then can you explain why you think that, for the lack of a better word, lifelessness is a better option than the living, blossoming world we live in?" I asked as I sincerely wished to understand my creator and how she had strayed so far from her virtues.

"Beauty comes in many guises. Certainly, I appreciate the appeal of a rose and

the elegant swiftness of a hawk. But these are unruly things, and unruly things cause pain to themselves and each other without mind. Humans, likewise, do such horrible things. And with intent, no less. Slowly, I came to see there was an equal loveliness in absolute order. In the unchangingness of eternal ice. When all is immutable, no one needs to go without; no one craves, covets, or envies. All have what I assign them equally, and they are content. No one can change themselves. Only I can mold them and the world then. I will lead them to a future that is even better than what you have now seen the past to be."

"You would tame the world because you cannot accept that you can't rule everything in it for its benefit?"

"Thorny is the flower of my creation." Istrata laughed. *"You would judge me? Very well. Follow, and I will show you all the ways humans hurt themselves, no matter how hard you try to offer them a reasonable way of living."*

As before, I took hold of the strands she gave me. I could see people killing each other. I could see them lie, cheat, wage war, and do all those despicable things many only secretly think of. Each time she tried to prevent a mistake or another injustice in her court, people would find excuses as to why other high-ranking members just could not be brought to justice. Maybe the offense was against someone who didn't matter in their eyes, or maybe the offender was the person everyone liked enough to brush off their horrible deeds simply to keep their comfortable reality.

I knew all the things she showed and felt as she did. Her logic was unwavering. If people could not grow and develop to cherish this world and each other, what was the point of them? She had built them a paradise to live in, and yet they still squabbled and killed for the pettiest of reasons.

The trouble was, as flawed as they were, in her mind, she loved them too much to simply kill them all, and thus, she had chosen this road. A road to take their will for as long as it took for her to change them to be good by mandate. A world of stagnation with no organic, free development to force into an existence a world where, through mutual suffering, people would finally shed their base needs. By force, not by will. By squeezing them into a mold of her making, not by voluntary growth.

There were no words to describe how I felt about her plan. I knew myself capable of the same. But would a forced peace for creatures who had no will of their own be worth anything? She would take everyone under her spell and bend them to her own will until all was as she wished. Until all behaved well enough for her, like her.

"And then? After all life follows your mind exactly? What then? Will there be a point where you undo all? Let them live again?"

Istrata looked at me, puzzled, like it was a question she had never considered.

"Why? Why would they want to be free? To make more mistakes and misery? To potentially undo all I accomplished? I'm offering you all a world with nought but contentment. You will have all you require to exist, and you will want for nothing. You will not need to work, not eat, not sleep, not fall in love and despair. You will exist in the most comfortable state you can imagine. Can you not see it? Can you understand that no one needs to worry about anything once I take over them? Would you not wish to escape the pain you know is coming if you refuse me?"

Istrate looked at me as if trying to figure out if someone finally understood her.

"I have seen the world through your eyes. I agree; it is a horrible place at its worst. But... I cannot see your way as the solution. If we do not suffer, we do not develop, and if we do not develop, what point is there to life, to existence itself? I don't care how many times they will deceive me; I believe they can improve, and when they do so on their own, it will be truly wonderful."

Istrata's brows furrowed.

"You are far too young and far too hopeful then to see them for what they truly are. A failed creation of the Enforcer. A stain in her plan. You would doom me to an ageless loneliness as well. Why do you creatures defy me? Can you not see the prize at the end? Do you really not understand it and simply fear the change? A world where everything is provided for you."

"I can see it. I just don't believe in it. People are infuriating, but if the change and development do not come from them, what is it worth? They will not be granted souls; they will not find new lives and purpose. Everyone will merely exist. That, to me, is terrifying. To simply be and be nothing but a clump of flesh to bow to another. To mindlessly sit as your base needs are taken care of by a so-called benefactor that allows you to sit and rot. It would be a wonderful world if all did only good and everything would be fair... I'm just not naïve enough to believe that will ever be possible."

"Naïve?"

"You have great intellect, no doubt, to have done all you have and wrestled this world to bend to your will enough to create something that was not meant to exist. But you have not opened yourself to the world; you constantly fight it. I see now that you did all those good things, not because you were good but because you felt they would entitle you to things. To be the judge. You cannot do good if you hold the other person as a moral hostage for your perceived noble deeds. I…feel nothing but pity for you."

"*Entitled? Pity? I will show you how wrong you are,*" she promised coldly. "*You, a mere construct of my will, a placeholder for my soul, would defy and scold me. The next time we speak, it will be when I come to devour you.*"

Then, I felt it. She had awoken. It was like a wave of nausea rippled through our very existence. We were soon out of time. While she gathered her bearings, I would need to investigate, and for that, I would need Arvida.

Riestel barged in after my conversation with Istrata. The look on his face told me he had felt it as well.

"Yes, the Queen has woken," I stated. "I was talking to her when she was roused."

"What did you say to her to wake her up?"

"Nothing… I just declined her courteous offer. I might have offended her a bit."

"Of course, I would not expect less. We aren't ready." Riestel shook his head.

"I doubt she will immediately have all her pawns in a row. But we must become more alert, and we must begin to set up defenses faster," I mused. Waking after being asleep for hundreds of years was likely not something you shook off in mere moments.

"You seem very calm despite this," Riestel remarked.

"I…am… I'm at peace, really. I know her now, and there is nothing more she can do to tempt me to her side. I was always afraid she could somehow take me over or awaken me to her truth. That she would appear to me like a true sage or a god. But she can't. She is just another misguided fool like I am— like we all are. A dangerous one, but still a fool. She was so furious at me like she wanted to stamp me out. I imagine she has always hoped for validation of her path being the correct one… I understand what that feels like. I was the one who she wanted praise from. After all, if a creature created of you cannot understand you, then who can? Also, earlier, I found a small meadow bustling with life. Flowers, bugs, and the like. We can do this. We need to do this."

Riestel nodded, seeming quite happy with what he heard.

"Where is it? I want to show it to Elona."

I told him the location of the meadow, and just when I thought I was safe from him picking up on anything else about my mood, he turned back from the door.

"You seem sad," he noted. "I don't think an encounter with her would have caused that. What did he do this time?"

"Nothing."

"Liar."

"Really, nothing."

"Your chance of fooling me is about the same as a lark's falling tailfeather causing a storm."

"We just...talked. About the future of us, of this world, everything really. It was unexpected and draining. I was able to purge him, though it will diminish his powers. For a moment, he was the man I fell in love with."

"Good, we don't need him to be a liability amidst all else," Riestel said, his voice a little hushed. A part of me wanted to say that everything was likely drawing to a conclusion between Rime and me, but I wasn't ready. Furthermore, I wasn't sure if I'd be truthful saying it when I still felt a small glimmer of hope for the relationship. I needed some time to see whether my feelings for Rime would begin to fade or if I would miss him even more. First on my list was still finding a way to save him.

"Send Arvida my way, would you?" I requested. "I'm jumping into Istrata's memories to see if I can find anything useful."

"I will. But I insist on being present for safety now that she is more aware."

"Of course."

X

A rvida didn't waste time after being summoned. She was always curious to participate in any endeavor or challenge. It still amazed me at how poorly I had judged her in the beginning, though she was partially responsible for it, manipulating my feelings the moment we met.

"What will you do?" Arvida asked while strumming her slender fingers on the windowsill.

"Everything to help him, nothing more," I answered.

"Your answers are getting to be worse and more cryptic than Riestel's, you know. Honestly." She laughed. "What did you summon me here for?"

"Sorry, I guess his ways are rubbing off on me a bit. I need you to act as a dampener for me."

"A what?"

"A dampener. I will attempt to go into Istrata's memories again. But I know that if I get too nervous, she might catch me, especially now that she knows I'm not agreeing to her plans."

"Alright. I can keep your heart stable, at least when it comes to her. Not sure about the boys."

"Good skies. What are you on about?"

"I can sense your emotions, you know," she reminded me.

"I… We… I slept with Rime a little while ago."

"Isn't that a good thing? Why do you seem so out of balance?"

"It was a farewell. At least it felt like that. If you must know."

"Oh, I'm sorry. I should have just waited and not poked my nose right into it… But since I already did…and you aren't going to hate me anyway, no matter how much you scowl at me, did you tell Riestel?"

"Absolutely not. Do not dare to either."

"You are still pining, then."

"I wouldn't say I'm pining. Wait…truly, this is not the time or the place for this conversation," I decided, a little annoyed.

"You should tell Riestel."

"Why? You are such a meddler. Did he put you up to this interrogation? He already suspects something is going on."

"No." Arvida giggled at my frustration. "I'm simply of the opinion that he is a very good match for you. I want you to be happy. When you were with Rime, I took no sides, but…"

"I can't be happy if Rime dies without a future."

"Understood, but don't get all nearsighted about it. Remember to look to the horizon. Past the clouds."

"Listen. I do appreciate your care, and I hear you. Riestel…is… He is so much more than I first thought, but that is no excuse for me to behave inappropriately. To cross that final line, I mean, I know my behavior has already been worthy of a scolding. Rime is still wearing his fasting bracelet. As am I. We are bound. That's not something I can just forget. I don't think he would want me to either."

"Will you break the fasting, then? Once things are decided?"

"I know it is sometimes done, but it doesn't feel right, not at the moment."

"Something to think about," Arvida urged. "I know it is not easy, but I am one living example that it can be done and that one can find a new life after it."

"I'm happy you have, but you hardly loved your husband. At any point in your relationship. Can we please move on from this? There are much more important things to do."

"I shall bury this subject and obey your instructions to my best ability now that most of my curiosity has been satiated." Arvida looked more mischievous than was called for as I was getting increasingly uncomfortable.

We sat on the floor by the nexus after Riestel arrived. Arvida sat right behind me with her hands resting on my shoulders. I could feel a numbing of all my base emotions. It was a peculiar sensation for all feelings to subside and quiet, leaving only a purely sensible version of my consciousness awake.

Plucking my way through the different threads and strands, I was trying to find the earliest memories the Queen had about the substance. When I found them, it was easy to see the changes in her. She had been lovely and selfless, too lenient even, before meddling with it, but once her curiosity got the better of her, she let it and so much more in.

I watched her face as the sludge entered her channels. She looked confused, horrified, and ecstatic. She hadn't allowed herself to use souls, only general life forces before it, so injecting this dense shot of power and energy simply washed through her in a ball of lightning of pleasure and pain.

After it had cleared out, she was sweaty and trembled a little, but it was easy to see it had opened a whole new world to her, a world she would not give up. I watched her from the shadows as she experimented with it on herself. It made her character more inflexible, more intolerant of other ideas, and more judgmental. And all those things together must have corrupted her thoughts and made her feel even more isolated and disconnected. Instead of turning in to see if there was something she could do, she turned outward to see what others should be like to please her.

It was a bizarre feeling, following a person so like me in most ways from one life event to another as she constantly chose the path that led her further and further from what she had originally desired. A connection with the world and the people, someone to understand her and see her.

She became so blind that she even lost sight of Riestel and how much he had adored her. She loved him deeply. I could see and feel that, but in the end, she was so adamant about her course of action that there was no room for that love in her world. She was so disappointed in people; she began to see their faults in him too. When she died, there was a fleeting moment of pure love in her for him. It had been the last thing she had felt, but after that, all had become cold and lifeless in her existence, like her corpse.

Now, to do her justice, it wasn't just her mistakes that drove her. It was Elona. No one gave her hope for her daughter's recovery, so she turned to a substance with so much potential. She froze Elona's frail body in a horrid stasis of suffering to heal her and raise her to her side later. Even though Elona now had a second life, it wasn't due to her mother's efforts, and even though Elona was a happy little thing, I couldn't help but think that sometimes it might be kinder to let hope die. The only reason Elona's soul may have survived as intact and uncorrupted as it had was probably that she had been so tiny and not truly in this world yet.

For days, I searched in and out of memories, only stopping to eat and sleep. Arvida simply followed, not complaining once or breaking my concentration.

She did her task like an invisible spider that I could only sense as a slight tingle on my skin.

Then, on one particularly gray and cloudy summer day, with my skin dewy due to the high humidity, I stumbled on a thread that seemed different from the others. Sickly. Like the beginning of a disease. It stung and cut when I touched it. Carefully, I followed it, weaving through and between all other of her memories. The closer to the end I got, the less it felt like I was in the lighter world. Going forward was taxing. I had to push instead of just gliding.

The strand led me to the very moment of her death, but something was very different this time. I saw Riestel's pained face, and I saw Istrata collapsed on the floor. Riestel caressed her face, then stood up and fled.

All was quiet in the room, yet there was an eerie presence. As the mouse, my sight was limited, but even though I didn't want to take unnecessary risks, I needed to know what was going on. Clearly, I was in Istrata's memories still, but she was dead or at least very much unconscious. Something was very wrong. Then, it revealed itself. A shadow of thick ichor moved among the stone walls. Slowly, it stepped out of the wall. Istrata's skin was as pale as the dead eyes of the blackest hollows. Her being rippled like heavy oil when disturbed. She hummed a cheery tune.

Istrata disappeared from my sight as the Knights of Saraste barged into the tower. They gathered around her body, looking confused. One of them asked the others if they were now free of her. Another wondered if they could now heal as they had never felt anything but pain after her experiments where ichor was first born. Then, the shadow spread around them and pierced its way into their channels. Each knight fell on their knees around her, and she took her form once more. They were her creations; she would not let them go. It had to mean that she was the one to make them claim her death to their credit so the world would forget and not seek her out.

The knight's bodies trembled a little, and the black ooze dripped from their ears and eyes. Then they woke up, got up, and walked away. She had control over them through the heavier world. I wondered if that is why Irinda had been driven to such folly as a ruler. Istrata must have been whispering in her ear all the time. Rime's connection had not been known to most, but he had mentioned once that when he saw me, he knew me somehow. I was sure the Queen had no control over him or his father, but whispers through dreams were still a powerful tool to influence a person.

After the knights left, Istrata crouched close to her body and took out some instruments. Cutting and forcing her way into the lighter world with them, she exposed her soul tether. Her lifeless eyes looked at it with contempt. Holding a knife to the tether, she paused. Then, with one quick flick and a yank, she severed her connection to it. She was quiet and still, like made of stone, for a long time. Then she let out a small laugh.

She had, in essence, made another vessel for her consciousness of this heavy tar or within it. All her memories transferred, all her emotions. The joy of it being a success was clear. She studied her hands and the now hostless soul. Then she let go of it, and I saw how the soul dashed toward a strand that connected to the island.

Something grabbed my tail. Istrata lifted me in the air.

"My, my, I had not expected you to be this observant, let alone capable yet," she said, looking at me and the scene of her former triumph.

"This is my second birth. I see you have understood it well. And you are correct; the same method I used could be used to mold him a heavy soul. It would allow him life after death. There is but one problem...little mouse. And that is simply that I will end you here," Istrata said and wrapped her fingers around my mouse body. She squeezed with ever-increasing force.

It wasn't my body, of course, but it was my soul within it, and the pain was just as real. I tried biting and clawing, but it was like she didn't feel anything. Her grin widened.

"Such a thoughtful gift to bring yourself to me. Maybe, after all, you understood I am right. Even if only subconsciously."

Before she cracked my vessel's spine, the last thing I saw was Riestel behind her, reaching his hand toward me. He hit the mouse with his palm, and my soul detached. The last thing I heard was Istrata's surprised voice.

"Love? After all we have worked for? This is how you betray me?"

I woke up to bright blue eyes studying my face as Riestel lay next to me with his hand clasping mine. He greeted me with a tentative smile.

"I'm sorry, I was a little late," he whispered. "Thankfully, Arvida noticed something was wrong and alerted me."

"The mouse is gone. I really liked that body."

"Well, it was a choice between your soul or the mouse husk. I'm truly sorry I made the call to your benefit," Riestel noted snidely. "Actually, I'm not. Learn to live with it."

"So... I have a question..." I hesitated, looking around.

"I'm guessing you wish to know why you are in my bed."

"Well, I would be lying if I said that wasn't a little baffling to me."

Riestel chortled and gave me a chillingly sharp glance, just like in the library years ago. It sent shivers down my spine. In a purely good way this time.

"I merely helped your soul to let go of the husk and enveloped it to protect and speed it away from Istrata through the lighter world so she could not chase you. But as we needed to hurry, you slammed back quite violently and lost consciousness. Like once before when... Anyway, I brought you here to keep an eye on your condition. Just in case she had something up her sleeve that I did not notice at first."

"Right, because the infirmary wouldn't have been a more suitable option."

"Let's just call having you in my bed a small award for such a chivalrous act."

"I should thank Arvida," I decided and tried to sit up. The blood vessels in my head felt like they were going to burst, and I could feel my grasp on the world dimming again. Riestel caught me and laid me back on the pillow. He poked my nose.

"Not so fast. Dying inside a husk can kill just as well as dying in your own body. Take it a little easier. One would think you are in a hurry to get away," Riestel said, acting hurt. Then his expression changed. "Something is not right. You aren't scolding me for being opportunistic and contemptible."

"Well, you are doing it for me right now. Saves me the trouble."

"Right... You aren't near clever enough to fool me with that. I'm sure... Never mind. I'll get you some water."

I curled more under the covers.

"Here," he said and sat back on the bed. "It might actually ease your heart if you'd just tell me what is going on. Lean on me a little. I'm not all bad."

I drank the water, partly hiding under the silky, bright orange floral cover. I felt ashamed of all the emotions I was feeling. I inched my way to a seated position while keeping the cover as a hiding place.

"You look extremely silly, like a fat caterpillar," Riestel noted. "Did he leave you or you him? Not that it matters to me." A smile crept onto his lips.

"Neither, we just...fell apart," I whispered and started to sob. Every negative emotion and insecurity just welled up simultaneously. It overwhelmed me to the point of simply breaking down. Riestel took my hands and pulled me to him. He pressed me into his embrace, and we just sat there for the longest time until I was still and quiet.

"Are you all out?" he asked gently.

I shook my head and stayed in his arms.

"It seems like you are. We can't just sit here all day."

"Why not?"

"Well, I can't actually think of a reason I couldn't, but the longer you stay here, the more likely it will be that I will turn out to be less of a gentleman than I would like."

"A gentleman, really?" I snickered and wiped my face.

"I have my moments. You can't deny that."

"I guess you have," I conceded and stared at him.

"Alright, out," Riestel told me and hopped off the bed. "Right now." He pulled me up.

"You don't need to throw me out, good skies."

"But I absolutely must."

"Why?"

"Because you are an emotional wet wreck. And as much as I would like to push you on that bed right now and run my hands on every inch of your body to cleanse it from his prints and claim as mine, I think you need time."

"You don't get to decide what I need and what I don't," I huffed.

"I do, being the wiser of us."

"Right, you know I heard a lot of rumors about you in the Temple, and not one of them was about your grand wisdom."

"Alright then," Riestel said, as his expression became serious.

"Alright, what?"

"Sit back on the bed. If I can't order you around, and I'm so wrong."

"You absolute jackass, you are trying to goat me into doing it, aren't you?"

"Adorable. Now, seriously, get out."

I narrowed my eyes with annoyance and walked by Riestel. As I stepped past him, a slight case of folly took over my thoughts. I turned around and pressed my cheek to his. A delightful chill rushed through me. We turned to meet each other's gaze.

"Out already." He sighed. "Truly, you evil little creature."

"Going," I whispered and took some distance. His pale face had the most charming hint of rose on the cheeks. Riestel grasped my hand as I passed through the opening.

"I will never allow you to leave me once you come. Just know that. If you choose me, it will be for all eternity, no going back and forth," he said and let go.

"Isn't that a little possessive?" I asked, feeling like my lungs had forgotten how to breathe.

"That's the deal. Like it or not."

"I'll consider myself warned then."

"Good."

Once outside his apartment, I felt a little giddy. Then I grimaced at the thought of this all being a very strange mating dance. I shook my head. I needed to get a hold of myself. As much pleasure as it would bring to yield to the more romantically inclined desires, I didn't want it to begin like this. To begin? By the endless skies, I was truly headed toward him, wasn't I? I felt a jab of guilt in my heart for having the audacity to comment on Launea's quickly developing feelings for Nissa after we had lost Simew. Though, in my defense, I had known Riestel for longer than I had known myself. It was a slightly mind-boggling concept.

XI

T he head of the Noble's district, Usko Maherol, was seated opposite Rime
in his office. They had been talking for a while before I managed to find
my way there. Truth be told, I was late because I did not want to be here. Usko
had been a good ally, and I remembered him as one of the few decent people
we had come across in the Nobel's during the civil war, or the Tearing of the
City as it had been named after.

"Good, you came," Rime greeted me and helped me into a chair by the table.

"A pleasure to see you again, Consecratoress," Usko said and nodded. "I
brought you and your husband a few tokens from the people of my district."
He gestured at a tray full of elaborate perfume bottles and bath salts. Rime
looked a little uncomfortable at the mention of our relationship, but neither
of us said anything.

"Thank you. I do like seeing you once again, but I fear you will be utterly
displeased with this meeting," I replied.

"Well, it was always rare that a summons from the ruler means anything
good. It was so in Irinda's time as well. All good news is public; all bad tend
to be told in hushed voices behind closed doors. Do not fret. We have lived
through many dark times. I am no stranger to odd requests by those who
rule."

"That is the way it often goes," Rime said. "However, this time, the secrecy
is due to the extraordinary nature of this conversation and how people might
misunderstand us if this was openly discussed." Rime sat back in his own
place. "This is something very different to a request for riches or... Well,
whatever it is, you nobles provided Irinda with. And there is absolutely no
reason for you to agree to any of it. It is a dark ask, and we would rather not

ask it unless forced."

"Ominous." Usko massaged his wrists. "Please, I do not wish to waste anyone's time, so just cease with the cushioning and tell me what you want to say."

"Are you aware of the old verbal treaty that created the noble cast?" Rime checked. "All the way from the Witch Queen's era."

"A verbal treaty? What a concept. No, I cannot say that I am. What I do know from the pages of history is that we made a deal to always support and show loyalty to the rightfully elected ruler should they not deceive us or neglect their duty to the land. We had absolute reign on our internal affairs and their never-ending favor in return."

"It cost a little more to become a noble than that," I noted. "In essence, the price of a title and riches was to pledge your entire line to be used as the ruler sees fit, whether as a soldier or a sacrifice. Whether they needed your body or your soul...to sacrifice."

"Alright, that I did not expect. To labor the point, you mean that we were essentially fattened up for sacrifice in the old days? Groomed to lay our lives for a greater good or evil?"

"That is the gist of it," Rime replied.

"Well." Usko sighed and unexpectedly chortled. "I never thought about it, but considering our brutal traditions and the near blind devotion to our families that causes us to kill ourselves and our kind in those games sounds like something planted in our society to condition us for this." Usko pondered with a grim look. "Our ways have always been rather extreme and called for sacrifices to move up the food chain, though, in the previous leader's reign, these may have brought a little too much pleasure in the form of games to some. But the tradition itself makes sense, hearing that."

"We aren't forcing anyone," Rime stressed. "We simply need to have all our options open."

"Why are our lives needed?" Usko asked, a little nervous. Overall, he was taking the discussion incredibly stoically. I would have stormed out by now.

"If we have to fight, and if we have to fight on for days or longer, against the Witch Queen, we may run out of...things to use for sustenance in that fight," I explained with an ill feeling in my stomach. "I may need to feed on lives to battle her, as the world is so weak already. If I take more than it can afford to give, we may never be able to resuscitate the earth."

"And that would doom us all, no matter what class," Rime added.

"I see. Not the news I would like to receive. You have, I imagine, planned out other options?"

"Naturally, you and your people are hardly our first port of call. However, if it does come to that, we would rather have volunteers than..." Rime said.

"I understand. I cannot say what my people will think about this, but I will hold a meeting and inform them. They can make up their own minds after that. It is a hefty price you are asking for something that was agreed on many generations ago. They might feel like it is not their responsibility to live up to such a bargain. Especially as there is no proof of it... Other than this nagging feeling in my consciousness that this explains our ways too well."

"There is no part of me that would want to go down this road," I clarified. "But for all the years that I have spent with Rime, I've come to learn that preparation for as many possibilities and outcomes is a must if one wishes to stand as the winner."

Rime didn't show much emotion from hearing my words. He simply looked down and took a deep breath.

"I will relay your feelings to the people," Usko promised. "I do not doubt that they remember how appalled you were at our customs when you came to negotiate with us the first time. Anyone who remembers that will understand that you are not as Irinda or my predecessor Yannit was. That there is a true purpose for it and that it is not merely for the amusement of bored hedonists."

"Thank you," I replied. "I wish we had never needed to have this discussion."

"That we can agree on." Usko nodded and got up. "But I know you both, so I am not offended nor afraid. I bid you both farewell, and we will meet again when I know their answer."

As Usko left, Rime cleared out his table of the papers and things they had discussed before I arrived.

"Wait," he ordered. "I have things we need to talk about."

"As you wish."

Once Rime finished his tidying, he gestured for us to head out. It was a pleasant suggestion. Talking while walking outside made everything a little easier. We snuck out from a side door into the sunset-colored evening. The heat radiated from all stones and buildings that shone with a honeyed, orange tint. We sat down on the warm rocky side of the mountain in the partial shade of a wonky pine tree.

"The Witch Queen fashioned herself a new soul of the heavy matter. I learned that just a few days ago," I told Rime, as I wanted to offer some hope. "It is a vessel, a place to anchor her consciousness to keep her living and to continue her existence. She calls it a heavy soul, but it really isn't. It can't be reborn; it is more like a construct. However, it would be possible to replicate the process. At least, that is what she hinted at. It would allow you to—"

"Stop," Rime told me wearily.

"But it would let you live."

"Would it?"

"Well, it would keep you alive." I readjusted my stance. It was wrong to say it would let him live. There was no telling what it would do to his nature in the long run. I had already seen how he had changed when filled with the ichor. It would change him again for the worse, just as it had changed her.

"I'm fine with my destiny. You don't need to fight it for me," Rime assured me.

"But I do."

Rime sighed. "Why?"

"Because I will always love you, and I think the world will be a much worse place without you."

Rime shook his head. "What does that change?"

"We could just make use of it until we can figure out how to make a real soul for you. Just until we figure it all out. We've only just begun to study it all," I told him and was startled by my own words. Would I doom him like Istrata doomed Elona?

"No, I mean that it will not change anything. Who are you trying to save me for?" Rime stared at me.

I sat still in slight shock. I knew he had made up his mind, but the coarse way he voiced it was a lot to take in.

"Look, I've had years to come to terms with my lack of soul. I do not want to have hope for another outcome when I know it is against all the laws of this world. You said yourself that even the Source cannot do anything. Let it be. Please."

"I'm sorry," I whispered. "I shouldn't have brought it up."

"Just leave it."

"Alright. What did you want to discuss?" I relented. I had wanted to perhaps ask him about our child also, now that we were alone and not in a hurry, as always. Just a few questions, just a few details, but now, it felt like I'd be simply causing him unnecessary suffering. If the child was safe and happy, that needed to be all that was important.

"It seems the plague in the Slums has finally died down..." Rime began. "The trouble is, it seems that all the inhabitants have been killed by it. I will travel there and would like you and Riestel to accompany me."

"Is it safe? What if whatever caused the sickness is still there?"

"I've gone over this with Moras. He is certain it is safe. The last life signs in the Slums were detected a month ago. If there are no living there, the disease will have died as well."

"Why do you need us to come?"

"Just in case. You do remember the symptoms? The black ooze from the eyes? I started to think about it one night after you cleansed me. What if the plague wasn't a plague? What if the people there were simply...full of it like I was? That could mean—"

"That could imply she might already be in the city. That she has always been here."

"Exactly. What if she never left, and the plague was a symptom of her starting to awake?"

"It is certainly possible. She loved the Needle more than many other things. She wouldn't have wanted to go far. When do we leave?"

"Tomorrow, if possible."

"I will tell Riestel if you can really stand him."

"That won't be an issue. This is more important, and with both of you there, I'm sure we can get to the truth."

The next morning, we boarded our carriage. Rime traveled with Usko in a separate one to escort him home courteously. And to avoid me, obviously. I felt as if I had fallen into some strange limbo where I couldn't really see the correct way out to end the awkwardness between us.

A part of me felt I should just bare all and stick this out to see if he would feel the same as before once this was all over. Perhaps he was pushing me away just in case there was no saving him. Another part of me felt like honoring his wishes was the correct thing to do, even if there was a chance of a cure. His dream of another life, away from all of this and us, bothered me.

As we crossed over to the Temple, an invitation was brought to us from the main temple. It was as good of a time for a brief visit as any. We had been meaning to inspect the new grounds and the people. Rime urged us to make a detour there as he would carry on to the Nobles and that we would catch up at the gate to the Slums at the latest.

The rebuilding was nearing the end. What had once been a huge, foreboding façade was now made from large open windows, giving passers-by a small glimpse of the temple life.

One of the Temple's instructors, Liike, was in the front garden waiting to greet us. His hair had always been a little colorless, with a glass-like quality to it. Now, it was as gray as a wisp of a raincloud.

"Are you enjoying the new look of the place?" Liike asked as we got out of the carriage. It felt good to see him again. After starting out as someone who disliked me and fought me, he was now one of my most trusted allies in the Temple.

"I am. It is like a painting, an inviting painting."

"Much improved," Riestel agreed.

"Did you have anything particular to talk to me about?" I asked Liike. I could see Kymenes coming our way as well. He had forgiven the injury I had caused him, and though his abilities were now much diminished, he was still content to teach.

"We merely wanted a bit of your attention; after all, you have been sending us many instructional letters, and we have been turning our teachings to something truer," Liike replied. "We felt your visit was overdue and took this opportunity. I do apologize if it caused any inconvenience."

"No, not really. I am actually happy to be here, but we must carry on soon, so I urge that you will only keep to the things that matter," I replied. To my surprise, I did not find walking about the temple building and its gardens in any way unpleasant. The new, softer, more inviting style seemed to wash away my less-than-ideal memories of the place. We were shown around the new garden. It was lacking plants, but you could see all the flowerbed locations and other elements to grace the area in the future.

As we walked, I spotted Merrie out in the garden. She was planting small, gaunt seedlings a little way off from the path we were walking on. Her face had a bit of dirt on it but it just seemed to brighten her smile even more. I could never get the image of her picking a piece of bread apart as we traveled through the city during the war out of my head.

"Isa! May I walk a moment with you?" Merrie asked cheerfully.

"Are the guards not traveling with Rime?" she asked. "We heard he was on the road as well."

"We are barely traveling with Rime," I replied. "Anyone, in particular, you were hoping to see?"

"Oh, maybe."

"You know Heelis and Arvida figured out—likely weeks ago—that you are more than just friendly with Veitso," I told her.

Merrie gasped, looking more than puzzled. "But? How? I mean, the last time we were all in the same place was the night of the coup."

"Do not ask. They are practically mind readers when it comes to these things... Is he good to you?"

"What a horrible thing to ask!" Merrie giggled. "Like you would assume he wasn't."

"That was absolutely not my intent."

"Indeed, sounds more like something I would say," Riestel interjected as he meandered behind us.

"In that case, I must apologize even more. I truly did not mean to imply that," I explained.

"I know." Merrie smiled. "He is wonderful. He writes to me all the time about how much he likes me and what he's doing, and where. I know he's a bit of a joke at times for some people...but I see a good man in him."

"People are many things to many people. I'm glad he has found someone to see beyond to surface. It is a very nice thing."

"It is. I just don't know how to reply to him, so I just tell him about things that go on here. I'm happy he seems content with that," Merrie said and pursed her lips. "You've known him for a good while. Should I be more forward with expressing my feelings?"

"I'm not close to him in that way." I dodged the question. "Just do what feels right. If something is holding you back, you should probably figure out what that is instead of reciprocating his feelings because you fear he might get bored of you. From what I can tell, there is very little chance of that happening, anyway."

"Yes, I see," Merrie replied, hiding a most pleased smile by turning away a little. "Tell him I'm thinking of him if you see him."

"I will, but I'm afraid we must continue. You all are doing a wonderful job here. Everything looks lovely, and all that I heard about the new classes of history and theory of the lighter world sound like a vast improvement to what was previously."

"It is. The youngest are so happy with the changes. With the knowledge, they find their connections easier and have a confidence none of us ever had. Farewell, I wish you'd come here a bit more often."

"I will try," I promised as Riestel ushered me toward the carriage.

"Was that really a necessary use of our time?" Riestel asked once we sat down on the bench.

"Absolutely. Arvida and Heelis would not ever forgive me if I did not bring them some gossip when I return. You have no idea how much they live for these things."

"Right. So, you assume this friend of yours does not try to inquire about my feelings and intentions toward you every time she comes to look after Elona?"

"She does? I can't believe she'd be that daring," I answered, smiling. My appreciation for Arvida just kept increasing. If you put aside her hunger for digging into people's personal lives, I was more than sure she was partly doing it for my benefit, which gave more weight to her previous kind words about Riestel.

"And she doesn't even bat an eyelid doing it. If she weren't so wonderful with Elona, I'd defenestrate her for prying."

After the Temple District, we passed many familiar places but stopped at none to reminiscence, just barely at a few suitable barracks to rest and eat. Rime continued the journey in another carriage. He always had some reason not to join us. Riestel definitely didn't mind. After a few days of traveling, I decided to stop letting it bother me. Perhaps it was for the best, anyway.

"Have you ever been in the Slums?" I asked Riestel as we were nearing the end of the road.

"A few times. I never needed to live there, thankfully."

"I can't imagine what it is like. At all. I mean, the Worker's was already bad enough. Who even lived in the Slums?"

"Well, it didn't exist as a living quarter when I was young. It was just a place where all garbage and sewage and whatever else disgusting comes out of a city flowed to and was meant to be further processed or disposed of. I can't remember exactly when…but one of the Knights of Saraste, as they began to rule, decided to use it as a punishment for political adversaries. You and your entire family would be just dragged there and forgotten."

"So, the people who lived there up until the plague were their descendants?"

"I would imagine some, at least. The practice was stopped after a few decades of purges as the knight family that took the throne consolidated their power. Though, I would imagine it was still used as a punishment for criminals long after."

"Did you know Istrata controlled the Knights? She created them. That's when she first encountered the ichor or created it. I'm not sure which. I suppose, before the experiments that made them soulless, she originally established the order as a façade of a counter-balance to her rule to keep people from saying she had too much power."

"No, I did not know that, but it explains many things."

"Governor Irinda's obsession with you, for one."

"Perhaps."

"The thing is… I'm now forced to wonder if Rime hears her whispers."

Riestel frowned.

"That must be painful," he said. "But I don't see her fingerprints on him. Irinda's insanity was similar to Istrata's. Rime is just…he is affected differently. His persona, true it has changed, but it has only changed in the limits of who he was. Irinda began her reign as a relatively amiable Governor, a friendly, open person, but then she began to change into someone else."

"I'm relieved to hear you think he isn't under her spell."

"We must remember that she has tentacles in many places but not everywhere. She isn't omnipotent, not even immortal yet. I would trust the Captain. Of course, the more he uses the connection, the more he may be at risk of her advances. Still, he is as hardheaded as they come. I would be very surprised if he would succumb to such things."

As the carriage stopped, I felt a little better. Riestel's words were comforting and logical enough. Rime had changed, but he had not acquired any new, sudden desires, goals, or characteristics. He had always been quite a hard-natured person. Withdrawn and a little sullen. There was a tender side to him, but it had always been overshadowed by the other elements.

XII

T he large gate to the Slums was without any decorations; just huge iron
bars slapped across the thick wooden beams to fortify them. We weren't
going to travel through it. A small sideway was enough for our three-person
entourage. Just staring at the dark gate as we waited for the captain of the
area to come and let us through filled me with a sense of dread. I wasn't sure
if it was just the thought of Istrata possibly being there or if it was me truly
sensing her.

Riestel and Rime were clearly feeling the same way. Rime paced up and
down the bare lot in front of the gate. Riestel leaned on the wall, with his foot
constantly tapping on the stone surface. As the captain arrived, he exchanged
a few pleasantries with Rime and then went on to open the way. He told us
that if we should, against all odds, find any survivors, we should alert them so
they can provide food and aid if the person seems healthy enough.

Stepping through the wall to the Slums, I felt a similar curiosity as when I
had first gotten free passage in the city. This was, after all, the last place I had
yet to see. The circumstance could have been a more pleasant one. Not that
a visit to this place would have been something wonderful, even on the best
of days. Moras had advised us to envelop ourselves with our skills, though he
was more than certain that the contamination risk was almost non-existent,
especially if it wasn't actually even a disease.

The side gate led us through a guard tower with much fewer amenities
than those I had seen in the Uppers. We emerged on the other side to a narrow,
unpaved area behind crooked shed-like houses made from a mishmash of
wood pieces that were of different lengths, widths, and colors. From the little
I could see walking this narrow path and peeking around the openings, the

Slums were a disheveled forest of huts and tents. It was eerily devoid of sounds made by people. The only noises we heard were from seagulls and crows. Rats simply avoided us, though you could hear them scutter further away.

"The air is much fresher than I would have thought," I remarked as we ventured further toward the larger gate area.

"That is because the people have been dead long enough to dry up in the heat. And, I would assume they have mostly been eaten by the rats, beetles, and other scavengers," Rime explained, unphased.

When we reached the official gate area, the sight was anything but heartwarming. Many had died right at the gate, waiting and begging for supplies, as those given clearly had not been enough.

"Better not look any closer," Riestel told me and positioned himself between me and the view to the gate. "There is no reason to torment yourself. Hey, guide, what is our plan?"

"There is no plan. We walk around and try to see what is going on and if we can link this to the Witch Queen."

"Shouldn't we examine the bodies at the gate in that case?" I asked.

"I'm sure we can find some individual ones. No need to go knee-deep in it," Riestel remarked and opened a door to a nearby shack. "Exactly as I said." He sighed.

"I'd suggest we do not enter any buildings we absolutely do not need to," Rime advised. "Can you see any marking on the body, or is it too far gone?"

"It is not perhaps ideal. I'll look in a few more."

We walked further into the forest of huts and shacks. The best-made ones had strange makeshift windows fashioned of the bottoms of different colored bottles stuck together with, as far as I could tell, bits of clay. Some had no windows, and some had fabric or bits of paper in place of glass, though they might as well have been just holes plugged with anything at all rather than actual attempts at making a window.

Riestel looked into several disheveled houses before gesturing us in. As I followed him in, he snapped his fingers, pointing at the body. I conjured a flame for him to see better. I left Riestel to check on the deceased, as his skills were more suited to determining the proper cause and looked around the hut. Well, if one could call it looking around. I stood in place and turned my head. This room was all that there was. There wasn't much to see. The walls had cracks; the floor was bare earth, apart from where the sleeping area was. There were a few wooden cups on a block of wood.

There were some other broken items, clearly rummaged from the refuse and waste brought here from other places: a child's porcelain doll without a leg, shoes that didn't match but were of roughly the same size. I felt truly ashamed for the city and angry at myself for not delving into this earlier. Living in luxury for the last years while others weren't offered even a fighting chance was hard to come to terms with. I knew this place existed but had done nought. Maybe I had not been willfully blind, but blind nonetheless.

"It's not a plague of any sort," Riestel said and opened his eyes. "You were correct in your suspicions. She has been filled to the brim with ichor."

"Does that mean the Witch Queen is here?" Rime asked.

"From all I can see and sense," Riestel replied. "She is. We also know she is awake, but if she were capable of action at the moment, she would have been on us already. She already tried to kill Isa once."

"She what? Why wasn't I told?" Rime demanded to know as he turned sharply to look at us.

"Well, Riestel got me out in time, and you haven't exactly been easy to talk to."

"You should still tell me. I must know these things," Rime insisted angrily.

"I will tell you next time. It wasn't as dramatic as it sounds. I would have mentioned it, eventually."

"Fine. Do you agree that she is here?" Rime sought affirmation. I could see he was anything but happy to let the previous subject go.

"I'm sure she is," I confirmed, as there was no doubt in my mind that she was in the city. Right here in the Slums. The revelation was both exciting and worrying. Finally, we knew something tangible about her location. It would allow Rime and the others to plan more specific strategies for defense and confinement. I wiped my palm on my dress. Just the thought of the Witch Queen having been here, so close, all this time, made me anxious. She had always felt like a distant thread, maybe some nightmare that would never even materialize.

"Then why is she not making an appearance?" Rime wondered. "What is keeping her from coming after us?"

"She hasn't been awake for that long yet," I replied. "As Riestel said, if she could come to us, she would. She might still be recovering. I would imagine awakening after a few hundred years takes a bit of time to gather your senses."

"Could be." Rime sighed. "Alright, as we've established that, should we look around a little more to see if there are further clues?"

"We can. I'm not sure there is much need." Riestel shrugged. "Our time would be better spent getting ready."

I stepped out into the narrow lane, which was illuminated by a small ray of light. I stopped in my tracks a few steps out of the door.

"Irinda?" I uttered hesitantly as a chill ran through me.

Both men rushed to look where I was looking. There she was, the former ruler, standing with a slightly crooked posture as if her left leg would have been bent. She was still wearing the clothes and armor we killed her in. Despite her much-diminished beauty, it was clearly her. The porcelain skin and long red locks were exactly as they had been when I saw her the first time.

Staring at a person whose death was your doing was, to say the least, a little disturbing. Irinda seemed strangely calm to encounter us. Her expression was blank. We all gathered a little closer to each other in preparation.

"The Queen bids you welcome," Irinda strained to say in a monotone voice. "Her grace is a little preoccupied and cannot meet you. I am her messenger for now. And her sword."

"Why would you bow to her?" Riestel asked, clearly loathing what Irinda had become.

"Why?" Irinda repeated. "It is as it should be. Mother Eternity promised that I would not die and perish. I am here. You killed me, yet I live. She raised me as she vowed."

"You would let the entire world be engulfed by her taint just to exist?" I asked.

"She has her plan; I serve," Irinda answered without emotion.

"Do you really want everything to be the same forever?" I continued.

Irinda cocked her head and looked at me with empty eyes. It was like she didn't understand what was being asked.

"Do you truly want a future that is without any growth, feelings, or changes? Forever the same?" I tried again.

She still didn't answer, just stood quietly, swaying a bit from side to side.

"She isn't herself, is she?" Riestel whispered. "There is not much of her mind left in there. It is almost like a puppet acting out a role. It might have Irinda's memories, but it has limited capability of organic, independent thought, if any. She gave up herself for her body to live. I find that tragic."

"What does your master want to tell us, then? She must have something to say if she sent you," Rime cut in.

"Yes," Irinda replied and closed her eyes for a moment like she was listening to something. "She has a message to give you. I am to tell you that if you do not grant her access voluntarily to the Needle and all of her domain, she will drown the entire city. She would request that her dominion over all these lands be acknowledged and that you would allow for the world to be healed, yourselves included. It is her opinion that you three are all suffering unnecessarily."

"You colossal bitch!" Riestel called out. "How do you dare to lecture me about suffering when you are at the very root of it? If you ever have the gall to show yourself to me, I will kill you good this time!"

I had never seen Riestel so enraged that he would use a direct insult rather than a snide remark or a sarcastic quip. Even Rime looked a little taken aback.

"She regrets that her actions have influenced you in such a profoundly poor manner. She would remind you that her goal is to save Elona."

"She is saved. By us! Elona lives, laughs, and grows. If that is truly what you are after, you can step down right now and stop. Cease and move on, as you should have long ago."

There was a long silence after Riestel's words.

"It does not change her course," Irinda stated. "She will improve on the world, and Elona will live for an eternity beside her without death ever bothering her."

"You are nothing but a liar! Betrayer of everything you ever stood for!" Riestel yelled. "You are not a mother to her!"

"Should we really antagonize her now?" I whispered and touched his arm.

"I'm done," Riestel replied and turned his back on Irinda. "Apologies."

"She would give you a pardon if you would just trust her. She still adores you. Please think of what you planned and hoped for. And you, soulless one," Irinda said, turning to Rime. "She would raise to lead her armies if you would accept. She finds you a perfect vessel for her endeavors and would offer you eternity in her care. You could live as she does and never again worry about anything."

Rime didn't say anything. Riestel scoffed and shook his head.

"As for you, the so-called Emissary of Fire, appointed by the high and mighty Enforcer itself... You, I have every permission to kill, as you have refused to function as a part of her plan."

"And you? Are you just functioning as a part of her plan, or have you any thoughts for yourself?" I asked. Irinda had been a proud ruler, and though we had fought on the opposite sides, I would have been pleased if she had not disappeared completely.

"I can think on my own well enough, little ones," she replied.

I could tell from the word choice it wasn't her reply.

"The Queen will allow the gentlemen to think for a moment, but she would ask that you would, as a courtesy, allow her to take what she created from herself with her at this moment."

"Well, you can tell her, worthless, cowardly shadow, she will have to kill me to get to Isa," Riestel said, turning sideways to Irinda. "And I will be more than pleased to wipe you off the face of this world while we are at it."

"I cannot yield to that request either," Rime concurred.

"Then I must take her by force now that you were gracious enough to bring her right to us, for if she falls, you will all fall."

"Try all you wish," Riestel sneered and steadied himself.

Irinda opened her arms as if she were getting ready to embrace someone.

"Arise, helpers, arise, my kin," she called, smiling.

The ooze began to flow from the skin of the dead, and then the piled-up bodies reanimated. For the first seconds, they seemed comically stiff and wobbling, then the movements improved and became strong and fluent.

"We must get to the side gate now," Rime ordered. "Isa ahead, Riestel, keep them at bay at the back."

"I would remind you that I am not your underling, but considering the circumstances, I am willing to cooperate," Riestel stated.

"Be quiet or be helpful," I told him.

"Now, that's an order I can live with," he smirked. "Such passioned words, milady." He formed several sharp ice-discs. They struck and cut down limbs and people easily enough, but the figures were pouring from all directions now. Riestel blocked off some alleys with ice-barriers, but there were always some small routes among the huts that allowed them to find us. The puppets that did fall simply united with the black viscous goo as it, too, crept closer.

I burned what I was able to for us to push forward. Rime handled those that slipped by me or Riestel. He impaled them and threw them away through hut walls. The ichor was up to our ankles soon. Walking became like wading through mud. Except this mud stung and grabbed at us.

As one more figure right in front of us turned to cinder, we reached the small gate. I began opening the locks with the keys Rime handed me. Certainly, I could burn through it faster, but what would keep them from chasing us after that? When I got the locks opened, black, claw-like hands charged up at us out of the ooze as Irinda stepped closer. They pulled me down into the mud.

Rime kicked the gate open and yanked me from their reach pushing me to safety to the other side. After that Rime ushered Riestel through.

"Prepare," Rime whispered in a hurry. He slammed the door shut. I heard him place the locks back. Riestel and I looked at each other in confusion.

After we waited for what seemed like ages on the other side, there was still no sign of Rime. There were no sounds coming from the other side, either. Dusk was approaching. Some drops of ichor squeezed through to this side from under the door, but no more than a puddle of water after rain.

"We should tell them to fortify all doors and gates," Riestel finally said. "If Rime decided to stay there, I'm sure he had a reason and a planned way out."

"I know he can travel through the heavier world or between the two at least... I just can't believe he... Why would he? What if Istrata's whispers got to him? He used the ichor so close to her, maybe..."

"Do you believe that?" Riestel asked. "That he would be so easily and quickly taken over?"

"No. He is much stronger than that."

"Then stop thinking about what he is doing and start giving orders."

"You are right."

I hurried to the local captain's quarters. He was a little annoyed that we had taken so long to return, as he wanted to retire for the night.

"Here are the keys," I said and handed them to him. "But you won't need them anymore. Tell every soul in this district to pack whatever food and sustenance they have and head to the Crafter's. Pass the order to the Harbor as well. Before you and the soldiers stationed here leave, you must see to it that all holes, all gates, doors, and the like are sealed as water-tightly as possible."

"I'm sorry, what? Why?" the man asked.

"We are going to be attacked, and they will come from the Slums. That part of the city is lost," I informed him.

"Shouldn't the War Council be telling me this?"

"He has no time to spare. Is his consort and the leader of the Temple not enough authority for you?" Riestel inquired, with his expression turning cold as ice.

"I...of course it is. I will begin," the captain agreed.

"We will make sure the gates above you are opened and that there will be places to locate to. Just get to the Crafter's as soon as you can," I stressed.

"And what if people do not want to leave their homes?" the captain asked.

"There are always some. If you have time, you may try to force them out. If not, make sure they understand that staying will be a death sentence," I told him.

The captain nodded and grabbed his coat.

"We should head to the Crafter's," Riestel suggested. "We can't do much here."

"Fine. Yes. We must. He told me to prepare, so we will. But I'm not exactly sure how."

XIII

O nce we passed the Crafter's gate, someone banged on the carriage door.
"Stop!" Tammaran insisted. His demeanor was frantic.

I gave the driver the order to pull to the side and got out.

"Is Rime with you?" Tammaran asked with a tense voice instead of greeting us.

"No, he..."

"He went through with it then. Ocean be calm and speed him back," Tammaran muttered. "He asked me to give you this. Did he say anything?"

"What is this about?" I asked, a little overwhelmed as Tammaran handed me an envelope as thick as my wrist.

"Did he say anything?" Tammaran ignored my question.

"To prepare."

"Right, I will begin immediately. Please read. I need to get to the Soldiers. I will send updates on the situation once I have some," Tammaran promised, bowed, and jumped into the lighter world before I could ask anything else.

"I'm so confused," I sighed.

"Everything is normal then," Riestel remarked.

"Really? At a time like this?"

"Especially at a time like this." He smiled. "Let's go to my kin's house. You will have all the privacy you need there to read that. We need a place to rest for the night, anyway. My back can't take another night in a carriage."

"I always forget how old you are."

"Cruel woman. I'm not old; I'm ageless."

"Just take me there, gray one."

Riestel grinned and ushered me back into the carriage. Then he told the driver where to head. I sat quietly, squeezing the letter. Again, there had been some grand plan for all this. Was the letter to explain my role or another apology for yet again leaving me out in the dark? I wanted to rip it open, but I did not want to read it in front of Riestel without knowing what it was about.

Riestel's relatives warmly greeted us, and fresh bread was shoved in our hands almost before we made it past the threshold. His aunt, Ombra, was a little miffed we hadn't brought Elona with us but quickly caught on that this wasn't a regular social call. She shooed everyone back to work.

"The spare room we keep for Riestel is all tidy and looked after," she informed me. "It is up the stairs and to the right. Riestel has something to tell me, so we'll stay here. No one will bother you upstairs for a good while."

"Thank you," I replied and headed for the stairs. Ombra quickly shuffled to catch up with me.

"Can I let him come up after we chat, or do you want me to keep the lad out and busy until you come down?" Ombra asked quietly.

"You can let him up after he is finished talking to you," I told her, as I'd have to face Riestel sooner or later after the letter, and in some strange way, it felt comforting to know someone would be there soon in case the letter made me sad or angry.

The guest room Riestel used when staying here was full of sturdy, made to last from one generation to another furniture pieces. There was nothing unnecessary in them. Each form was only chosen to defy time and use. A small, triangular window opened to the street. I lit the old, slightly dusty candles and let in a bit more moonlight.

The chair didn't look comfortable enough for the reading experience ahead, so I sat on the bed and pulled a pillow on my lap. I carefully peeled the envelope open. There were eight other envelopes inside it and one paper. I took the paper out as it was the only one addressed to me and not sealed by Rime's official signet.

Isa

Ever since this darkness has been crawling in me, I've heard faint echoes. Now that I have learned all about her from you, I'm sure it has always been her, but I have never answered her. She has been relentless, prodding, poking, trying to figure out how she could connect with me. More now than ever. Offering me things. I wonder if that is why you felt so familiar, and I wonder if that is how I was at the right place with an opportunity to find you. I would rather it was destiny.

Knowing we might find her in the Slums, I took every precaution for this scenario. I have set up all defense orders and every single move needed for now. They are enclosed, and I trust you to follow their distribution and execution. I feared that if I were to discuss them with you or out loud to anyone, she could somehow hear of them. Therefore, I could not take the risk.

I do not know when I will make it back, but I have every intention to return. I leave the city to your care while I am gone, as you are the only person I would entrust my life with, and I know you will fight for everyone's survival. This journey, should we have established that she indeed is there, will buy you time to set everything up. I will talk and negotiate with her as long as I can. Be ready.

Once I appear, I would ask that you burn as much of the tar out of me as possible, whether I ask it or not. Whether I can ask it or not. Do so. In whatever state should I appear back to you, I pray you will trust me one last time to do the right thing.

– Rime –

No confessions of love or goodbyes, mainly instructions. It was, strangely enough, a relief. One of my worries had been that it would be a much darker letter, but he was, as he had always been, steadfast and goal-orientated. Whatever the ichor was making him into, the Queen would have it no easier to turn his head or coax him into anything. His will, I hoped, would be as unbreakable as it had always been.

The confession of him likely having known me through dreams and whispers planted by the Queen didn't shock me. He had always accepted my ways and talents too easily compared to most people around. Not that he was most people, but for a person who was adamant about doing the right thing, aiding and falling in love with a troublesome firebug wasn't likely high on the list. It didn't even taint my view of our relationship because I knew whatever else might have happened, and whatever else still might happen, he had, at some point, loved me. Perhaps he even still did. Just knowing of me from the Queen wasn't what had brought us together.

A knock.

"Is it safe to come in?" Riestel asked.

"I can't believe you knocked. When did you learn manners?"

"Oh, they come and go. Bad habit, won't do it again. I know you prefer me entering as I please."

"Right."

"So?"

"Well, you can read it if you want," I told him and held the letter out. "There is also one marked for you. Here."

Riestel took the paper and the envelope. He skimmed the letter and then cracked the seal of his letter. His expression stayed almost unchanged throughout, but I could feel the air cool around him. He wasn't pleased.

"Tomorrow, we will run his errands," I decided.

"You will follow his plans?"

"To the fullest. I had been worried about his state before the letter, but… It is so purely him. There isn't even a trace of someone or something influencing him in it. And before you say it, yes, I know things may be horrendously different once he surfaces. He might not be himself; he acknowledges that too. But I believe that until his decision to stay in the Slums, he has been acting purely and solely as himself."

"I agree." Riestel sighed. "But his heroics are making me look bad, so I'm going to stay unimpressed."

"Duly noted. Can you now distract me from all this, please? Tomorrow and all the days after that are threatening to be long and arduous."

"Certainly. Maybe I'll tell you a story again? Make room."

"You aren't sleeping in here with me."

"Yes, I am. This is my room, and you are the one in my bed. Once again. One could think you have some weird obsession with my sleeping arrangements," Riestel smirked and removed his shoes and outer clothes. Then he paused.

"You can't sleep in full clothing. Try to relax a bit. I'll get another blanket, so you will have some protection against my charms."

While he rummaged through the closets for another cover, I took off some of the more uncomfortable clothes and jewelry. The thin green summer silks with flower embroidery were comfortable enough to sleep in. I tucked the blanket around me tightly.

"One would think you are related to a sea urchin with that shell," Riestel noted and sat next to me on the bed. "Feeling secure enough, or do I need to erect a fence between us?"

"Just about."

"It just melts my heart to hear how relaxed you are around me."

I crossed my arms and inched as far toward the wall as I could. Riestel stretched and laid down with his hair spreading across the humble, coarse linen pillow like a river of silver and light brass. I felt so utterly horrible being so close to him and having to keep my desires in check. Rime had said, "That's alright," but it wasn't. Why was I so weak-willed when it came to Riestel that I constantly allowed myself to be pulled toward him?

Riestel lifted his left hand slightly over his ribcage, palm upwards. The air cooled a little as a white, icy fog appeared from his fingertips.

"This is something I learned ages ago," he told me and scooped me beside him with his other hand.

As Riestel told a story of a white swan whose wing had been broken and its mate who refused to leave her, whether it was to the winter or wolves or hunters, the icy crystals and fog formed and moved like set-pieces in a small theater locked in a snow globe. As he finished, I drifted into a comfortable sleep.

The morning sun was almost hostile in her brightness. I wiped my eyes and began to realize the position I was in. We were a nightingale's tail feather apart, with my leg wrapped over Riestel's pelvis. Then his eyelids fluttered open. I heated up instantly.

"I could fry an egg on you." Riestel laughed, but he didn't exactly look or feel any less affected. There was an uncomfortable silence. Then he moved his hand to stroke my cheek.

"If your annoying husband had not written me a personal letter, this would be the moment I break," he whispered. "But because there is a bit of scoundrel in me...he can't expect to make demands without a small price." He pressed my head forward but stopped just as we were about to kiss. It was unbearably tempting to lean in just a hair's width more. There was a slight sweetness in his morning breath like he would have just drunk honeyed tea.

His hand followed my thigh, and my skin shivered. It made me sigh softly. I found myself pressing against him by instinct as if I had no control over my body. Then he stopped and withdrew with a half-startled look.

"Time to cool off, I should think," he said and sat up. "Otherwise, I will feel like a complete jackass for the rest of my days."

"What? You can't just...?"

"You'd want me to continue? I can be persuaded," he said, planting his palms on the bed and leaning close.

"I..."

"You would, noughty," Riestel jokingly scolded me to take his mind off the possibilities. "I'm going for breakfast...before I'll have you for breakfast."

XIV

The kitchen was an absolute mess of flour and leftover dough. All the bread for the day had been baked before the first light and was now being delivered, so the house was quiet and empty. Riestel was cutting a few rolls in two, still shirtless. Then he buttered them and handed me one.

"What did he ask of you in the letter?" I asked. "It must have been something to do with me."

"Not really."

"Don't try to lie."

"I'm not trying. Either I am, or I am not."

I bit on the roll as he was being impossible. The way this man vexed and annoyed and yet absolutely supported me was ever so curious and something I would never get used to. But I was grateful he had stopped when I might not have had the strength to, nor even the desire to, in the moment. This morning would have felt tainted if he had not. The bracelet on my wrist felt twice as heavy as normal.

"Water or... Never mind, there is only water right now. Do you want some?" he asked.

"No, thank you. This is fine. Did you tell them yesterday about the evacuation?"

"Yes, they wanted to deliver their morning commitments so no family goes hungry before the word spreads, but they have begun preparing for the move. They will be among the first out of here. They are also telling others of the situation."

"Will people listen to them?"

"You can be sure they will. If they don't, Ombra will personally carry them by their trousers over to the next district."

"I can actually imagine that…" I answered, amused. "I'm glad they will travel soon."

"You are?"

"Why wouldn't I be?"

"I imagined they are mostly annoying to you."

"So are you, but I still…" I managed to stuff the rest of the roll in my mouth before completing that sentence.

"You still what?" Riestel asked, eyes gleaming like a snake's as he walked over and leaned on the high baking table, inching his way toward me.

A soft slipper hit Riestel.

"None of that in my kitchen!" Ombra said. "Even though I'd be ever so happy to have more of Elona's kind, this is where I cook, so take it outside." Riestel fluffed his hair and took some distance. The great Consecrator of Saraste reduced to a mere awkward schoolboy with the flick of somewhat soft footwear.

"I see your throwing arm is still as accurate as ever."

"Lot of practice with this lot," Ombra replied with a wide grin and gestured to the younger men of the family who were outside by the window checking the horse cart. "They are at it like rabbits; they are if you give them a moment of respite from work."

"You really should learn to keep such remarks to yourself if you presume I will house you," Riestel told her.

"The high and mighty will just need to put up with me, or otherwise I will sit my wide behind right down by the fireplace here and let you deal with your conscience then," she replied, unphased.

"You know I wouldn't leave you." Riestel laughed. "I'm actually looking forward to having ordinary people about in the Peak."

"Good, or I would chase you down the alley with the slipper. Did you feed her?"

"He did," I interjected.

"Fine, lad. I will get the district sorted for you two. Go on beforehand. I imagine there's a lot to do."

"We'll leave in just a moment," Riestel said. "Just making us a parcel for the road."

"I'll leave you to it then. You will hear us once we arrive."

"I'm sure I will with your croaking," Riestel said, and they hugged.

The Crafter's District connected directly to the new Center Square, tentatively called the King's Circle by most, that had been created for the new palace. The Uppers still had their gates and walls, but some of the structures between the Lowers had been demolished. This was why all people who wanted would be offered a place among the Uppers for the duration of this battle or war. I preferred to call it a battle in my head. A war meant a long, drawn-out conflict, and I truly hoped we would be able to avoid the slow grind.

We stopped for a moment to see how the construction work was progressing. The foundation was laid, and the walls were being erected. The head of construction showed us the blueprints, beaming with pride over the craftmanship. Certainly, there weren't enough decorations to his liking, but whatever there was to build, he would do it with the utmost quality and care. Riestel rolled his eyes so many times I was surprised he didn't get dizzy.

To me, seeing the castle form just felt unnecessary. If Istrata attacked, it would be caught in the middle and fall back to rubble. But stopping just for "what ifs" wasn't that sensible either. We might be wrong. Perhaps it would be finished and provide shelter and refuge instead.

As we entered the Temple District, my mind made a rather surprising decision. It was something that I had wanted to do for a long time but had not had the endurance to face yet.

"Can we make a small detour?" I requested.

"If you wish," Riestel agreed. "Where?"

"To the Laukas manor. They have something I want."

"An uninvited and unwelcomed visit to the King of Façades. Sounds delightful. Do you think they'll serve tea?"

"I wouldn't advice drinking it if they did."

"Mayhaps the prudent thing to do," Riestel sneered as he knocked on the carriage roof to alert the driver.

The manor was as fine as it had ever been. There was a line of people waiting for an audience all the way to the street. For a moment, I wondered if I should wait for mine and not abuse my status, but while I weighed out the decision, Riestel had already gone to the yard, and before I could catch up, he had evidently lectured the guard into submission. Judging by the poor man's expression, he was feeling like he might like to make a career change.

"We can go in," Riestel announced and gave the guard a sharp look. He certainly wasn't going to open the door himself. There was an annoyed choir of sighs from the line after us as the guard caved in and let us through. Riestel turned on his heels and faced the queuers.

"If anyone should oppose us going in, feel free to complain to me after." He smiled and nodded at the nobles and officials.

"You are terrible," I scolded him.

"And you are thoroughly amused by it."

There wasn't much to deny there.

Alerted by the servants, Friti came to receive us in the foyer.

"I bid you a warm welcome, Consecrator Aravas. Consecratoress Elona, what brings you here?" Friti asked with a forced smile as she stood in our way. "Did you ever receive our letter?" she continued to ask with her small nose turned up.

"I cannot recall that I did," I lied, as I wasn't going to admit to burning it. "I'm delivered bags of them daily. I do not go through them myself. Only the ones that are specifically brought to my attention."

"Oh, and I'm the terrible one," Riestel remarked in a hushed voice, all too pleased.

"Well, you should really have a word with your staff then. I cannot imagine anyone dumb enough to throw away a letter from the King's wife!"

"I shall ask about it. Perhaps it was just an oversight."

"It's quite a burning question, isn't it," Riestel said and sidestepped just enough that my flick only caught his garments.

"Well, enter then. We have a long day of visitors ahead. It would be rude to keep them waiting any longer than necessary." Friti gestured toward Frazil's study.

"Actually, I merely need to speak to you and your daughter, Ghila."

Frazil appeared on the stairs and stared at us. "So, you would come all this way and not even greet me? I had to come down to see if I recognized the voice correctly."

"I hardly think I'm a welcome guest in your world," I answered honestly.

"Nor I in yours, but we should learn to co-exist, should we not? We cannot avoid each other forever."

"Alright then, I will discuss what I came here for with all of you if you wish."

The family gathered in the study. Ghila was the last to arrive and looked a little uncomfortable in our company. The servants brought some meager refreshments.

"I do regret I have no time for pleasantries. I need something from you, and I need it today," I told them.

"What?" Frazil asked.

"The jewelry you had made for Ghila's wedding."

"What! Out of the question," Friti yelped. "How dare you come all this way to... to... rob us, quite frankly."

"They were never yours to begin with," Riestel remarked.

"What does that mean?" Ghila asked, a little annoyed.

"I'm not blaming your husband," I explained quickly. "He may not have known where they came from. But they were, in fact, ripped out of a living creature. The aroch woman he brought here. They are a part of her like your nails or hair are of you. I would like to return them."

"How can stones come from a living creature?" Ghila gasped, surprised. "I didn't know that was possible."

"It is, and they do. The arochs will come to this city's aid soon. They will give their lives, if necessary, to save ours. I would like for her to be whole again. It would be a wonderful gesture to make."

"But... I... We did not know they were taken from her in such a manner. Besides, they have been fitted to the jewelry. They are ours now," Friti objected, even if a bit shaken.

"Mother... I will give mine," Ghila said. "They are beautiful and dear to me, and I would not wish to part with them, but I would not wish to wear them either, knowing where they came from."

"You have a kind heart. I'm glad," I told her. "Can you fetch them?"

"I will," Ghila said and got up. "Mother, shall I get yours too?"

Friti's ears were bright red, her lips pursed tightly.

"You'd hardly want to run into the aroch they were taken from while wearing them," Riestel pointed out. "Who knows what they might do?"

Friti glanced at Frazil but still didn't utter a word.

"Yes, get them too," Frazil finally answered on his wife's behalf. "I will have new ones made, whatever kind you'd like."

Friti's ears began to return to a normal color, but she wasn't happy with any of us. If she wanted to, she was welcome to dislike me for all eternity. When

Ghila returned, Friti excused herself immediately and left without saying farewell.

"I'm sorry for Mother," Ghila said a little hesitantly. "She isn't happy with much these days. We are still royalty and live better than most. I've tried telling her that but to no avail."

"It will take time," Frazil noted. "The new palace will help her mood. Did you visit it?"

"We did. It will be grand. I hope you will find it sufficient," I said as cordially as I could.

"I'm sure we will. I am actually beginning to enjoy my circumstances," Frazil said, shaking his head a little. He did look more rested than I had ever seen him.

"I'm glad. We will depart now, as there is a lot to do."

"I know about the evacuations. Do you have any need for help?" Frazil asked.

"You are free to help in any way you wish in any of the districts. I would imagine the officials would be overjoyed indeed to have a more experienced person to turn to. It is for the city, after all, so I have no reason to judge you as lacking when you offer your services," I answered.

"Good. I will play my part and perhaps gain a bit of trust back," Frazil assured me.

As we stepped out, I felt relieved that there had been no argument or need to threaten them. Maybe Frazil had understood what times we were heading into and realized he was not the leader that was needed, no matter how badly he had wanted to be the absolute ruler.

Once we were back at the Peak, all orders were handed out. We could feel the entire city wake up, and the air became tense with anxiety. We had told no one that Rime was unaccounted for, just that he was busy. Well, no one but his guard. The letters were mostly for them as they contained detailed instructions on how to proceed with what district. I had been allowed to read all of them once they had finished.

All districts up until the Temple could be sacrificed if the adversary was deemed to be too much, and we needed to move to use the tactic of divide, stall, and destroy. Then, the battleground would consist of the Temple and the Peak. They had the most differences in elevation, and thus would be the easiest the use for guiding and stalling the enemy where it was wanted.

Most of the guard took to their tasks immediately in their specified districts. I hoped that Rime would return soon. I did not want to have to lead us through these times. Obviously, the military strategy was Veitso's area, and I would have all the support in the world for all other matters—except for Rime's support.

Traveling had kept my mind in check well enough, but being back at home, it wasn't so easy not to obsess about Rime's whereabouts. Riestel tolerated my pacing and constant talking about the situation well. When I felt too guilty using him as a sounding board, I went to Arvida and Tammaran, who had finished his duties in the Soldier's.

Looking out from the Needle, I could see streams of people arriving. It was a very different sight than before when affluent visitors had poured in for the coronation. Now, from everywhere in the Lowers, people found their way to the three upper districts. Most seemed a little baffled about the exercise. We had not divulged the whole situation as we did not want to cause panic. People were smart, though. The many rumors heard echoing on the streets suggested an attack. They were just wrong about the attacker. We would have to start working against the rumors of an aroch army. But how honest should we be?

Arvida peeked her head into the chamber, wearing a yellow dress. "What am I needed for this time? You could just once invite me purely for my company, you know." She almost never wore any other color, but anything from brown mustard yellow to sunflower yellow to cream, she would wear with joy.

"I could, but I can still enjoy it as a side benefit." I smiled. "I need you and all others with your talent. You keep in touch with them, I assume, or at least can get them gathered somehow?"

"I can. Why?"

"I need to… well…influence the people a bit faster than I could otherwise."

"Because of the Queen's presence?"

"Yes. The arochs are coming to support and help. People fear them, so suddenly having them appear here might cause chaos and unnecessary clashes."

"Understood."

"And not just that. I need rumors to spread that a peace has been forged between us, as well as what the cause is. You need to get the idea of another, stronger, more dangerous enemy growing. One that forces us to unite our forces. If we just announce that a dead Witch Queen is about to rise and attack the city, people will either not believe us or..."

"Yes. I see the necessity. Will you come and walk with me then? See the master at her craft?"

"Certainly."

"We should really have some air of officiality. Do you remember when you handed out bread with Launea to the poor? Maybe we should have something to give them as a welcome gift. That way, we would have a natural reason to approach people," Arvida suggested.

Arvida went to the kitchen with an order from me while I changed into my most humble clothes, which reminded me much of my time in the Merchant's. Arvida would not get close to people being trailed by a fully temple-clad consecrator, after all.

A bit later, we had a whole cart full of small, sweet, nutty cakes. Well, if one had the gall to call them that, as the cook had cut out more than a third of the nuts in the recipe due to shortages. At least they were tasty. A servant guiding the small patchwork patterned horse pulling the cart trailed us. We approached the former ruler's private theater, which was now dedicated to housing people. It had massive statues of Saraste holding up the façade, with masks and symbols of other important deities appearing in the ornamentation that was present on every inch of the structure.

It was a rather lovely example of too much of everything. The finest waste of money one could imagine. Of course, now it would give shelter to around two thousand people as the stages, floors, and every nook and cranny of it had been converted for temporary lodgings. There were a few families unpacking in front.

"This looks like a good place to start," Arvida said and grabbed a basket from the cart, shoving it in my hands. "Hello, travelers. Which district do you hail from?"

"From the Crafter's," the father replied. Everyone in front of the building glanced at us, a little weary. "What's it to you?"

"We are here to bring some treats to welcome you all here for what will, hopefully, be a short stay," Arvida told them and smiled. She could when she wanted to, look absolutely mesmerizingly pretty and open, which didn't happen often. Mostly, she preferred to look sour to keep unnecessary people away from her, but when she smiled a genuine smile, her entire aura changed.

"They are from the Consecratoress herself," she cooed and pointed to the basket. "Just one for each, I'm afraid. There are so many to come here."

"From the Consecratoress? You mean the one up there? The Fire Witch?"

"Indeed," Arvida confirmed, and they flocked to us.

"Have you met her? What is she like?" a woman asked. "Some say she feeds on souls, and some say she heals the land."

"Such odd rumors. I can assure you that she is quite amiable to those who treat her well, nought to fear from her," Arvida told them. "If it weren't for the clothes, you'd never even know you had met her. She doesn't behave all high and mighty and only travels with a huge entourage like Irinda did. Very smart and seeks to improve the lands. Of course, she can be hot-headed and a little rash at times, but what can you expect from a fire consecratoress?" She laughed.

The people nodded approvingly. Arvida ordered me to circulate with the tarts with a big grin.

"Really? It's a relief to hear that." The woman sighed. "You never know what you'll get with a regime change like this."

"Yes, I hear you. We have had so many poor rulers and Temple heads in our history. It is ridiculous!" Arvida agreed. "I would not worry about the current ones. They have a good, clear vision for the future. If only this situation had not befallen us, we would be seeing many wonderful changes already."

"Well, I almost fell on my bloody ass when I heard the walls were coming down, and the King was to move to a place where people could actually reach him," a gaunt-faced man with very tanned and callous hands said.

"Yes, they are hoping to allow for movement between the classes. Why couldn't a master crafter who sells his skills live among the merchants or nobles?" Arvida pondered.

"I've been a carpenter for all my life. My work's always been good enough for the Uppers but not me." The man huffed and crossed his arms in front of him. "It'll be a fun day indeed to get to see what my clients look like. Never met anyone of them. Just get the damn drawings by city couriers and send the stuff back through them."

Arvida kept smiling and chatting as I went to each and every one with the basket. I could hear how she slowly turned the conversation toward their fears and, little by little, alleviated them. The people gasped a little when she casually told them that some arochs would seek refuge here too.

"I know, it scared me the first time too, but what worries me more is the threat that forces us to make peace and fight side by side," Arvida told them.

"What do you think it is?" they asked almost simultaneously.

"I couldn't say. It is not something that is told to most people."

"Is it something to do with the plague and land withering?" they suggested. People were surprisingly observant.

"It could be," Arvida pondered and nodded. "It would threaten all that exists."

The chatter grew louder for a moment, and everyone seemed like they had stumbled on some unspoken truth. In a way, that was true. They just didn't know that was the purpose of our visit.

After Arvida and her kind had worked their areas, it took but a few days until we heard the rumor begin to circulate on its own. Many actually felt it made more sense for the arrangement to be from a new threat as the aroch issue had been slowly fading in importance in their minds for decades, as everything involving them had always happened far away at the Borders.

XV

Arid and her kind made an appearance in the city soon after the rumors had taken hold. People were careful and suspicious, but very few showed outward hostility or malice. There were, of course, some that had lost loved ones at the Borders and had no intention of making friends with them. Even those people accepted their presence after a few days.

The reason behind the fast quelling of any objections was perhaps that it was known I had rescued some of the arochs earlier from execution and apparently be-friended them. Many thought that might have triggered the road to peace, and whatever people thought of the arochs, most were content with the idea of the conflict finally ending. The few that weren't were wise enough to keep quiet to avoid my attention. To ease the tensions further, we had the arochs assigned to very particular places and houses, away from most regular citizens. The Temple welcomed them courteously, as did the Peak.

Whenever Arid wanted to talk to me, I would first hear what resembled a windchime as she didn't want to just jump out and frighten me or charge right into my mind in the middle of a thought. She showed me different locations in the Peak and Kerth that could be considered holy by their standards. Of these places, we would choose the strongest for them to make their stand in, and they would align the rest to feed more power to the chosen location. I approved of their plan, not that I ever had any intent not to. If they were noble enough to make the sacrifice to save us, I was not going to stop them.

Arid also told me that she had brought a few of the seeds from their home. I could use them should I wish to try to converse with the Source. She encouraged me to do so, as she believed there was still more for me to learn from it. She was very likely right. There was something that I felt the Source was holding back on.

Following Arid's advice, I went to the place where life was the strongest in the Peak. The small meadow had changed since my last visit; the flowers that were in bloom then were now maturing their seeds, and the grasses bearing ears were turning to a light yellow. I sat on its side and leaned on a rock. As I chewed the seed, I began to drift into sleep.

"Welcome, Emissary of Fire. I had hoped we would speak again."

"The Queen has awoken. If there is anything that can help us, I need to know it now."

"Yes, I felt it. Do you doubt that I have not been honest?"

"I don't know exactly; I just think you have more to tell."

"You may be correct. It is something I have not even shared with her or the arochs. The arochs, because they have not needed the knowledge, and her because, thankfully, she betrayed me before I was able to."

"Will you tell me now?"

The Source flickered as it stared at me.

"I must, mustn't I? Hear me then. The Queen knows the nexus is the key to molding this world in any way she pleases. It will give her access to all its structures, and she will corrupt them all. I know she believes that she can undo all that she will do now once she has changed the very nature of humans to what she wants them to be... But I know that will not be possible. You cannot let such rot in and expect to heal it when you are the very root of it."

"A doomed plan, then."

"I suspect she knows this in her heart of hearts, but the taint has changed her permanently, and as it makes everything more rigid, it also makes turning the heads of those affected much harder. It is like talking to a wave and trying to ask it to turn. The motion and intent were set at the start of it. There is no turning it except by force."

She was describing Rime as well. I knew that much.

"What she does not know... Is that the nexus is the heart I was given to exist here? It is my connection to this world. Once it is devoured, I will be free of this world and will fly to the next, and the person or persons bearing its powers will be guiding this world. And once this world is spent, they will be like me and leave it for new worlds. If she should take hold of the nexus, the entire existence will slowly be threatened. If she notices that it can open other worlds to her, she will move forth

to them as well. As of now, she does not know the true nature of it. Otherwise, she would be more obsessed with it than with the world."

"Why did you keep this a secret? It's not as if we possess the means to destroy the nexus."

"For one, should someone take it before I know it will be a suitable match, I could still try and find a contender. Another reason would be that if someone merely forces the connection, they may die a death resembling the veil madness some consecrators face if they forcefully attempt to pierce through to the lighter world. You are a power-hungry one, so telling you this before being able to confirm that you are fully ready is a risk I am uncomfortable taking. But there you have it. Risk taken."

"How is a person supposed to know they are ready?"

"It will call to you. It will draw you in like never before, like the song of an enchantress. Like the desire felt when you lean in for your first kiss. For the moment, the rest of the world will fade, and you will only see it. Should you answer it, it will fuse with you. There is pain, bliss, and every other feeling there to be had. It will take several times. It is not a process that will be completed overnight. And it will change you in all ways imaginable."

"I don't understand why you could not tell me this before."

"Because, Emissary, I wished you would make your mind up first based on your true wishes, not lust or the need for power should the nexus present the opportunity to you. There is no part of me that would wish a person to need that power and take it because of that. A calling to serve would be the ideal."

"You are right. I do not have that. But I might need the nexus."

"At least you are honest with me."

"If I can take it, even if it is not calling to me yet, and I decide to take it despite that, are there consequences?"

"Only to your mind and heart. It will be a burden to make such a pact of servitude should one not be inclined to it."

"But wouldn't it at some point be that, anyway? You cannot convince me that you have enjoyed every moment of your long existence."

The Source laughed as if a thousand merry voices were carried to me from afar.

"Truly, that is a statement of wisdom. You are correct. I have cursed this existence a few times."

"Is there any end to it?"

"*There is. A voluntary return to the cycle through any world. A shedding of all your memories and things that make you, you. But my mind always seems to find reasons to go on. Maybe one day I have truly seen enough.*"

"What were you originally? Can you remember that?"

"*Indeed, I can. You will get access to such memories as well. Although, I am not sure you would remember anything more than you do now, as your individual beginning is this life. We have never had a person created as you have in this kind of position. To answer your query, I was a bird. A white and gold feathered pheasant in a king's garden. I loved him dearly, so when an assassin approached him, I threw myself in the way and awoke in the lighter world with a newly formed soul.*"

"That's...a tragically lovely way to begin, I suppose."

"*A very foolish one too.*" The Source smiled. "*But it simply takes a massive amount of will and emotion to create a soul, whether in one single moment or throughout one's life. I see you are at the end of the seed's effect; we will resume at another date if you still need me. And thank you... For asking me who I was, not one person has ever done that.*"

The Source faded as I opened my eyes. For a moment, I thought I saw Rime in the shadows further away, but when I wiped my face, there was nothing. The discussion with the Source weighed on my mind. If I wasn't drawn to the position for other reasons than power and knowledge, would I make a horrible choice in the end? But if I did not take the role before Istrata could reach the nexus, then she would eventually figure out all its potential uses. That was for certain the way she was.

Walking back toward the side entrance, I noticed a strange but pleasant smell in the air. As nothing was pressing, I tried to see where it came from. A little way to the side, closer to the reservoir, a few dozen arochs were gathered around a fire. They had small pans over the flames.

They all turned in unison toward me.

Arid waved. "Come!"

"I have something for you. I will be back in a moment," I told her when I remembered the gift I had picked up from the Temple District.

I hurried to the Needle. The stairs that had felt so magnificently grand to scale for the first time were really becoming a pain to go up and down every day. The scenery was worth the climb, but as a living place, it wasn't ideal.

The pouches I had secured from the Laukas family were sitting at the table close to the door. It felt like crossing out an old sin to be able to return them to Arid.

"I didn't know you ate like we do," I said once I got back to their gathering.

"Only sometimes, only special things. Take," Arid urged.

"What is it?"

"It...a gift of trees. Try," she said. It was a wonderful gesture for her to keep trying to talk to me our way.

"Alright, let me give you these in exchange."

The moment Arid touched the pouches, her face lit up, and she breathed deeply.

"How?"

"They are still attached to metal frames as they had been made into jewelry."

"Not worry," Arid sighed and emptied the small bags on the sandy ground. In unison, the other arochs stopped to watch her. She extended her hand over the gems, and the metal melted away. Then, one by one, the stones lifted in the air around her, swirling in a golden light. Once she was pleased with their positioning, they pressed into her skin, into the places where they had been cut, pried, or pulled out from. As her body accepted them back, each of them became illuminated from within her.

There was a wave of relief and deep love from the other arochs. The ideas "Queen," "Mother," and "Whole" could be picked up from all the chatter. Arid had always been striking, but now she was mesmerizingly strange and wonderful to behold.

"Eat, it cold soon," she told me. "Peel."

She took one of the hard nut-like things from the fire and popped it open by pressing on the sides. Inside was a cream-white mass that had a sweet, almost floral scent. The taste was like slowly cooked, dense milk with a hint of warm spices. The effect it had was that of pouring a whole bottle of wine on one's brain.

One by one, the arochs sat down with a pleasantly calm expression hinting at a smile. Arid pulled me to sit as well, and then she took my hand in hers.

"It is fruit from Evertree. Mother of trees. Eat too many, die, eat one, get hugged," Arid explained with gleaming eyes.

I could barely hear her words as I glanced up into the sky. There was a feeling of limitlessness, a sensation that all was as one. A terrifying, deep love for the world and all living could be felt everywhere. It was almost contagious, curing away all resentment, grudges, and fears. Afterward, the mind felt clear and unimpeded.

"Is this how you feel about the world?" I asked Arid.

"Many times. Not all. But many." She turned to me. I could feel her encouragement and a subtle plea. Then she told me, in thought, that if she could bear the burden, she would, but the position was not possible for her to claim even if it would have been her greatest pleasure. She also believed that it should be someone who knew human hearts and understood the evil as well. And even though I was a made creature, like they were, she was fully of the opinion that I was just as worthy as any true human.

"I know," I whispered. "But I cannot make such a promise yet. I know what is at stake, but if I can avoid it, I would rather avoid it. Maybe we can fight this and then focus on finding someone truly suited for it once Istrata isn't killing off all others of my inclination. There are so many things worth staying here for," I mused, though the thought of someone else suddenly taking my place at Riestel's side was surprisingly vexing.

"If only got power, would you?"

"You mean if I could only have the power and knowledge and none of the responsibilities?"

"Yes."

"In a heartbeat."

Arid chortled and seemed to drift into her own little world.

XVI

R iestel's relatives settled rowdily and fast into the rooms appointed to them. The servants who were only accustomed to nobles of the Peak were ever so confused as to why such people were housed close to us. They simply thought it another way for Riestel to cause them trouble—which, of course, could very well have been one of his secondary motives.

On her second day here, Ombra almost threw out the head cook from his kitchen to make her breakfast the way she wanted, but after arguing for a good while, they had suddenly stopped and broken into laughter, and now she was allowed to do as she pleased. Kindred spirits, apparently.

"I believe most have arrived. Should we soon head back to the Lowers or the Center?" Riestel asked. "They will be the first places she will launch an attack at once she comes out."

"We should," I agreed.

"We can stay at Ombra's while we wait for signs," he suggested.

"I would prefer that to the official guest rooms of the army. Just the two of us?"

"Well, only if I can trust you to keep your hands to yourself. I know it's difficult, but let's keep a resemblance of honor."

"I will not touch you with a ten-foot pole," I groaned.

"Good, then it is settled. I've been told that the first-line consecrators and army members are present in the center already."

"I should burn all the stored ichor first. I don't want to leave any here while we are gone."

"Has Moras agreed to it? It will hamper his experiments."

"I don't need his permission."

"I didn't say you did, but wouldn't it be wise to tell him?" Riestel suggested. "I will gather all the essentials for us to leave. You have a chat with him."

Moras was a little taken aback when I told him what I wanted to do. He understood why but was noticeably anxious about the thought of having to pause his tests.

"If she appears, I do not wish to have any large pockets of the substance behind us. Just in case, she might be able to use it somehow. I'm not saying she can, but..." I explained once more.

"I hear you, I'm just... I'm just so close to figuring something out. I didn't want to tell you about it yet."

"Tell me what?"

"Well, those machines that we use for the emptied souls. They've been able to grind souls for fuel, right? And grinding them, they have created more of the suffering mass and spat that out everywhere into the world, from the lighter world to the forced heavier world. Your husband can do both. He can rip out souls and energy from the living in this world and chew them to fuel his powers. When he does that, he creates more of the ichor in him and pushes it out as a leftover. But he can also use that, and he can draw it from the heavier world itself. Of course, it cannot be used in a similar manner to pure energy and the life force; it is simply used by molding it into different things. Other creatures, weapons," Moras explained, drawing a myriad of small arrows, current markers, and channels on a board. "What if we can find a way to make the machines transform the heavier substance? I'm not saying I can suddenly build you things to fight with, but if I could modify them to pull out the substance from the heavier world and at least filter it somehow to a slightly better form to use."

"Do you think it would be possible to empty the heavier world that way? Completely?"

"Yes, in time. Then, we could seal the scars to prevent any such substance from forming again here or from forming a new plane. It would help with the revitalization as well. Slowly, yes, but anything more would be good, right?"

"It would," I replied. "Have you done actual tests yet, or is this just a hypothetical thing?"

"I have not. I'm simply trying to study the machinations and how I would need to modify them. I'm still calculating things."

"Understood. So, you are requesting that I leave you some in case you are able to find a test-worthy solution?"

"If you do not deem it absolutely life-threatening, yes, I would request that."

"I will allow you to keep some, but all other tests must be put on hold. As I understood it, you are merely refining things at this point, yes?"

"Correct. Thank you."

"Then I will leave you with one of the smaller containers," I promised with a sinking heart. If he found a way to empty the entire heavier world, we would have a good chance of stopping this catastrophe from repeating ever again, but it also meant that Rime would lose whatever it was that acted as a substitute for his soul. But that was the permission I gave; Rime would have done the same.

Burning the storage of the black tar took much out of me. I slept through most of our journey back. The first night, we would spend in peace, just the two of us, then we would go to the lower walls of the district where we could keep an eye on most of the Lowers.

"Stretch," Riestel told me as he rubbed my hands in Ombra's abandoned house. "I've never met a consecrator who dances and doesn't before you. You never let your body heal and rest."

"I have you to fix that."

"What if I go on strike?"

"As if you'd miss an opportunity to make me squirm."

"True enough, it would be a challenge to resist," Riestel smirked, but then his expression changed to a darker one. "This feels eerie. Like the beginning of the end."

"I know. I feel it too." I sighed. It was all I had been thinking since we returned here. Everything was too calm to last.

"Do you think Rime will come back?" I asked.

"I think he will do everything within his power to return to you. Even if just for a moment."

"Why would you say that? What did he write to you?"

"Enough for me to know he is one of the finest men I've ever had the misfortune to meet."

Riestel's words squeezed the breath out of me.

"You have to tell me what he wrote," I insisted.

"No. I am merely safeguarding his words in case he does not return. Then and only then, I will let you read it. And, unfortunately for you, I intend to honor that request to the fullest," Riestel told me with an uncharacteristically somber expression on his face.

"You are cruel."

"He is the cruel one." He huffed and shook his head.

"I suppose he is," I agreed. "I didn't see it in the beginning. But his cruelty always serves a purpose."

"It does. It almost elevates it to a noble characteristic. I should have liked to have a friend like him. I'm slightly envious of his guards. I've never had many friends, and those I did have had come and gone."

"You are unnerving me, talking like that." I felt a chill run through me, even though the evening was mellow and warm.

"Let's go up to the roof. I want to say something to you, and I want to say it in a place that is removed from all of this."

"The roof?"

"You know...the thing over most houses."

"I know what a roof is—"

"Good, I was worried for a moment. This way."

The small upstairs corridor had a little hatch in the ceiling, and from there, he pulled down a ladder. It was a very rickety old thing but held our weight. We had to bend through the attic to another triangular window with small hooks on the sides. Riestel unfastened them and pushed the window open. Then, he took a small stool and placed it under the window. He quickly climbed onto the old shingle roof and then held out his hand for me.

The evening sun hit the roof with a dry and tender warmth. A quilt of similarly colored roofs spread out below. It was a comforting sight somehow. The ocean was bathed in the sunlight as well, with a few sailing ships casting their shadows toward the Harbor.

"I used to come here often. I'd stare at the sea endlessly until father or the neighbors would shout at me to get down. It felt like it was calling to me as a child. Like I was meant to be one with it."

"And then you manifested water gifts?"

"Yes. I just knew it. It started with raindrops. I could bend them or make them fly upwards. They'd cure my wounds."

"Did you like the Temple when you were taken there?"

"I did. It was a place of peace and learning. At first, then I met her and, everything started to look as if there was a curtain of happiness hiding something. Everyone and everything had a façade. I found it unnerving. Now, I wonder... I wonder if it truly was as she painted it, or did I begin to share her disconnect and delusions?"

"I know the feeling."

Riestel reached out and took my hand in his.

"Do you know what is strange?" he asked.

"You."

"I can be." He smiled. "I'm going to be serious for a moment, so bear with me."

"Depends on the topic."

"You and her mostly."

"If you must."

"I think I do, just so I don't regret never saying it. When I met her, I was drawn to her right away. Then again, who wouldn't have been with her lineage and patrons... She could have been the ugliest maiden in the kingdom and had suitors crawling out from under her petticoats for her pedigree alone. Soon, I loved her enough to dedicate my life to her or, subsequently, to her plans of 'making the world a better place'. If only I would have listened more carefully."

"You couldn't have stopped it even if you had."

"Maybe not. Anyway, when I found her the first time after her death, I felt as if I would go mad. I grieved and carried on one version after another, all miserable and resigned. After that, I simply indulged in the world, hardened myself, and consumed whatever and whoever I wanted. Suddenly, you happened. You happened. You, not her. Not even in the slightest could I have ever mistaken you for her. I didn't know what to do or what to think, so I carried on as always. Testing, prodding. I didn't dare to think this time it would be different. I had never considered the option of a soul becoming someone completely new, not just a suitably different version of her with all her memories, feelings, and ambitions. The strangest thing was that I knew, almost right away, that you were the other half the Source had been waiting for. That I had been waiting for. It was strange coming to terms with my destiny not being at all how I had thought."

"The other half?"

"Needed to complete me."

"That's quite the assumption to make," I said quietly and avoided his eyes.

"It took me a while to accept my future didn't lie with Istrata anymore. I fought it, thinking I had waited for her for centuries, served her for centuries... She had to reappear. She had to be it. She had to be... But she wasn't. She likely never was. We never managed to naturally create the electricity you and I accidentally sparked just by being close. We had to focus and force it. She never yielded herself so openly to those feelings or the fire. I know you said you felt her love for me, but what good was a love expressed only within? It never reached me. Even the passion you hated me with in the beginning was warmer than the love she left me with."

"You speak so bitterly about her these days."

"I'm not denying I wasn't head over heels in love with her during the first life and that there weren't moments of pure bliss. Obviously, I was, and there were. I wouldn't be here otherwise. I wouldn't have been so blind and tolerant. I'm merely saying that what I felt for her faded like a mirage, an infatuation for an ideal that makes room for something true."

"I don't know what to say to that," I replied.

"No need to say anything. I just wanted to express it. This is might the last half-decent place for a rather serious confession of the romantic kind as I'd rather not pour my heart out knee-deep in corpses or other fun things or blurt this all out with my dying breath should the worse come to pass."

"I think most people would consider a confession of the romantic kind something other than talking about their sort-of-kind-of-dead former lover."

"I'm going to give you the benefit of the doubt and assume you are simply being mean and not oblivious enough to have completely missed my point."

"Very gracious of you."

XVII

Being around Riestel, after hearing him lay it all out, was curious. He was exactly as he always was: a little rude, snide, and constantly getting on my nerves as if he had been born with that gift. It wasn't that I had ever doubted that he had feelings for me. But the realization of how deep everything between us ran was a little frightening and, strangely enough, made us distance ourselves a little.

The construction of the palace in the King's Circle had been now partially halted by the decrees Rime had left behind. Instead, there was a huge urgency in building funnels, walls, and whatever could be used to direct or split the enemy. It was to be our first proper defense line. For now, we patrolled the lower walls at Crafter's daily, looking to the Worker's and the Slums for any sign of Rime or Istrata and to stall any progress until we were better prepared if she should begin the assault.

Riestel did his very best to keep me from slipping into a sullen, depressed mood. He woke me up each morning and walked with me tirelessly everywhere while I kept staring into the distance and waiting. It had been over half a month since Rime left us. Half a month of silence and an uncomfortable lull in all action. Preparations were going well; all those who had wanted to be evacuated had been evacuated. There were always a few stubborn families who simply refused to listen.

Some of the still living members of the disbanded Black Guard had arrived at the Crafter's as well. I could see them pace about the walls and structures with the same frustration and worry as I. Veitso was feeling particularly edgy, so he diverted his attention to getting as much wine and spirits for the evenings as possible. He had decided that if we had to wait, we might as well make the most out of it in a similar fashion to how they had spent any free evenings on the Borders.

Once the sun began to set on our camp consisting of tents, piles of resources, and some empty, borrowed houses, the air acquired notes of autumn. A slight hint that the warm season would begin to wane soon. The other consecrators and most soldiers were on the larger square or closer to it than us. There were altogether a few hundred of us, so just the bare essentials for an outpost of sorts.

Tammaran lit up a few fires to cook on. Veitso arranged his rather impressive haul of all kinds of beverages on the table close by. By the look of it, he had been sampling them a little earlier on. I helped him bring out some glasses, as that gave me an excuse to find a moment alone with him.

"I hear you write lovely letters," I told him.

"Letters? I...uhm...I do?" he replied, all flustered and with his cheeks flushing from more than alcohol.

"Merrie told me she is very fond of them. She said she wishes she could express herself better and that she hopes to see you soon."

"Really?"

"Really. I would suggest, though, and I know this may seem rude, for you to slowly lessen this kind of pastime if you wish something more. She is the sweetest person I know, and I fear to pass these regards to you because I'm unsure how much of your time is spent with... well, passing the time by drinking."

"That's a bit unfair," Veitso muttered. "We only see each other in these rather dire circumstances. I'm hardly drunk all the time."

"I just needed to ask so I can be happy for you and not worried."

"Yeah, okay, I get it," he grunted as we stepped closer to the fire.

Veitso took the glasses from me and put them on the table. I sat next to Riestel on a log by the fire.

"You're telling me that he is the strategist of the bunch?" Riestel whispered as Veitso fumbled with a few bottles.

"You don't need dexterity to be smart," Tammaran noted from behind.

"Obviously not," Riestel agreed. "But one would think a man of such a reputation could count how many hands versus how many bottles he has."

Tammaran looked over at Veitso, who was currently searching for one of the slippery bottles from behind a log he had brought out to sit on.

"Well... Let's just say that I at least attempted to defend his honor." Tammaran sighed and walked over to help Veitso.

"They are a curious bunch," Riestel noted.

"I'm sure they'll like you; shall I go and ask if you can play with them?" I suggested and grinned.

Riestel looked positively mortified. For once, he was the one out of his comfort zone. After the bottles were set in a manner that pleased Veitso, he focused on pestering Samedi to watch the sausages and bread over the fires.

Watching the flames was soothing. Every once in a while, the wood cracked, and sparks flew up. Samedi went to hand out some of the warmed breads to all the people they currently worked with. The assistants and army members found their way to other suitable sitting places or returned to their accommodations. The evening air filled with a relaxed chatter of dozens. Only Tammaran, Veitso, and Samedi sat down by the fire with us.

"If you got to wait, make it comfy," Veitso told us. "No point in worrying too much. He always pops up eventually. No other way about it. He will be back." He looked at Riestel with slightly squinted eyes. I got an uncomfortable feeling that as I had meddled with his life, he felt he now had a similar right.

"I'm glad you are so confident," I replied as Riestel simply ignored the attention, except for leaning a little closer to me to spite the messenger.

"It is his way. He always takes calculated risks," Samedi noted. "They usually pay off—"

"Hey, mister ice magic man," Veitso interrupted his friend, addressing Riestel. "Can you make this drink a little colder?" He shook a bottle in his hand.

The moment Veitso finished his request, Riestel's eyes flashed white, and Veitso's hand was frozen tightly to the bottle. He scratched his head with the handle of the knife he had skewered a sausage with and currently held in his other hand.

"Not exactly how I imagined it," Veitso said and laughed. Then he clinked his hand against the log to shatter some of the ice. He picked up the shards, plopped them into the bottle, and proceeded to warm his finger over the flames.

"You're quiet for a mighty consecrator," Veitso remarked to Riestel. "Are you shy, or don't you like us? You know we have much more reason not to like you than you us."

"I have nothing to contribute to the discussion," Riestel said, sneering. "I am merely here to—"

"You're trying to get into her favor, aren't you?" Veitso took a jab.

"I do not have to try," Riestel retorted smugly, giving him a cold smile.

"Veitso, hush," Samedi ordered. "You wanted to have a relaxing evening, so don't ruin it."

"Yeah, but it ain't quite right, is it?"

"And who are you to judge that?" Riestel said, straightening his posture.

"Look, I know you have Rime's best interest at heart," I interjected before they would ruin the entire evening. "And I appreciate you for it, but you fully well know what he did to cause this rift. This situation is in no way Riestel's doing. If you need to blame someone for it, blame me. I'm the one letting him closer."

"Sorry," Veitso muttered. "It's just that you make a real fine couple. I was hoping you'd work it out."

"I like that you worry for us, but leave it to Rime and me to settle."

Veitso nodded and took a swig. He still kept an eye on Riestel throughout the evening but refrained from talking to him. Samedi came to sit closer.

"We are just all a bit worried, no matter how calm we may seem. Rime was our leader for years. It is still bizarre that we are apart now. Each of us focusing on something different."

"I think he would have liked to have kept you all closer, but there were none but you he could trust with the districts at this point," I mused.

"We know," Tammaran agreed, then he tilted his head and frowned. "What is that? Can you feel it?"

There was a slight shake in the ground. The tremor was so faint I needed to close my eyes and place my hands against the earth to convince myself I actually felt it.

"I can… There aren't earthquakes in this region, are there?"

"No, there aren't," Riestel confirmed.

"It stopped," Tammaran said and straightened up. "Strange."

"Maybe you just had too much to drink!" Veitso suggested, happy to accuse someone else of his sins of the evening.

Tammaran sighed. "I'm not the only one who felt it, you half-soaked log."

Then, we all jumped up as the stones on the ground shook violently. Samedi began ushering people to leave as fast as possible, not that they needed much prompting. I covered my ears, as it was almost like the ground was screaming. The vibrations seemed to come from behind us. When we turned to look, the ground bulged, and black ichor spewed from it.

"Back, get back," Riestel yelled and created an ice-barrier to contain the liquid.

The shaking stopped again. From the middle of the pool of black ichor and earth rose a hand, then another. A dark, dripping figure pushed himself out of the ground.

"Rime?" I asked and took a step forward. Riestel grabbed my hand.

"Don't go closer yet," he insisted.

"Rime?" I called again. I was sure I recognized him. Why wasn't he answering me? Did he not hear me? He had to hear me. Did he not know me anymore?

The figure hobbled toward us, then it lifted its hand against the clear ice and collapsed. I could see a small glint of silver on the wrist.

"It's him. Help him out!" I ordered, hoping that there was enough of Rime left to save. I had to take the chance, even if it was a trap.

Veitso and Tammaran charged over as Riestel shattered the ice. They reached out for Rime and pulled him out of the sticky ichor. Rime seemed to be unconscious. At least he wasn't an immediate threat.

"Clean him," I requested.

Riestel hummed a low note and made a pulling gesture with his hand from the sky to the ground. A shower of heavy raindrops began to dilute and push the ichor away. I crouched down beside Rime and wiped some of it away from his face. He looked pale, almost gray. He opened his eyes, which were blacker than the ocean's depths. His breathing was shallow and labored.

"Get him indoors, somewhere safe," I demanded. "So, he can be kept hidden for a few days."

It was the only sensible thing to do for Rime's safety and ours.

"My quarters should be the best for it," Samedi suggested. "This way, I'll check that there are as few people on the way as possible."

Samedi ran ahead from corner to corner as Veitso carried Rime on his shoulders in a mostly straight line. The speed at which he could sober up from almost unconscious to somewhat functioning never ceased to surprise. Riestel stayed behind to wash the ichor away as much as possible.

Veitso lowered Rime onto the carpet in Samedi's room.

"Leave, all of you, please," I requested. "He is going to yell in pain in a moment. You need to cover that if you can."

"The wooden walls are rather thick here," Samedi said. "Tammaran and Veitso will be outside to figure something out if they can hear it. I will get my people to patch the ground."

Rime was barely breathing, so I began the process as gently as I could. First, I burned it off his skin, which improved his color a little. When I started to inch my way into his channels, he moaned and tried to wave my hands away. Did he even know where he was? Did he recognize me? Was it even him anymore? I got up and backed away. This was unsafe. I needed him to be held down.

"Can you get Riestel?" I asked Tammaran.

"What do you need him for?"

"Do you want me to try to heal Rime or not? If you do, get him," I told Tammaran and shut the door. Of course, they disliked Riestel. Of course, they were trying to back their friend, but I didn't have the time or the patience to discuss my motives at this moment. Rime needed to be himself, or as close to it as possible, and fast. Before anyone truly started to wonder where he had gone, and definitely before, his father would smell that something wasn't right. Whether Frazil was content in his part now, I wouldn't want to arouse his previous ambitions with rumors. It was the last thing this city needed on top of everything else.

Riestel closed the door behind him before Rime's guard could ask anything or try to come in.

"He's in a bad way," Riestel noted. "Full of it."

"I can burn it out. I need you to restrain him. Anyway, possible, until his eyes return to normal."

"Alright. But it will leave frost-bites on him if you take too long."

"His skin will heal, and even if it doesn't, it is hardly the most important part of him. Just do it."

Riestel positioned himself on the floor at Rime's head. Then he fused his hands and feet with ice to the floor.

"Rime, can you hear me?" I asked. "I'm going to begin cleansing you. It will hurt as it did before. Try to hang on."

I placed my hands on Rime's hands and pushed into the fire and my consciousness. Forcing the flames to the most peripheral of the channels, I moved with steady pressure and pace. Rime groaned and twitched. Riestel got up a few times to wipe my forehead so the sweat didn't sting my eyes. The further I went, the more Rime tried to resist it. The ice holding him down became darker and contaminated. He got one hand loose for a moment, but Riestel didn't waste any time forcing it back and reforming the shackles.

"Focus on your task, not mine," he reminded me. "I have strengthened them."

Moving to the larger channels, I could tell something was different than before. This ichor was thicker, truly tar-like. I could also feel the Queen's fingerprints on it. She had fed him with herself. That's what it felt like.

As I had cleared out his right half, he began to breathe in a more relaxed manner. The pain still made him moan and, at times, grunt. The left half of his body went faster. Riestel dared to diminish the ice thickness and width.

I cleared as much of his head as I could. For a moment, I considered if I should enter the main channels and try to clear them a bit. I reached around his heart. There was an odd nodule at the junction of the main channels. It was surrounded by a thick crust of hardened ichor. I stared at it for a long time. I wanted to poke it but stayed my hand. Perhaps it was the point that was connected to the heavier world. Like our soul tether was to the lighter world. I backed away, as it would be better to leave the main channels alone. Any mistake in them could be fatal.

Veitso lifted Rime to the bed after I allowed his friends to enter the room.

"We'll take turns to watch him," Samedi promised. "We will call you as soon as he is awake."

"I need to be here in case I did something wrong and need to try to fix it," I said, refusing the offer. It was a lie. I needed to be the one in the room in case Rime had been turned to the Queen side. His friends would never believe it or see it before it was too late.

"Then let us get you something to sleep on, and we will guard outside."

"I will stay as well. He may need other kinds of healing," Riestel decided. "I assume you can find enough supplies to accommodate that."

"We can..." Samedi replied, dragging Veitso out with him.

XVIII

R ime showed signs of a rising fever during the night. I was going to ask his friends to bring in cold towels, but Riestel ushered me under covers and ordered me to rest. It wasn't an easy thing to do with one worry after another coming to my mind. It was horrific to think that the moment he closed the gate might have been the last time I saw the true him. If he would wake up and be like Irinda, it would tear my heart apart. When morning came, Riestel was still sat by Rime, circulating cool water on his forehead and neck.

"Good morning, lazy worm," Riestel said, arching his back to turn to me. "The fever is almost gone. I would think he will wake soon."

"Have you been up all night?"

"Well, he wasn't going to cool himself off, was he? It wasn't a terribly bothersome task. I can meditate and heal at the same time when the symptom is as simple to cure as this."

"It's still not a proper rest. You should sleep too. It's still rather early."

"I might slumber for a moment. You don't need to cool him off anymore. Just wait," Riestel told me and got up. He walked over to my mattress. "Up."

"You have your own place right there. The one you demanded they set up for you."

"It doesn't have your scent. Now, let me sleep, or you'll seem ungrateful."

"Fine, good skies, you are needy at times."

"I'm simply choosing the most comfortable place for my nap."

Riestel tucked himself under the covers comfortably as I went to sit next to Rime. Riestel fell asleep almost immediately. I felt a slight urge to throw some small object at him, or maybe I could braid his hair and make it all frizzy.

Riestel's face was so peaceful as he slept, and he had been a wonderful help, so the desire to harass his well-earned rest subsided quicker than usual.

The morning came and went as Rime remained asleep. I was running out of ways to distract myself from the unanswered questions. I wasn't the only one anxiously waiting to see Rime wake up. The former guardsmen came to check on him and us as often as they could. But nothing changed. Riestel monitored Rime's condition.

"The fever isn't coming back, from what I can tell," Riestel said.

"Then why isn't he waking up?" I asked. Someone was running in the hallway.

"My guess is that he is just exhausted. I can't find any physical issues," Riestel mused.

The door slammed open.

"It's starting," Tammaran announced, trying to catch his breath. "The Slums are overflowing."

"Go and look," Riestel told me. "I'll keep him comfortable. Promise."

"Thank you," I replied and glanced at Riestel and Rime. If I had met them both on the same day without any history between us, which one would I have leaned toward?

"Stop comparing us in your head and hurry," Riestel ordered without looking at me.

"I was not."

"Definitely were. And the answer is favorable to me, I'm sure."

I closed the door on him and hurried after Tammaran. He guided me to the highest point in the wall toward the Worker's and handed me a looking glass. He pointed toward the gate and smaller doors. The black ichor was forcing its way through all crevices and pushing on structures.

"The gate will yield under the pressure," he stated. "Or it will just start pouring over the wall."

"The Queen is doing it slowly to make a point." I sighed. "With the amount she has at her disposal, she could shatter that gate."

"She's toying with us?"

"I am merely guessing. I don't know that more than you do. It is equally possible that she doesn't want to expend any more strength than she has to."

"Do you want us to go in there and begin burning and cleaning what we can?"

"No. If she is playing, she can drown everyone with a flash flood of ichor, and we'll lose too many. Let her take the Worker's as slowly or as fast as she desires. You can burn all you can from here once it is within reach, of course. I will begin my chore then as well."

"Understood. I will ready all suitable people and the incendiaries that can be used long range."

"Good. If there are still any left in the Worker's, let them know that now is the last moment to leave and that all who still choose to stay will not be rescued under any circumstances."

"Is that a command? To leave all to their own devices? Even if they would make it to the wall?"

"They won't make it if they stay and only run once their rooms flood... If you are able to hoist someone over the wall, then by all means, do so, but I highly doubt that she will allow for it. For her, advancing slowly and causing anxiety and panic among us will only lead to an increased number of souls that are already tainted and suffering once they die. To kill those trying to escape at the last minute... It will simply increase her influence. And when people see others fall, they may succumb voluntarily if her whispers and promises reach them."

"That is the worst reason for a slow advance if there ever was," Tammaran said.

"I hope I'm wrong."

"Do you think we will ever see her? Or will all just play out through proxies?" Tammaran asked.

"I'm sure she will show herself, eventually. If we survive long enough, and when she does, it should give us hope."

"Hope?"

"If she comes to get us, it means we have been effective. She needs to risk herself to defeat us. If we make it that far, we have a chance."

Tammaran squinted at the sight of the ichor pouring out from the Slums and nodded.

"I will keep you informed should you wish to return to Rime," he offered.

"I would like to be there when he wakes, though I would not mind walking in there to find him conscious."

Riestel got up when I returned. He wanted to get some fresh air and stretch his legs. Once he had gone, I realized there was a window covered by drapes in the room. I had been so focused on what was happening that I hadn't really paid any attention to the surroundings. Surely, I could let some light in as we were on the fourth and highest floor of this temporarily claimed residence.

The wooden frames were painted with a light dusk pink. I could see directly above the wall that bordered the Worker's. People were hurrying everywhere. Consecrators patrolling on the wall, trying to assess when they might be able to begin their work. I could see Riestel out on the wall too. He was staring into the distance. One could only imagine how badly he wanted all this to be over with, to finally have a life that wasn't affected by the Queen or involved cleaning up after her.

What would it be like? To become a god with him? Would any love last for ages? Would we even tolerate each other after a few centuries? I think I knew the answers to those questions.

"Isa? What are you looking at?" Rime asked. He sounded groggy and rough. I turned to him, feeling a little embarrassed I had been staring at Riestel and not looking over Rime.

"Welcome back," I said with a forced smile. "I wish you would have warned me before doing that. Are you thirsty or hungry? Does it hurt anywhere?"

"Hungry, fine otherwise."

"I'll have something brought to you."

"Did you get the letters?" Rime winced as he tried to move to a more upright position. Of course, that would be his first proper question.

"I did. Everything is set in motion and prepared as ordered. You just need to clear your head and get well."

Rime sighed and gave up on trying to sit up. I sat on the bed next to him. His eyes seemed a little unfocused but mostly clear of the ichor. He didn't seem to be in a talkative mood, not that he ever was someone you could describe as chatty. This time, it just irked me in an entirely new way. Did he expect me to interview him about all that happened? Why couldn't he just volunteer the information and not have me yank it out of him?

There was no way he didn't know we all wanted answers. Craved for answers. Instead of making a fuss about it, I went to tell his friends that he was up and needed nourishment. I stayed outside by the room's door, waiting for them to get here with the food.

"Have you been in the hall all this time?" Samedi asked as they appeared.

"I have. I'll go for a walk as he will be glad to see you all. If he has anything to talk to me about, let me know."

"All right... Is everything fine?" Tammaran checked, looking a little uncomfortable.

"Yes. He is healing."

"Between you two?"

"No, but that is not your concern. See that he eats properly and rests more. If he tells you anything about his time away from us, I would like to know. I'd even say I deserve to know."

"You can come with us," Samedi suggested.

"Unless he has something to actually say to me, I do not need to be there," I replied, fully aware of how childish I was being.

Looking over the wall, the ground was slowly being dyed black by the oozing substance. There were still some locations where normal earth was visible. I was so angry I could feel my veins thump in my temples to the point of feeling dizzy. At that moment, I jumped down to the Worker's side. People yelled after me and ran to see if I needed help to get back up.

Positioning myself in the middle of the only larger swatch of land that was clean, I clenched my fists and felt my entire body tense up. Fire spewed forth from my feet and hands to all directions my dance directed it. I reached out to every house, every alley, every nook and cranny I could find and get to. My muscles trembled from the strain, and I wanted to give up.

Once I felt I couldn't lift one more finger, I breathed deeply for a while. Then I continued. The fire forced the ichor to sever its bonds and become the gritty soul-sand-like substance after a small amount of lighter energy was released into the cycle. I could see that the created grains did not get eaten back into the ichor. It was lost to her for now. I took some in my hand and reached into them until the bonds broke once more. They gave a crude, painful sort of energy to use. But right now, it felt good. It allowed me to continue and burn my anger on something useful.

I don't know how long I danced among the flames, but all the ichor had been cleared from the nearby areas. It would return soon enough, but at least I had made a small dent in her stores. Even standing seemed straining once I stopped. My limbs trembled, but I felt good. Pure and lucid.

"If you are quite done with this spectacle, need a way back up?" Riestel yelled from the wall.

"Please."

Riestel formed me an icy staircase to ascend.

"I'm guessing he got on your nerves," Riestel said as he helped me step off the ice.

"Royally. I just do not get why he is like this. He keeps putting this artificial distance between us. Whether we are lovers, we are still married, and we always had an understanding about supporting each other. Now...he's just... shutting me out."

"I gave him his letter back. I'd assume he will seek you out to talk soon enough. Or you could just go to him and tell him he is being an idiot and behaving poorly toward you. Like I did before I found you out here burning half of the city."

"You did what?"

"You heard me. Now, march up in there and have an actual conversation. If he tries to avoid something, press on. Otherwise, even I will die of old age before you two settle things properly." Riestel sighed and pushed me toward the building Rime was still resting in.

The door creaked as I went into the room. Rime was sitting and reading to catch up with all that had happened while he had been away. Samedi was opening and sealing letters for him.

"I see you are well enough to work," I noted.

"Getting there," Rime replied, avoiding my eyes and concentrating on his reading.

"Take a breather from those," I requested. "Start with the important things. Did you meet her?" I was as calm as possible. "What happened after you shut us out?"

"A sharp choice of words," Rime remarked and finally looked up.

"Deserved. Answer me."

"That was the reason I stayed there. To meet her, to buy time for defenses to be finalized. I figured if she was there and we all walked in, it would make her begin her attempt, as she wouldn't be able to hide anymore."

"Your desire to sacrifice yourself for us all is getting to be a little suicidal," Samedi scolded him.

"It is not my intention as such. It is simply that I'm the only one who can go to her realm. First, I stayed hidden, making her seek me out. She knew from Irinda that I had stayed behind, and she was curious enough to focus on me. I let her find me after a few days of avoiding her the best I could. She was very keen on talking about finding a like-minded soul. Someone to understand what she wanted to do. I played along as much as I could without giving her an answer. She offered me eternity at her side, a life of sorts."

"Were you tempted?"

"Of course he wasn't!" Samedi interjected. "How can you ask something like that?"

"Because I have to."

"Isa is right to ask it. Yes, I was tempted by the thought of being gifted a life after this one. It is the one thing I've envied others for during my entire existence. But seeing what she means by life... It isn't an option. It wouldn't be me. It would just be my body and some residual humanity and memories. You all heard Irinda speak. All of them are frozen, stuck in a loop of their final thoughts and desires. It is easy to direct them to attack the living as the amount of envy and the thought of having been wronged are etched to their very nature."

"Were there others? Besides Irinda?" I asked.

"Yes. The ichor itself consists of the people of the Slums and more, so many dead and twisted remains. It is somewhat conscious. It can form into an ocean or to individual creatures by her desire and has limited capabilities of thought."

That was the last thing I wanted to hear.

"I wish I would have been born earlier..." Rime sighed. "Then I could have tried to prevent this city from becoming such an unequal place, to prevent people from splitting into smaller tribes almost and losing a sense of who we were as a nation, what we could accomplish together. We have created those masses for her."

"You are much too hard on yourself. She would have gathered momentum with or without you having lived earlier. She created the conditions for the suffering to linger and not be torn into the cycle to be purified and move on. Time was always on her side," I reminded him.

"You are right." Rime took a deep breath. "There isn't much else to tell. We know her goals already. She doesn't have any grand strategy. She is purely expecting to squeeze us to death slowly and steadily and join anyone who wants to avoid the pain of her mass."

"Then we can't let her dictate the pace she will use her resources," I remarked.

"Exactly. We need to force her to expend more so we can get to her. One thing I did learn is that while you can move through this world and the lighter one, like breaking the water's surface, this is not the case for them at all. To get to the heavier world and out of it, she requires a tremendous amount of energy and power. It takes much for me to pierce my way back here, but for her, it is a much more demanding task, like breaking through a steel gate. She cannot create new openings quickly. She uses already existing ones, ones that she has prepared."

"Can we use that knowledge somehow?" I wondered.

"I'm not sure yet. But it was an interesting find."

"Maybe we could lock her out of the important ones?" Samedi suggested. "Not sure how, but right now, Rime is the only one who can access the heavier world with her. He cannot fight her there alone, so we have to force her to this side."

"Good." Rime grinned. "You are worth your weight in gold."

"I appreciate the acknowledgment, but it is hardly a workable solution," Samedi replied.

"You need to go to the Peak then, as soon as you can travel," I said to Rime. "You need to talk to Moras and the arochs. We need a way to close the wounds. They are the best option we have for figuring out how to close them. Unless I should just try to burn and scar them shut? I'm hoping there might be a less attention-provoking way. We will take care of everything here."

XIX

T here was a sense of relief among all after Rime's return. He walked the walls and inspected all things and units in the area so that he was seen and heard in case there had been any rumors circulating of his sudden and rather long absence. He would head to the Peak to converse with Moras and the arochs on the doorways the ichor was forced through to our world. The rest of us would stay in the Crafter's and cause Istrata to lose as much of the ichor as we could.

The ichor had climbed a man's length up the wall and was now a black lake below us. Houses of the Worker's were half filled with it, and some of the lowest buildings only had their roofs visible. The Slums looked like a black tarp had covered it. The ichor didn't behave like a normal liquid. It could be poured to fill an area, but it could also just creep along any surface like some quickly growing organism.

"Is it time to lower it?" Riestel asked.

"I think so. Let's annoy her," I concurred.

The ichor was a bit easier to get a hold of now. The amount of daily practice I had with it made sure of that. I still had to painfully force it to ignite, but keeping it burning and getting the fire to spread had become easier. As the sand-like residue was formed, Riestel's waves and spirals of water rinsed it to a purer form and lifted it to the wall to store and use. If the first time I had burned the ichor as an experiment, I had needed half a day to get through a barrel. Now, I could clear a small lake in half the time with the help of others.

People gathered at the wall to look as the oily substance lowered and withdrew. Obviously, we knew this was only the Queen testing our determination. Once she realized the slow pressure to make things seem irreparably lost to make us want to surrender would not work, we would see something much worse. For now, I was secretly grateful she was hoping to win an easy victory.

It wasn't that Istrata's tactic was without merit. The idea of having to keep backing up and withdrawing toward the Needle as our living space continuously diminished was unnerving and stressful. And it would test the commoner's will especially. There would be a point where we would have no place to run.

We had made it clear to all military and temple personnel still with us in the area that withdrawing should not be thought of as defeat for now. Everyone had been talked to so people would be clear on the agenda. Still, I think most felt a little better every time we were able to lower the surface visibly. People hoped that it would be all we needed to face from the Queen. I hoped that as well, but I knew better.

After bathing and changing into my regular green temple clothes, I tried to rest, but it was a futile exercise—my body was willing, my mind wasn't. It kept playing different catastrophes over and over and then tried to figure out the best ways to counter them. Eventually, I would just find myself taking longer and longer walks alone to quiet my thoughts.

One night, I noticed Riestel and Rime sitting off to the side of a campfire. No one else was close to them. Rime kept his gaze adamantly on his boots as Riestel kept talking. Trying to listen, I circled behind them as quietly as I could and sat down in the shadows cast by a few crates.

From the fragments I heard, I surmised that Riestel was trying to push us to a conclusion. I knew it was a good thing, but a part of me wanted to stay in this in-between where things were still possible either way, at least in theory. Emotionally, it was a poor place to be, but I was scared about the outcome.

The next few days were spent fighting the ever-rising ichor. It had started to pour faster. Istrata was getting angry at us. The good thing about her fixation on getting her own way was that she became easily emotional, tapping into all of those betrayals and all those disappointments she had ever experienced. It made her dangerous, but it was also her biggest weakness. Mine as well, really.

As the evening came, a soothing bath awaited, as always, when I stopped. Riestel prepared it every night to help me regain strength and rest easier. The humble wooden tub in a guarded, hastily erected shed became a sanctuary of sorts. There wasn't much of anything to note here to the naked eye. The floor was just earth; the walls had small gaps and had been covered by a light fabric to keep prying eyes from seeing too much. There was just the tub, a few stools, a thin-legged, unstable table, and some lanterns.

Underneath the simple surface, it was a spot of slightly stronger life-flow as picked out by Arid. She had studied the entire city for places of respite and sanctuaries that would sustain and hold the longest. Now, the arochs were scouting for openings to the heavier world for us, as I had requested Arid to help in that endeavor.

With concentration and Arid's help, I began to sense the ebb and flow in places. We communicated easily over distances as she constantly kept me up to date on their findings. They had found about ten true openings and several smaller ones they couldn't quite make up their mind about and would need Rime to check if they led to a pocket or the heavier world.

The shed door opened and closed.

"This brings back memories." Rime sighed and walked to a small, sturdy oak stool. He sat down and hung his head for a moment, gazing at the wet ground.

"Those memories are among my most treasured," I admitted.

"As they are mine," he replied and looked up. "I wanted to have time for more such things. I'm sorry."

"About something you did or what you are about to do?"

"All of it."

"I'm not. Whatever you did and whatever you will do, I will be happy to have spent my time with you."

"You do not need to make this easier for me." Rime grimaced and shook his head. He was tense and seemed like he could bolt at any moment.

"Just tell me. You are needed by the arochs. We do not have time to waste on silence."

"I came to free you. You were not mine to take for my own, and now we are both paying for it," Rime told me softly and swallowed.

"I gave myself quite willingly. Nothing was forced on me," I comforted him while trying to keep my own heart from breaking in front of him.

"Nevertheless... It must be done," Rime said and removed his fasting bracelet. "Here. Keep it or curse me and throw it away."

"Do we need to go this far?"

"Yes. You are hesitating to walk the path meant for you because of me. The world hangs on it. You must head toward your destiny, no matter which of us is left behind. I acted poorly and coldly toward you because of that. Your stalker has been quite adamant that I must change my ways and confront this instead of trying to make you leave me by making us both miserable by lies and hurtful acts. I'm usually never like this. I always confront things as the need arises. But I couldn't this time."

"I'm not sure I want to be let go."

"Unfortunately, I'm not giving you a say in it... Like I didn't give you a say in many other things. You need to become more for all our sakes, and I'm the one keeping you from that path and keeping you human," Rime said with a slight tremor in his voice as he placed his silver bracelet on the small table on my folded clothes. Then he smiled, even though his forehead and eyes frowned from an entirely different emotion.

"End of an era," he whispered. "Please, Isa."

I couldn't look at him as I extended my hand toward him. His warm fingers took hold of my wrist and gently opened the lock. He weighed the jewelry on his palm. Then he took out a thin silver chain. He threaded the bracelet on it and put it on his neck.

"This way, you will still be close to me and give me strength. I must go now. We will either meet back here or when you retreat."

As Rime left, I could hear a strained, quiet gasp. Once my eyes dried and focused, I looked at my wrist. It felt unnaturally light, almost unfamiliar. It seemed like it should have a scar in place of the bracelet. The dark, secret path had spit me out, and I had lost sight of it. No way to return. Only one way forward now. Even though there was an odd, melancholy freedom in the air, relief as the decision was made for me began to spread. Amongst all that, I felt I had just lost the final chance at a life I had truly wanted to experience.

The morning came, and I woke up shivering in my bed. Riestel was sleeping uncomfortably in a chair close by. I could barely believe it was him and that he had not somehow weaseled his way to rest directly at my side like he usually did at every opportunity.

"Did you carry me here?" I asked as he was roused by my movements, making the bed creak.

"Well, I had to, didn't I? You were being all dramatic, sitting in that small tub for hours, just staring off into the dark and not responding to anyone. Do you have any idea how frightened the guards were when they noticed that and couldn't get you to reply?"

"I—"

"I know. Just gather your strength. We need all of it. This isn't a time to get sick or pine away."

"Harsh."

"There is nothing else to do," Riestel said with a hint of true compassion in his voice and a sullen look. I would have thought he would be in a far better mood after what happened, and I definitely hadn't expected him to just sit there chivalrously all night. At the very least, I had thought he would have tried some annoying way to wiggle his way closer to me now that I was awake. And yet, there was no attempt at that. I didn't know what to think of Riestel when he was like this. The one time I could have used some of his more questionable attention to heal my wounds, his behavior was flawless.

XX

Rime had timed his talk and departure impeccably. There was no need for any awkward side steps in the alleys or silences when meeting unexpectedly, as he had left before I even had proper clothes on that morning. The longer time would go on, the less likely it was that either of us would be tempted to go back on what had happened. The new reality would set in bit by bit and permanently.

"Do you harbor any grudge against me for pressuring him? I know you saw us talk," Riestel asked as we climbed the stairs of the wall on our morning tour. He was keeping a fair bit more distance between us than usual.

"A little."

"Well, I'm sorry, but I'm not apologizing."

"I did not think you would." I sighed and found myself smiling involuntarily. "But I'm still going to put it out there that you are an absolute king of the jackasses."

"I've never had the title of a king before. I suppose I would make a good royal."

"A royal pain." I brushed my hair to the side and slowly tried to get closer to him.

"I do try to exceed in anything I do, so..." Riestel started and fell silent as we reached the top. "Well, that's unnerving."

The black goo was half a man's length from the top of the wall. It had crept higher than ever and faster than ever. That, however, wasn't what Riestel was referring to. Under the oily surface, there were trails left by shadows that swam within the substance. They were hard to catch, like the glint of a fish's scale in murky, muddy waters. Just in reverse, a glimpse of the darkest black.

"Rime is able to pull creatures to do his bidding and form them to his image. It is not surprising she has figured out how to do the same," I sighed.

"Obviously. But it isn't exactly a pleasant thing to witness," Riestel said.

"Do you suppose they are remains of people or just her creations?" Tammaran asked behind us. His habit of appearing from thin air never ceased to catch us off-guard.

"I would suspect they were once someone," Riestel replied, getting a little tired of Tammaran's habit of just popping out whenever and wherever. "Why else would she have gone to all the trouble of luring people to her side?"

A few guards were looking at the ichor as well. They were pointing at something.

"Please get back a little," I urged them. "It can rise more any moment."

"Oh, right," the closest of them said and nodded as one peered over for one last look. A black figure with features from both a human and a centipede shot out of the water and grabbed his leg. None of us had time to help him before he was pulled off down and under. Riestel took hold of my arm.

"Don't try to dive after him. He had his mouth open going in, he's already full," Riestel said.

The remaining guards looked as if all their blood had been drained from them. Tammaran walked over to them and ordered them off the wall.

"I will go and talk to them to settle them. But what should be told?" he asked.

"Just be honest, though, ask them to keep the sightings to themselves for people's safety. They must know that if they spread such tales, people will go and look," I requested.

"I will make sure they understand that."

"Do we start moving to the next wall?" Riestel wondered. "It might spill over at any moment."

"No. I will clean it up once more. At least that way, we can have an orderly retreat," I decided.

"As you wish," Riestel replied and kicked a bit of loose dirt into the ichor.

I turned toward the Needle for a moment. The sun was making it shine so brightly it almost hurt the eyes. A wave of bitterness welled in me. We had been so happy, so close to attaining a lovely dream. Now? Now, I had to become, as he had said, "more." For his sake and everyone else. To attain such power had once been a deep desire of mine, but now it was a duty that was solely mine.

I had never been as human as a regular-born human, and letting go of the thought of living life as such a creature was a hard thing to do. Then again, I suppose, none of them were actually free to do what they wanted. In that brief moment of clarity, the thought of becoming a servant to the world felt, for the first time, not entirely unpleasant. Having only one path forward gave certain undeniable focus and peace of mind.

Breathing slowly and deeply, I began my dance. The power collected easily without any emotion caused by my hesitation, distorting, amplifying, or diminishing it. I noted everything around me clearly, the very core of people's beings. The nexus wasn't yet impressed with my determination, so instead of waiting for it to approve me, I called it toward me despite the warnings.

At first, it didn't respond, but as I softly presented the opportunity to it and coaxed it, it began to grow in my mind. A small piercing ray of light hit my forehead from the Needle. Through it, the nexus swelled to a large star-like fire that filled all my senses. A part of it flowed into me, and as it did so, a faint tremor moved through all my cells as the Source's heart made a permanent connection to me, rearranging and adding things, waking up dormant parts.

The skin on my hands began to itch as small, ornamental scales with a golden tint rose to the skin's surface. I could feel a shield-like invisible wall form around me as they appeared. A projected form of them hovered three inches from my skin all around me like tiny golden leaves fixed in the air to create an eloquent armor.

With my last step in the dance, I dove back first toward the black sea. The scales indeed held up a barrier between me and the ichor. Just moments before the dark swallowed me, I called a globe of fire around me and smiled as I realized it was a very light-yellow flame. I spread my arms, and the flames burst forth. Riestel shielded himself with ice on the wall, letting out a short, excited laugh. The black ichor burned and screamed. The only drawback was that all the buildings for four blocks to the sea's direction had been crushed and burned to ash as well.

The ichor at the edges didn't come pouring down like water. Instead, it stood like a gelatinous wall, waiting to see what I would do next. The scales shimmered and faded. As Riestel lifted me back up with his water, the ichor began to creep back to the scorched area.

"Unexpected, yet impressive. Are you really ready to walk this path?"

Riestel asked, eyes gleaming, excited.

"Ready?" I repeated. "Hardly. But I'm not being given a choice, and for this time, I will yield to the will of the many. If I don't, none of us will have a world to live in, will we?"

Riestel lowered his head a bit, frowning. Then he nodded.

"I got to make my decision when all was still well; my heart aches that this is not a joyous thing for you. You will find much pleasure in it, I assure you," he said. "We both will."

"Riestel?"

"Yes?"

"Please don't leave me alone. I can't do this alone."

"You are wrong," he said tenderly. "You are capable. I'm a witness to your strength. But you do not have to. I will be here until all time ends, whether tomorrow or in a thousand lifetimes. Whether you like it or not, we are now connected through the world itself," Riestel said, taking my hand with a comforting smile on his lips. Then I felt it as he pressed my hand on his heart.

"Wait? You've fused with the nexus? You must have. That changed your body to have wings and claws, right? In the battle against Irinda, you used those gifts. But you said you cannot use it."

"I can't, not like you can. I have my own ways. And yes, partly. You can control your gifts and how they manifest in you should you not wish to look as the Source intended."

"Is it the same nexus?"

"Obviously. The other half of it. It is right here," he clarified. "The part that stabilizes the things you make. The Source told me once that it had always wanted one thing. Another one of its kind. Honestly, it could have chosen just one to fill its place when it was still making all of this, but it chose a pair for this world so that we would never know the pain of its yearning."

"I never imagined gods could be lonely."

"She will be happy now, at least for a while."

"Have you fused with the nexus more than once?" I asked.

"Yes. Once in another life, a few more times after that. I lack the last connection because I was waiting for you and Elona. I didn't want to become even more distant to human troubles before everything was well."

"You held off from becoming a god for a person who despised you for the better part of the first years. She knew you and a daughter you didn't even know still lived... We really do have some issues, don't we?"

Riestel laughed brightly. "You have abandonment issues, and I'm clingy. A perfect match." He smirked, still holding my hand on his chest.

I waited for him to continue and try something like he usually did in these situations, but he didn't. He was being supportive, loving even, and pledging to be forever there for me, but why wasn't he trying to... Well... A part of me had just imagined that he would immediately attempt to grab me and pull me away from everything else the moment my relationship with Rime had ended. And I had to admit; he had pushed me so close to breaking my oath so many times that my curiosity about how his touch would feel when permitted was getting to be overwhelming. But I wasn't going to let him know that.

We cleaned out the other side of ichor a few more times, and each time, it rose back faster. We should soon move to a higher position when we could still manage it calmly. One could ask why backing up and cramming ourselves into a more and more enclosed area was a good idea. The reason was to draw out as much of the ichor from the heavy world to ours as possible. It would never end before the last drop was dealt with, and we didn't yet possess any other reliable way to get it here in large quantities. In the name of honesty, I suppose Rime could draw it out in vast amounts, but it would likely be his end.

The risk was, of course, that we could simply drown in it, but any plan had its drawbacks. At least, with this plan, our final defense would be easy to solidify and hold for as long as possible, as she would constantly need to push further up and keep it rising with her mind, which would take up much of her concentration.

Tammaran hurried to us. "Do we go straight to the King's Circle? I need to get the wagons rolling if we are going today."

"You can send all those that are not assigned specific support duties to the Circle. Have the consecrators and burners stay a little higher at Crafter's in case they are needed. I will try to stall the ichor here a few more days," I replied.

"Understood. I will stay behind with you. Samedi ja Veitso will head to the Circle with the rest."

"Thank you. Any news from the Uppers that I might not have heard from Arid?"

"Maybe, the last I heard, they have located more openings in the Noble's. They are coming downwards now to identify any still in other areas in our control so we can do something about them. You need to decide the order in which you'll try to close them... If you go to the Peak and start there, Istrata can overwhelm everyone here. If you start from here, she might be able to push the ichor down on us from the Peak," Tammaran weighed the options.

"It isn't much of a discussion, though, is it?" I sighed. "If we lose the Peak, we lose the plan. If we lose the thousand men and women here in the Lowers, we can still win."

"Cold," he replied.

"I know, but I can't focus on individual lives, not even yours."

"Understood. But I do wonder what kind of god that will turn you into," he pondered, looking away.

"I'm not saying it because I want to. I'm saying it because I have to. And it will make me what I need to be. My role isn't to make people happy. My role will be to keep a balance so you can make yourselves happy and sort the world mostly as you please. I will be a cold god with no comfort to offer you. You do realize, if we make it through this and the world can still be healed, that I will be the one causing the calamities for you all after that? I will be the one to decide there are too many people and that a volcano should erupt. Riestel will be the one to offer you ways to survive me."

"That is a little...unnerving."

"I'm merely being truthful. I know you can handle hearing it, but please do not tell others what I will become."

Tammaran turned to me and took my hand in his.

"I'm your friend as well, not just his, and I will not fail you either. My possible progeny may curse your name, but I, or Arvida, never will."

I couldn't say another word to him, so I merely nodded. Tammaran smiled and let go of my hand.

"I must get going," he said and bowed his head a moment. "While you are still with us, try to see the worth in every soul. It is all I ask."

His words were sweet poison. I understood his meaning. Just because it was a risk to save someone, it didn't always make it the wrong choice, even in a perilous situation. How much did the chance to save one life matter in the face of the safety of many? The heroic types might answer that you should save everyone, no matter the situation. Every tale was filled with such triumphs where the hero or heroin snatched people from the jaws of certain death. Of course, we only heard the stories where they had succeeded.

XXI

W hile still in the Crafter's, I followed the Source's instructions. The merge would take a few times to complete, and the next one should never be done in haste in order to not damage my body or soul. I needed to be able to call up the skills at will before the next step. My skin looked perfectly normal in the daylight, with no golden scales anywhere. Closing my eyes, I could feel them attached to my lighter being. Drawing them to this world on command was much harder, though very similar to the sabers I had once formed there.

I practiced dutifully whenever I could. I also noticed that the hotter flames did not need more fuel compared to regular orange fire. That meant that I could utilize energy more efficiently. It was more than good news with our limited resources. And they were limited indeed. It was getting to that point where I could feel the world's reserves diminish every time someone other than me or Riestel used their skills for more than healing small ailments. Riestel used incredibly small amounts of energy whenever he did. Somehow, he was able to multiply the power within himself.

For the next five days, I danced with Riestel by the wall. He pushed, pulled, directed, and froze the ichor as needed while I burned it for him to wash and purify further. After hours upon hours spent together and him behaving like a perfect gentleman, apart from the normal snide remarks, I found myself trying to lure him into temptation, whether it was by "accidentally" winding up too close to him, gently brushing his hand while I passed, or keeping my eyes locked on to his.

Riestel was clearly enjoying it, and yet, each time, he just allowed the moment to pass. He couldn't have just stopped wanting me? After tormenting and harassing me for years? After making me have all these feelings and talking Rime into giving me up? Not that Rime had needed much encouragement in that after having made his mind up.

I was given some respite from this wonderful new feeling of my self-confidence crumbling in front of him as it was time to pull back to the center of the city. It would be the first proper defense line. One we would attempt to hold as long as possible or until the end if things went well. Sitting in the carriage, I tried my best to position myself in ways that wouldn't be overly obvious. I was trying to get Riestel's attention, but still enough to make his eye wander. To my great annoyance, he mostly stared out of the window with a faint smirk on his annoying face.

When we arrived, the King's Palace was halfway done but completely abandoned, with workers off to do more important things. It looked like a brand-new ruin. A fortified wall stood between us and all the Lowers. Every gate leading there would now be shut and jammed. Rime had come to the Circle with Arid and a few other arochs. He had requested a meeting at our earliest convenience.

In the large blue tent, Rime had a table and all his ink bottles, correspondence, and seals laid out as he liked. He was using the black guard captain's attire again with the high white collar. The stripes and chains on his shoulders were the only things that betrayed he wasn't just a captain. I sat at the table. He looked well enough and not at all bothered by my presence. Riestel followed me in and sat next to me, leaving a prudent gap between us.

"This is what we've decided on," Rime said without greeting us and pointed to the city map. "We found openings at these locations. You will need me or Arid to get you close enough to burn them shut. Yes, I know, that is the sophisticated tactic we settled on... I suggest the arochs. They have fewer things to worry about overall. I will stay here to coordinate things. I would request Riestel to stay here as well. If the Witch Queen begins an attack while you are away, he will be the only one strong enough to hold her advance until you get back."

"I have no objections," Riestel agreed.

"Neither do I," I added. "Are things... well?"

Rime looked up from his map. His eyes were starting to darken again. He must have spent much time in the ichor when trying to find the openings.

"Yes. Thank you," he replied. "There is nothing you need to worry about here. Focus on the task given. You should leave today. The mass hasn't reached us here, so we won't have a better opportunity to take care of as many as we can. We need to leave her with just a few in the Lowers."

I sighed. "Today? Alright. Let us get it over with."

"That is all for now. You may leave," Rime said, then he took a deep breath. "I am sorry to seem rude. I do not have time for personal matters. Nor do I wish to bring up anything from the past for now. I'm glad to see you are well and more than happy to hear you have taken the necessary steps. Please know I will always be here to help."

"Honestly, I wouldn't have expected anything else. I will leave you to your duties and attend mine," I answered, trying to keep any emotion from showing. "Are you coming?" I asked Riestel, as he was still sitting.

"In a moment, we have something to talk about without you."

I stepped out of the tent. I had felt a little guilty for trying to flaunt my charms at Riestel for the last few days, as it had been so soon after taking off the bracelet. That feeling was gone now. I had been removed almost surgically from Rime's life. He was doing everything he could to keep me on the road he had decided was the right one. I needed to respect that decision. I loved him deeply, and I would do whatever it took to save him if I could, but I would never be his again. Would I want to if he changed his mind? What if Riestel would never claim me despite all his talk? No, in that case, I would walk this path alone.

For a moment, I stood outside the tent, trying to decide if I should listen in again, but they were very quiet. They must have sensed me lingering, so I eventually walked away from the tent toward the arochs. Arid was delighted, as always, to see me. She almost purred when she bombarded me with images of how she had felt my connection to the nexus take place. Her whole being beamed with hope.

"We travel by jump?" she asked.

"Yes, as fast as possible."

"Go now?"

"Soon. I want a word with Riestel first."

"How do you have a word?"

"It means to talk."

"Oh. Funny," Arid replied and said the phrase a few times quietly as if to see what it felt like in her mouth.

As Riestel stepped out of the tent, he headed toward his designated quarters. I caught him before he disappeared inside the palace's finished parts.

"What did you two speak about?" I asked.

"We went over the tactics on how I should stall the ichor should it begin rising substantially once you burn her doors shut."

"Nothing else?" I pressed, leaning on his arm a little.

"No. We did not talk about you if that is what you are asking," Riestel remarked and hesitantly took some distance. I was pretty sure he was lying.

"You should go," he insisted.

"Fine. Apparently, both of you want me out of the way as soon as possible."

"I'm sure we can survive without each other for a day or so."

"Hard to imagine based on how you chased me before my marriage ended..." I muttered. "But I guess it is not as fun anymore."

"What in the highest skies are you on about? Did I not just promise to never leave you a few days ago?"

"Forget it," I sighed and returned to the arochs. I wanted him to want me as before. I needed to feel wanted. Having accepted the end of my time with Rime, I felt lonely and small, and the way Riestel was suddenly declaring his feelings but not acting on them just made things worse. I knew it was petty of me, but I just couldn't seem to stop myself. Maybe they were both right. I should go with Arid and concentrate on that.

"I'm ready, let's go," I told Arid.

"Hold on," Riestel demanded from behind. I had been so focused on my pouting that I hadn't even noticed he had followed me back.

"You don't get to try to pick a fight about something I can't decipher and then leave," he admonished me.

"I'm just in a bad mood... I'm sorry. I don't really understand it myself," I deflected.

"Should I believe that? I feel like there is something more here."

"Leave it. Please."

"If I listen and believe this is nothing, will it blow up in my face later on?"

"It might," I replied and bit my lip because he made me smile.

"That's better," he remarked, a little relieved. "Keep safe and return to me," he continued and stepped closer. Finally. Then, he patted my head in a patronizing way and left. I wanted to scream in frustration, but the unnerved look on Arid's face made me take a deep breath and do my best to calm down.

Jumping from area to area was easy this time. The arochs had established channels between anchored locations, so I merely needed to follow them. There were only a few of these openings to the heavier side in very remote corners in the Peak. They also seemed relatively unused, at least that is what the arochs believed. Perhaps Istrata had thought it would be too risky to use them often. She had been aware of Rime, so he could have sensed her out as well.

"How do we do this?" I can't see them nor reveal them," I asked them.

"We have the key to structure from Source, create tunnel, painful, send fire in," Arid replied. Then, she sent in the images to make sure I knew what she meant.

"The first one is here?"

"Yes. We start with smallest. Ready?"

"Do it."

Arid and her mate drew sigil-like figures in the air. Everything became heavy around us. Then, slowly, they seemed to grab onto the very basis of our reality and pull it. A black hole was revealed as the scenery distorted. There was only a thin membrane holding the mass back. I gathered the fire and released it toward it in a straight, narrow column. Slowly, the membrane began to thicken and form a scar. Once it was fully melted and patched, I stopped. The scar was like a crisscross of molten metals sprayed on a surface.

"Will it hold?" I asked.

"Yes," Arid answered with a smile. "Good done. Sturdy. She won't come through."

"Do you think she noticed what we did?"

"No. I think these old. Not used. She will sense in other places."

"The Temple?"

"No... Noble. Those fresher, more used."

"Of course, that makes sense. There were and are many suffering there due to their practices."

The openings in the Peak were fast and easy to correct. To my relief, it seemed that the arochs were good at estimating the danger of sealing each of them. We sensed nothing out of the ordinary nor saw anything concerning throughout our work in the Peak and all the Temple area. In the Noble's, their mood changed. Arid guided us to the least used openings, hoping that we could get some of them done before Istrata noticed. We still had a few to deal with in the Merchant's and the new center afterward.

The doorways in the Noble's were wider, and the membrane oozed like a festering wound. The first ones were closed with no issues. I could see the arochs getting tired from holding the structures open and Arid's pain as she used all her strength to keep all structures revealed as long as was needed. Trying to get her to take a break was as futile as trying to persuade me in the same situation, so we both just kept going.

There were only two more to go in the Noble's. The first was in the Winter Palace, the great glass greenhouse that had once been used for garden parties and horseraces in the winter. Now, it was used for simple things: root vegetables and any others that would keep through the next winter. The hole was located in the same area we had installed the valve into with Tammaran so we could drain the suffering from the lighter world at the location. Obviously, it was the perfect place for her to gather more of the mass.

Arid took a deep breath and pulled. Their brows furrowed, and muscles tremored as they kept the portal revealed like two statues by its sides. The moment my flames hit the doorway, I felt something wasn't right. I braced my feet and centered myself as black long tendrils shot out and grabbed my arm. If I hadn't been ready, they would have pulled me over and in.

"*Do come into talk,*" Istrata said. Her voice was muffled and distorted as if we had heard her through water.

Her tendrils were strong and hardly reacted to my fire. The bones in my hand and arm felt like they were about to break from the pressure as my hand was pulled through the membrane. I snuffed out the flame and concentrated on resisting her as hard as I could. The arochs helped by holding out one of their hands in front of the opening to block my way. There was nothing more they could do as if they let go of the doorway. It might close on me and cut my arm off. As I watched my elbow sink into her world, the scales shot out and pushed the ichor of my skin. The tendrils sizzled on contact and loosened. Yanking my hand back, I let the white flame ignite while still partially in the other world. It caused the opening the melt shut.

The arochs let go and collapsed to their knees. I leaned on my thighs and tried to catch my breath. Arid shook her head.

She huffed. "Must move on."

"If she is at the next one... she will eat us alive."

"Maybe."

"She will. The only chance is that she doesn't yet know which we've done and which not. Can you really handle more without rest?"

"We must," Arid insisted.

As we hurried to the last opening in the Noble's, the fear of being too slow gave us much-needed energy. To our luck, the last one, though large, was not guarded yet. After closing it, we headed directly to the Merchant's District.

Close to the first opening was a market. I could hear faint chatter around the corner. I had heard there were some families here refusing to leave their shops and homes. The arochs weren't pleased when I walked over to the corner, wasting time, but they were too exhausted to complain and sat to rest.

The small market had a few carts, and there was a familiar smell of roasted nuts and seeds.

"Do you have any left to sell?" I asked from the men standing about. They were all well-dressed, but their faces were gaunt. It wasn't something that I had often seen here on my travels. The Merchant's class was well known for being just a little more round-faced than most others.

"That's what we are here for, Miss," the eldest of the men replied. "What can we do you for? We don't have the best delicacies we used to; all of them have been taken to the Peak. But we still have some very nice pumpkin seeds."

"Those will do. Do you have anything to drink?"

"Just water."

"Can I take some?"

"Yes. If you're buying something."

"What can I pay within these times?"

"She's a consecrator," one of them noted. "You can see from the clothes."

"I am indeed."

"Are you going to the Lowers to defend?"

"To the Circle. That is where the first large line is."

"Have them. I don't have the heart to charge you then. All being led to the slaughter, you are. Poor things. Now, don't get me wrong, I realize that orders are orders, but this whole strange business with the goo and the Queen and all that... I'm sure we could figure out some deal with her and prevent this city from falling apart. There's been enough battling over the rule for decades."

The others nodded approvingly.

"Why do you say we are being led to slaughter?" I asked.

"Well, I mean... We've heard that only the new witch can fight it, so what are all of you going to do? Just slow it down."

"Exactly," I replied. "That is exactly what the others are required to do. To slow down the progress, so I have enough time to fix this. I appreciate the free seeds and water, but if I ever hear you spreading this defeatist mentality and uncertainty when you know nothing and are dumb enough to stay here and wait to drown..."

"That's not very polite. Give those pouches back."

"No. I need the sustenance, and you will die if you stay here, so losing them will not hurt you in any way in the long run," I told them and headed back.

I could hear the men argue amongst themselves, and then I heard footsteps.

"Open the wound. We will deal with this one, and then you will eat," I ordered the arochs. The merchants came round the corner as the arochs pulled the structures open. I didn't wait to see if Istrata was there. I pushed the scales out and placed my hand on the membrane from within the wound. It scarred much easier like this.

The merchants stood behind us, mouths gaping, one shaking his head a bit.

"What is that? What are those?" the eldest asked.

"They are arochs. And that black abyss is what the Witch Queen will drown you in until you melt into it and become a suite for her to dance around in, so I suggest you start hauling your families out of here and fast instead of chasing me for payment. Unless you want to try to negotiate with the Witch Queen. I can reopen it if you'd like?"

"No, please don't."

"And no need to thank me for trying to save you, the horrid witch that I am."

XXII

The arochs accepted their fate and sat down to eat and drink once we made it to the next doorway. We all felt an urgency to carry on, but I needed to take care of their wellbeing. I still remembered how awful the coughing and fever had been when I had overexerted myself trying to escape from the Merchant's to safety while being chased by Irinda. The memory made me smile. It was the time when my feelings for Rime had been at their purest and strongest. It made me happy to find that I could still get joy from them, that they weren't tainted by all that happened after.

As we tried to use the small break to its fullest by nourishing ourselves and closing our eyes just for a moment, the opening near us began to bleed. That could mean two things. Either Istrata was coming, or she had realized she couldn't predict what door we would try to shut next, so she would open them all and allow the ichor to pour out everywhere.

"Quick, expose it fully," I ordered. Arid and her companion did as told. Every time they touched the ichor, they shuddered and winced.

No tendrils. Just darkness. This one was easy to close. The next one gushed on the cobblestones like a small river rapid. The arochs stayed back as the doorway was already in the open.

"Should we get someone to help?" Arid asked. "We are no use."

"One of you go see if this is going on everywhere. Let them know what is happening if they don't know already. The other needs to stay, so I find all of them if some are still hidden."

"I will stay," Arid decided. Her companion disappeared right away.

We hurried from one doorway to another. They were all spewing the ichor forth. Shadowy, oily figures could be seen trying to inch their way out with the doors. The last opening in the Merchant's had an odd-looking pile of the substance blocking it. Walking closer to it, I could tell it was a creature of some kind. An amalgam of people. They hissed and reached at me through the opening as the entire creature tried to push itself out.

I wasn't going to let it through. The noise as the exposed parts burned was painful.

"Was that the last here?" I checked.

"Yes," Arid replied, looking disgusted with the remains. "Unholy," she whispered as her metallic hairs chimed nervously. "They must cease. All of them."

"Then let's head back to finish the ones in the center."

We both gasped when we got to the center. Riestel was on the wall, extending it by a man's length toward the sky as the dark ocean kept rising on the other side. We could see a few openings that had other oily-skinned creatures, some with human traits and some more insect-like, coming out of them. The consecrators were trying to block and slow down all that came from the doorways.

I ran to the closer one. Heelis was cutting up whatever came through with granite discs. She grimaced as one of the figures grabbed her hand and twisted it.

"What are you waiting for? Burn it!" she yelled at me. "Try not to hit me if you can!"

"Then duck and fast."

She managed to just get grazed by the white fire. A few of her locks were singed. The creature released her, and she ran away from the opening.

"These things are ridiculously sturdy. I can hardly dent them," she told me, winded. "And even when I do manage to cut them up, they just stretch back together if we can't light them up or freeze them before that."

"Then allow me to uninvite them." I smiled and armed my hand with the scales. Heelis ripped the ichor apart in front of me to allow me a clear path to the opening. There were relieved sighs around us when the thing scarred shut and vanished.

"Have them try to burn the rest with regular fire," I told Heelis.

She nodded and shooed me on to the next one. The few other fire consecrators that existed were doing their best to burn the matter flooding the ground. The stream was steady and strong. If I would attempt to clear it, it would take ages to reach the scar.

Rime came running toward us. "I will get you access to it," Rime said. "But you will need to jump straight in there."

"Do it."

Rime stepped into the ichor. It seemed as if he was contesting the will of it. Then he parted it. I passed him quickly and half-submerged myself in the stream. The scales had a dim glow that allowed me to find the membrane more easily than just by feeling it out. My hair and clothes dripped off the substance once I emerged back. The scar faded instantly from view.

"Let me get that off you," Rime offered and ran his hands around me, gathering each drop and then flinging it to the pool that was left behind. "Just in time. There are other openings in the area, but they are under control for now. Those with ice skills are taking turns holding them. You should help him next," Rime suggested and pointed at Riestel. "He's been holding that mass back for hours alone."

"I don't know if I can handle that much."

"Then we'll all drown the moment he falls."

I had been working on the openings for over a day now, but there was no rest in sight. The black sea pressed on the thick ice barrier. Riestel's eyes were closed, his forehead furrowed. There were beads of ice on his forehead as he kept the gigantic wall of ice spanning the whole width of the city in place.

"Hold on, just a little longer," I whispered and touched him. Riestel nodded ever so slightly and seemed to relax. His face no longer looked as worried, and he detached one hand from the wall and placed it on me. A soft, healing pulse coursed through me. I could feel the scales respond to it and implant more securely.

As Riestel let go, something chimed softly in the air. I looked around, but no one else seemed to hear it. Then, there was a small flash of light from the Needle. I could not look away as it filled my mind anew. I raised my arms toward it and called the nexus. The connection was instant. A flush of burning, raging force coursed through. The painful feeling resembled the sensation of when Istrata's statue had opened my fire channels in the attic. Thankfully, the agony was fleeting this time.

Stepping through Riestel's ice, I was engulfed in the dark. Hands were brushing against my feet, trying to grab me to pull me down to the bottom, but the scales burned them with each touch, and they slithered away to heal. I sensed the coarse stone wall under my feet. There wasn't much room to move, but I could still get into the proper stances. I needed to gather power before I ran out of air behind this small barrier created by the scales around me. Each movement felt as if I was pushing against water.

The fire gathered within began to heat me, almost to the point of burning. When I simply could not bear it anymore, I let it out to the front and sides. A bright blue flame tore through the creatures and evaporated the ichor. Air had never tasted sweeter. Seeing the sky above me and the rooftops below me was a huge relief. The black sea was still covering a large part of the Crafter's and Worker's, but now it was below the stone wall again. Not by much, but enough.

Riestel detached from the ice barrier. We both sat on the wet stones, leaning back onto our elbows.

"What did you do when you touched me?" I asked once I felt more stable.

"I helped the scales to settle by healing the areas they attached to," Riestel answered and stretched out on his back. "They open and close you to the world like a protective veil. Because they stabilized, the nexus allowed for more of it to transfer into you."

"Why didn't you just do it when I got them?"

"Because it wouldn't have worked at that time... You needed to get control of them first. Once they were a part of you, I could help by healing," he explained and massaged his neck.

"That must have been exhausting, holding the wall alone. I'm glad you are alright," I whispered and touched his arm, leaning in a little.

"I'm not alright; I'm practically a hero here," he insisted with a weary laugh, then he glanced down at my hand and withdrew his arm. "It was not as bad as you'd think. I was just having a hard time concentrating, not knowing where you were and how you were doing."

"Water?" Arid asked as she appeared on the wall and held out a bottle.

"I'd rather have wine." Riestel yawned. "But thank you, that will do. Are we needed somewhere?"

"No. All well for now," Arid replied as she stepped back into the lighter world.

"Your friend is very handy. I should get one," Riestel said and turned his face toward me. His tired smile was oddly adorable. Adorable? I must be going out of my mind.

"She can be."

Riestel rolled to his side and hovered his fingers over my cheek. Then he traced my neck with his fingers just above my skin.

"If only we had some better privacy…" he whispered.

"Why?"

"Well, I can't be seen falling asleep here after this. People would think I was a weakling," he answered with a smirk and got up. "Coming?"

My mood plummeted. I was tired of all the innuendo. Riestel was brazen enough for me to assume that if he wanted to kiss me, now that I was not tied to anyone else anymore, he would just do it despite the circumstances. At least he was courteous enough to offer his hand, but I was too annoyed to accept it.

Once I stood up, I could see Rime looking up at us. He waved for us to come down. The square, the streets, and everything around was a mess of splotches, pools, and residue left of the ichor. People were sitting, staring off into nothing, and trying to cope with what they had just seen. They had been told what to expect, but having a corrupt mongrel of a creature staring at you from another plane of existence and then trying to pull you in and drown you was a little more harrowing once actually experienced.

As Rime walked before us, he kept stopping by soldiers, servants, and temple folk to exchange a few reassuring words. In that respect, he was exactly as always. Looking out for those he was responsible for.

"You both did well. There are four openings left in the area. They are controlled and can be dealt with once you have rested. I have given orders to use everything we have here to burn and lower the ichor while you recuperate. If it should start rising more than we can handle, I will alert you. The cooks have started on food. I will be on patrol if needed," Rime brought us up to speed. "Go around the corner. We have set up tables there. Eat, have a drink, and rest, but do not wander off in case we require you."

There were indeed rows of very plain tables and benches in what would eventually perhaps be one of the palace gardens. We sat down, looking around in the calm space. The cook brought us some broth and bread.

"Let me know if it needs something. It hasn't been simmering for as long as I'd like, but the War Council made it clear he wished we serve you before announcing a break for the others."

"I'm not sure if he's being polite to us or sparing the others of our company," Riestel replied with a snide smile. The cook didn't know what to say, so she simply backed away to continue his chores, looking flustered.

I sighed. "Speak for yourself."

"I usually do. I am pleased that you are alright," he said in a softer tone. "I worried so much I almost lost concentration a few times, as no one told me anything about your progress."

Even though I knew that Riestel had a tender heart beneath the mountains of cold mockery, it always confused me when he said things like this. I rarely minded quietness, but sitting at the table with nothing to say was making me nervous.

"How did your arm hold up?" I asked to get him talking.

"Better than my old one," he answered. "I don't really feel the difference between them anymore. The Source said the ice will gradually heal to a fleshed-out arm with skin and all should I keep at it. If I want to, that is."

"Why wouldn't you want to?"

"Well, I can think of a few things," Riestel replied and smirked. "Have you ever played with ice pieces?"

"What?" I asked, barely managing to swallow my mouth empty before speaking.

"I'll take that as a no. Something to try later on."

He was doing it again. All this flirting was wearing my patience thin.

"Are you finished with the food?" he asked.

"Almost. Why?"

"I'd just like to look around. We might not get many chances to see this area without some pompous architect lecturing at me about the tensile strength of materials."

"Didn't we get an order to stay here?"

"Well, we wouldn't be going far. Just a stroll. It will help clear the mind before trying to sleep," he promised. There was a mischievous glint in his eyes, but I couldn't really tell what it was about.

"A short one," I agreed.

XXIII

We sneaked out of the yard to this maze of small alleys and passages, clearly designed to keep servants out of sight and out of mind. It would be a grand palace if it ever got finished. The groundwork was flawlessly done. Everything was at exact angles, and every detail, no matter how humble, had been constructed with care. But it wasn't the Needle, nor would it ever surpass it; I secretly smiled.

There were dozens of rooms and corridors waiting to be furnished and fitted with doors. We weaved through scaffoldings and ladders and climbed over piles of supplies. After a few dead ends, we found a staircase that led to the highest floor yet built. It was unfished and basically just a walless platform. We stood at the highest stable point of the palace's half-finished structures. Even in this state, the building towered over its surroundings with pomp that suited Frazil and his wife impeccably.

Riestel stood at the very edge, as he often did. The lazy, mild wind swept all worries away as it caressed the skin. A few tiny ocean swallows were trying to find insects far up in the sky among the sparse, wispy clouds. Their dives were a pleasant distraction.

"It's nice to explore a bit," Riestel noted. "Takes your mind off things."

"We are going to get into so much trouble if they need us…"

"If they truly, truly need us, I'm sure Arid can track us. She senses you, does she not?"

"She does," I replied. I hadn't quite gotten used to the idea of Arid as my shadow. According to the Source, Arid was linked to me in the lighter world by design. She was the strongest of the arochs, and she would guard me with all he had.

The thought made me feel a bit better about our momentary escape. Although, mostly, I didn't want to let Rime know I was being this irresponsible or who I was with. Not that the "who" wasn't more than obvious. It wasn't because I was afraid it would hurt Rime. He was doing a well enough job at that with his own choices. I didn't want him to be disappointed with backing me up all this way. If he ever lost faith in me, it would break my heart more than the conclusion of our faded romance.

Looking at Riestel, there was no way to push down my feelings anymore, nor any reason. The speed and strength of them taking over me was still surprising. I constantly had to remind myself not to stare at him. Riestel pulled the ribbon off his hair and allowed the wind to play with it. His hair and skin were slightly damp from sweat. If we kissed now, he would likely taste a little salty.

"What did you mean when you said that I could choose my appearance?" I asked Riestel as we stared at the emerald sea beyond the black mass surrounding us.

"What word didn't you understand?" Riestel quipped and smiled radiantly.

"I understood all the words, thank you very much," I muttered and considered if I should try to lean closer to tempt him just once more. If he behaved like the jackass only he could, I always had the option of pushing him off this floor. The thought brought a bit of comfort in case I made a fool of myself. In the end, he didn't even seem to notice.

"Well, I meant exactly what I said. You can mold the way the gifts appear. If you do not, you will resemble the Source's design at some point in the lighter world, with characteristics of many created creatures. That soul expression will then carry on over to this world when you use your skills."

"Do you use the scales for defense as well?"

"Yes, I find them functional, as well as esthetically pleasing. Even on you."

"Right... Thank you so much."

"You're welcome. It's not every day you get a compliment from the most eligible bachelor in the whole city...or world, should I say?" Riestel grinned and cocked his head a little to the left. He rolled up the sleeves of his winter sky blue, finely woven linen shirt. The muscles of his arms were well-defined but slenderer than a soldier's.

"I'm not sure how many would be interested in a centenarian..." I jested but felt an odd increasing desire to actually offend him. His inaction irked me more than I cared to admit. So much more. I wanted to rush headfirst into this new era and not dwell on the hurt. I was free, and I was going to make the most of the rest of my days. Obviously, it might not be the wisest course of action, but it was the only one that brought me joy right now. And I needed some joy.

"My head feels less foggy. We should return and get some well-earned rest. I expect the ichor will rise substantially over the night," Riestel said as he kept looking at the horizon instead of me.

"I don't want to, yet. I can feel the autumn in the wind. This may be one of the last truly warm evenings," I protested. We would not be going back until my mood improved.

"What would you like to do, then? There isn't much here to see yet. I think we've covered most of it. I mean, we saw that stone pile, the other stone pile, and the piled stones."

"I could do you," I answered, staring at him without blinking.

Riestel's expression was priceless. It was a combination of shock, amusement, and confusion. He coughed for a moment, and when he finally turned back, there was a clear red hue on his face. I knew he would turn it into a jest.

"Have you been secretly drinking this whole time, or is the exhaustion making you all weak in the head?" he asked and squinted, trying his best to distract us from what I had said.

"No? Alright." I sighed. "You can't complain later that I never offered if we happen to die," I told him and turned to walk away.

When he began to follow, I stopped and turned quickly. Our bodies softly nudged into each other. Just a kiss for the love of the skies, I urged him in my mind. There was nothing that should have been holding him back. All the times he had made me feel things I had wanted to avoid and push down but eventually couldn't, were still waiting for fulfillment.

"This is a strange side of you," he whispered and bit his lower lip.

"Well, I've been spending so much time with you; something must have rubbed off."

"Are you claiming that I would ever blurt out something that crass and straightforward?" Riestel asked, genuinely a little miffed at the thought.

"Then should I have suggested that I could perhaps lay with thee in a romantic way before the whole world ends?"

"That's even worse," Riestel answered and shook his head, laughing at the phrase.

"Fine. Forget it."

"I will absolutely not forget this conversation for all my days to come," he said, wiping the corners of his eyes. "Wait? What? Are you actually angry at me? Isa?"

I walked away without a word.

"Would you stop? What has gotten into you?" he asked as he followed me down the stairs.

"Nothing."

"Nothing? Certainly seems like something. Be honest," he insisted, walking dangerously close.

Honesty? The mere thought of having to confess anything to him about my feelings made me speed up my steps. What should I say? That a part of me had wanted him since the day he kissed me in the library among all the threats he made and that I was tired of waiting but too cowardly to admit to such things sincerely. Not happening.

"I'm so entirely confused and annoyed," I finally said. "You have been chasing me for as long as the sky goes on, and now that there is nothing in your way, you…you…just stand there," I admonished him as we reached the doorway out to a small woodland area.

"Is it not too soon to…" he said. "You two have barely been apart for…"

"We were drifting apart much longer; you saw that, and you were pushing us apart. Where did you find your morals suddenly? You had no trouble trying to make me fall in love with you before I was free to do so."

"That's a little harsh," Riestel huffed as we walked among the trees. His brow frowned, but his eyes had a curious, almost sinful shine to them. His mouth betrayed a small amount of delight.

"Is it? Really? You partly forced his hand in officially ending this, and now you act like you have no interest in me at all besides this odd back-and-forth courtship we have been at for years, even when we shouldn't have allowed for any of it."

"Isa… I'm merely allowing some time—"

"For what? For me to heal? Or time to pass so it doesn't seem like you are swooping in on someone else's leftovers?"

"How dare you accuse me of that?" Riestel asked, sounding well and truly irritated by now. Glancing back, I could see his expression had changed from partial amusement to an icy stare. The smarter person might have stopped here.

"Prove me wrong," I replied.

"You are acting like a child. A very spoiled one at that."

"And you are not acting at all! I feel alone and scared, and now you are making me feel unwanted!" I scolded him and turned around again to escape. Riestel grabbed my wrist and yanked me back into the shade of a few elm trees.

"You troublesome little... Look at me!" he commanded. The moment I gave in to the order, he pulled me in tighter and closer.

"I pressured you for ages, I waited for you for ages, I pushed you to this conclusion with him. Just as you accused. Do you really think I would just suddenly stop wanting you? You utterly silly creature. I merely wanted to know, for my sake, that once you came to me, you came to me for wanting me, not purely for comfort, because I knew the next time we kissed, I wouldn't stop. You have no idea how difficult it was to get up from that bed in the Crafter's with you entangled over me. And I thought, if it happened before you were ready, you would resent me," Riestel whispered in a harsh, annoyed tone.

I tried to distance myself from him, feeling a little taken aback at what I had just started. Riestel shook his head and stopped my wriggling by leaning in ever closer. He pushed me against the tree trunk and stared into my eyes, leaning into me with his entire body. His breath grew heavy, and a slight electric wave made my hair stand up. Time seemed to stretch into a frozen eternity of hazy desire as I gave into the slightly salty kiss. My cheeks flushed to a burning red from the rushing blood. Once the kiss ended, his face lingered by mine, with our cheeks caressing.

"That at least shut you up," he remarked. "Anything more to add?"

"But why kiss me now? After I was being all horrible," I asked, trying to mask any obvious signs of arousal and likely failing at it miserably.

"I promised you ages ago that I would not proceed until you begged for it. And that behavior, my dear, if anything, was begging for it," he smirked victoriously. "I feel very warm and fuzzy on the inside now that you yielded to that demand."

"I hate you."

"If you say so. But you love me much more than that."

"Debatable."

"Lovely. No turning back now, whatever you feel."

"What?"

"Did I not just say what would happen the next time we kissed? And yet you kept on pushing for it. You have to bear the consequences. And before you ask, yes, I mean exactly what you think I mean."

Riestel took my hand and pulled me through a small wooden gate to the right of the forest. My stomach knotted up, and my heart pounded in my throat. I couldn't believe I had said all those things. And I couldn't believe he had actually managed to lure me to make a fool of myself because I thought he wasn't paying attention to me. All the time pushing me into telling him exactly what he wanted to know about my feelings. Maybe he really was the smarter one. He would never let me live this down.

The yard on the other side had a thicket of yew trees surrounding a modestly sized steaming hot pool carved straight into the rocky hillside. The ten or so people there were a little startled at us barging in and began a frantic search for towels. Riestel didn't even glance at them. He herded me gently with unyielding determination toward the water through wisps of fog as he took off his blue shirt.

"Out. All of you! Now," Riestel ordered.

"What? You can't just barge in like this. We all have our turns," a man replied, annoyed. "This is the army's private bath. You have no rights here."

"Really? Can't I? Who's going to stop me then?" Riestel asked and halted, tilting his head menacingly to the side. If someone would ever be able to kill with just a mere glance, it was Riestel.

"Sir, that's the consecrator who held the wall alone, the ice wall," another man noted. "I think we ought to leave."

The high-ranked soldier eyed Riestel more carefully and decided to grab his coat and run.

"You are never going to stop, are you?" I sighed.

"Stop what?"

"Enjoying acting like a cold-hearted lunatic."

"A man needs his hobbies," he said gleefully. "And we don't need an audience for what I'm going to do to you. Or do we? I could be persuaded."

"I...don't know if we should stay."

"Too late. You are getting what you begged for," Riestel told me in a low, soft tone and froze out the fence and all exits now that the previous party had fully vacated the premises. "Try the water. I bet it is a natural hot spring. The army always hogs the best locations." He unwaveringly pushed me against the edge of the carved tub. Then, he had the water pull me in.

Riestel undressed himself, never taking his eyes off me. As he climbed into the hot water, I felt like jumping out. And yet, I stayed put. The situation felt unreal. We had been at this threshold many times and backed off equally many times. It felt like something should stop us now, too. Maybe a guard will barge in somehow and announce we are needed, maybe Arid will appear, maybe... I looked around, but there was no sign anything would or could disturb us now in this private garden of ice and fog.

"Here, kitty," Riestel called and extended his hand. "I'll be nice if you come now, but if you make me chase you a moment more, I will bite..."

I took his offered hand, and he pulled me to him. Gliding his lips on the skin of my arm all the way up to my neck. Sitting straddled on his lap left me nearly speechless. I took his face in my hands ever so tenderly. I could finally look into his eyes without guilt.

"Why the tears?" Riestel whispered as he drew the individual drops onto his warm hand and washed them away. His blue and ever-hue sifting eyes were now like deep, dark, bottomless pools with a silver sheen to the edges compared to the lighter, cold blue he usually had.

"Because I'm where I was always supposed to be, aren't I?"

"I think so," Riestel answered, and his cold ice-hand slipped behind me as the current of the water gently tugged, loosened, and unlaced my clothes.

"I'm going to purge you of him," he said in a low, humming tone. "You are mine now."

The vibration from his humming made the water ripple and caress me as if it were an extension of him. Riestel ran his hands slowly on me. His fingers had a very different feel than I was used to. A light, caressing, lingering manner. And he found his way everywhere. Every touch was drawn out to tease pleasure and impatient desperation.

"Consecratoress, you are getting rather red," he whispered with a wicked smile. "Should I stop?"

I shook my head, and we kissed again.

"I can if you should be unsure still... Don't be shy. Tell me and look at me as you say it," he demanded, making me stare directly into his eyes.

"In." It was the only word I was able to say in this trance state. The electricity crackled in the air around us.

As he pressed his lips against mine, the water lifted me and lowered me on him. As I felt him, my mind went blank. Everything else ceased to exist. There was just his body against and in me. When a wave of pleasure resonated through me, something wonderful happened. My lighter body responded to his. It felt like our very cores were melting together in the same rhythm as our breath mixed. Looking at his face, I could see an expression of pure joy as he ever so slightly sucked his lower lip in, guiding my movements. We clasped our hands together as he tensed and sighed.

As the electric charge subsided, we sat quietly entangled in the water. I felt so relaxed, clean, bright, and giddy; it was astonishing. At the same time, I could barely look at his face. The level of intimacy had been something that I had never experienced or anticipated. I felt completely exposed and uncomfortable about it.

"Was that proof enough that I still want you?" he asked, caressing my hair, his eyes half shut, looking like a well-eaten fox.

"Don't ruin the moment," I pleaded and pressed my fingers to his mouth.

"Because if it wasn't, we can go again..." he insisted, mumbling from behind my hand with the widest sincere smile I had ever seen on his face.

"You might break a hip at your age if we do..."

"I think it will more likely be my jaw that will hurt because of this, but I won't complain. There was no way to keep both promises, so I chose the one made earlier," Riestel pondered and frowned and then gazed at me. "Worth the price."

"What does that mean?"

"Nothing. Shut up so I can kiss you."

"You don't get to say shut up."

"Alright, you are allowed to make some noises." He smirked. "Do you want to return or stay here for the night? These places usually have blankets and such available."

"We really should return..." I answered, looking around the icy walls. It was like the outer world didn't even exist at this moment.

"We are staying. Don't even try to argue. I know that tone. You want to pretend you want to do what is right by some strange arbitrary standard, and yet you want nothing more than to stay and take your mind off things. I believe we have the right to a bit of mortal happiness in the middle of all this. Once it is all done, whether we lose or not, these are your last days, weeks, or months as the person you are now. Don't you think you are allowed some human experiences, even weaknesses, too? I will be your shield for it. They can blame me."

Riestel built us a soft bed from cushions, blankets, and towels. Lying next to him, feeling his skin on mine as I drifted to sleep, was a new kind of paradise.

XXIV

R iestel had been the first to wake up. He had dried our clothes and cleaned up any ice that had not melted during the night.

"I'm afraid reality calls," he said as he sat down by my head after noticing I had awoken. "You looked almost peaceful when sleeping. Had a good night?"

"It was okay." I smiled and got up to dress.

"Just okay? I must be rusty."

"Have you ever considered you might not be as good as you think?"

Riestel stood up and hugged me from behind.

"Now, I know it went better than I had hoped for," he whispered and bit my ear gently.

"What could give you that idea?"

"The simple fact that you are being pricklier than ever. It's your happy place."

"It is not."

"It definitely is." He laughed and grabbed his shoes by the laces, chucking them casually over his shoulder. "Let's go, love."

"Love? That is incredibly old-fashioned."

"Well, according to you, I'm a relic anyway, so learn to live with it."

"Do not start calling me that."

He was all mischievous smiles this morning.

"Fine." He took my hand. "What about 'dove'?"

"Absolutely not!"

We meandered back to the square. The black mass was just visible on the other side of the wall of ice, but it hadn't risen at an alarming rate. Riestel let my hand go as soon as we spotted other people. Of course, Rime had to be out and about this early. Heelis was yawning on a bench nearby, listening to the orders he was giving.

"See, I told you, they would have come looking if we were truly needed. This we can fix soon and be in a better position than last night. Not that there are many positions better than last night's positions," Riestel said quietly, quickly brushing my cheek with his nose in secret.

I could feel my face turning red.

"We should tend to it right away," I said.

"You mean the ichor or trying to find a better position than last night?"

"Be serious," I tried to say with a straight face but had to turn away to keep myself from smirking. The moment came to an abrupt end when we saw Rime coming towards us. His expression was tense and angry.

"You utter bastard," Rime growled as he reached Riestel. "I should have known better." He hit Riestel straight in the jaw. Riestel took a step back from the force and pressed his hand on his face. He opened his mouth to feel out if everything was still working.

"What are you doing?" I demanded.

"Nothing to worry about." Riestel spat out a bit of blood. "That was almost entirely deserved from his perspective."

"You just couldn't honor the agreement, could you?" Rime accused him and looked like he was about the hit Riestel again, so I stepped in between them and tensed up.

"I think we need to do this. We should have done it ages ago properly." Riestel stepped past me. "Clear the air a bit," he hissed. Then he spread his glassy wings and swiped Rime to the side with one beat of them. I backed out of the area.

"Do your worst then," Rime replied as he got back to his feet. The black tendrils shot out of the ground and wrapped around Riestel's wings.

Heelis walked over, clearly enjoying the unfolding scene.

"Should you try to stop them?" Heelis asked, stretching her sides.

"Probably, but I don't think I will."

"Oh, exciting," she said and chortled. "Why not?"

We both ducked a few icy discs and a spray of gooey ichor.

"Because it is, and it isn't, about me."

"Right…that makes no sense to me."

"Just enjoy the entertainment so you have something to tell Arvida later," I advised, looking at Riestel's hail of ice-spears tearing through a black wall.

"You can count on that," Heelis promised with a wide grin.

"I'll start with the ichor while they are at it."

"You aren't even going to watch?"

"I wasted time for a whole night already. And they'll keep going longer if I linger here."

"You did, didn't you? Noughty girl!" Heelis shamed me, giggling.

"How would you know what we did?"

"I was around the arochs last night. Your little dalliance had quite the effect on Arid. I didn't know you were that closely connected."

"Excuse me?"

"Just try looking her in the eyes the next time you see her."

I left Heelis to witness the physical debate taking place, feeling a little uneasy. I couldn't walk for very long at any point without glancing at what was going on. They had demolished much of the square by now. Those courageous enough were peeking from corners and houses to see the fight. I could see Riestel throw a cloud of sparkling needle-thin ice particles into Rime's face, which just made Rime more annoyed. He would charge, hit, and slam Riestel. Then, Riestel would do something underhanded and pay back everything in one graceful move. He was, by the look of it, actually enjoying himself. They both were.

I climbed over the ice on the wall. I could have sworn that the surface was a little lower than it had been when we arrived. That couldn't be a good thing if I were right. When I prepared to start, the ice-wall shattered as Riestel was flung through it. I couldn't grab him as he went past and saw how the ichor swallowed him. Rime appeared next to me and the breach.

"Enough!" I ordered and halted him with a wall of fire. "Stop, or you will fight me next."

Rime returned to normal, and I jumped in the ichor after Riestel. His silver scales had him floating in a shimmering cocoon. Once we reached the bottom, I cleared the ichor from around us.

"See, I told you it would be the jaw that would hurt the most." Riestel sneered and coughed a little. "I didn't expect he would turn this into a serious fight."

"Right, because he is notoriously stable these days. Did you both get it out of your system now?"

"I did, could have done without it, honestly, but I thought I owed him this much."

"Why? For the love of the skies, seas, and every other saying there is."

"I had promised him that if he set you free, he would not have to witness our...romancing...that I would abstain from courting you further until this was all done."

"I cannot believe you two. You idiots!"

"I suppose we had to have something in common for you to love us both," Riestel remarked and winced. "He has a very good left hook. So, which one of us are you more annoyed with?"

"You have a long think on that," I told him and concentrated on the ichor further away. I took every bit of frustration out on it. Then, I returned to the wall and marched down to Rime's tent.

"Let me get this straight. You fast with me for advancing your plans, you let your father think he has kidnapped our children by allowing them to be cut out of me, you drive me away, ask for our bond to be cut, and then after I finally give up and leave you, you come and attack the person who is still standing beside me!"

All color washed from Rime's face. I had never seen him this uncomfortable.

"I overreacted," he admitted.

"You overreacted? Gods! That is the most insufficient answer. This is not about you punching Riestel. Whatever I feel for him, the skies know he has probably deserved it plenty over the years. This is about us. You have no say, no say, anymore about what I do or who I do, for that matter. You gave that up. You have no right to try to run my life anymore, and that entails making deals like the one you had him agree to."

"I..."

"You're hurting. I know that. But you chose it. I would have stood right there until the end with you, whether it was in battle or decades after, once you had grown old. You pushed me to confront my feelings for Riestel."

"I didn't want to force your hand to stay with someone when you had feelings for another."

"Yes, I had feelings for Riestel. But it was you I loved when all this started. Truly, I did. It should have been my choice, and now you will never know if I would have stayed with you or gone off with him because now... Because of all that has happened, I allowed those feelings to grow, and the first option isn't there anymore, as you took it away."

"Understood. I'm sorry," Rime said, his voice breaking just a little.

"Anything you want to add? If you're mad at me for any of this, now is your time to say so."

"No. I should focus on more important things."

A hurtful lie, as far as I could tell. There was clearly something he was desperate to say, enough so that he picked a fight with Riestel. Maybe he still loved me; maybe he regretted everything. Maybe, but he had no right to say those things anymore, and I did not wish to hear them.

The square was back to a somewhat normal state, with people a little wary of us. It would be a good time to take care of the doorways that were still left.

"Arid," I called and grimaced when I remembered what Heelis had said, hoping Arid wouldn't reply for once.

"Here," Arid said and stepped out into the visible world. She was definitely avoiding eye contact and had a bit of a bronze blush on her cheeks.

"Right, so...I... I'm just going to ask. What did you see last night?"

"Not see. Feel. I felt you. Electricity." Arid smiled. "Elation, creation."

"How?"

Arid chimed a little. She extended her hand and closed her eyes. The answer was clear. She was the first child of the Source, and now that I was taking over the nexus, that bond transferred to me. She would always know if I was happy, pleased, angry, or sad, and she could convey that to the world in my stead if needed.

"I see. I did not realize the link was that substantial. This will be a permanent thing, then?"

"Yes, but not so strong. You will learn to mask. Hide, not all, but details."

"Good. I really did not know it would carry on to you. I would have stopped if I had known."

"It was"—Arid snickered and blushed with a deeper bronze hue —"exhilarating. We do not have that. I felt only love."

XXV

In the warm evening, I headed to the second last opening in the district with Rime. It was him or Arid, and somehow, it was less awkward in his company than in Arid's right now. Oversharing had never been one of my flaws before, and to do so involuntarily and in such a situation... Also, Arid's response would have been more tolerable if she had not been so genuinely excited and innocent about sharing the moment. Not to mention all the questions she had about our human ways.

It was no pleasure to walk in silence with Rime either, but I could not think of anything to converse about. Rime was not helping with the atmosphere at all as he kept to his own thoughts, merely pointing the directions when I needed to turn. It was a blessing the journey would not take days.

Other consecrators had been keeping the doorway blocked the best they could by ice and earth. Liike, the former Temple council member who had once initially sided with Irinda, was particularly glad to see us, as he had been holding the portal shut for half a day while his students rested.

"You may release it," Rime said as I armored up.

When Liike allowed the barrier to fall, no ichor came through. A shadowy hand touched the membrane, and a moment later, Istrata pressed herself against the membrane with an eerie, inviting smile. She was clad in a flowy dark dress that moved with the oily substance around her. Or maybe it was all a part of the ichor. Her eyes were dark but had a shine to them; her skin was glowing, and her hair was flawlessly bunched up with rose pins.

"Hello, child." Istrata waved her hand slowly. *"I have to say, I am rather impressed."*

"Better step back. I'm closing this one now."

"You may do so. I have judged you slightly more capable than I had surmised."

"Did you come all this way to pay me a compliment? I'm touched."

"You may take it as one if it will allow you to sleep better," Istrata replied calmly. *"Let me look at you properly. I suppose I could have done without the small inaccuracies, but you do not look terrible. I haven't yet decided if I should destroy your form or inhabit it once this is done. Being in a body made from this matter is rather tiring when walking the middle plane. It would be convenient to have you as a vessel. Well, not you, of course, just the husk with you ripped out."*

"You are free to plan. Just don't cry if things don't go your way," I replied, a little unnerved. Being separated from her only by a see-through membrane made all things much more real.

"I have all the time and power in the world to slowly strangle you out of existence. I merely walk around your people to offer them an option, a pain-free entry to a grand new world. For those who listen and embrace me, it will merely feel like falling asleep," she promised with a coy smile.

"Close it. Do not let her run her mouth while there are others present," Rime advised.

He was probably right; there was a chance we could learn something if she kept talking, but there was also a chance she might lure people to her with rumors if it were to seem we were fighting a losing battle.

As the blue flame hit the membrane, Istrata pulled back and smiled again. Then, she was gone, and we did not see her at the last opening either.

"Did you notice the ichor's surface had lowered even before I burned some of it today?" I asked Rime as we headed back.

"No, are you sure?"

"Absolutely sure. And the fact that she suddenly showed up to try to get under my skin makes me think it is not a coincidence."

"Well noticed. Such things are rarely unimportant. Any idea what she could do with the ichor?"

"You might have better answers for that question than I. When you use it to call forms... Does it condense?"

"It does."

"Then that is what she is likely doing, right? Instead of drowning us, likely she threatened just now, she might attack with her creations. Whatever they are. With the amount of ichor she has, that will be a substantial army."

"That is plausible. I will go and scout. Can you find your way back from here?"

"I can. Be careful."

"Always." Rime sighed and stopped to look back. "Thank you."

People were either getting ready to sleep or were having a late meal as I returned to the base of our operations. I grabbed a flaky bread roll and some butter. Climbing the wall had quickly become a daily routine. Whenever I had a moment, I checked the level on the other side. It had diminished again. Was she just tired of playing with us, or had we actually made a big enough dent that she wanted to change her approach? It was an impossible question to answer as we had no true estimate of how much she could lose and still have enough resources to win.

Eating the humble little bread roll gave me a surprising amount of comfort that evening, and even more than that, just sitting on the wall alone without anyone allowed me to find some clarity on my situation. I should find Riestel and let him out of his misery. He probably still thought I was angry at him. In reality, that had not been the case for even a few moments. Did I think they had been ridiculous to go as far as they did? Absolutely. Did I understand why they did it? Kind of.

I found Riestel sitting by a fire, legs resting on someone else's supply bag. He glanced at me and inconspicuously made some room on the bench. We sat there for a good moment side by side as he tended the fire.

"How are you feeling?" Riestel inquired, adding some firewood to the flames. "I at least hope that you have no regrets about us becoming more... well, deeply involved."

"I don't," I assured him. Anytime my mind wandered to the other evening, I could feel my face flush.

"Good. That was my biggest concern."

"Because of Rime?"

"Obviously."

"I think... I think it was over far before I admitted it was."

"Really, when?"

"When we laid on the field with the arochs the first time. I..." I began and stopped myself.

"You can speak to me about it. I don't mind."

"I don't know if I should..."

"If it bothers you, yes, you should. I know fully well you had a consummated marriage. It won't hurt my feelings to hear about the relationship. I'm not that weak. Not that I have any particular wish to discuss it, but who else are you going to talk with?"

"It's just that he had been changing for a long time before the final moment. No, that's not quite correct. He was allowing himself to change his mind about me and our future because he thought it was necessary. Maybe he was right to do so, but it started to be too much. He was leaving me behind. That's why it hurt so much, and it was difficult to deal with, to let go. If I had been a part of it all, things might be different, but he shut me out. I still want to help him and heal him, and I believe he loved me very much. Just not enough."

"He still does. And maybe too much."

"Why would you, of all people, say that?"

"It is the truth, and you should never doubt it, but you both say the exact same thing, just from a different perspective. He said he felt that he had trapped something that wasn't truly his. That would never be truly his. He wanted it more than anything but always felt there was something wrong. I can imagine how hard it is for him to look at us. It must be rather painful to love something and know it will eventually leave you. I suppose some people would hold on as long as possible."

"He isn't those people."

"Definitely not. He knows the amount of agony he caused, but it hurt him more to watch you drift away."

"Is that why you made that promise not to court me while this battle raged? You had to know you'd end up breaking it. I've never known you to do that before."

"I did not... Fine, yes, I did. The moment I said it. But I tried my best, and your overly obvious flirting did not help one bit."

"My what?"

"Oh, let me bend a little this way..." Riestel laughed and posed.

"I did not!"

"If you did not allow me to keep my face by denying I'd break my promise, you aren't going to get out of this."

I sighed. "He's being two-faced, though. He says it was because I was drifting away, but he's the one who let go first."

"Does it really matter?" Riestel asked. "The result is the same. It was always going to be the same; it was just a matter of time. And you can't possibly know what he saw to make that judgment. The way he described it was rather poetic. He said that once he calmed down after realizing we had a connection and who we were to each other, he felt as if he was holding on to a bird's leg when the other called to it to fly."

There was nothing to reply to that. I had never considered that my taking Rime's offer of marriage could cause him to feel so desperately sad. It made the ending even more bitter.

"You should talk to him someday," Riestel suggested. "Just to hear his side."

"He will never tell me things this directly. Everything else he can say and face, but things of the heart do not come naturally to him."

"He may if you are still there when he needs you. I would very much like the wound to be closed for both of you. But he isn't getting you back."

XXVI

As everyone in the command chain had convened the next day to discuss the situation, Riestel had suggested that we take a risk and try to shut some more openings, those that were now in the middle of the ocean of ichor. That would extend the distance Istrata would need to move the substance to get to us, as making new openings in the fabric was time-consuming, and we would likely be able to pick up on them quite fast. It would allow more time for us to deal with the waves. Most also agreed that it would become a ridiculous cat-and-mouse game if she put in the effort to make new openings, only for me to shut them down right after. As far as we could reason, it wouldn't benefit her or us.

None of us was particularly excited about the potential excursions out into her territory, but the plan was still found to be best to execute for now. Rime would have his men, Veitso in particular, focus on simplifying and hastening our supply lines to withstand a coming attack better. Some of the arochs had already evacuated to the Peak as they would be more valuable in the defense of the Peak should we have to retreat that far. Arid wished to stay and observe, which was allowed to her.

"How do we approach the doorways, then?" I asked. "We can't just travel in the ichor, and jumping through the lighter world might be too inaccurate."

"I will locate them while I look for signs and clues about what she is doing," Rime answered. "After that, we need a strong consecrator with ice or earth manipulation to basically move us forward in blocks. You need to conserve your strength for closing them and any ambushes we might run into."

"Will you start soon?" Riestel asked. "She should also focus on claiming the rest of the nexus for herself. Her powers will grow from it, and having her absorb it will make it harder for Istrata to ever get her hands on it."

"It will take a few days for me to get locations on the doorways," Rime estimated. "She can use those for anything she wants. I will also have to calculate the best routes we need to take based on the city drawings. That will give Isa four to five days in total to use her connection with the nexus. I would allow for more, but we cannot know how things go. We can stall if things look promising when we get that far. Are we all agreed? Good."

After his fight with Riestel and a few days to cool down, Rime seemed to be doing better. Letting out all that frustration must have helped. Or maybe it was I who was different, having finally accepted what had happened and gotten a sense of closure. Riestel's advice and perspective had sharply reminded me that I was not the only one wronged here. It made it easier to think of Rime in a fond, though more distant, manner and interact with him. The only thing I had ever wanted was to understand all that caused our fate. Now, I felt more at peace with things and was able to gradually let go of all the negative emotions gnawing at me.

"Have you given any thought to what you wish to look like once you have all your powers?" Riestel asked on our vigil at the wall.

"What?"

Riestel shook his head and looked at me as if he was questioning my intellect once again.

"You know how I have wings when I choose to and how the Source looks like a mix of its favorite creations. What will you choose to look like as a god? If I'm the only one with wings, it will make me look an absolute pompous fool."

"Well... you are an absolute pompous fool."

"Very funny. Answer, please."

"I haven't."

"Well, you should. I'm not saying you have to change, but people like a bit of flare. And they definitely listen more attentively when you look the part."

"Wings...?" I mused. It felt like a weird dream.

"I don't think I'm ready to change that drastically. Not that I wouldn't want to fly, but I don't think I'm ready to take on an appearance of that caliber."

"You don't need to have them out all the time. I certainly don't. You should still start to mold yourself unless you are happy to just see what the Source planned for you. You are taking in its gifts and its heart; it will mold your body in the lighter world to resemble the Source's wishes unless you make something else from the gift. The scales, for example, are directly from the Source. I would assume that something changed within you again when you forged the other connection."

"I didn't notice anything new."

"Did you search for it?"

"No," I replied and closed my eyes. At first, there was nothing, but then it occurred to me. I felt pressure in six points between my shoulder blades like I would possess new channels and muscles there. It was a very faint feeling and could have easily been mistaken for just a stuck back.

I sighed. "You're right."

"I have them too, but I chose to have two wings, not six."

"We will look so strange to people once this is done."

"You do not have to. Like I said, you can choose your form. You can stay as you are if you want to, and you can mold it later as well. You control it from the lighter world. But if you put no thought in, you will become the Source's kind. I'm hoping you'll suddenly wake up with horns, though. That would make my year."

"I don't want horns! I think."

"Well, then, step into the lighter world and start forming your own visage. If you choose the ways you manifest, you will resonate with all the Source's gifts faster, as they will feel more familiar and right for you, not just something superimposed on you. You don't need to use them here, only to allow them to form and accept them. The wings are a whole trial on their own to master if you choose to have them. They do not matter for now; it is more important to get to the stage where you can proceed further. For that, you only need to open the new channels and keep them open so they become a natural part of you."

I would have thought I would have been more excited about the prospect of wings and other fun additions. Power in all its forms had always called to me. Yet, I found myself hesitating to accept and embrace all that came with the nexus for the simple reason that it would distance me from the human world I had learned to appreciate and those that I had grown to know and love. There had been a part of me that never thought I would find a place where I felt at home and people who I felt close to. Now that I had that, giving it up seemed like a very steep price.

"Do you think there is any benefit to looking so different?" I pondered.

"Well, depends on the perspective. If you want to be able to blend in and see the world, simply keep those traits hidden, as I do. If you want to make a point of your powers, appear as you truly are," Riestel said and shrugged. "You will have your powers in either form. I do recall a certain consecratoress from a certain temple in the Noble's that used to mesmerize people just to scare them at the end of her performance. It is an act as any other act for an eager audience."

"Will you let them all show once all is done?"

"I rather like the idea. I think I might, for official godly duties anyway," Riestel mused. "But you are stalling. You should be focusing on them to establish proper channels and allow them to strengthen so you can get to the next item on the list."

"What will that be? Do you know?"

"Each time, you'll get stronger in some way, whether with your channeling or your defensive capabilities. I don't think all our gifts will be similar in their function, so I cannot predict them for you."

"You have done it four times, right?"

"Yes. For me, that was enough to get to the final cusp. I received the scales and the wings."

"What else?"

"The claws were my addition on a whim, so you need not worry about getting those."

"Could you just tell me?" I groaned.

"You will likely start seeing the reflections of the lighter world on objects in this world. It means that you can see places and things more like the arochs. You can see where the lighter world touches this one, the holy places. It is a very different kind of beauty."

"But I already see the lighter world if I concentrate."

"I know, but imagine seeing it seeping into this one, seeing the souls of people shine from them as easily as you see their bodies. Seeing the holy places glow compared to the rest of the world. It will make you love the world even more."

"Anything else?"

"You will receive a dual consciousness, which means you will be present in both planes at once and can act in both. The last one is that you will have the ability to detach fully from your body and keep all your memories, even if the husk dies. Even if this body, your original body, dies. You can regenerate it anytime you want and access the previous memories, which is not possible for humans as they are reborn. The memories do not transfer between lives, even if the soul might hold them."

"I cannot even imagine how that feels. Aren't you at all worried about the end result?"

"Not really. I've been on this road for decades. I've had time to adjust, and it was always my destiny, was it not?"

"I suppose so. You just had the wrong counterpart."

"Exactly."

I tried imagining what I wanted to look like as a god, but it all seemed ridiculous. Too much. On Riestel, everything looked fine. He looked exactly like he should with his wings. The thought of suddenly walking around with them gave me a slight feeling of embarrassment. Embarrassment? I had never feared that before. The number of times I had made a scene in the Temple alone... Why would I be embarrassed now? I was on the cusp of something only a few in the entire existence would ever get to experience, and I was embarrassed to show it. This would not do.

Closing my eyes, I drifted to the lighter world. I looked at my form. It was indeed starting to look like the Source in some respects. I had not wanted to become Istrata, nor did I want to become the Source. Thus, I began molding myself on my whims. Would I ever show anyone other than Riestel what I would eventually choose? Perhaps not, but at least I would be me.

XXVII

It was decided we would attempt to close the doorways in the Crafter's. Everything else was too far and presented too many risks. Riestel would stay behind to erect an ice-wall if needed to keep the center safe, as he had done before. Rime and Heelis would accompany me to the openings. I pulled Heelis to the side as we waited on Rime.

"You do not have to risk your life for this," I told her. "I know Rime gave an order, and as he is the acting…"

Heelis cut me off by slapping the back of my head somewhat gently, as she sometimes did to her children when they were not paying attention.

"I'm here because you told me to support you when you do right and tell you when you are being an ass and doing wrong. I know, despite our falling out, you care for me. As a mother, the best thing I can do for my children is to leave the world in a better state than it was, even if it means giving my life for it. If you ever question that decision again, I will hit you with a boulder," she added as Rime arrived. "Are we clear?"

"Yes, Mother," I muttered.

Heelis began her chore by simply calling the earth to rise as narrow pillars for us to find footholds like skipping along stony waterlily leaves. She made them fast to disturb the ichor as little as she could and removed all after us to leave no trace. On a sunny day with less pressing matters and with a less poisonous mass around us, it would have been an amusing bit of pastime.

Rime gave Heelis directions as he was the only one of us to properly feel the wounds in the structure of the world. I could sense them vaguely as a strong uneasiness and a sense of something being wrong, but I had no way of pinpointing them accurately.

"Make a space here. We are right above it," Rime ordered.

Heelis pulled a stone circle of about two horses' length from the ground to cut the portal off from the mass. I burned out the ichor trapped inside before we all dropped down. Rime pulled the opening out for me to see. It was much larger than the previously encountered ones but no more difficult to close. Heelis lifted us back to the level of the surface, and we continued to the next one.

As we traveled, the oily ichor began to ripple. We could see shadows dash about under the surface. Heelis made the stepping stones a little larger and higher to prevent anyone from getting suddenly grabbed and pulled in. My skin itched as I felt the scales ready themselves. The more in tune I was with the nexus and the more power I had from it, the worse my aversion to the dark matter became. It was abhorrent and repulsive. I wanted it gone, and everything restructured to the way this world had been. Looking at Rime was difficult, as I constantly felt the ichor in him.

In the beginning, his darkness had been a curious thing, a strange, inviting thing. Now that I knew myself and I had a desire to exist as myself without having to repeat the cycle of death and rebirth as another place-holder for Istrata's soul, it was everything but that. Maybe a part of the infatuation had been Istrara's desire for the ichor and the power it gave her. It had been so strong once she had given into the temptation that it must have left an echo in me. Or perhaps there had been a longing in me to simply break the cycle by risking death in his hands. Whatever it had been, it was almost gone now.

"The next one. It is larger than the previous," Rime announced. "You need to make the circle twice as wide."

Heelis crafted another circle for us. "Not a problem."

"Stay up on the rim. Every time we do this, it will be more dangerous, so no reason for all of us to go down," Rime told her.

"Understood," Heelis agreed and stayed higher to serve as a lookout.

The oozing opening was wider indeed but also as high as a two-story building. I felt unnerved, peering into it. There was a distinct feeling of being watched. As the fire began to seal the wound, everything was quiet enough. Nothing tried to attack from the opening.

"Hurry!" Heelis yelled. "There's a huge number of figures pushing on the walls of the Circle. Riestel just conjured the ice-barrier!"

"Keep yourself safe!" I replied.

"I…" Heelis began. "Get out! Now!"

Rime and I turned to look up. Two graceful, granite-like hands fashioned of the ichor and as tall as a wave that can drag a ship down arched above us. Heelis was nowhere to be seen anymore. The hands paused as they blocked the sky from our sight. Then they reached toward us.

"You need to finish it from the other side," Rime said and grabbed me.

"I can't, I'll die there."

"I will get you out before that. Trust me."

It wasn't like I had a choice if we wanted to succeed in closing the doorway. I took a quick, deep breath as Rime embraced me and jumped into the black opening just as the hands crashed down. I was able to scar the doorway from behind. The pressure on the scales was enormous, and I could hear a sizzle as they burned Rime.

The endless darkness slithering and prodding, trying to break through, wrapped ever tighter around me. The scales couldn't resist it in all places, and where it got onto my skin, it stung like a row of biting teeth. My lungs were burning as the air behind the scales was becoming thinner.

Rime pulled me through the ichor as fast as he could. The horrible thought that I might die here, in complete darkness with the ichor flowing to my lungs, was unbearable. There had to be something I could do.

"Isa, stop struggling; you are making it worse," Rime ordered calmly, but his voice had a tired ring to it. "We will make it."

I shook my head, barely able to understand his words. The scales gave up one by one, and each time I felt the ichor press on me with a ferocious sting. First, they failed around my legs, then my body, hands, and finally, I watched them disappear around my head. I was able to hold my breath for a moment. The pressure made it impossible to resist for long. The ichor rushed into my lungs.

At the edge of my consciousness, I saw the island. I was floating toward it, holding on to a silvery thread. Did it mean I was dying? Going back to the very beginning to be born into a world with no hope? My feet touched the island's ground. It sent a small ripple throughout it. I could see figures start to form and houses rise. The thread I was holding was thinning.

When I tried to call for help, a sunlit wave wiped me off my feet and pulled me with it. It flooded my body and pushed all the ichor out. I coughed violently on the stone pavement and gasped for air.

Riestel lifted me into a sitting position and hugged me. "I'm not letting you go that easily."

"Will she be alright?" Rime asked as he stood a little way to the left with his hands crossed over his chest and his gaze on the ground.

"She will. Thank you for bringing her back...to me."

"Good. I will get everyone sorted out to withstand the attack as best we can," Rime told him. "How long will the wall hold without you to reinforce it, or can you return to it soon?"

"In a moment, it should hold until that. Go." Riestel turned to me and brushed my hair from my face. "We are under attack from them. You are not allowed to scare me in such a manner. I forbid it."

"I saw the island. I almost returned there," I said quietly and shivered at the thought. It would be a fate worse than death to have to start all over again and lose everything I had gained in this life.

"I would have stolen your spirit back if the cycle would have taken you. I don't want any other version of you. Just you."

"Heelis! Did she make it back?"

"Yes, she is fighting as we speak."

"Fighting... An attack? What is going on?" I asked as the situation was sinking in.

"A little while after you left, the creatures came with a large push of a wave. And then there is the matter of Irinda..." Riestel explained as he helped me up. "Are you in any condition to fight?" He frowned. "I don't know how I feel about you going right back into it."

"Does it matter? I need to."

"You don't, we can retreat."

"Without causing her losses? I don't think so. Where is that subservient mechanized bitch?"

"That way." Riestel pointed with a sigh. "Do not overdo it. We do not have to win this battle."

"I know."

I didn't have to go far to see Irinda as she was perched on the wall behind the ice. Her delicate frame was again suspended in a contraption of Istrata's design. The former sleek scorpion fashioned to hide between the two natural worlds now looked like it had been covered in a dark, moving, organic mass. It dripped and left a trail of the ichor, but the matter surrounding it did not diminish.

An eerie, stifled wailing sound permeated the air as the scorpion's stinger hit the ice. The wall cracked, and pieces of it fell on both sides. Riestel unfolded his wings and charged to hold her out. The wailing sound rang across the city as Irinda unfurled a flurry of blows to the barrier. She was too late to damage it further. Riestel had pressed his hands against it and pushed it to grow higher and curve toward the outside to keep her from trying to climb it.

"A little assistance!" Heelis screamed at me.

I turned in the direction of her voice. At that moment, I realized they had breached us from somewhere. Heelis was attempting to cut down figures made from the ichor. They were all human origin, but they moved slithering like snakes, and where they might have once possessed feet, they had just a shadowy tail. None had discernible eyes, but it didn't seem to stop them from making very specific attacks.

As Heelis tore them apart with her stone knives, I began to force the fire into them. The sound they made was repulsive. It was a combination of a gurgle and a child-like cry. Heelis leaned on her thighs after all had been burned.

"I'm getting old." She huffed. "There are more wreaking havoc over there. They got into the resting quarters… Thankfully, it was rotation time, so most there weren't sleeping yet."

"I will get them; stay safe." I headed to the door.

The destruction on the inside was quite complete. All the furniture had been smashed. Windows were in pieces with ichor, and red blood spattered all over. I followed the sounds and went around room by room, helping all that could still be helped. I tallied over fifty strange creatures before I was certain they were all dealt with.

Returning outside, I could see people being gathered to be counted and patched up. The younger temple folk were pale and shaken, huddled together.

"There are some still indoors to be helped," I told the soldiers. "No enemies."

"Understood," a woman replied and ran to check.

We had taken a risk and suffered because of it. Istrata had likely waited for exactly such an opportunity. I went around the square and through the nearby alleys and houses. On returning, I noticed Arid huddled close to a water barrel. For a creature much taller than most humans, she looked small and frail.

"Are you alright?" I asked and kneeled by her. The wail echoed across the block.

Arid covered her ears. She was shaking. "Walking doorway. Must kill."

It was like she was in physical pain just by its mere corrupt presence.

"Go to the Peak, get ready," I ordered her.

Arid looked at me. I could feel her hesitation and shame.

"Please, you can't help me here, and you certainly can't help me later if you die here."

She nodded and disappeared.

I heard Tammaran calling my name from somewhere around the corner.

"Here!" I answered and walked to a more open area to look for him. As he saw me, he gestured for me to follow.

"We have everything set up for you to begin dismantling them," Tammaran informed me.

"Are we really going to follow that plan? What about Irinda?" I asked.

"Let her focus on Riestel for now. She seems to be rather pigheaded about getting through from where he is. Riestel will allow this part to break the moment so we take on the ichor and the creatures as we rehearsed, so you will only face an amount you can handle at all times."

"I think we shouldn't waste our time on this." I hesitated. "We should simply fight her."

"There is no reason to change plans. We had a bit of a moment of chaos as Riestel had to be called down to save you. They got through only because of that. Trust us. Have we ever let you down?" Tammaran asked.

"What if she breaches the ice?"

"She won't for now. Worry about that later."

"I just... Fine. Start." I relented. It was our time to bleed them more actively, and yet, I couldn't get Arid's panicked request to just go after Irinda out of my head.

Tammaran and the others, whose task it was to observe and decide the routes the mass of ichor and creatures of all kinds were allowed to traverse, gave the signal to have them pour in from our chosen location.

It didn't take them long to notice the weaker spot in the ice. The black mass pushed and clawed at it until Irinda came and punched through it. The front legs of the device pushed through the opening, but it was too small for her, and Riestel's ice was too hard for her to make it any larger than he allowed.

As Irinda backed off, clearly getting annoyed at us, the ichor flooded down like a waterfall of oil and strange lumps. The dark river and the creatures it carried rushed into the system of maze-like corridors and chosen alleys built for this exact exercise. Most were sent to me for disposal as their own pressure pushed them through burning areas.

I stood by the last opening on a slightly higher piece of flat rock. As the river reached me, I began the dance. I could feel the lighter world around me begin to empty. Did we really have enough force or souls for this plan? After the ichor came the creatures. Most had gone through many of the traps or faced other consecrators, so what ended up here at my feet was a sludge of torn limbs and undiscernible parts trying to stretch back together.

After I had disposed of as many as I could and began to make small errors, I gave the signal for needing time to rest. As the others took note, the ichor flows were directed to pits, some frozen, and some smaller streams directed at the few other fire consecrators that we had for softening the matter. The bulk was let out into the river below us. This way, it flushed with great speed down the rushing river that traveled under the city and to the Slums and then to the sea. It would dilute the ichor at the same time and give the creatures in it a long way to march back.

All went smoothly; everyone played their assigned part, and crude soul sand kept on piling behind me. Everyone seemed to have found their legs after the surprise of the first uncontrolled breach. People from the Temple encouraged each other to get more done and were happy they had an effect.

While I was allowed the luxury of small breaks, it was difficult to rest looking at Riestel holding an entire ocean back, with Irinda determinedly harassing him. He did have some help from other ice-skilled temple folk, but I knew there wasn't a moment he was not the one doing the heavy lifting. He wasn't as taxed now as he had been before, apparently simply because he could give it his full attention, knowing I was safe. Our connection was definitely a double-edged sword—giving us strength and making us weak.

There was no doubt that Riestel was strong, but how many days could he possibly hold with minimal breaks while we dabbled with eroding the ichor little by little? I knew they had calculated it before all of this, but I couldn't quell my doubts. No matter how many days I would do this, it wouldn't be enough to stop them. Everyone looked so pleased with their tasks like we were making a difference. There was no other way about it in my mind. The plan had to go, but it wasn't a decision I could make alone.

Rime was in his tent, meticulously going over the progress and measurements. He seemed satisfied with everything so far.

"Should you not be resting?" he asked when I interrupted his tasks. "Is there a problem?"

"We need to kill Irinda now. This isn't the right time to focus on the mass," I said.

"Why?"

"It just isn't. Trust me."

"That is not a good enough reason. Everything is going well. I know it seems like we aren't doing much, but we are making progress each moment. We all agreed this was the best course of action, did we not?"

"Yes…"

"Why have you changed your mind? If you want me to change orders, you must give me a reason. A hunch is not a reason," Rime demanded. He was right, but it irked me that if we had still been together, it was likely he would have been persuaded by less.

"Because it sounded like something that should work, but it is not going to. We will simply wear ourselves thin, and once we are tired and weak, she will get through, and we will never even have the chance to challenge the Witch Queen. We need to strike Irinda down hard and fast, even if it means losing the center."

Rime frowned and stared at the tent walls, tapping on his desk.

"The calculations…" he sighed. "They are done by the best we have, and you would have me throw them away for a 'maybe'?"

"I know. But we didn't figure in her sending Irinda clad in that, did we? She isn't just one more fighter; she is a moving doorway, that's what Arid said. It took all of us to take her down the last time. What happens if Riestel loses his grip even for a moment and she breaks through when we are not prepared, or I'm exhausted? You must have thought of it. We have to defeat her first. The Queen will not come before she is gone. I'm not saying abandon the plan. I'm just asking to postpone it. We can do this later, even afterward. You always asked me to trust you without justification."

"You are understandably frustrated." Rime sighed. "It won't do anyone good if you falter now."

"I'm not faltering. Let's say we manage to spend so much of her reserves that she feels she has to make a personal appearance. Do you want to take on her and Irinda at the same time? How would that work?"

"Fine. I will discuss this with Veitso. Today. Do not do anything rash before that, please. This isn't about who is right."

"Are you implying that I should just stay quiet about my doubts"?

"No," Rime groaned. "Isa…" His tone was quiet and warm and brought back many lovely memories. "Please understand that changing course now will create a huge risk. All of our people need to be given new orders, new tasks, and a whole new direction. It doesn't happen with a flick of my wrist. I know waiting is not your strength, but a large ship doesn't turn course as fast as a small rowing boat."

Rime had a point; he always had a point. This time, though, I knew I was right. He stood up and placed his warm hand on my shoulder. Despite sensing the ichor in him, a wistful wave of emotion washed through me. I placed my hand on his and nodded. Out of respect, I had to wait for their decision.

XXVIII

R ime did as he promised. Veitso and he ran the tactics and calculations again.

"You can stop pacing and come in," Rime called.

"Are you done?" I asked.

"Yes," he answered.

"Well?"

"We think we should continue this for a moment. A day or two," Rime told me.

"See, we can drain them while we switch to take her on. We'll send most away to prevent any stupid losses," Veitso explained. "Let's continue whacking them while we get people to safety."

"I don't know if that will be soon enough." I sighed. There was just something about the situation that made me uncomfortable. Mainly the lack of trying to from Irinda's side. She pestered Riestel, but I didn't think she was truly trying to push through yet.

"It is the fastest we can do it in an orderly manner without the risk of unnecessary casualties," Rime stressed. "We have no clear reason to hurry and cause panic. Anything that can be done thoroughly should be done so. Do you not agree?"

"I don't know what I think at this point," I replied. "I'm not going to argue the matter with you. I don't have your experience in handling things like this."

Soldiers like Veitso hated this sort of battle. He had no other motive to keep it going but victory. They had all been trained to defend us, and now they had nothing to do but to plan. The Temple's consecrators and students were now the ones protecting them. It was a full reversal of duties, and it didn't sit well with many. It was one of the reasons I relented on the issue. If they were ready to continue like this, despite it going against their very nature as our defenders, I should listen to them. I should listen to them...right?

After hearing their judgment on the matter, I climbed up to Riestel. I wiped the sweat off his brow and fed him small pieces of bread. Irinda paced on the other side. When she noticed me, she stopped all movement and simply hung there silently, staring at us. I suppose she still considered Riestel her pet and wanted him back.

Riestel opened his eyes for a moment and gave me a shifty glance.

"You are planning something," he noted. "I can feel it."

"I'm not. I'm just trying to talk myself into listening to those who know more than me."

"And how is that working out?"

"Honestly! I'm not planning anything... Well, I mean... I'm just thinking about things that might happen and how to respond to them."

"Right, and in your expert opinion, what would be the definition of planning?"

"Could you just focus on your task?"

"You came here to distract me," Riestel huffed, amused, and turned his attention back to the wall. "You want me to drop this ice curtain and see if we can kill her permanently?" he whispered in his silkiest voice.

"No... I mean, they promised to get things moving on that front..."

"Just say the word, and I will."

"I can't. That would lead to unnecessary casualties."

"What if I want to lower it?"

"Do you?"

"Well, I can't say I'm enjoying sitting here day in and day out listening to that scream again and again."

"No, stop talking me into it."

"Fine. But you know where to find me once you change your mind." Riestel laughed as I escaped. "I am certain it won't take long."

Had I ever gone against Rime's wishes? Was there even one time that I had done so? I had gone to the Temple and left him behind, but he had benefitted from that and had not objected to it either. Everyone else I had opposed at one point or another, but we had always listened to each other and found a route together. He was trying to do that now, too. Was my hesitation caused by that or because their plan made more sense? If the person saying I should not fight Irinda yet had been Frazil, would I have listened and waited? I had to be able to answer that before I'd act.

The allotted time to rest came to an end, thus the task began anew. When this trap had been laid, the first creatures to emerge from it were trying to attack and scrape at anyone they could reach. Now, it was mostly a lazily flowing river. If any creatures were present, they simply lay waiting to be dismantled. It wasn't right, and it was lulling people to think the worst might be over. There was not one part of me that believed it was true.

The oceans of ichor I had seen in my dreams when I had been more connected to Istrata were definitely not infinite, but compared to the amount we processed here, they might as well have been. We had reserves to last an entire year to slowly and constantly fight her. However, the idea of living with a tightening noose around us for a whole year or longer unnerved me. She had always placed her trust in time.

It wasn't a question of doubting the chosen tactic; it made sense to try to weaken an enemy who was so much more powerful than us. There was another way, too, one that suited me better. To strike her hard and fast with everything we had and to not allow for her to set the pace. It was, of course, potentially an even more suicidal route to take. The best thing about it for me was the thought of pushing her off kilter. Now, we had two tactical minds, Rime and Istrata, two people of immense patience, against each other.

After my shift, I went to Heelis as I knew fully well what would happen if I returned to the wall to Riestel. Heelis was tending to a small, trampled garden in a nearby alley, just in case the people who lived there could someday return to more than a destroyed life.

"Do you think I'd be making a mistake?" I asked her quietly. "Be brutally honest."

"You'd need a fortuneteller to answer that," she said and shook her head. "I've followed a lot of rules in my time in the Temple. Those I agreed with and those I didn't. It's not in my nature to oppose those higher than me in their decisions... Not that I ever kept quiet if I disagreed...but I did not challenge their decisions after voicing my opinion."

"You can just say if you do not want to answer."

"Let me finish. The thing is... I've seen you almost destroy the Temple on a whim, following whatever feeling you followed. Same with the city. People too. One might quite justly think you were the harbinger of difficulties. Destruction even."

"Well, this took a light-hearted turn, thank you."

"Now, now, you told me I had the right to air out everything I thought when you released me."

"I'm still listening. I am not?" I sighed, very likely pouting a bit.

"And I can't say that all things have changed for the better; not all the consequences have been positive... But that is not to say they are fully your fault, either. I mean, if one pops an abscess and the puss spreads and causes smaller infections in the nearby tissue, but the abscess begins to heal, and so eventually does the patient... Isn't that worth enduring the other lesser negative effects and maybe the eventual scar? That thing there, beyond the ice... I would not mind dying to rid this world of it and its Queen. I hope I won't, but isn't almost any consequence worth it if we can then begin to build again?"

"You know how I feel."

"And now you know how I see it. Is that enough?"

"I don't know. I've never been this unsure of what to do."

"You know fully well what you feel you need to do. You just don't want to take responsibility for it if it proves to be the wrong choice. In all seriousness, I love that you came to ask me of all people this, but you are aspiring to become essentially a god compared to us. Should it not be solely your decision? How will you manage the world if you will bend to our will and seek our guidance when you are the one entrusted with our lives? If you don't know how to manage the task, then we are all done for now or a little later."

"I..."

There was only one answer to that.

"Thank you." I squeezed her hand. "I'll go grow a spine now."

Heelis smiled. "Regretting that you gave me full speaking rights?"

"Very close to it."

The last steps to Rime's tent were the hardest I had ever taken.

"Can I come in?" I asked.

"You can, as always."

I stopped halfway, holding on to the draped tent door.

"I'm going after Irinda," I told him, looking down at the ground.

"Excuse me?"

"I'm going after her after I rest for a moment. I will not spend one more minute draining the reserves. It is a waste of my strength."

"Isa, look. We already agreed on this. There is no point in going over this anew. You agreed on it."

"I shouldn't have."

"You what?"

"I should have held my ground. I know you are the War Council, and I have absolutely no doubt you are the best this city has ever had to defend it. However, this is my battle. This is my war. This is not something even you, with your years in the army, have ever faced. I can feel something is not right, that something bad will happen, and soon if I do not attempt to correct our course. It might already be too late."

"The army can't function on feelings."

"I'm well aware of that. But I'm not asking permission; I'm simply announcing what I will do. If you must stop me, you will need to do so by force."

Rime stared at me with an expression I could not quite decipher. Disappointment or relief? He got up and walked to me. Just a little closer than he had been for a long time. It was a strange thing, as before, I would have battled to keep my desires in check. Now, I had to battle to hold on to the love I had for him to not withdraw from sensing the heavier world in him. It was like the magnet between us had been turned around.

"Then go. I will get as many to safer ground as I can."

"Just like that? You aren't mad?"

"If I was, would it change anything? I can't lift a finger against you. I'd be undermining everything I've done to save this city. Its future is entirely tied to you, is it not? Your way may work, even if it would not be my choice of action, so the best I can do in this situation is to try to ensure it will work. I promised to support you a long time ago, and that has not changed. Just give me a head start to get as many people to the Temple area and give an all-out order to withdraw higher."

XXIX

I flicked my fingers nervously at my side. Riestel was getting ready to shatter the barrier. The last time, it had been a difficult match, with some of us dying and getting maimed. This time, I was stronger. Much stronger. It should be a more even match.

"Are you sure you can keep up?" I asked Heelis.

"I won't let you down. And you have Riestel to back us both up if I should mess up, but I won't." She grinned and scratched the old scar on her neck. "I hope I won't get a bigger one, or at least not on my face. I like my face. I have a nice face."

Riestel sighed. "Would you two cease chirping so we can start?"

"We are waiting for you, are we not…" I remarked.

"Well, pardon me for making sure you are paying attention. It is not as if we are dealing with a matter of life and death," he replied and snapped his fingers.

The wall burst into a mist of ice particles. Irinda's machine teetered from side to side like she was unsure of what to do. It only affirmed my decision to try to settle this part here and now. For a moment, I wondered if I should try to talk to her once more, but decided it would be a pointless exercise with her soul and personality having essentially succumbed to be tools for another.

Heelis lifted some initial earthen platforms around Irinda for me to use. The idea was to keep her on the other side of the wall so she would not notice we had almost cleared out the entire Circle. Irinda had been quietly dangling from her contraption for a long time now, just occasionally waking to harass Riestel. As I crossed the remains of the shattered barrier, she twitched and shook her head.

Irinda turned to Riestel and said, "When I win this time, you have been promised to me. She has no use for a traitor, but I will take you in."

Her voice, though mostly hollow and void of emotion, had a slightly more personal ring to it. Like an echo of her former self. It was unsettling and compelled me to feel a modicum of pity for her. Riestel was having none of it, as his reply was to pierce her contraption's leg with an ice shard. She didn't seem to mind. The scorpion shook a bit, but soon, it drew more of the ichor over its frame and repaired itself as the ichor on it moved and pulsated.

The fire bit into the machine reluctantly. The carapace was made from an incredibly dense ichor. It was soon clear that Irinda could no longer produce fire or any manifestation of our powers with the scorpion. If only she had not gained new abilities, this would have been over in the beat of a swallow's wing. The wail that emanated from the tail slashing forward and hitting things was unbearable at a short distance without the ice to muffle it out. The air that carried the sound hit our bodies in sharp waves that would stun those who did not manage to cover their ears.

Once the shrill sound passed, the machine's feet jabbed at whoever was the closest to it or seemed the most affected by the wail. The ichor surrounding Heelis's small islands reached and grabbed at us. She increased the height to help keep our balance.

As the hands could no longer reach us, another problem appeared. The ichor withdrew and condensed to melted, doll-like figures. They climbed and ran as proficiently as any human form. They were easier to disperse and burn than Irinda, but the amount of them meant that we were spending more time trying to evade her and them than attacking.

As we danced around Irinda and between the dozens of husks and exchanged blows, I could slowly feel out her structures. Once I found what I was looking for, I crossed my wrists. Riestel stopped on a piece of earth. I felt a cold rush of air toward him, and then an icy gust froze out the sea of ichor and the creatures caught in its way.

I charged at Irinda so she would not have the time to attack Riestel, who needed to stay still and focus on containing the others. The machine's legs melted in the blue fire and brought her closer to the earth. She did not seem particularly affected by all of it, and when I was close enough, I saw a smile adorning her face.

The gleaming ice surface beneath us shook. Several black masses shattered through to the surface. Riestel withdrew his consciousness from holding the forms in ice back to what was happening here. The masses trembled and shifted and then condensed into several other contraptions resembling Irinda's scorpion or into more spider-like vessels. They looked disjointed but moved fast. They chittered quietly, mimicking Arvida's gifts. Their voices pricked right through the skin and conjured up a cold terror from within. The only cure was to resist.

"Why not welcome a few more of my brethren?" Irinda asked. Her eyes were bright and lustful. There was no doubt who was present in her for the fight. The melted legs began to repair themselves.

"Withdraw and fight as we go." Riestel grabbed my arm. "It is too risky taking on all of them on their turf. Let's try to move toward the Merchant's and drop them if they follow and as they follow. Retreat like you would in a panic. Make them believe we think we cannot take them on."

"Heelis, run!" I screamed, and we all scrambled to the other side of the wall and ran into the alleyways heading up the city. Soon enough, the pounding of the multitude of machine legs reverberated through the stones, and the unyielding chitters trying to drum up panic spread through the streets like a cold wind that reminds you of a night terror sitting on your chest.

Rime had left us horses a few blocks away. They were a little startled at us running at them from the nearby street corner but calmed down as soon as we got on. They were the fastest kind of army horses, bred for messengers that moved between units and command. They were tall with slender but powerful muscles and had a silvery sheen to the tips of their hair. Their splotches of reddish brown and white gave them an endearing, funny look. Even their speed would eventually falter as the unrelenting and untiring contraptions followed, but we had no intention of outrunning the machines.

"Let's take the first two down," Riestel suggested as we could see the machines spread out more from each other to cover the ground to find us. They could not sense us as easily as we could hear and feel them. We stopped and hid the horses behind a sturdy stone storage house.

For a moment, everything was quiet, and then the first of the machines jumped over us, almost bending the earth below due to its weight. Riestel slashed its feet from under it with one clean movement. Heelis quickly brought down a building to hold it in place. It was not as well made as Irinda.

As it struggled in vain to free itself from the elemental shackles, I placed my hands on the temples of the once-human creature using it. I forced the flames inside, to where its heart had once existed and where now was only a hole that led directly to the heavier world. Nothing changed in its expression as I burned it shut. The blank eyes simply closed, and the head went limp. Once the machine was useless and the creature was mostly charcoal from within, we stared at it.

Heelis sighed. "Lucky it behaved so carelessly."

"Is that what I think it is?" I asked and turned over a slightly melted medallion.

"Yes," Riestel confirmed as he touched it. "She or he was a Knight of Saraste."

"But they were lost to history ages ago!" Heelis replied.

"They were indeed." Riestel showed her the medallion. "But she made them back then for her purposes. They were not made to protect us from her for balance like we all once believed. Look at the engraving. Whoever this was, they were born only a few decades later than Istrata had us believe she died. She's kept all the emptied souls she could procure for this battle. No wonder the Knights disappeared at some point. Some of the families must have objected to being used and hidden from her or just stopped the practice and let that part of their line die out. Irinda's could have been the only one that volunteered for this as long as they did."

"How many of these will we need to fight?" Heelis asked, with her eyes darting around the area.

"There is no way to know," Riestel answered. "We saw a handful; I would wager there will be more. They aren't all as skilled as Irinda. This one had no idea what it was charging at. I'm not even sure you could say it was conscious. I would theorize that the older the creation of hers is, the fewer faculties it has preserved. The first ones would have been practice runs. Simple dummies."

"You might be right," I said, "but doesn't the Queen control them, anyway?"

"I doubt that she can hold them all in her mind at once and decide all movements simultaneously. Not even the Source can split her attention between more than a few issues at a time and keep full control of them," Riestel reminded me. "Let's keep moving and picking off the ones we can."

We did not head straight toward the Merchant's. Instead, we took our time to see if the others were trying to find us. I cursed myself a little for not pushing to do this earlier. If we had moved on Irinda the moment she appeared, we might have gotten her down before the others arrived unless they had always planned to appear once we made a move. If we had kept going with our first strategy, we might have been too tired to fight once they would have all appeared on their own time.

Despite the unpleasant revelation of having to fight more of Irinda's kind, I felt calmer than in a long time. I had trusted my instinct, and it had proven the correct thing to do, well, more or less. Maybe it was all that was asked of me. Of course, some would argue that I caused this again and that without me acting foolheartedly, we could have avoided the withdrawal. Maybe. It was their right.

"One is near," Heelis whispered. "I can feel it making dents in the ground just by moving. No...there are two. Neither is Irinda. They have a different weight and gait to her."

"Bait them?" Riestel suggested.

"Why not?"

"No," Heelis interjected. "There are even more coming...behind them."

Heelis was right. I began to sense them too, not through the ground but as a heavy wave through the structures of this reality. The sea of ichor was moving and rising in its entirety. Pushing to cover us all.

"Heelis. You need to make haste to the people traveling before us. They need to pick up the pace. Everyone needs to evacuate from all other areas than the Peak. We are going to go all in, luring her out in their wake."

"Lure her out? You mean the Queen? Are you sure?" Heelis asked, looking uncomfortable. "This is not the plan made."

"I know," I said. "We will stall and take down as many as we can, but we can't hold or draw them all. Our people need to get a warning. Otherwise, it will be an absolute mess. I will try to reach Arid, but it is still difficult to communicate clearly with just images. They might get overrun without proper warning. Please go now."

Heelis squeezed my hand for a moment and took off with the horses. As she disappeared, I tried to focus and tell Arid about the situation. She responded, but I wasn't sure if she understood all. Before I had time to clarify, the two machines Heelis had warned us about hovered near us on opposite roofs of stone buildings. The houses barely withstood the weight suddenly thrust upon them.

Riestel pointed at himself and then at the closer enemy with his index and middle finger—almost as if he had made a blessing gesture. When I nodded, he shot out a barrage of hail and ice that simply drowned the entire roof and fractured it. The still-frozen creature fell into the building. As soon as it was incapacitated, Riestel charged at the other one and targeted its legs. The machine swerved to avoid him but too slowly.

Once it stumbled to the street and was suitably shackled to the ground, I made my way to the creature that hung in the harness in the middle of it. The claws snapped at me threateningly, but Riestel's grip was too strong for it to extend them. The creature was similar to the earlier one with nothing inside it, nor did it react much to anything said or done to it. The other one was still helplessly encased in ice when I brought the first to an end. Riestel cleared a route through the icy cocoon directly to the heart.

"This makes me suspicious." Riestel nudged the machine a bit with his foot. "For a regular soldier, they would pose a big threat, but..."

"I know... These might be older, cruder versions, but I have a feeling she's still toying with us."

"The few times I disagreed with her toward the end and was brazen enough to voice my concerns, she would be relentless in hammering in her point until the other person simply gave up from exhaustion. Somehow, I get the same feeling from this."

"She does not seem to direct them fully at us."

"No, we need to hurry and cause havoc along the way. I would imagine they will push all the way to the Peak if they can this time," Riestel pondered.

Traveling through the first parts of the Merchant's, we had killed over ten of these dark, mindless wanderers. The cooling evening in the wholly abandoned section of the city felt oddly comforting. It was like walking through the ruins of a once great culture that had just disappeared, leaving cooking equipment on the stoves but no clues as to where they had been whisked off.

Looking up at the sky, the first evening stars shimmered through a wispy, torn-looking curtain of dirty grey and pink clouds. Riestel took my hand in his and hummed as we strolled along like nothing was pressing going on. Whenever I glanced at him, he conjured a bright smile. When I managed to steal a glimpse without him noticing, his face was tired and pale, and his gaze followed the ground and not the sky.

"You don't need to smile for me," I whispered as we stopped to rest by a small wooden bench.

Riestel turned to me and cocked his to the left.

"I'm not smiling for you. I have no reason to pretend to support you or believe in you. I'm smiling at you…because looking at you brings me joy."

His words had no hints of insincerity or mockery.

"For a fledgling goddess, you can be pretty clueless at times," he added, as I should have expected after such sweet words. "What is that expression?"

"Pure unadulterated frustration."

"With me?"

"You are the only one here."

"Really?" He gasped and looked around like he was completely oblivious to the fact. "Alone with a recently divorced woman? The scandal. Whatever should we do?" He grinned with a mischievous look about him and sat on the bench. "Scurry to me, little mouse, and I will pet you through the night."

I nuzzled against his side on the bench and yawned. My eyes felt so heavy. There were urgent matters to take care of, but we both needed a break.

"You would rather sleep than play with me? The audacity." Riestel huffed, amused. "Go ahead. I'll guard you."

XXX

T he sunrise was far more beautiful than it had any right to be on a morning like this. Having an increasingly strong connection to the lighter world and this world seemed to reap the benefit of needing much less sleep to renew my strength. Riestel still sat silently as a willing pillow. His eyes were narrowed as he had spent his time in a meditative state to replenish himself.

"Not much of a guard, are you?" I remarked and poked his jaw.

"There are other ways to keep alert," he replied and batted his eyes open. "Would you look at that? I'm smiling again," he whispered and gave me a gentle kiss.

"Emissary!" Arid yelled as she appeared. "Happy alive. Come, I will ease the way."

"Could you see them from above? How far are they?" I asked.

"Yes, many crawling. Many going to Peak." She grimaced. "Eat all left. Give hand. Jump. Heelis safe. Holding at Temple to give time."

Arid allowed us to navigate easier and faster with our bodies intact through the lighter world toward the Temple. We hit four contraptions with their vapid drivers on their way up the city as they were careless enough to wander on their own and not very alert of their surroundings. There were a hundred or so of them crawling and scaling the roads and structures ever higher. Some had chased down lingering groups of soldiers and people who had not left despite warnings. Their remains told of a death that may have been quick but hardly painless.

As we reached the Temple, the fighting was spreading all over the place. The soldiers there were of use this time. Even if they could not do much about the ichor, the structure underneath it was possible to twist and damage with explosives and weapons. I didn't see any consecrators, apart from Heelis, helping them. The bigger dilemma, as we soon noticed, was the absolute panic among people and the disorganization it caused.

"We need time to kill the ones that have reached us," Rime told Riestel as he hurried toward us. "You need to get up there."

"I'm getting tired of putting up walls everywhere." Riestel sighed. "It is unimaginably boring to just sit there."

"We don't have time for your quips and complaints," Rime admonished him. "Either you help us or leave us to die, but make your mind up quickly."

"You should know I always play hard to get." Riestel sneered and bowed mockingly. "Clear the wall!" He shot up with his crystalline wings spreading out against the sky. The sun's rays split into every imaginable direction, painting the entire area with multi-colored dots of light. For that moment, he looked like hope incarnate.

The soldiers and consecrators that had been levelheaded enough to act faced with this sight of mechanized insect-like creatures fused with the resemblance of human remains almost fell off the wall as they hurried to comply with the order. Riestel had slowly and surely built himself a façade of coldness, even cruelty, so whatever he asked, he got and as fast as possible. Now that I knew how warm he could be, it pained me that he had spent centuries slowly distancing himself from others. Then again, I suppose there was no other way. No matter what, we would both lose this connection with those we now cared for. We would remain and remember; they would die and hopefully be reborn. Even Elona.

The moment Riestel's shoes touched the wall, a crackling sheet of razor-sharp hard ice cut and pushed all that was on the wall down or into pieces. After the initial clearing, he quickly thickened the structure and sent it curving outside. He remained there, hands pressed on the ice like a mighty bulwark against the black tide. Looking around, I noticed some of the fighters dropping to their knees or pressing their hands across their chest and giving a silent prayer.

Rime grabbed me by the wrist.

"Would you focus a bit?" he demanded, frustrated, as he pulled me toward a warehouse surrounded by consecrators in blue-hued uniforms that were a mix of their old temple clothes and army jackets.

"I'm sorry. I was in my own head for a moment," I replied.

"I asked if you managed to kill them on your way here. We have not been able to deal any damage that would keep them down permanently," Rime said in a low voice as he opened the door to the warehouse, and we stepped in. Half of the temple folk working with the army were huddled there. They had orange hues in their clothing. They looked unnerved and unsure.

"Yes. I have to burn the hole within them shut. It's like the doorways. You must cut them down and shield me so I can get to their core. They do not heal after that," I replied. "It connects them to the Queen in the heavier plane and all any resemblance of life they had."

"Alright." Rime sighed, relieved, and turned toward a group of about a hundred consecrators waiting in the building.

"Offensive temple units!" Rime called. "I know this has been a rough, rough start to our cooperation, but the Consecratoress is here to help you now. She will fight with you, she will back you, and you will back her."

Their faces hardened, and their posture improved. They nodded to each other encouragingly. The fear caused by hesitation seemed to loosen its grip on them.

"Show her that you are worthy. Show everyone the Temple can carry its own weight and more," Rime told them.

"Yes, Sir!" most replied as they had learned the army's way in their joint exercises. Some were still struggling a bit with the idea of having to shout a response, so it wasn't as sharp of an answer as from a veteran unit. A couple of the answers were a little late on the cue, but all seemed ready to do their part.

"Divide into groups of two units by ascending unit number and start tearing them down. When you have one in a vulnerable position and pinned down, call out, and the Consecratoress will assist you as soon as she is able," Rime gave them more specific instructions.

The men and women arranged themselves with an efficiency I had rarely come across in the Temple. Each group headed out with the order to attack the nearest unharassed creature, plowing its way through the regular soldiers. We followed them out. You could see how relieved regular soldiers were to see the temple coming to their aid.

"Why weren't they already fighting?" I asked.

"We couldn't find a way to kill those damn things. Why would I waste the offensive units in a purely defensive battle? And...we were holding out for you to appear. They have trained under me, but it is you they follow. You needed to be here for them to perform at their best. You may not have noticed it, but the changes in the Temple have brought you a following more loyal than any leader could hope for. Go and help them."

"I'll go."

"Good. We will both go."

One by one, they fell. As I sealed the last ones, we could hear the now familiar wail of Irinda's stinger. She had been in no hurry to get here. The streets and parks and squares were filled with broken men and pieces of the machines as more of them gathered outside the ice. Rime gave the order to clear and burn all bodies as soon as possible. If there were even the slightest chance the Queen might be able to use them, we would not allow for it, even if it seemed cruel to send them on their way without their families being informed or giving them the opportunity to say farewell.

Dancing and burning the bodies didn't move me the same way as when we had gone against Irinda. It had become routine through the years of having to unravel souls and bodies. The fragility of lives, the momentary nature of it from one creature to another, was pitiful, and yet perhaps beautiful for the exact same reason. Even if they gained a soul, death was the end of that particular expression of them, which would never reoccur.

I sat on the ground among the embers in the waning evening as most everyone else shuffled—tired and shaken—to their accommodations. A faint crescent shone in the sky. Being chosen for this task, or forced, meant I would never again be reborn. I would exist with all my memories of my mistakes and losses. Obviously, there was a comfort in knowing that the cycle of rebirth to the island would be over in that case.

For the first time, I began to understand why it was by design that death erased the persona and memories. It was a blessing to a creature who had attained the promise of eternity. Certainly, the souls carried a mark of their experiences and some unearthly wisdom that could permeate the current conscious, but not to such an extent that they could not be gifted a life where they could experience everything anew. The first time you walked on dewy grass, the first time your best friend hurt you, the first time you felt a connection with someone.

Tammaran and Veitso had been watching and waiting the whole time I sat there. I could see and feel that Veitso was anything but happy with me despite his participation in honoring the fallen.

"You are free to voice your concerns," I told him as I stood up.

"You caused many deaths with this rushing," Veitso said, averting his gaze. "We should have stuck to the plan. It was all going well."

"Perhaps," I replied and looked him over. Veitso's upper lip twitched as if he had more to say, and he seemed disappointed. Now that I was no longer Rime's, he was becoming belligerent. Who could blame him? Not I. There he was, making all these plans to the best of his ability to serve his friend, and here I was, making his hard work obsolete and causing losses. And yet, even with all the compassion I felt for him, Riestel's example led me down a different path.

"But that is not for you to judge," I stated and stared at him.

"What?" Veitso huffed and leaned backward a little. "These are my men, and Rime's dying here, and I don't get to complain?"

"No. You do not. Their lives, your life, all lives here fall to my domain," I told him as a feeling I had been fighting stirred within me. A feeling of entitlement to this world. I had always craved power; now, I had more than my fair share. My decisions were not up for debate at this point. If we survived, the future generations were free to judge me as harshly or as kindly as they saw fit. This was not the time for my trial.

"Tammaran, do you remember when I told you what I must become?"

"I do," he replied, lowering his gaze.

"I cannot delay it for the sake of a few people."

"A few people!" Veitso raised his voice in dismay. "We lost two hundred at least because you wanted to begin a fight out on a whim."

"I'm not denying that my actions led to the losses."

"Then you admit being wrong?" Veitso pressed. "We need to work together and in a smart way."

"No."

Veitso's face went pale. I had never seen the jovial man so appalled. Tammaran tapped his friend's shoulder. Veitso shook his head, adamant to continue the discussion.

"Whatever your status, I won't let you mess with my people. You brought Rime nothing but trouble either, and yet he follows you like on a leash. I don't get it."

Veitso's words were harsh and maybe deserved. He had been kind to me many times over the years, but I could not say we had become friends, so this reaction was not surprising for a man whose whole life was the army and those he trained and commanded. In his eyes, I was quickly becoming a liability.

"That's too far," Tammaran told him and squeezed Veitso's shoulder a bit, trying to turn him to walk away.

"It's not!" Veitso objected.

"What would you do then?" I asked and allowed the fire to shine forth from my eyes and my skin until a blueish aura surrounded me. "Will you try to destroy the only weapon you have against this enemy? Or if not that, will you try to subdue me, bind me as Frazil attempted?"

Veitso took a step back from the heat.

"You are asking me to obey you when I'm the one attached to the world's very core structures? Do you feel the pain every day and moment that this realm is in? I can do more damage to the enemy than all of you combined. And you would dictate to me how to resolve this?"

"I'm saying that you should listen to those more experienced," Veitso held his ground.

"And I will when I find it is the correct thing to do."

"That isn't listening," he complained.

I knew I could silence him by telling him that Rime had eventually approved my decision. It was a route I didn't want to take, hiding behind someone else's back. They would have to understand sooner or later that I was no longer someone accountable for individual destinies.

"I'm not sure if you are being unnecessarily or commendably hard-headed," I told him. "This is not a negotiation. I will do anything and everything I deem necessary, just as you are doing now, trying to reel me in. You may be responsible for your units, but I am responsible for life in all of its manifestations. If we lose…you humans…I will weep for it for centuries as a failure and grieve you all, but if losing you means that I can save what will help me build everything anew, I will not hesitate twice."

"You are not human." Veitso spat. Tammaran let go of his shoulder, clearly startled that Veitso would go so far while he was sober. Everyone was used to him speaking his mind and putting his foot in his mouth whenever he drank, but this looked to be unexpected and new even to Tammaran.

"Indeed." I sighed, feeling as if he was questioning my very right to exist.

"You do know I have never been a human? And I will never have the chance to be one because I was formed to be a vessel with the only purpose of dying when the time was right. Would you like to trade places with me? If you can think of a way to make me human if you can think of a way to grant me a life where I can be happy and not have this burden, by all means, tell me. If you can give me a destiny that is not an eternal prison of servitude, tell me! If not, leave me alone and bite your tongue because I will be your *god whether or not any of us wants it.*"

The last words I spoke startled me as I could hear an echo in them, like when the Source or Istrata spoke. I felt a rush of forced power gush into me from the nexus, and a wave of energy shot out from my body, clearing out any unwanted impurities.

Veitso and Tammaran stared at me with eyes wide open as they scrambled to their feet after the blast. The entire area was alight with a green flickering light that, at times, bent to a cool blue and warm orange. Small multicolored embers floated to my field of vision from behind. I sensed the change. Looking over my shoulder, I could see six wings of flame. I turned around just to make sure they were actually attached to me. One pair of orange, one of white, one of blue. Then they were gone, and the mixed green light faded.

I could feel the lighter world moving within and through me, carrying a subtle, restoring light. It wasn't like the healer's gift; it was more that I was turning into the nexus, becoming a connection between the worlds. With it came feelings of elation, ascendence, and pure power. It was an intoxicating combination that spoke to my very essence, to the part of me that always wanted more.

"Are you happy now?" Tammaran asked Veitso and gave him a backhanded slap on the arm. "Or will you keep at it until you are the first person to be smote for being an idiot to a goddess?"

"Forget it," I requested. "We both went too far. I know you care, Veitso, about everyone here. And I care, too, just from a different perspective. To you, the people are the world and the thing you are trying to save, the most precious thing. I cannot fault you for that in the slightest. I do not have that luxury. If she corrupts the lighter world or crushes it or, in any other way, destroys it and gets the nexus, her will is going to seep into other worlds beyond ours."

Veitso's face was hard to read. Tammaran patted him on the back. Slowly,

Veitso turned away. Tammaran gave a short nod to me and began escorting his friend to their sleeping quarters.

XXXI

Sitting at the same table with Veitso the next day was rather uncomfortable. He avoided any eye contact and didn't speak like he normally would about anything that popped into his head. Rime surely knew already what had passed.

"We have the very same situation again. Riestel is holding the line, and we are waiting for something, anything we can do. I assume there is no point in suggesting we go back to the slow attrition of the ichor reserves?" Rime asked.

"Don't have a clue," Veitso muttered.

"No, no point," I affirmed.

"Then you have something that you would like to try or for us to do instead?" Rime checked.

"Well, it took surprisingly long for her to get the ichor up after we closed the nearest doorways. Enough that she moved on to another plan. Now, we have the machines trying to break through. She can only have as many of those as there ever were children made into emptied souls from the families that agreed to the practice. We counted around a hundred. There won't be many more, if any. Once those are down, she will need to proceed with another tactic again," I surmised.

"So, our target is to dispose of them as fast and with as minimal casualties as possible," Rime simplified the thought.

Veitso perked up a little.

"Yes, hopefully we can achieve that," I agreed. "However, you need to relieve Riestel from his wall duty. I will need him for the attack."

"What for? He is the only shield we have. If he disengages from the ice, all of them will charge at us," Tammaran remarked before Veitso could. "I'm not against the idea, but I would like to know what would happen to warrant such a risk."

"We have been experimenting and practicing. My fire, though hot enough for many things, is no match for lightning. When we…combine our skills, it shoots out at the ichor and unbinds it and forces it to soul sand quicker than anything else we've encountered."

"Lightning?" Rime echoed. "You never told me that before."

"It wasn't something we could reliably do until now," I replied, hoping he would not feel betrayed that I had not kept him up to date on everything.

"How accurately can you control it?" Rime asked.

"There is no way to control it once it crackles out. But we can control the direction it initially shoots out to."

"There is a chance they can evade it in that case or that it could hit our people. Any ideas on how to either improve accuracy or shield the other fighters?" Rime quizzed, looking at Veitso.

"Right, well, spears." Veitso eventually grunted. "We could make double-ended spears of the ones that have metal tips by fusing two into one. If we also put in a metal strip to join the ends, it should draw and guide the lightning into them."

"Do we know which metal is the best for this, or are all equal?" Rime asked.

"I'm no smith or scholar. I just know most metals attract lightning," Veitso replied.

"Ask Moras. He'd know," I suggested. "I can send Arid unless Tammaran wants to go."

"I can make the trip," Tammaran assured. "There is nothing I can do here for now, and as much as I respect your aroch friend, I think it will be easier to convey all that is needed if I go."

"Can Riestel hold on for long enough for us to get this equipment made?" Rime checked with me. "It will take at least a few days, even if we use existing stocks from the army and just do a coating on them."

"We can relieve his burden by having all others who share his talent take over parts of the wall," I presumed. "I believe he can last long enough, but once he lets go of the wall, he will need a moment to catch his breath, so that will require planning and whatever help and backup is possible."

"That is our task to plan. You can go and talk with Riestel," Rime told me. "If he has any reservations, tell me or Veitso as soon as you can so we can find a solution or formulate another course of action."

"Does this mean I get to make a plan and stick to it this time?" Veitso muttered. He was becoming a bit more animated, which I took as a sign of him accepting that while our concept of saving this world differed, it did not need to mean we could not cooperate.

"Yes, I would like it," I replied. "I'll leave you to it."

Riestel was sitting cross-legged on the wall with his hands on the icy barrier. His muscles looked a little strained from the constant strikes against the towering ice-shield. I could feel him drawing power from the surroundings. Now that there was so little of life and souls left compared to the size of the world and what it needed to keep fertile, I could feel it all draining away anytime anyone used them. Keeping the wall up, as much as it protected us, spent our resources, even with Riestel's skills, at a rate I was not content with.

"Your steps have become lighter, though I'd still recognize them anywhere," Riestel noted, smiling with closed eyes.

"I told them about the lightning. They agreed that we should try to use it to our advantage. They will construct weapons to help conduct the electricity into the enemy."

"How long?"

"Days. Tammaran is on his way to begin the arrangements. Can you hold on until?"

"Of course." Riestel sneered to hide his hesitation. "Any break would still be appreciated."

"We will try our best. For now, you can have some of my strength," I said and sat behind him, hugging him with one hand. I poured out some rough sand next to me and focused on refining it. A slow, light current of energy transferred to him through me. It circulated in him, mimicking a good night's sleep.

"When did you get this ability?" Riestel asked, opening his eyes. His body relaxed, and I could feel he needed a little less force to uphold the wall.

"When I was arguing with Veitso. I got so frustrated that I think the nexus thought I was in danger and forced the next connection..."

"Accidentally then, should have guessed. The way you stumble into success at times is truly entertaining." Riestel snorted. "Don't overdo it," he requested gently.

"I won't," I promised and felt a lovely, relaxed tiredness take over my body. "And you'll be disappointed, no horns, but I might have manifested the wings. Though, I'm pretty sure mine are of the ornamental kind, not functional like yours."

"You could make them functional through the lighter world."

"Maybe someday. I just want to get all this over and done with first. Promise me something?"

"What?"

"That we'll still have a life of some kind if we manage to win. I mean…do we have to be gods every day and every moment from now till eternity?"

"It is funny, is it not? You were all power-hungry in the beginning, and now you fantasize about trading it away for a normal life. Not that I think you actually would, given the choice. You are just having a moment of doubt. And that's fine. You have every right to grieve the life you have just lost and the life you will lose once all of this passes."

"Did you ever regret accepting the Source's deal?"

"No, not really. I have always wanted to see what is beyond all of this. To see what only a few can ever see. I did second-guess myself at times after all that went wrong with Istrata. I cursed my undying body when I realized what had happened. If it had not been for Istrata's spell and me getting caught up in it, I would have been reborn many times by now, waiting for a suitable person to ascend with. That is the only part I resent. The waiting, every agony caused by her. I have never regretted agreeing to become the Source's heir. I don't think we will feel the same uninspired oldness once we become what we are meant to be as I experienced being trapped in this long life."

"You really believe that?"

"We can always pretend to be mortals and walk among them if we miss such a life. The world does not need us watching it every second. Besides, the idea of someday getting to travel to another world as the spark of creation… Wouldn't you like that? Think what it must be like gliding among the stars of the sky and choosing where to go next and what to make next?"

Looking up into the sky, I could feel the titillating beauty of the thought. Leaving a world that had run its course and heading into the unknown. Maybe the Source was right as well. There was almost always something yet untried to make one wish to delay death one more time.

"Show the wings," Riestel asked.

"I don't know if I can."

"You always say that, and then you do it, anyway. Have some faith. You don't always need to explain the possibility of failure to avoid embarrassment before you even try."

"I don't..." I objected as Riestel glared at me. "Fine, I admit I may have that tendency."

I closed my eyes and lifted my hands to chest level, palms facing each other, fingertips a nose width apart. It helped me slip into the between. It felt as if the wings were placed on me like a mantle that fused with my skin.

"So?" I sighed as they appeared behind me in the middle world.

Riestel's smile was like a sun ray piercing through a foggy meadow.

"Do not change a thing," he replied.

There was a murmur from down below. As I looked, I realized I was seen far and wide in this form. The soldiers didn't know what to make of it, and those from the temple had kneeled and began a prayer. The strength of their thoughts and wishes passed on to me. I could feel it shift the currents in the lighter world. Was that why Istrata also tried to convert people to her side and not just outright kill them and add them to the ichor? To influence the world in a more subtle way to work in her favor?

Looking down at all the people, I could see little lights and ripples emanating from them. It was like a small vigil of souls in the making. Behind them, partly hidden by a corner, was Rime with his left hand clenched around something by his heart. I couldn't see the object, but I felt it. I had carried the bracelet for years. His mouth moved in silence, but there were no lights around him.

Once Rime finished his prayer, he glanced up at me. I pretended not to have noticed him as I knew he would feel uncomfortable. He stood there for a moment and then disappeared into the shadow-filled alley.

The next day, I spoke with Arid and gave her the task of taking my first personally crafted edict to the Temple's current overseers. In it, I gave them the order to gather all people who they could to begin holding daily sessions to send out their purest and most well-meaning thoughts into the world. If Istrata had deemed it worthwhile, there was no reason not to attempt to counter her at every level we could.

While waiting for Tammaran to return with news, we tried to isolate some of the creatures and their machines, but there were so many that they almost always managed to escape. The other consecrators, who were brave enough to agree to attempt to venture to the other side, just weren't enough to hold them properly if there were more than two or three of them. Whenever we attacked a lone one, its companions would quickly swarm us.

We believed that Istrata was likely looking out of each of them to control where they went based on where I was. Our suspicions stemmed from the fact that when we had attempted to use another group for a decoy, none of them appeared to aid the targets. They knew the others could not permanently kill them.

Despite the numerous failed attempts, we managed to bring a few of them down when we had Heelis along. She was one of the few Temple's instructors still capable of fighting. Most of those who had survived thus far had sustained too many injuries during the city's internal turmoil to use their talents to their fullest. The next generation wasn't yet at its peak form. It also seemed that this waning of the souls affected their powers too. It was harder and harder for them to call enough life forces from their surroundings. It was slowly getting to the point where it would make more sense to simply have them stay back and not consume the scant forces that still were available.

Rime, Veitso, and Samedi had been sitting at the planning table for most hours of each day, just repeatedly going over even the most unlikely scenarios and what to expect. It was agreed that no matter how we would proceed, we could not hold on to the Temple district. There was only one place left to retreat to. The Peak.

A slightly damp late summer morning finally brought with it some awaited news. Tammaran appeared to announce that a shipment of silver-glazed spears was on its way.

"I'm sorry I didn't come to tell you earlier that we were already working on them. I wanted to use all my time to help where I could. The first have been loaded onto the pulley carts in the walls. It will be a day or so until they reach us," Tammaran explained.

"You did the right thing," Rime thanked him and gave him a short, brotherly embrace. "I have spoken to all those I feel have the capabilities of helping in this battle. I have given the order for everyone else to move up to the Peak. Only those fully prepared to die should stay here for the breaking of the ice. Even if we manage to defeat them, there are no guarantees that the ichor won't drown us."

"Why are you telling us this?" Veitso muttered. "You know there isn't one of us that would leave your side whatever the battle. Even the prancing prince arrived to help."

"You uncouth peasant." Samedi sighed. "I swear the last thing I'll hear in this world is him mocking me with some equally unamusing nickname."

"It is my duty to offer a choice," Rime stated, cutting them off before they had the chance to begin another round of affectionate bickering. "If there is nothing more to add from anyone, then get to your duties."

I heard a faint whisper tickle the air around me.

"Emissary of Fire. Please come."

The Source had never reached out like this, and I could hear it was immensely difficult for it.

"I will. Just give me a moment to find a place," I told it.

"Who are you talking to?" Tammaran asked.

"The Source. I need to speak to it."

"Then use this tent. We are clearing out. I will step out as well," Rime suggested. "I will see to it that no one bothers you."

"Thank you."

I placed a moss flower on my tongue and slipped through the world to the Source. It looked fainter, transparent.

"I can feel my freedom creeping closer," it said wistfully. *"You are one step away from becoming what was meant for you and I from being banished from this world."*

"Have you ever gone back to any of the places you've created?"

"I have not. Though, it is possible to do if one is willing to suffer the agony of birth to a mortal frame for one life. Though, as the vessel is quite randomly chosen, you might not even know you are a god in disguise, so it serves very little purpose other than getting to fulfill a sentimental itch by taking the chance."

"I'm sorry. I shouldn't be wasting time with these questions. You called me here for a reason, yes?"

"My heart has been heavy with thoughts of the one you loved before. The emptied soul."

"I'm still hoping to find a way to heal him. It is the least I can do for him. Istrata can guarantee a continuum, but he does not wish for such an existence."

"It is wise of him. I do not think you can heal him. However ... I have been

revisiting the time of creation and what I set into motion there. The fundamental laws. I may have found hope for you. Let me explain: There is no rule set against someone gaining another soul if one should be stolen or destroyed. I'm not sure how it could be done for him, and I do not know how it would attach to him as he is so fully a creature of the heavier world and more and more with each time he uses the powers gained from it."

"Understood, and yet it could be done?"

"There are no laws in place to prevent such an occurrence. You cannot heal him, but you could make him anew."

"Would it be him?"

"That is a tricky concept. A soul can be born when a person truly excels at something. However, if they are so passionate about something, they simply force it to exist. This happens in the lighter world."

"He would need a connection to it. He doesn't have one… Still…"

"A glimmer. It is all I can give. I wish there were more."

"It is more than I or he had yesterday. Thank you."

"I am happy that my final moments in the world can be of assistance," the Source said, smiling, and gently pushed me out of her space.

The joy I felt on waking up was boundless. I knew the hope was almost nothing, like weighing a single mouse's hair against a heavy stone, yet my heart grasped onto it like it was my life on the line. A connection to the lighter world. That was the first thing he needed. I had no clue where to start, but if there was a way to force an entire new heavy plane into existence, there had to be some way to make this happen.

Should I tell Rime? Every part of me wanted to give him something to hold on to, but I knew he would resent me if I brought this knowledge to him. He had specifically told me not to give him hope to not hurt him even more. I would have to abide by that wish for now.

The silver spears had reached the Temple area. They had been loaded on carts and would be at our disposal at any moment. All the defensive units of ice-skilled consecrators had taken their spot on the wall. Slowly, they would take over sections for Riestel. As the enemy noticed Riestel detaching himself for the barrier, they began to bash it with everything they had.

Riestel walked down and sat at the root of the wall on pillows brought to him. He fell asleep almost instantaneously despite the worsening ruckus. Behind the worshippers of Saraste on the wall were Heelis's kind. It didn't matter what kept the enemy out for now, so if any of the ice parts seemed to yield, they would help as they could with earth or metal. Ado's servants were also employed on the walls to hold the structural integrity for as long as possible.

We could hear the horses. Rime and Veitso hurried to unload the carts with a few of their most trusted men. The spears were distributed to teams of consecrators who would be in charge of delivering them to their targets. I sat down beside Riestel and took his hand in mine. Then I closed my eyes and focused on breathing as slowly as I could.

Our fingertips pulsated, resting against each other. My hand gently floated as the pulsation became stronger. I could feel his heart's rhythm through it.

"It's time," Tammaran said. "If you have gathered enough strength, if not, we will try to hold on."

"We will see," Riestel answered and stood.

"Rime has ordered the teams into their positions. Just one word and the barrier will drop," Tammaran told us.

"Hold on, let us get started first. We need a moment to gather." Riestel yawned. "Is the square cleared of people?"

"Yes. Everything is as you have requested it. All those with an accurate throw have been positioned around the roofs. You only need to allow for the signal."

"Well, then... Would the lady do me to honor of this dance?" Riestel asked, turning to me with a thin smile and presenting his hand.

"You're so old-fashioned," I said and walked to the center of the square. "Hurry up."

Riestel rolled his eyes. "The youth these days..."

We had practiced the lightning call many times, though not at this magnitude. To really make it work on a large scale, we needed to mirror each other as closely as possible. I took off my shoes, as did Riestel. The sandy earth was warm and pleasant. I could see other consecrators and some soldiers in the structures above.

"Nervous?" Riestel asked.

"Yes, but in a very good way." I smiled. "Begin."

We positioned ourselves facing the opposite direction with our hands bent at the elbow and palms together. Riestel began humming a note that made the ground and air ripple. I mimicked it as I could. Then we clasped our hands tighter together and began to flow from stance to stance, always keeping at least the very tips of our fingers touching.

The fiery hot air and the freezing polar wind went under, over, and around us, gathering strength and speed. One movement reached away, and the next contracted and led us close again and again. The gathering powers began course within us. I could see small flashes and crackles on Riestel's skin and between us.

Above us, the summer clouds began to gather into a swirl and condense into darker storm clouds. The repetitive wavelike motion of the dance brought on a very trancelike state where time itself seemed non-existent. I could see my hand move, and behind it moved a hundred other hands in the same pattern. I could see my skin beginning to glow, and the next step I took lifted me into the air from the gathered charge.

"Let it break!" Rime yelled.

All consecrators on the wall dropped down, and a moment later, the first machine broke the barrier. Fifty or more of them battered their way through and pushed to our side. Heelis and the other advanced consecrators attacked them to keep them from getting us right away. They came closer and closer.

"Throw!" Rime ordered.

The silver spears were launched by hand and by gun at all and any machines on the square. Riestel and I stopped into a contracted stance with our free hands across our chests to keep all that we had gathered from fizzling out. Every muscle in my body burned.

"Release!" Rime gave the command.

We both straightened our bodies, and as we extended our arms to the side, an arc of lightning shot out in both directions. We dropped to the ground as a deafening rumble accompanied the flashes, jumping from one rod to another. It was a bizarre sight to behold. The heavy dark clouds began to murmur above us, and suddenly, natural lightning struck at our location as well. Like a local primordial storm.

"We need to find cover," Riestel said and dragged me toward the nearest stone building. We huddled in the doorway, partially looking out to see what was happening.

All of our people on the roofs were gone from sight. Hopefully, some had managed to avoid getting hit. I knew the lightning we released had hit some of our own. I had felt it as their souls were released. It was a tactic that was always going to produce casualties. Being aware of each of them was an unwanted side effect. What most moved me was that I could feel none of them begrudging their fate.

We watched as the machines sparked and burned as the lightning still jumped between them, slowly lessening in force. Every hit left a burst of soul sand after it. There was a distinct, fleshy scent of smoke everywhere. Buildings began to burn from the embers and small fires.

Through it all, I could see Irinda standing on the wall, looking at her kind writhing and squirming and melting. She swayed there quietly and then disappeared back to the other side. A moment later, the black ichor flooded over the wall, gushing and raging. Lightning still struck from the sky, burning vast amounts of the ichor as it hit the conducting weapons. Any dark creature hit by it disintegrated in the blink of an eye into millions of tiny particles that floated in the air like a pastel-colored mist.

XXXII

T he stone building sheltered us from the brunt of the weather's fury. Most still alive made their way here as many of the wooden structures burned. The Temple's previous damages had been only just mended. Now, another of its areas was destroyed. These had been mainly storage houses for all merchandise coming from the Lowers, so the destruction wasn't as culturally significant, even though almost comparable in scale otherwise.

"Well, that definitely worked," Tammaran remarked as he caught up with us. "Didn't expect it to take down that many."

"We fried a lot of the bastards! Merrie would have loved to see that." Veitso laughed, seemingly in a better, more forgiving mood toward me. Samedi nodded behind him.

"Do we step back to the Peak now?" I asked.

"Yes," Rime affirmed. "We cannot rest if we do not retreat. And I'm sure Riestel is too tired to erect the barrier again."

I slapped Riestel pre-emptively on the arm as I could already hear his brain brewing a lewd joke to annoy Rime.

"What was that for?" Riestel asked and looked at me ever so innocently.

"You know very well," I replied.

Riestel nodded and shrugged, smiling to himself.

"Well?" Rime pressed.

"It's not an easy thing to admit to," Riestel smirked. "I usually always have enough energy for erecting things."

Tammaran turned half away, pretending not to be amused. Samedi and his delicate ears had apparently not registered anything either. Veitso was staring at Rime to figure out if he should laugh or not. The answer was not exactly hard to decipher.

"Get to the corridors," Rime ordered dryly, ignoring all mischief around him. It was very clear who the responsible one in the room was. Despite the inappropriate moment for the jest, it was, all in all, a much-needed moment of relief. The amount of damage done to the enemy was nothing to sneer at, and a moment of levity let it sink in better.

Looking at the other consecrators that had survived, I couldn't have been more impressed with the change that happened in the Temple these past few years. They were no longer a self-righteous sect that only used their skills for entertainment and riches. Of course, their having to fight for mere survival wasn't what I had hoped either, but at least they were beginning to find their worth again.

We could have saved time and traveled through the lighter world, but that would have meant leaving those unable to withstand such means of relocation without any support. The decision was made to guard the others until they could reach a safe distance and then to jump to the Needle. Of all the consecrator units we had here to help us during this siege, only about fifty people were left completely unharmed, and we weren't about to let them fall behind.

Rime led us to the nearest point in the wall between the Temple and the Peak that connected to the cargo lifts that would get us up to the Peak. The pulley system connected lifts could fit around six to seven people with no loss of a proper amount of personal space at one time, with a good number of supplies in the middle. We waited for our turn and watched the survivors get on them. Some were shivering from exhaustion, and some looked tired but relieved to be going to relative safety. Some looked unphased and ready to take on more.

I remembered looking at the soldiers during the civil war. Paying attention to the individual fighters. Now, I realized I didn't even know any names of the people in the units most closely operating with us. They were as faceless to me as the enemy. This was the first time I was even looking at them as individuals. Living in the Needle, being so focused on the nexus and the lighter world, had isolated me from this city and the people. I was just as blind to its true condition as Irinda or any other ruler before her. It was disconcerting how fast such a gap was formed.

"What are you overthinking now?" Riestel asked me as he got on the second last platform and offered his hand.

"Everything, as always."

There were still five of the consecrators left, but they looked hesitant to get on.

"You are free to join us," I invited them. "It will be safer to travel on this than the last. They will collapse the corridors and tunnels leading up after the last one."

The consecrators got on quietly, only nodding as a thanks. The platform nudged sharply and then began a steady climb through the damp tunnels of bricks and carved rock. A while later, we could hear a loud explosion and a rumbling sound. The entire structure shook a little, but at this distance, only a few pebbles fell from the roof.

"How long have you trained with the army?" I asked from the unit.

"Since the cooperation started… Consecratoress," the eldest, a brass-haired woman, answered. "I'm not quite sure how to address you." She looked a little worn and pallid.

"As you would any Temple member," I told her.

"No," Riestel interjected. "You may refer to her as the Emissary of Fire."

"Really?" I groaned. "I don't need more titles."

"And yet, you will have to have some and get used to them." Riestel shrugged. "You could, of course, just use the goddess's moniker Nef'Adhel. You are taking her place from the world's perspective."

"I like my own name. Thank you very much."

"You may like it and use it, but the world won't," he said gently. "Besides, Nef'Adhel is a title, not a name."

"What?" the youngest consecrator gasped.

"Indeed." Riestel smiled. "It simply means 'Fire of creation' in the old language."

"Will you start calling yourself by Saraste then?" I asked, annoyed.

"I might as well, really."

"Is it a title also?" a straw-haired consecrator asked as he was playing with a few colorful pebbles in his hand. He bowed his head immediately once he realized he was looking into Riestel's eyes.

"It is. It means 'Gift of rain' or 'Gift of life.' Either one is an acceptable translation," Riestel explained. "That should give you people enough options to choose how to address either of us."

"Yes, thank you," the eldest answered.

"Emissary, we were wondering," the young man began. "Did we make enough of a difference?"

"You did better than I could have asked for," I replied. "If the Temple is made of your kind in the future, I will be content."

"Don't look so pleased," the woman said. "The Emissary did not answer the question directly. That can't bode well."

"And how should I answer it when I do not know if you did enough? We will only know that once I am dead or the Witch Queen is dead. Do you want me to lie and give you a false sense of achievement and safety?" I asked, a little taken aback at her impolite demeanor. The other consecrators looked surprised as well.

"Don't waste your breath on such," Riestel told me. "The complainers will not be satisfied no matter what you tell them."

"I...meant no disrespect," the woman answered after Riestel's words. "It just—"

"I don't care what you meant," Riestel replied without so much as looking at her. "But that poisonous attitude will cost you your own life or the life of one of your wards here. Bravery can do the same, but would you rather die as the one holding the line or the one who let it crumble and turned to run?"

"Apologies. I will consider my words with more care," she said and sat on the moving platform away from the rest of us.

I eyed her for a while. There was something that wasn't quite right. I gestured for the young man to come closer to me so that we were as far from the woman as possible. He moved to me carefully, keeping his gaze down at all times.

"What is your name?" I asked the youngest quietly.

"Utonie, Emissary."

"The woman, your unit leader."

"Hazsa."

"Is this typical behavior for her?"

"No, not at all. She is usually very humble and polite," he answered, glancing up at me.

"Was she injured, or did anything happen to her during the battle?"

"She was knocked unconscious for a moment," Utonie recalled. "I wasn't right next to her then. Tifer might know more. He's the shorter one of the two men."

"Get him for me, please."

Utonie bowed and did as asked. Tifer was a stocky man with a hairline that had somewhat recently decided to vacate his forehead. He walked to me and stopped a few feet away without uttering a word. Riestel inched his way closer out of curiosity.

"Your unit leader. How did she get injured?"

"We were fighting one of those spider-creatures with a human inside before the lightning in the earlier attempts. She got a blow to her right temple and fell to the ground. We got the thing under control, and then you came and killed it. We rushed to her. At first, we thought she was dead. She was not moving or responding. Then she came to before a healer reached us."

"Did she behave differently from then on or?"

"A wee bit. She performed all her duties, but her motivation... I do not know how to explain it. It is like she has already decided we have no chance."

"Riestel," I whispered. "Could you check if she is still, in fact, alive?"

"You think she's carrying the ichor?" Riestel asked quietly.

"Maybe. I can't sense it clearly."

"I will have a look," Riestel said and moved closer to Hazsa. The woman gave him a sharp look but didn't attempt to distance herself. Riestel took hold of her neck and forced her to her feet.

"What are you doing?" Utonie gasped.

"Just having a look," Riestel replied and turned to Hazsa. "I wonder if we might have a spy among us," he continued as the woman's face began to frost over.

"Please don't hurt her!" Utonie pleaded, taken back by Riestel's actions.

Hazsa tried to grab Riestel's hand and pulled it away from her skin. When that didn't help, she reached her hand towards her group as pleading for help. There was something amiss with her theatrics. The fear did not come across as genuine to me. The members of her group were panicked but kept their distance.

"I'm not hurting her," Riestel replied. "There is no her to hurt. Is there?"

On hearing Riestel's words, Hazsa's hands fell to her side.

"You killed her!"

"I did not," Riestel protested. "Show them."

Hazsa's eyes twitched open and a black drop of ichor come out from her eye and her mouth. She turned her gaze to us. Then she smiled lopsidedly and started to laugh. At first, it wasn't familiar, but slowly, I recognized the rhythm and pitch.

"Poor little ones, so afraid. Allow me to reassure you, she died painlessly, devoting herself to me. Now, she will stand beside me in an eternal, woeless existence."

Hazsa's skin shifted and crawled. Her face changed to the Witch Queen's.

"My regards to the dying," she said and tore herself free from Riestel. Then, she slumped over like a disregarded doll with no bones and fell off the platform.

"Hazsa!" the consecrators called and ran to the edge. Their leader's body lay on the tracks behind us, bent unnaturally from the spine.

"I'm sorry to say, but she has been gone for days," Riestel told them, then he walked over to me. "Her mind was taken. I think some of the ichor must have gotten into her wounds to give the Witch Queen a direct path to whispering to her. She was controlled in the same manner as Arvida does it. When she received a fatal blow, she was a convenient spy for a moment."

I sighed. "That's all we need."

"If she can get the ichor into people, she can affect their mood and actions." Riestel shook his head. "The rest of you, come. I need to make sure you are clean."

The consecrators aligned themselves into a row. Riestel pressed his index and middle finger on each of their foreheads.

"All clear. It was just her," he announced.

"Good. But we should check as many as we can once we get up..." I decided. "Look, I know this was very likely a worse surprise for you than the enemy appearing. I would still beseech you not to talk about this to your peers or others. The enemy feeds on sorrow and pain. The more uncertainty and lack of commitment we have, the more ground she gains. She likely took her as a means of lowering your morale, and I don't blame you if she succeeded. I hate keeping secrets from people... Still, I must ask it of you."

"We, uh, we will do as you require," Utonie agreed. "At least I will."

The others nodded and sat down to offer their leader farewell prayers. Riestel and I made ourselves comfortable in the opposite corner. I had begun to converse with the others to remind myself not to forget individual people and their worries, but I had only managed to remind myself why I had distanced myself from them. To look them in the eye and share their grief was debilitating and distracting.

Once we reached the Peak's opening and the platform ground to a halt, the consecrators got off and bowed. Rime helped to secure the platform while we disembarked.

"Where's your unit leader?" he asked. "We need to have a meeting."

Riestel took Rime to the side and gave a quick rundown of things.

"Right, Tifer, you have been promoted to unit leader. Follow me," Rime said as they returned, then he looked over at me. "I will catch up with you later. You can go to the Needle for a few nights if you wish, but be on alert."

XXXIII

B ack in the Needle's highest room, I stared at the nexus. It had diminished to a dense, small star-like knot. Taking its powers and structures into me hadn't seemed so significant until now. I must have only barely scratched the surface of things that had been passed to me. The nexus seemed anxious, like it wanted to complete the merger at any moment.

Sitting at the desk with a journal in front of me, I began to list out all the things I knew of souls. In principle, they were the very essence of intent, passion, or any feeling strong enough or manifested long enough to make the person's life force evolve into a more permanent structure in the lighter world.

Undoubtedly, a new soul would be possible to make, even rather simple, now that one knew the mechanism. The trouble was there was no apparent way for Rime to do it. He was only in contact with the heavier world and this world. Souls were profoundly a quality of the lighter world. Something was needed to build an organic link from him to it. To grow it back where it once existed.

Even if Rime exhibited all the willpower or emotion required to birth a new soul, unless there was a connection from him to the lighter world, nothing would happen. If we could forge a new connection, would there be enough time for a soul to form? Those born of an immense outburst of emotion were in the minority.

What if the energy did not come from him? The thought occurred to me, staring at the strands that connected to me. There were so many. They contained whole lives and contained much power. Out of respect, I had never followed a strand between Rime and me to the very end on his side, into his versions of the memories. Maybe it was time to invade his privacy for a good cause.

Traversing one of the strongest paths available to me, I ended up on the street, just outside the tavern, where he had succumbed to the pull between us. The memory made me blush and wet my lips. Falling for him, for whatever reason, had been wonderful. After lingering in his embrace within this small fond memory for a moment, I carried on. The strand thinned, becoming extremely narrow at the end where it should have connected to him.

Of course, there was nothing there. Except all strands that led to him ended exactly at the same point in the lighter world. At that strange hole in the very fabric of creation I had seen long ago the first time. Then, I had thought it was his soul, but in fact, it was the heavier world pushing out from him. It was a curious thing.

Reliving the moment definitely stirred up regrets and longing. But there was no way back. He had given up, and I had given up. With Riestel, I felt complete, but I would always miss Rime and how I had felt when he had loved me. The scar created by the affair would never close fully.

"A scar?" I sighed out loud. "Anything removed makes a scar?"

The thought vexed me for a good while, but nothing came from it because as much as it seemed like a key, I also knew Rime's body had no elements of the lighter world visible. I had seen him through all possible lenses. There was no trace of the lighter world in him. Examining and cleansing his channels definitely should have revealed if there was anything left. I broke the pen out of frustration.

Then, I realized there was another pertinent question to answer. Why could Istrata still use her strands in the lighter world if she claimed not to possess a connection to it? I had seen her severing it. No, that wasn't quite right. I had seen her sever the connection to the soul I now carried. Could she still possess a basic connection to the realm itself? Like those who lived but did not possess a soul yet? If she did, it was very likely that it was due to the difference in the creation methods she used for herself and the knights. But it could be a step closer to the answer, could it not?

It would require tapping into her memories again, which had not ended in a very encouraging way the last time. It was a mystery that needed to be answered. There was no point in using Arvida to mask me. Istrata already knew that trick. I would need to charge in as fast as possible and get out as soon as possible. The timing of such an excursion would also need careful consideration. Istrata would have to be extremely preoccupied for it to be a success.

"Yes?" I called out as someone knocked on the door.

"I have all the drawings of his channels here, as requested," Moras said as he entered.

"Wonderful. How are things?"

"I am feeling a little more hopeful. I was able to construct devices that can generate an electrical discharge in weapon form. That means we can give regular soldiers something to fight with as well."

"How do they work?"

"Well, you see, I figured materials of different qualities could function similarly to you two. Then I just tested. The machines to empty out the heavier world are still a work in progress, but I am sure I will get it right eventually."

"I believe you will. When mapping out the War Council's channels, how many minute ones did you still note, and were there any that seemed different?"

"Well, you can see here. These are the main ones; the metallic enhancements and controls are inserted into them. Here are the second-tier ones and then the negligible ones. I'm not sure what would count as different. I haven't encountered his kind that often. Just him and his father."

"Just any that would have characteristics the other channels don't. Honestly, I don't know what I'm looking for either. It could be anything."

"Let me have a look. If I recall right, there was one that didn't seem to lead anywhere. Here, look, it's a very short little line and just stops. It could be just a natural flaw, or maybe there was too much pressure at some point in him, and it was born of that. The only thing that makes it odd is that it has no purpose."

"Istrata's theory was that the heavier world simply takes over the pre-existing channels in a person. If he was born with this particular channel, one could think his father might possess it?"

"Yes, that is a fair assumption. But even if he didn't have it, it could still be a natural phenomenon."

I leaned closer to a shadow in the corner and listened for a moment. "Yes, do that."

"Do what?" Moras asked.

"Not you. But assuming he had it, we could at least be sure of the natural, hereditary nature of it."

"True."

"If I get his father to your laboratory, can you check him for it?"

"I can. Though I hardly think the new ruler is one to waste his time on things of this sort."

"He doesn't have to know, does he?"

"Are you asking me to drug and examine the King?"

"No, no. I'm simply asking you to check and maybe never mention it to him afterward."

"I...fine. But how do you expect me to pull that off?"

"I knew I could rely on you. Please get ready." I smiled.

"Now?"

"Yes, Tammaran just said that it won't take long as they have evacuated to the Peak like everyone else, and he checked Frazil is alone at the moment."

"I...certainly," Moras said, stuttering.

"I will follow along in just a moment. Do remember your drawings. I do not require them for anything else."

Moras locked the door to his laboratory as Tammaran and Veitso dragged in Frazil, inconspicuously wrapped in a cape, looking like a soldier who had had too much to drink. Getting Tammaran and Veitso to do my dirty work did not require one bit of effort after explaining the reason behind it. There wasn't really anything they were not prepared to do for their captain.

Moras pulled the glove Frazil used to control his darker tendencies on Frazil's hand and proceeded to feed him to see where everything was. The rest of us paced. As he finished, Frazil was still sleeping soundly from Veitso's tea recipe.

"He does not have it," Moras finally said.

"That means it is more likely something individual to Rime," I surmised. "I know, I know, it still could be from his mother's side." Moras was clearly about to say that it doesn't prove anything beyond a shadow of a doubt. "How about otherwise? How similar are they?"

"Quite similar. Some differences in the peripherals, and, of course, the War Council has much larger channels."

"Similar enough to say the channel structure might be an inherited quality?"

"If I had to say yes. For the most part."

"So, something else might have caused that little dead-end... Thank you, gentlemen; please smuggle our esteemed guest back as quickly as you can."

"Did you figure anything of use out?" Tammaran asked.

"Not yet. I feel I'm close to it, but I'm still missing something. Can I have the drawing where the dead-end shows? I changed my mind about not needing it."

"Take it," Moras offered, looking very happy to get rid of us.

Back in the Needle, I circled the redundant little channel and put the drawing up on the wall. My brain felt like it was about to explode from trying to connect the dots. There was no forcing the revelation. I would have to return to the puzzle later—if there was a later.

XXXIV

The ichor was rising behind us, mockingly slowly. The machines, Irinda included, had perched themselves on the highest points in the Temple, oozing ill will. At first, we didn't understand why they stayed there. Then, the reports started to come in. Guards and soldiers positioned on the walls told us about their peers and citizens starting to feel a deep hopelessness. People would go up to the wall and stare at the machines, crying, as if mesmerized by a nightmare.

After listening to the sorrowful call of the machines long enough, people simply walked off the wall to their deaths. We had to station Arvida and her kind to counter the effect where they could. There was no way for them to cover the entire wall, so we had to restrain those caught trying to join her in any way we could. More often than not, we had them locked into houses.

It wasn't easy to keep morale up when many were living in cramped temporary rooms, and everyone could now witness what the enemy was. The Temple held prayers for all every day, and it seemed to alleviate some people's mood, even those who simply passed by the buildings when prayers were said. We would need to give the citizens something to believe in, and soon. Our best chance would be to attack Irinda while there were still untainted regions below the Peak.

All soldiers capable of resisting the oppressing mood of the machines were handed out Moras's weapons. They would still be quite vulnerable to the ichor itself but a good enough fighting force against the creatures. It also meant that all the remaining consecrators could focus on the ichor in whatever way they saw fit.

"Do not even try to keep track of the forces," Rime reminded me. "I and the guard will see to them. Go after the machines, only the machines, and be like a rabid dog about it. Riestel and Heelis will prevent their escape."

"You told me all this before," I said.

A chime alerted me that Arid was coming. She slid out gracefully from the lighter world.

"We are at the places and ready," she said to me.

"Alright. Thank you."

"Not needed, created for it."

"That doesn't mean the deed isn't worthy of being praised or thanked," Rime interjected.

"We will make fortress for you to defend when ready." Arid smiled. "We only need your spark to help release it."

"Keep an eye on her and get her to your people when Irinda falls," Rime instructed Arid.

"Yes. I do so," she replied. "Many should come and watch. It will bring hope, I think. Beauty brings hope."

"You want an audience for your sacrifice?" I made sure I understood correctly.

"Yes. They will see miracle."

"Time to move," Rime ordered. "All is in place. Let us not waste the opportunity."

The soldiers and the consecrators poured out from the passages and doors of the Peak's wall into the Temple area, charging directly at their designated targets. Riestel ascended the stairs to me after Rime had joined his troops below.

"Need a ride?" he asked.

"Really?"

"Why not? He did say you needed to act fast," Riestel grinned and hugged me. Then he stepped over the ledge with his wings folding open, and the fall changed into a fast glide. I held on, looking at the sky and then the fighting below.

"That one. Let's start with it," I told him as one of the machines was heading toward a group of our men in a neighborhood park. They were fighting lesser creatures by a small ornamental water fountain.

"Alright," Riestel agreed and let go.

As the spider-legged creature looked up, Riestel tied its hands with a long glistening chain. He yanked on it forcefully, and the creature's chest was exposed. I ignited the flames over my sabers as I drew them out. As I landed on the creature's middle section, where the human part was fused into the machine's carapace, I plunged the sabers in. They hissed and sizzled as it squealed and collapsed.

"They are all turning this way!" Riestel warned me and came down.

"Good," I said under my breath as the first one jumped at us from a far.

Riestel slammed it with a house-sized ice slate, and it crashed through the walls of a red brick house to the side of the park. Two others, more scorpion-like creatures, appeared on the other side. I surrounded them with a wall of fire and leaped in. Dodging their quick jabs and the ichor they oozed was draining, but they soon made enough mistakes to allow me to cut through their legs and torsos. As each beast fell, I made sure to close the hole in them.

Once they were down, I ran to the ones disabled by Riestel's freezing gifts and finished them. More and more joined in. Our troops simply withdrew from the park and stayed at the edges, hindering the smaller creatures and preventing as much of the ichor from getting to us as they could. The whirr and zap of the charging weapons was a constant background noise.

There were around twenty machines in the park now, all slight variants of one another. You could see the development through the ages as Istrata had made them. Riestel began a rapid game of tag with me. The purpose was to evade and gather charge. The lightning was our best weapon, but it sucked out substantial amounts of life force. We needed to use it sparingly. We had wanted to use it for Irinda, but if we waited for much longer and many more of these contraptions made it here, they would soon force one of us they make a mistake or an undesired turn. Riestel knew it too.

The next time we passed each other, the air crackled, and small streams of electricity licked both of us. I shot out a signal fire straight into the air, and a hail of silver-tipped spears rained down. Riestel and I forced our opposite gifts to meet one more time, and then it all released with a magnificent boom. The lightning evaporated the first two, then pierced through the following five, leaving them smoking and immobile; the rest were knocked into a stupor.

"Where is she?" I asked Riestel. "Almost all others have come here."

"I can't see her either," he answered. "There can't be many more. Can anyone see, or has anyone seen the largest machine?"

An echo of the question went through many chains of people, but no one had any idea of Irinda's whereabouts. Then, it became abundantly clear. The screams and shouts reached all the way to us as the few undestroyed machines had scaled the wall and crossed over to the Peak instead of fighting here.

"Arid!" I yelled.

She jumped out and grabbed my and Riestel's hands. We came out to the right of Irinda as she was tearing through a fully occupied house.

"Tell Rime not to change his tactics," I ordered Arid. "They can do nothing here. Go."

Arid nodded and left.

"Let's make sure the next breath she draws makes her choke on her own blood," Riestel said. "Lightning or traditional?"

"Fire...it will have to be enough. We are down to very few reserves."

Irinda had four other machines with her. The last ones of their kind. With each movement, she dropped and slathered the thick ichor around her. It stuck on the dead and dying at her feet and quickly melted them into the same mass to be added to their forces. That's why the lighter world was draining faster than we had calculated. We were losing life force and souls directly to the viscous matter. The corruption was spreading ever faster and stronger.

Irinda and her companions were demolishing everything around them like they were trying to clear space. We attacked them fast. As we got two of them down, Irinda and the other two left had positioned themselves in a triangle, and the ichor they leaked was creating a protective sphere around them. There was a tremor in the ground. Similar to what we had felt when Rime appeared. Then it happened again.

Riestel and I attempted to cut the ichor chain around them. They repaired instantly. The ground screamed so loudly I could feel it in my bones as the three scorpion machines connected their tails. A horrible, ice-cold, sinking feeling came over me. They were summoning something. Someone. A black abyss tore open between them. Deeper and darker than any cave. There was no averting one's gaze from its unnatural pull. I could feel her in there.

I took a step back as my heart raced. It was the battle I had wanted, taunted to happen. To force her out, but standing on the precipice of the final moments made my skin feel too tight, my throat dry, and I wished my feet would carry me far away, swift as a swallow in a gale. Riestel took my hand.

His face was washed of color, and his eyes filled with worry and sadness. His posture, however, was defiant and sure-footed.

"The end is near," Riestel whispered. "I finally get to rest or live."

I wrapped my arms around his waist from the side. His heart was beating even faster than mine. I closed my eyes. No matter how much fear there was within us, we had no right to show it. The machines stopped and the ichor chain shield around them dropped. They backed off from the abyss with reverence.

From the darkness came a hand, then another. All dark as the ichor itself but beautiful, graceful, and marbled with cataract grey veins. Istrata pushed herself out from the ground. She towered over the scorpions, smiling wistfully at us as her tresses waved in the air, looking more like conscious extensions of her body than hair. Her eyes were shadowed, hollow, skull-like. Her dress was like an oil-soaked canvas clinging to her body. Her presence exuded a chill I had only ever encountered near the mass graves after the civil war. A haunting echo of life that is driven by pure hunger.

"I can't tell if it is her or just another creation," I sighed, squeezing Riestel's hand.

"I can't either. I can sense her in it, but..." Riestel replied.

"My, my. The world seems much smaller than I remember it." Istrata sighed. *"I see that my attempts to push you to a more peaceful solution have been more or less vain. I truly did wish you would all come to your senses."* She addressed us as much as she addressed each and every soul in the city. *"I will wait right here for all those who wish to seek my forgiveness and a painless existence in my embrace. Have your current rulers told you that I am here to offer peace, eternal absolution from your daily woes? I suspect they have not."* She showed a warm and reassuring smile. *"My world may seem dark and frightening to step into, but it offers you a chance to welcome paradise. I know many of you have forgotten me, so perhaps you might listen to a more recent ruler. You all respected her once. Would you speak to them, my dear friend?"*

Irinda nodded and positioned herself in a higher place so all around could see her. As she did so, Istrata looked directly at me, and I could feel her thoughts say, "I only need one moment of doubt, and they are all mine. You could save them by handing yourself over."

"My subjects," Irinda began with a commanding voice. Her presence straightened to reflect a portion of her old regality and grace.

"I ruled you for most of my life. I know I made mistakes; what ruler would not sometimes err? For the most, I did good. Even those of you who hated me as a ruler cannot say that the new regime has brought anything better with it. Chaos, suffering, change, constant uncertainty. That is what you have been given. I have pledged my entire existence to a cause that granted me life after defeat, after death. Not a mere hope of a soul and a continued life, but an assured one!"

"Arid... We need your miracle now. She will have them walking to their death otherwise," I whispered.

"Agreed. Hurry," she replied, scowling at the Queen and her slave.

As interesting as it would have been to stay and listen to Istrata's play starring a soulless puppet regurgitating her thoughts, we would not give her the time or opportunity for an endless monologue. Arid took us to the Needle's root on the point where the bows began. All the aroch elders she had brought with her were there, sitting quietly, looking at Istrata.

They were not the only ones. People outside the Needle's bows and everywhere I could see in the Peak were outside, staring at the spectacle. Some of them seemed to lean forward a little, like hesitating to take their first step.

"You remember how?" Arid asked.

"I do. I will miss you."

"Do not miss. I will still talk in spirit," Arid replied and smiled.

As Arid walked to her kind, all of them formed into what I can only describe as a living statue. The two in the middle raised Arid to sit on their shoulders; the rest formed a base for them. The people who were not bewitched by the call of the ichor began to turn their heads to us. They alerted others to us as well.

Those who had succumbed to the enemy's lures began to creep forward toward the Queen's open arms. When they reached her, they simply melted into the ichor with no release of energy or their soul. Now and then, as enough people gifted their lives to her, one could see Istrata close her eyes and sigh out of the sheer pleasure it gave her.

"Don't tarry," Riestel reminded me and nudged me forward. "They are giving themselves voluntarily. Do not hesitate too long. I will be right here to settle them."

I laid my hand on the back of the nearest aroch, at the very base of his neck. As the heat from my hand passed on to the aroch, fine glowing lines appeared on his skin. It revealed a sigil. The fire tore into the aroch's very being as I moved onto the next. I stepped on some of them in their state of metamorphosis so I could reach Arid. She glanced back at me as I raised my hand. Her metallic hair chimed as she gave me a nod and a loving smile.

"Goodbye," she whispered as my hand pressed on her back. The gems in her skin became interconnected via a web of elaborate sigils. The fire spread through her to the others, connecting them all into one.

Then it began. I backed away as fast as I could. A wave of energy pulled out from the very core of creation gushed through the Peak, leaving all alive unharmed and pushing any corrupted away from us. The aroch's bodies fused together and spread out enormous, crystalline roots. They plunged into the earth and shot out at the very edge of the Peak, where the abyss had been opened, cutting the path to Istrata. Not all people could avoid getting hit by them, but it was still a better death than in the Queen's belly.

The spirit tree reached for the skies and sprouted branches and leaves. All glowing with the light of a thousand stars. And in the very middle, Arid entwined her body around the Needle. She became the heart of the tree, the ruling spirit of it. Her branches were soon adorned with a blanket of as many different colored flowers as she had had gemstones on her. Her branches cradled around the Needle like arms protecting a child. I felt the same embrace around me. An eternal link to her and the world formed with in me.

Istrata's expression was one of loathing as she witnessed the forest growing but for this moment, she could not reach us. Her anger wasted on already conquered surroundings. The roots, branches, and leaves pulsated with life as they formed a shielding chrysalis dome around most of the Peak with Arid as the center pillar. I could see a barrier of the energy of the lighter world surrounding it like a morning mist on a mountain. As everything became quiet, Riestel placed his hand at the base of the center trunk. A blue sigil flashed at the base, then it repeated all the way to the very top and solidified the transformation into place.

I could hear people cheering as they saw the Queen cut out from a way to reach them. Some simply stared at the trees in awe, and some cried from the sheer breathtaking beauty and horror of the sudden change their world went through. I gazed at the spirit tree. The connection to the world was overwhelming and pure. The shear force and purity of being forced my eyes to water. Life, strong and wild, coursing everywhere, and yet all of its expression could so easily be wiped away and forgotten if not defended.

The air filled with a whirring sound. Small bright dots appeared in the base of the Needle. As they connected by rays of pure light into a constellation of sorts, the Source's knowledge and plans invaded our thoughts. They poured in and forced my being and mind to expand far beyond the mortal body. Then the Source stepped out from the portal of stars. Looking at it directly was almost painful. The world bend around it, like a reflection in a faulty mirror as it moved to the tree.

"*You have done well, my firstborn. May you live and guard this world as you now are,*" the Source whispered with a hand on the spirit tree. The Source closed its eyes for a moment and pressed its forehead on the bark. I felt a pulse of deep love flow through the newly formed spirit tree. A mother bidding her child a last farewell.

"How can you be here? In this plane?" I asked and looked at Riestel, who was equally taken back by the Source's appearance. The Source turned to us with shining eyes. It waved its hand slowly in a large arch as if painting the dome's figure above.

"*Holy places are junctions where the worlds unite and cross. Now, the heart of creation has been transferred and established here by your actions. It is your throne, and am your ruler no longer. The place where you will be born into your roles as caretakers. The place where your very flesh will change and the last of your mortality shall be locked away. Look around. You are in both worlds at once.*"

I had not realized it. Everyone around us, in the regular world, beyond this hazy core, was frozen into time-like statues. Even Istrata in her fury.

"*Now, it is the time to create the final bond between you and the nexus. And that, my friends, must be done by releasing me and molding this place to your liking.*"

XXXV

The Source was sat at the edge of the space, staring at Istrata in silence. Its grief was tangible in this hollowed area. Riestel was pacing around the crystal tree's roots as Arid swayed me gently on a swing made of blooming vines. I couldn't hear her anymore, only feel her. Looking out, I could see Rime among the many, just like he would have been standing before me.

I closed my eyes and imagined a whole other life unfolding before me. One where he never left my side, one where we had nothing but time to get to know one another and travel. I isolated each and every dream and emotion I had had of him and for him and allowed myself one last dream. Then, I sealed them away.

"You can lower me," I whispered. "I have an answer for him."

The vine lengthened, and my feet touched the ground. Riestel stopped in front of me and grabbed the vines.

"And?" he asked, looking flatteringly anxious.

"Yes. I'm ready."

"And you are absolutely sure? No ifs, buts, or maybes about in that wonderful head of yours? I will not allow it if you cannot fully embrace it."

"Riestel." I sighed and took his hand. "As much as I will always love him… There is no doubt nor hesitation within me about you."

"You cannot undo this fasting."

"I am aware, although if you keep this interrogation up—"

"Alright. Let's begin." Riestel took my hand. "I would prefer to take you as mine in a place like this."

The bow's garden began to transform. Riestel did not do away with the Needle or Arid and the other arochs. Instead, a lush, ever so slightly overgrown grove illuminated by fire-bellied and winged bugs dancing and swarming in the air, and the trees grew around the established structures.

Bright ferns and soft mosses with darker, warmer hues of green or brown appeared around us. Colorful, tightly packed blooming thyme spread out to cover any ground still visible with fuchsia.

A natural pond replaced the fountain. Its surface was calm, and the floating waterlilies shimmered as if they had been painted with dust from the stars themselves. A few rays of sunlight sieved between Arid's branches and cast light all the way to the pond's sandy bottom between the waterlily leaves.

"Do you like it?" he asked.

"How could I not?"

"I almost forgot..." Riestel whispered, and his clothing changed to regal, flowy silks in the ocean's colors. Every stitch and embroidery was done with a silvery thread. He looked like a painting in some exotic storybook. A warrior poet, if there ever was one.

My temple armor of chains and fabrics began to morph into a dress of lace, the color of dusky pink roses. He ran his fingers through my hair, and small braids with lilies and roses appeared.

"There. Now you look like a bride should. You will have your armor back when we step out from here."

We walked to the opposite sides of the pond. The water area grew, and stepping stones surfaced. They led to a white, domed, floating gazebo on the water. There was a delicate pedestal in the middle where the nexus shone. The roof was covered by flowering wines of yellow and pink blossoms.

One stepping stone at a time, we neared each other. Once we met in the middle, a pure white peacock flew to the banister. It raised its head high and then pecked at its own chest. The blood did not drop to the ground; it floated into the nexus. As the last of the blood rolled off the feathers, the Source shimmered and faded from this world with a content sigh. Only the peacock husk was left on the ground.

I raised my hand and reached for Riestel's hand. Our fingers met in the nexus. A whirl of golden streams spread onto our skins as we clasped our hands. The nexus stitched itself into us, connecting us forever. Riestel's eyes shone with the brightness of summer day clouds. His wings unfolded, and his skin acquired a cold tint. I could feel my body going through the same process. The scales emerged, and with them, an elaborate, small pattern between his eyebrows. Similar to the sigils on the arochs. To Riestel's unending delight, slender aroch-like horns accompanied them. They started right at the temple and arched back like a crescent moon. At least I wasn't alone in getting them.

The nexus was spent; the Source was free and gone. The world would now survive or die by our actions. We looked at each other. As strange as Riestel looked with all the markings of a god, the Source and he himself had decided on, he was just as he always should have been.

"Allow me to give you one more thing." Riestel smiled and pulled me to him. "I knew this ceremony would take place, so I took the liberty of commissioning these. I do understand if you should not wish to wear it yet to not hurt him. It will not offend me. Well…a little, obviously, but not so much that I would start to hate you. For those times we live or visit in the mortal realm."

Riestel pressed his palms against each other, and once he pulled them apart, two chains linked to a dividable pendant appeared between them. He took the pendant and broke it in two. His side had the sun and orange roses. My side had the moon and red irises.

"It's gorgeous," I said.

"Do you want to try it on?"

"Not yet. I adore it, but not yet. I couldn't do that to him, not in the middle of all this."

"As you wish," Riestel answered. He was clearly a little disappointed, but I couldn't bring myself to wear the token yet.

"You hold on to it," he requested. "If I have it, I will keep offering, and I don't want to pressure you any more than I already do."

"Thank you."

The pendant drew my gaze again and again, but there were more pressing issues to attend to than swooning over a pretty piece of craftsmanship. I kneeled by the remains of the Source. It would be a shame to not remember it in some way. The peacock's bright white feathers called to me. Nef'Adhel was usually portrayed with a disc of sabers behind her, almost like the tail of a peacock. I plucked one feather and infused it with a blade. It was wrong for a weapon to possess such beauty, and yet, I made one from each.

"Are you going to keep this appearance out there?" I asked Riestel.

"If we step out from here like this, they will see the change having taken place in the blink of an eye," he replied. "It might be too much. Incremental changes would be better for people to process. As fun as it might be to have them gasp and gawk."

"You are right. I think I will leave this marking and the scales," I said and touched the pattern on my forehead as I looked at my reflection in the pond. I would have thought I would feel more unfamiliar and uncomfortable with myself looking like this. It was the opposite. I was no longer Istrata's copy. This was the first time my body was completely my own. It was a joyous thought that almost made me cry.

"Really? I thought you didn't want to have anything out of the ordinary showing," Riestel said, amused at my change of heart.

"I didn't. But this appearance isn't for me, is it? It's for them. For the people to look at us and feel they have something equally strong on their side."

"You are finally starting to understand." Riestel smiled. "Are you happy with this place, or do you wish to add something before we leave? I realize I did much of the adjustments."

The heart of our dominion was more than I could have wished for in terms of beauty. Riestel's creation was far more detailed and thought out than mine might have been. Did it lack anything?

"I want it to be as much yours as it is mine," he said. "Paint it any way you like."

"Perhaps just a few little things, though I'm not sure if I can make them," I mused and touched the pond. The water rippled, and a school of white fishes with lilac side stripes and orange fins appeared. I bird began to sing somewhere in Arid's branches. Butterflies of different colors and sizes found their way to the flowers, as well as plump little bumblebees.

"Now, it's perfect," I told him. "Arid will have company while we are away. I don't know if she can see or sense them, but I hope she can."

"I'm sure she does. Let us go. The Queen has moved a little," Riestel noted.

He was right. Time moved ever so slowly outside, but it still moved. Her eyes were now fixed on us.

XXXVI

S tepping out from the Heart caused a modicum of pain. The serene and the sacred were replaced by screams and cries emanating from the ones trapped outside the chrysalis and their loved ones on the inside, trying to find a way to rescue them. Rime was standing right at the barrier formed by the chrysalis and the thick, wall-high roots of the enormous tree. His three closest guard members stood by him, pulling people up and through the shimmering field to safety.

"I'm not sure if we are safe or trapped," Rime remarked as we arrived. "But at least we live to fight. What will you two do now?"

"The lightning is our best weapon," Riestel answered. "But we cannot do it from in here, and we will need time and resources outside to call it."

"I will arrange as many distractions for the enemy as I possibly can," Rime said and straightened his back as he looked past us. Then he nodded slowly, keeping his gaze down for a moment. Tammaran, Samedi, and Veitso bowed their heads. I turned to see what the cause was.

At least two hundred nobles in their best attires were making their way to us. Usko was at their head, clad in fine, decorative banded mail with bright, expensive fabrics flowing from the sleeves. Each of the nobles had gilded family crests shining on their chests. It was easy to tell they were armed with Moras's inventions. People of all walks of life were bowing as they passed by, approaching us.

"I have come to pay the price," Usko announced as he stopped right below us. "We are well armed, and we will fight until the last breath. Do not let that breath go to waste. Once we are compromised, take us before the Queen does."

"Will you fight as well?" I asked.

"I will. How could I ask them something I would not do myself? We were given the title. Let us now prove that the title is not the sole thing that makes us noble," Usko replied as all the nobles behind him crossed their arms over their chests and bowed.

"What about Nyssa and Simew's children? You would leave them?"

"I have provided them with the best start to life I can. They will hopefully miss their uncle, but in order to miss their uncle, they must live."

"I will not take this sacrifice lightly."

"I know that." Usko sighed. "Just make it as painless as you can if and when the time comes."

"You have my word."

"Good. Where do you require us?" Usko asked Rime.

"You are sure you wish to do this?" Rime checked as he jumped down from the root to face Usko.

"Do not make me second guess myself in front of my kin and peers," Usko told him with a fatherly smile. "Where will we be of the most help?"

"My soldiers will charge out against the mass of creatures once the Consecratoress clears us a path. Follow them. Our task is to keep everything at bay while they summon the lightning. It is purely up to us to ensure they have enough space and time; the Temple units cannot participate as they use too much of the life force," Rime explained. "It will be a hard battle. We are no match for the endless mass."

"I will relay the orders to my men," Usko promised. "We will be right there to back you up."

"You will not be forgotten," Rime told Usko and shook his hand before the nobles went to join the troops.

Looking outward, the chrysalis was almost fully covered with the creeping ichor, but it could not find its way in yet. Some light still broke through to us.

"We need to begin," Riestel said and turned to look at the sea of people counting on us for help. "Time for a bit of theatre. I'll be right back." He smirked.

Riestel walked into one of the last beams of light falling on the root, and of course, he just had to run his hand through his hair to emphasize the effect his pretty visage had on people. The pompous godling, not that I minded the show; after all, there was nothing unpleasant on the eyes about him.

"Pray!" Riestel yelled as his wings unfolded and his scales shone like moonlit waterdrops on his skin. "Pray for the world and yourselves to keep you safe! Pray that you will not drown in the night! Pray that the only light you have in this sorrowful midnight of our world will not go out!"

Those who had been able to resist Istrata's calls to follow her dropped to their knees or lowered their heads with their fingers, touching their brows in prayer. The individual pleas began to change into the Hymn of the Revered with Riestel's lead. His clear, soul-cleansing voice rang out above all. It was a slow chant-like prayer written to no specific god. It had been rarely heard in the temples of this city. Perhaps for that reason, it carried still some ancient feeling of holiness the Temple's corrupt ways had not managed to tarnish.

"We seek the blessing of the holy. We seek shelter from the winds. We seek land to call a home. Lend us strength to live, lend us courage to prevail, lend us a kind heart to heal."

The words echoed around the Peak, and the more people joined in, the more the air filled with tiny, floating particles of energy. Their faith and hopes were creating lighter energy from nothing but their wills. The amount was meager, but the sight was astonishing and made my heart soar. The dust particle-sized globes gathered around Arid's branches and were siphoned into her, giving the chrysalis more strength to keep the Queen out.

"Are you ready?" Rime asked as he climbed back to us.

I sighed. "I don't think I will get any readier whatever happens or does not happen."

"Then we will begin the moment you step out."

"The moment I step out…" I repeated. "No time like the present, I suppose. See you on the other side of today."

"I hope so," he agreed. "The additions are quite lovely." He pointed at the scales.

"They are just a few of the changes… This is me now," I said and allowed all the gifts to show.

Rime stared at me in the green-hued light. He drew a deep breath and smiled. "Thank you for fulfilling your task. I promise I will fulfill mine, so you still have a world to rule afterward."

"What does that mean?"

"It means exactly what I said. I am the one who commands the soldiers, after all. Do not stall now. Everyone is waiting."

It was indeed time, as we were only a few rays of light away from complete darkness. The chrysalis around us allowed me to pass through without any effort. I pushed off into the ichor, and as I slowly sunk deeper, I danced to Riestel's chant while I reached out to find the spring pox victims still trapped in their bodies. When I found their location, I drew from their lives all the power I could get. As the blue flame tore through the ichor's fabric and cleared a space that could fit a village, the army rushed out to meet the creatures and the still-standing machines. It wasn't an army of thousands like against Irinda, but it was still a great many men that we had been able to kit out with the new weapons.

Riestel walked to my side as the soldiers ran past us without hesitation to an almost certain death. The sounds of battle were all too familiar.

"Are you done playing god?" I asked Riestel.

"Who's playing?" he answered with a wide smile. "But of course, we do need a world. It would be rather depressing to be a god of nothing."

We could still hear the people chant in the chrysalis, so once more, we began to gather the force for the lightning. Reaching into the very structures of reality felt as natural as breathing after absorbing the nexus. I closed my eyes to dance blind as I needed my concentration elsewhere. As my body danced, my mind was alert in the lighter world. Every time a fighter of ours died, I reached out for them and pulled their life force within me before the Queen could envelop it in her ichor. I guided their souls to the lighter plane, but I did not allow them freedom just yet. In case we would also need to consume them. Riestel helped to gather and guide them.

Even in the lighter world, I could feel the ichor rise around us and swallow the bodies of the men and women fighting. The more peculiar thing to me was Istrata's inaction. She merely towered over her forces, looking down at us like pieces on a board. If she had participated herself instead of just directing them, we would have lost many men much faster. Not that she truly needed to do much. Her army was an ever-rising tide that we had no hope of winning without destroying her.

I returned my attention fully to the world as the lightning was released. The pressure and the rumble pushed everyone further from the point of release. The few machines fell with the first bolt. Then the world answered. The spiraling clouds above us joined the fight as natural lightning found its way down to destroy them to pieces and break the ichor's bonds. Istrata pulled away slightly to avoid the lighting, seemingly content to see whether

her creations could best us or we them.

We kept a close eye on the arcs of lightning as they passed through the guiding rods and spears. Finally, a large jolt hit Irinda's machine. After it passed through the ichor between us and her, she was stunned long enough for us to reach her from the cleared path. We rushed to her. She had once been a formidable enemy, and she still was the strongest of the machines, but facing her was only one step on our way to the Queen. A dangerous, unyieldingly annoying step, but a step we had to clear nonetheless.

This time we had no need to concentrate on the ocean of ichor and we had ample space to maneuver. All our actions were free to be directed only towards her. The wailing tested our nerves. The scorpion's legs our speed and awareness. The moment Irinda focused on Riestel, I burned through the ichor armor that shielded the machine's structures. When the metal frame was exposed and her attention turned to me, Riestel was able to shatter parts of her. Leg by leg and joint by joint, the scorpion creaked and tilted.

Once the machine was gutted all the way to the knees, it became almost immobile. The ichor sea rushed to her aid. I climbed the center husk, trying to keep from the ichor's grasp. Riestel pushed it away as much as he could. I reached the husk where her remaining human parts resided.

I placed my hands on the protective barrier and forced the fire into it. Molten cracks appeared and widened until it shattered and left her defenseless. I felt the Queen retreat from Irinda. Abandoning her in her final moment after she had given her soul and life to her cause. I placed my hand on Irinda's heart and forehead, a small light of recognition sparked deep within her eyes. Her head twitched. She frowned as if she would have felt the wounds that killed her once for the first time. She coughed up black ichor and began to cry like a lost child. Loud and uncontrolled. The pure panic in her voice made me freeze.

Riestel hoisted himself to us quickly. As Irinda saw him, her cries mellowed to a weep.

"Hush," Riestel whispered and smiled. "You need to rest; you've been used enough for one life."

Irinda reached for his hand, and Riestel allowed her to gasp it.

"You do it," she said. "Not her."

"Close your eyes," Riestel told her as he placed his free hand on her temple. Irinda took a sharp, shallow, pitiful breath and then she was gone, only a small puncture wound on her temple revealed how she died. The Queen straightened herself having decided to cast away her last knight and fixed her eyes on us. Just her stare alone pulled some of our fighters down into the ichor for them to emerge in the blink of an eye later corrupted and turning on us.

"Rime, contest her!" I yelled. "Riestel, chain her."

I charged toward the Queen. Rime waded into the black sea and plunged his hands into it. I could see many of the figures stop or even turn away from our fighters. Every muscle of Rime's body was working to exhaustion to wrestle control of the ichor from the Queen. Riestel's chains slithered on the ground, looking for their moment. Then, when the Queen turned toward Rime, the chains shot out and wrapped around Istrata's arms, allowing me one brief moment to lunge right into her body of ichor as the occasional lightning strike still wreaked havoc on her stores and creatures.

Lunging inside her, I saw her focus on Riestel. Black waves battered him and pulled at him. To control the chains keeping the Queen's arms from pulling me out, he could not defend himself. The army was of no use, all soldiers simply washed away with each passing moment.

Entering her ichor form, I felt a crushing pressure all around and lost sight of the outside world. I separated my conscious mind and, without discrimination, pulled all the force from the nobles I could. I opened my arms and released an orb of blue fire as large and as hot as I had the strength and capability to produce within her. At first, the flames seemed to stall around me, but finally, I managed to push it out from her form as it ripped in two. The entire Peak outside the chrysalis had all things taller than a one-story building destroyed, but the ichor was gone from an equal area.

I was flown out from inside her by the force. As I gathered to my feet, Istrata was bleeding ichor profusely. I stood among the destruction, listening and waiting. This was the most I could do with our current resources. If she had not died, I would have to use the souls of the soldiers and the nobles, as well as those of people inside the chrysalis praying and hoping to live another day.

Istrata's body, torn in half, tilted and fell slowly on the remains of a nearby building close to Riestel as he had been containing her. My fire had melted the chains from her hands. As she laid on the building, she suddenly opened her eyes and swatted Riestel away with such force he went through a pillar at the edge of the battle ground.

"Riestel!" I called out as the world seemed to spiral out of control around me. The Queen sighed and fell back on the building with a weary grin. Her eyes closed.

I started to run towards Riestel. He was on the ground, completely still. His wings folded over his body like a bird flown against a window. I could see Riestel's hair was stained with blood. My feet felt heavy and painfully slow as I scrambled over bodies and rubble to get to them. I fell to my knees at Riestel's side. I held out my hand to touch him but I couldn't. As much as I wanted to, my hand would not move an inch more. What if I touched him and he was dead? That was a reality that would kill me. If he died, I would be alone for all eternity. Just like the Source. Elona would lose her father, the world would lose the counter balance to me.

Rime kneeled beside me and lowered my hand.

"I will check. You do not need to," he told me.

"He can't die now," I whispered. "If he dies, I… can't… I…"

Rime placed his wrist under Riestel's nose. His face frowned. The world spun around me. My field of vision blurred. I tried to get up but fell back on my knees as a sharp, cold pain went through my heart. Breathing became difficult.

"Isa," Rime called. "Hold on. He's alive…" Rime rose to his feet and steadied me with a hand on my shoulder. "Because, of course he is." There was a hint of relief and disappointment in Rime's voice. "His breathing is stabilizing. He is healing himself."

"Why did you frown! I thought he was dead because of that," I yelled.

"I was concentrating," Rime sighed. "At least, I know how you truly feel about him now."

"Riestel?" I called and touched his face as my vision returned to normal. He shook his head a little and opened his eyes. The left one had a broken blood vessel, which began to heal fast as soon as he regained his wits.

"Don't scare me like that," I whispered and pressed my head to his neck.

"Have some patience. I can't heal with you fussing over me. Is she gone?" Riestel asked and got up. As he did so, the rose pendant fell out of his shirt. He moved to hide it, but Rime bent down and snatched it with his right hand and stared at it for a while before letting it go.

Rime turned halfway away. His countenance was sullen and sorrowful. It must have been awful having to witness my feelings for another this way.

Then, we heard laughter.

Istrata's upper body twitched and propped itself up with its hands, and the ichor she had bled began to slowly create her anew.

"You darling creatures," the Queen said joyfully. *"Did you truly think this was me? A mere reflection built of ichor. This was a most amusing experience. Let me just gather myself, and we may repeat it as many times as you wish. You will never destroy me when I reside in all the worlds."*

"There's no more... I can't take any more from the world... Unless I begin to destroy souls of the now living... I had wanted to save their souls at least," I uttered, feeling like a failure.

Rime grabbed my hand and pulled me to my feet and to the side a little.

"Do you have one?" Rime asked, annoyed. "Did you accept it?"

"What?"

"The other pendant of the pair. Do not treat me like a fool. I know a fasting token when I see one."

"I...don't see how this concerns you, especially now," I deflected, and Rime frowned disapprovingly. "Honesty, then...I'm going to spend an eternity with him. It didn't exactly seem like a proposal one should decline. The ritual that made us what we now are also bound us. You knew it would be like that, but I did not wish to wear the symbol until all of this was over."

"I'm aware. Do you have it with you?"

"She does," Riestel answered in my stead as I hesitated.

"Show me."

"Why? There is no point to any of this anymore," I insisted and looked at the Queen. She seemed to enjoy listening to our little palaver. She even made a gesture with her hand to keep on talking as she pieced herself together, humming cheerily.

"Show me," Rime insisted.

I pulled the pendant out from a pocket and offered it to him. Rime held it in his palm. Then he took my hands into his, still holding on to the jewelry.

"I want to tell you something," Rime whispered.

"Please, do not," I pleaded, as I felt like my heart was being stabbed.

"I have to. I will not have another chance. I am not mad at you, not even at Riestel. I have to get this off my chest."

"Let him speak," Riestel urged. "I'll just look away for a moment."

"Thank you," Rime replied to him as Riestel turned his head away from us.

"Isa," Rime said quietly. "Every moment I spent with you made me happy, this ending, this fate, the chance to bear a burden no one else can… I was always going to be consumed by this, but with you, at least, I mattered to someone as myself. To have met you, to have been loved, to have something left of me in the world, even if just a memory you carry, is something I never thought I would have."

"Why are you saying this?" I asked, trying to avoid his eyes and keep myself from falling apart.

"Whatever keeps that unholy thing alive is in the heavier world. I can get it out."

"No, don't. Please."

"You can let me go now; finding the cure, if there ever once one, is too late. We are out of time."

"I… I'm so sorry," I said, my voice faltering.

"Turn around," Rime told me, and without waiting for me to do as I was told, he stepped behind me and put the pendant on my neck. "It looks beautiful. Like it should have always been on your neck." He smiled. "Promise me two things. One, you will be happy without guilt. Two, make sure my guard has no say in what kind of statue I get. I will haunt you if you let them make it."

I couldn't utter a word. He leaned to embrace me tightly and pressed a kiss on my lips as he parted. My left wrist burned as my tears fell on it. Then Rime turned to Riestel, who was giving him a stare colder than the ocean's floor.

"You turned around too early. I'm not going to apologize for that," Rime told him. "Bring her the happiness I could not."

"Will do, War Council," Riestel replied without any mocking tone.

"Good. Now, I can go with my heart at peace and drag the Queen's remains out from the pits of the darkest ocean. I'm sure you can keep this oversized version of her amused while I do so."

"Certainly, I was just about to ask it to tea," Riestel answered and spat out a bit of blood. "You know, reminisce about the good old times."

"Do your worst," Rime replied with a hint of actual amusement. "But I do recommend stepping back to higher ground because I won't stop until every last drop is here in this middle plane."

"You will die," I said, looking down at my wrist where my tears had left a marking very much like a bracelet I used to wear.

"I'm fully aware of that," Rime replied and glanced at the sky. Then he closed his eyes and tore a connection to the heavier world, lodging himself between the two membranes as a living door.

"Rime! Stop! I will try again!" I pleaded. This was not right. He did not get to leave me and then be the one to die for this world. He deserved better.

Rime looked at me with his eyes darkening and shook his head gently.

"Let him go as he wishes," Riestel told me and pulled me away. "If you are to save him, you must hurry to end her."

"No!"

"Let him go!" Riestel pulled me into an embrace and flew us back to the chrysalis. I couldn't even see Rime anymore. There was just a constant stream of the ichor pouring out over his entire being. The only consolation was seeing Istrata's pupils enlarge and her movements become more frantic to repair herself.

"I...need to go to the lighter world. Right now," I decided as I recalled the Queen's words. "She said we cannot kill her as she resides in all the worlds. That means it is not just this or the heavier one. Something is still left of her in the lighter, too. If I'm quick enough, we might save him."

"Then go. I will keep piercing her cold, lifeless heart here as many times as it takes."

"Can you? She almost killed you. I cannot lose you both."

"Please, I was just distracted the first time looking at you, diving into her without any warning. Now, she will have my full attention."

"You get distracted by me a lot, don't you?"

Riestel smiled. "The proper amount a man should."

XXXVII

Entering the lighter world made me want to break down. It was so barren. Where before you could conjure up thousands of lights and spirits and imagine anything for it to come true, there was now a hollow wasteland of shimmering, sickly specs of light and power. Not much more could be used without this world dying.

Steeling myself to focus and fight through the hurt and fear, I managed to bring out the nexus and its strands from within me. Without any hesitation, I jumped into the Queen's memories. Pushing through to the beginning of the contamination. To that space where they all ended. Then I found it. The connection. She had separated her soul, her body, and her life force. The island. The island was her private, lighter world, hiding among all other structures. It had to be. That would have given her access to the cycle of souls, and that would have forced the soul I now called mine to always seek it out, to try to unite with her.

It was the tiniest, narrowest, an almost nonexistent connection to travel through, but travel through I did. The island seemed as real as anything I had ever seen. The people were stuck in time as statues. There was no movement, no breath. They were simply waiting to reset like pieces on a board. Walking there felt like a nightmare. It was the last place I wanted to be in, and I could see I wasn't supposed to be here. My presence, the way it was, was twisting things, similar to the memories one could corrupt.

Her ideal was different from what I remembered, so the two visions fought, causing all sorts of small anomalies. The neighbor used to have four goats as far as I could remember, and I was sure one had been black. Now, there were three goats and two halves of one. A dark-gray head just floating among the others and a black body lying down on the hay. The entire set piece was made from her gathered life force.

"Hello, Cowe," I said to the lifeless version of the man, still standing in the last position I remembered him in. Looking over my falling body. The churning sea below the cliffs looked like a heavenly gate compared to the idea of having to live here even once more. Reality or not, it had been my life.

"Burning you down will be a highlight of this visit," I told him and lifted my hand to ignite him, but no flames came out. Of course not. This was her lighter world. I had no powers here yet. I would have to destroy it some other way or change it to such a great extent that I could control its reality.

"You can try," Cowe replied and caught me off guard. "I had not anticipated you to make it all the way here."

"Ah, it's you." I sighed. "I'm not really in the talking mood, creator dearest."

"Neither am I. You three are hounding me on every level. I do so appreciate the opportunity to feel Riestel killing me over and over again. Very underhanded even for you."

"Well, honestly, killing you had been killing him for decades, so take a little responsibility for his enthusiasm."

"I think not. You will not be returning from here anyway," Istrata informed me with Cowe's voice. The people nearby began to move toward me.

"Die here, die everywhere. Unless you are like I am," she said with my pretend mother's mouth.

"I rather not. I have to get back to your former love and spend a glorious eternity with him," I said to annoy her and managed to find my sabers. They were forged in the lighter world, so they at least worked here as well.

Istrata smiled. "I will eventually overrun you."

The sabers were a better weapon than the pitchforks and shovels of the islanders, but fighting close to the cliff and having more and more of them show up wasn't boding well for me without the fire. A piercing pain forced me on my knees as Cowe's friend withdrew a stake from my side. The blood seemed all too real.

For a moment, I almost bought into the illusion, but then all the people froze. It allowed me to control my fear and shift focus. I could see that Riestel had just detached the Queen's head in the middle world. She could not keep her consciousness in all places at once. The shock of dying in one place meant that she was stunned in all planes. This brief pause granted me time to concentrate and remind myself of the quality of my wounds here. My side patched itself adequately.

"You know…I believe beyond the shadow of a doubt that you people were beautiful fluffy bunnies. And I distinctly remember that you were being held in a cage over there."

After a few attempts, some of the people finally transformed and were sucked into a caged area. At that moment, the Queen returned to her chosen host. She didn't notice it for a moment, but the squeaking and the furry paws gave it away soon enough, and perhaps the fact that I looked like a giant from the bunny's perspective.

"Truly amusing," she hissed as she molded herself a proper body within the memory.

"I was a little lonely with you gone. Is your head alright, or does it ache a bit?"

"Quite fine, thank you," the Queen answered with a faked smile. "I am sorely disappointed with your manners. Once again. How can someone who I gave the world to be so immature?"

"Do you not like bunnies? I'm not sure what that says about your character."

The Queen's crooked smile widened.

"Do you have any idea where you have come? This island is my creation from start to finish. Do you honestly believe you can somehow wrestle me for its control?" the Queen inquired and returned the people as they were. Though not all of them. Centuries had deteriorated her memory just as anyone else's. As they approached, I jumped from the cliff, as there was definitely a path there. I'm sure I had run that sandy path to the shore dozens of times to gather seashells.

"This trickery will not get you anywhere!" the Queen yelled as she erased my addition.

"I see it quite differently!" I replied and pressed my hand on the bedrock on the beach below. Caves. Of course, there had been caves. A winding system of caves, and it had not been bedrock. Sandstone. Indeed. The whole island was built on sandstone, I thought as I ran through the caves, sending ripples of change throughout the entire area.

The Queen's mind restored all the changes it could find, but every time she was stunned by Riestel wounding her fatally in the normal plane, I changed hundreds of things, things she would likely never even notice. I turned the island once again to sandstone and kept adding on the caves. Tunnels after tunnels. In a long enough time period, the raging storm around us and the waves that filled them more and more would cause it to collapse. Or had it already collapsed? Maybe it, indeed, had already collapsed, and everything on this island had fallen into the deep, cold embrace of the sea.

I hovered in the air as the island broke off piece by piece and was swept under the raging ocean. The feeling of power and freedom to destroy something that had been an endless prison to me was indescribable. The Queen appeared back, and the destruction stopped.

"Fine. You have broken my toy beyond all recognition." She sighed. "But I do not have need of it anymore."

A storm wind pushed me down toward the sea.

"I only need Riestel to succeed a few more times, and this precious place of yours will be nought but a broken nightmare."

"Indeed, you do. However, might I remind you that he is battling me alone, and I cannot die. He is at the very edge of his strength by now. Bleeding, panting, shivering... Once he falters, you are both doomed. Or are you so naïve to think that I have not hit him back at all?"

"He will not falter."

"He will. I know him."

"You do not. Not as you think," I replied and allowed myself to fall into the sea. Under the waves, I focused on the other plane for a moment. I could see the Queen was not exaggerating. Riestel was gorgeously defiant, but his exhaustion was clear as his hair was moist with sweat and blood and his body bruised. I opened my eyes in the middle plane and rushed to the edge of the chrysalis, where Heelis and Merrie stood watching all unfold.

"Help him," I ordered Heelis. "Get everyone and help him!"

"You said there isn't enough life to sustain us helping?" Heelis replied, surprised. "Will it not destroy the world as certainly as her deeds?"

"Trust me. Hurry!"

"Will you kill people to fuel us?" Heelis asked, slightly hesitant.

"Heelis!"

"Alright, alright," she yielded and touched the chrysalis. "How do I get out?"

"Pray to Arid. I have to go before I drown."

"Before you what? What is going on?"

"Help him!" I ordered and sat down, beginning to shift my focus back to the other world.

I could see Heelis yell my orders to Tammaran and him jumping into action. Heelis stepped through the barrier and ran to Riestel's side. At first, I could hear him tell her to get lost, but after a few equally friendly words from Heelis, they began to coordinate as other consecrators charged out to help them.

The sea was hard to get out from as, for the first few seconds I was back, the ice-cold waters stung and pulled me. It took all my wits to find my composure and find the correct way to the surface. The remains of the island were now covered in snow. Istrata had changed all to a winter scene. This was it. She was not trying to keep the island together anymore.

I began to change anything and everything I could think of while running away from her. The fabric of this pocket began to deteriorate. She was no longer the sole master of this isolated reality, which meant I was able to use my fire.

The moment she located me, a stone hand shot out from under what was left of the island and attempted to grab me. The ice forming on the ocean shattered into thousands of floating pieces. Some flew into the air and hovered there, as there was no one to keep track of the laws of this creation anymore. As Istrata had me running for my life, I kept imagining the entire globe the island scene was trapped in becoming smaller and smaller.

As I landed on a sliver of ice, my feet became trapped. The hand swatted me down like a fly and clenched into a fist. I tried to move but could not free myself. Bracing for the impact, I imagined a shielding wall. Covering behind it, I waited, but the punch never landed. I looked from behind my shelter. She had been stunned again.

Winded, I forced myself to take out my sharpest dagger, the one I used to carve things in the lighter world. I cleared a path to the bottom of the ocean and sunk the dagger into the very membrane that contained this island. I pushed and pushed until it yielded toward the middle plane, and all the energy that had formed the island began to siphon into a whirlpool emptying to the battlefield where Riestel and the others waited for the Queen to once again come to life.

The energy from the lighter world rained on them and the Queen's body. As all the ruins and bodies washed out and became pure energy, I detached myself and returned to my own body through the lighter world, making sure to tear an opening from the island to there as well. The amount of energy now flowing locally in the lighter world and the middle plane was considerable. Hundreds of years of her collected power. Riestel healed himself in the blink of an eye. Heelis looked around at the rain of stardust.

"See, trusting me is good," I remarked as I caught up to them.

"What happened?" Riestel asked as he embraced me, keeping an eye on the Queen's body.

"She is no longer connected to the lighter world. The life force she fashioned into the island is partly here and partly out of reach for her. She had created a threefold safety mechanism for herself. One part there, one part in this world, and one in the heavy world."

The Queen opened her eyes, a little disorientated as the part of her life force I had not been able to alter flowed into the ichor body. The ichor and lighter energy did not seem to co-exist well at all, but as they recognized, they were a part of the same creature; they kept trying to unite.

"What *did* you *do?*" the Queen asked, a little taken back at the sound of her own voice. "This *will* not *stop me.* I am *still not within your* reach."

"I would not count on it; the third part will be dragged out of darkness soon enough," Riestel gloated.

"Can you hold her for now?" I asked. "I have to find Rime before he kills himself."

"We have been holding for two days already," Riestel replied.

"I took two days?" I asked and felt my hopes dwindle. I had been so focused on getting the Queen out that I had not even noticed the hundreds who had given their lives in this arena of rocks and ice Heelis and Riestel had built during their attack on Istrata. The black sea of ichor had filled the entire city below us, and it didn't just creep on the surface of buildings, painting them in an oily dark sheen; it was truly filling every nook and cranny.

"You did," Heelis affirmed. "We still have some fight left in us."

"Two days?" I muttered, and a cold fear tugged at my heart as I ran toward the ichor sea. Rime had had the ichor flowing through him for two days. Two days of pure agony and pain.

Istrata struck her hand down before me.

"*Are* you not *going to play* with me?" she asked.

"You have plenty to entertain you. Out of my way!"

The Queen turned to Heelis, who had just flung a boulder at her. Istrata's face soured, and she called more of her army to her. They were everywhere now. Fortunately, pulling from the energy I had released from the island, I had no issues clearing my way closer to the point where Rime had been. I called the scales and jumped into the ichor.

Swimming ever deeper with the light from my scales helping me to navigate through the destroyed buildings. I swam and swam but could see no sign of Rime. Then I heard a faint call. However, it was more like a feeling than an actual call. Pushing through the heavy ichor and against a current of sorts and chasing shadows that tried to harass me, I saw the doorway where Rime stood. Seeing him there like a solemn guardian between our planes made me calmer. He had been able to hold on. Everything was still possible. His hand was holding tightly onto something within the opening. As I reached for him, he flinched in pain from the scales. His eyes opened, fully black. He nudged me to follow his arm.

I pushed my hand into the crushing pressure of the darkness. The ichor was thick as oil there, and the scales barely illuminated anything more than a finger's length from them. I saw the Queen's once human body. She was trying to free herself from Rime's hold, but he was not having it. Neither was strong enough to get the other one to yield. I grabbed the Queen's arm and pulled on her with all my strength.

The ichor attacked me and squeezed as hard as it could, but finally, we got the Queen through the doorway. I could feel Rime's body sigh with relief. A multitude of shadows attacked me and ripped Istrata from us. She quickly escaped toward the other two parts of her.

Rime positioned himself in front of the doorway to keep her from getting back; then, he nodded to me to go after her. As I swam a little way away from Rime, I turned back to look at him. He had closed his eyes, and the current of the black ichor flowing to our world increased. I wanted to take him back with me, back to the surface and the sun and stars. Every bit of me wished I could have forced him to detach from the opening, but that would have offered Istrata a way back to safety. Forcing myself to honor his choice, I continued to the surface as hope died within me.

XXXVIII

On the surface, I saw the Queen's body shield itself while it merged with the large ichor form we had been fighting all this time and the lighter energy from the island. The small, mortal body of hers melted halfway into the ichor body. The lighter energy stolen from the island and cast into this plane swirled around her and condensed into her human remains that had been hidden in the heavier world.

"Watch out!" I called to the soldiers as I could feel she gathered energy. "She can use the consecrator's gift again."

There was a sudden drop in the life force around us as Istrata let out a wave of orange fire. Riestel was able to shield most of us from it.

"How is that possible?" Tammaran asked as he ran to me with Veitso a few steps behind him.

"It is her original body. She hid it in the heavier world. The channels are there, but she has no more connection to the lighter world. She cannot use the power from there. Only what she can find from here. Like the machines, she can only use souls that still linger here."

"Did you see Rime?" he pressed.

"I did."

"He's alive then?" Veitso checked nervously.

"He's alive," I told him and lowered my gaze.

"He's alive!" Veitso repeated joyously. "Let me finish this fight, and we can get him home to heal." He had too much confidence for my liking.

"Yes. Certainly," I replied and nodded. I didn't want to discourage them at this point, but this was not the moment to get careless due to hastiness.

As Veitso returned to Samedi and they began changing the orders for a full-on attack, now that they had the consecrators at their disposal as well, Tammaran stood quietly by my side.

"Rime's not coming back, is he?" he finally asked.

"It might be too late, I don't know," I affirmed his doubts.

"So, there is a chance he could still be saved?"

"I don't know, alright? I wish I knew. I just…feel utterly powerless in trying to solve this."

"You are far from it. We need to act quickly if he is to have any chance," Riestel said and hugged me from behind. "Stop thinking and do your best."

"I owe him that. Let us put an end to her," I said, looking at the Queen. "I will keep the ichor away. You go for her."

I danced on the edges to keep the ichor from drowning anyone. The soldiers and the consecrators attacked her in waves with Riestel's lead. Their lives seemed so easily burned out or drowned by her. First, dozens, then hundreds of ordinary people. It was a game of speed between us, a test of who could get to the dead and dying first to take their souls.

I had lost track of everyone fighting. Having to use every ounce of my strength to diminish her resources and keep her waves from dragging us all to a watery grave made it impossible for me to focus on anything else. Riestel was the only one who I could easily tell was alive.

Istrata's face shone with twisted enjoyment over this battle. She showed no signs of tiring or slowing down. The longer the fight continued, the more people who had at first refused to fight made their way out of the chrysalis and joined us. I could see Arvida standing on the roots inside the chrysalis as the ichor was being burned out from its surface by the prayers of the people inside. Merrie was beside her, peering worriedly at the battling masses below. Then I heard Merrie cry out as she jumped down to the battlefield.

Her light wisp of a figure blew through the fighting like a spring zephyr.

"Merrie! Come back!" Arvida yelled. "Isa! Stop her!"

I had no idea what was going on and why Merrie, whose airy powers, though formidable but not at all battle-trained, would try to help us. Her kind had been specifically told to stay put and help people keep their hopes up. I could see she was heading to an area behind Istrata.

While running after her I realized, the only reason she would jeopardize herself like this was Veitso. His group had to be in trouble. Once I caught up with Merrie, we both saw a hundred creatures around a group of twenty men who were dying fast.

"I will get him out," I told Merrie. "Get to safety."

Clearing out he creatures as fast as I could while saving my strength for the Queen, I got to the troops.

"Come, let's get you to a better position," I urged them.

Veitso nodded. He looked tired and bruised. The corner of his eye bled, making it hard for him to see with his left eye. Merrie ran towards him.

"I told you to..." I began as Veitso pushed past me and slumped at Merrie's feet as he had blocked a spear of ichor flying at her. There was nothing to do to save him. I felt his death immediately. Merrie shrieked and stood above Veitso almost paralyzed.

"He's gone," Merrie whimpered, and her eyes welled. "I didn't get to tell him I loved him." She kneeled beside Veitso. "You promised to make it through! People do not leave me!"

"Merrie...You need to get back to the chrysalis. Right now," I told her after taking a deep breath to control my emotions. I wanted to scold her for her recklessness.

"No!"

"Merrie, I have to take him, or the Queen will."

"No! You both have eaten enough. Leave us alone."

"I can't. Please don't make me do this in front of you."

"You will not take him from me!" she screamed and got up. "I will fight you if I have to. He will get his sending off in a proper way."

I had never seen this humming happier than anyone girl so broken. She had been one of the first to accept me all those years ago when I needed to gain the Temple's trust. She had embraced me, annoyed me, and gladdened me.

"I must do it, Merrie, or the Queen will," I repeated.

"You will not!" she insisted and got up. As she raised her hands to attack me, I could see shadows moving behind her in the ichor. It meant that a creature of the Queen was condensing nearby.

"Merrie, I can still save you, but I cannot save him. If you stand down now, you will live."

Merrie frowned and whisked a sharp sliver of stone at my face with a gust of wind. I could feel a few lazy blood drops pushing out from my skin from the cut on my temple. Merrie's eyes were wide and gleaming. There was no talking her down. She had never faced much adversity in her life, being always praised, and it showed at the worst moment. Either I fought her for the chance of saving her and lost precious time, or I would take them both before the Queen did.

"Then I'm sorry, I have no time for this," I replied. "You were one of the kindest people I ever encountered. The world will miss you."

"What?" She huffed and realized something was behind her.

A creature of ichor lunged at Merrie and tore her throat open. Merrie stumbled a few steps and fell backward next to Veitso more gracefully than most living dancers could have. I burned the creature, closed my eyes, and took their souls.

The amount of energy given by them was more than most people. The pure power and life force released knew no sorrow or pain. It always brought with it a wave of joy. The pleasure derived from their deaths was a horrible thing. It was my body's natural response, but it made me feel so dirty. I prayed that no one had paid much attention to this scene. The guilt was enough as it was without witnesses.

I turned back to the Queen. The consecrators and soldiers around her looked tired and stretched to their very limit. Each attack cost us lives and ate at our morale. My body was stiffer and slower as well, despite the boost it had just received. The battle had gone on so long, all the way from the lighter world. Whatever the end was, I was too worn-out to be afraid of death anymore. An end would suffice. As the Queen threw back more fighters and took their souls for her sustenance, I decided to attempt to participate in the attacks while trying to shield people from the ichor.

"Aren't you tired of failing yet?" I taunted Istrata, getting her to turn towards me.

She frowned and cocked her head to the left. "And how *do you know*, I am failing?"

"Well, you did get kicked out of two worlds already. Only one to go."

"I do like *this side* of you," she replied. "Come then, *child*."

The smaller, mortal body controlled the fire, and the ichor body still controlled the sea and the creatures. As we danced around each other, I begun to find a rhythm with Riestel. We could weave around her, and even though we could not afford to call large storm bolts, we could summon smaller ones directed at her. The first hits sent her backwards and tore of a piece of her arm. She dove into the sea and emerged whole again.

All of this seemed like a waste. She had too many resources for us to ever win. We needed rest and food. She had no such hindrance. What did I know of her? Of the way she was made? Her connection to the lighter world and her entrance to the heavier world was fully gone therefore she could definitely be killed. Her mortal body, a base of her memories and her past, was entwined with the ichor. The ichor form was the least important one for her existence. A controlled armor she had injected into herself.

The battle ground was not the best place for thinking. Istrata caught my leg in a painful way with her fire. I was able to get to Heelis's as she quickly built stone cover while Riestel blunted her attack on me.

"Looks bad," Heelis said, frowning. "Do you need a healer?"

"No. I can't afford one," I grimaced. "I need to be out there." I took a deep breath and walked to the edge of the stone wall. My leg felt like it was still on fire.

A light, like a rapidly rising moon, illuminated the battlefield as I stepped out. It was the chrysalis. It had filled to the brim with the prayers of the people there. The entire battle quieted down at the sight. The Queen stopped to look at it as her forces ceased all movement. The serene blue light pulsed and radiated hope. The wind carried small shining particles, energy created by the prayers, over to us. The Queen instinctively reached out to touch one of them. The light sent ripples through her, and she withdrew her hand as if stung.

Like Istrata, I reached for one of the lights. I took it into my hand. The energy was soothing. It had a similar essence to Riestel's powers. Just to experiment, I pressed it to the skin on my leg. It spread like ocean foam and healed the skin. The bruising was still there but the burn was gone. Of course, the lights carried the energy of life itself. It was self-created, the very raw material of creation willed into existence for our benefit by the people wishing for our triumph.

Seeing and feeling it made my mind clear. Istrata was poisoned, the light essence of the world rejected the ichor. She needed to be cleansed similar to Rime, but I couldn't both strip the ichor armor and push this into her. Riestel had to be the one to cleanse her. He couldn't destroy the ichor, but he could wash it out.

Riestel was on the other side of the battlefield. Getting to him past hundreds of ichor creatures and Istrata's flames wasn't an easy task. When he noticed, I was trying to get to him, he started to make his way toward me. He was as sweaty and weary as I was but not even close to giving up.

"I have a plan," I whispered once I could touch him. The quick embrace felt like a safe haven.

"I'll try anything at this point."

"Did you see how she reacted to the light?"

"I saw her flinch at its touch."

"It is what we need. It is a healing power. It's your power to use. I will burn holes; you need to get the prayers to hit her when she is exposed and sink them into her."

"Are you suggesting we heal her instead killing her?"

"We need to heal her for her to die."

"Alright. I will siphon them from the chrysalis whenever I can."

With all my remaining powers, I called the disc of feather sabers around me and lit them with the blue flame. The constant demands of the battle weighed heavily on me. It wasn't easy to dodge her attacks, and she was able to block mine almost always but every now and then I managed to cut her. The burning sables ensured that the wound took longer to close. At those moments, Riestel charged at her and pressed a light to her skin. Each time it made her ichor form ripple and her mortal form seem a little less corrupted. The more prayer lights we forced into her, the more she hesitated with her attacks.

Slowly, she lost control of the dark ichor sea. All her faculties were occupied with keeping her ichor form and her being together. The more cornered she became, the more unpredictable and devastating her attacks became. Sometimes she didn't even seem to see us anymore. She merely released waves of fire indiscriminately into all directions. We ordered more and more people to back off to save their lives and keep her from gaining more souls.

Overwhelming exhaustion begun to set in. I could barely produce flames anymore. I simply felt empty. We were so close, and yet I felt as if I had nothing more to give to the fight. The Queen's ichor hand struck me to the ground. Heelis was closer to me than Riestel, so she took my corner of the field under her protection to distract the Queen as Riestel made his way to tend to me.

"Are you hurt?"

"Not badly. Just scrapes. I'm sorry," I told him as I felt lightheaded and unable to push myself of the ground. "I can't get my body to move. I'm so tired."

"Then you rest," he said and brushed my hair from my face. "I helped her to start this, I will help her to finish this." Riestel's eyes turned ice-white as he rose up.

"I can't let you go alone."

"And if you cannot even stand, what will you do against her? Shut up and breathe. I will send Heelis to shield you."

I watched Riestel run back out, and Heelis make her way to me. She had been an invaluable help during the battle, keeping her distance when required and stepping in to help when needed. The prayer lights hovered everywhere around this broken mess of a city. I had loved this city the moment I arrived. I muttered a prayer to the deep night sky with all the others. It was the first time in days I had had a moment even to recognize the time of day.

Riestel's ice-wings blocked the Queen's attacks as he slowly fought his way closer to her. His moves were still fluent and quick as he struck to her side with blades and hail and forced in more of the light. I turned to my side and watched as she pushed him off of her. Riestel landed awkwardly but managed to find his footing before the follow up strike landed.

Again and again, relentlessly, Riestel pushed at her defenses, ignoring his own wounds like an attack dog with a singular purpose giving her no moment of respite. I got on to my knees. The exertion almost made me lose consciousness. Heelis shook her head and pointed at the ground. She wasn't going to let me anywhere before I regained a modicum of strength.

We both gasped as Riestel avoided a series of ichor fists pounding in his wake. Then he lunged upward with the help of his wings until he was eye to eye with the Queen's mortal body. My throat tightened and my heart felt like it would crack my ribs. He was completely exposed to her.

As the Queen readied her fire with a swift motion of her hand and funneled it at Riestel, Riestel reached into the ichor armor and pressed a light directly to Istrata's forehead. He grabbed her shoulder with his other hand to keep her from throwing him away. His wings became a shield for his sides to keep the ichor's blows from his body and a silvery field from his scales engulfed him and the Queen. A steady, forceful stream of lights poured into her through Riestel. It was a mesmerizing sight. A stream of stars wrapped around them like a vortex with blue flames shining from inside it.

The blue flames and the shining vortex expanded and broke out.

Dissipating into a rain of starfire. The ichor shell collapsed as Istrata's body was filled with the purest of energy. As they fell from high, Riestel had to let go of her to land properly. Istrata's body hit ground with a thud. For a moment, she laid completely still. I forgot to breathe waiting to see if this was it. Then she twitched and mirrored my position, forcing herself on her feet. I did the same. Istrata limped towards me with Riestel following her. Her ichor form melted on the rubble in the background like a pile of dirty snow. Once we faced each other, she sighed and sat down in front of me and reached her arm to touch my foot.

"Child. I yield," the Queen whispered, spent and mortal. She took my hand, drew a deep breath, and smiled. "It is here." She painfully glanced at the chrysalis that now shone like a beacon over the remaining ichor. "At last, they had true faith… Thank you for fulfilling your duty so faultlessly, and I'm truly sorry." She closed her eyes with a peaceful smile. Her hand briefly squeezed mine, and then it slid out of my grasp as she fell over.

I never expected my first reaction to her death to be tears. But there it is was. I placed the Queen's hands on her chest and wiped my eyes. Kneeling next to her lifeless body and hearing the crowd cheer and seeing the ichor gradually lose its form everywhere, dripping down from all the surfaces it had covered and becoming merely an unsightly, toxic waste, should have been a true joy and wonder to behold. All I could think of was that should I have at any point lost my faith in people around me, the Queen's path might have been mine. The thought that followed was no more comforting. I just allowed Merrie to die for nothing. If I had just killed the monster and stayed to fight her, she might be alive at this moment. The regret made me numb to the relief everyone else felt. Then, the Queen's final words made sense.

"I think I've earned a rest too, since you made me do all the hard work." Riestel sighed, looking down at Istrata's corpse. "I hope she will as well. Forever, if possible. Why are you laughing? This would be a very inappropriate moment to go mad."

I could not answer him for a good moment as I kept laughing and crying out of frustration, anger, amusement, confusion, and joy. Arid began to open the chrysalis' walls like a blossoming flower in the morning.

"She got what she wanted… She became the thing they united over. Just look at the Needle. They all cared. They set aside their perceptions of class, rivalries, likes, and whatever petty things separated them in the past and prevented them from treating each other with the smallest amount of humane courtesy. They united and opened their souls to each other."

"You are right..." Riestel said and frowned. "You don't think...that was her plan all along?"

"It might have been."

"If that was the case, my words must have hurt her plenty," Riestel said with a pained expression.

"None of us could have known. I'm not even sure she remembered it herself until the very end. Until she felt their prayer. There is nothing we should have not done to defeat her. Even if her goal was this and not what she made us believe. She could have never awoken to change course with the ichor's corruption even if she would have been able to see she was going too far."

"What now?"

"Now? Rime!" I gasped and shot up. "Tell everyone it is over now."

I jumped into the calm ichor below. There were no shadows, no creatures in it anymore. And there was no current. I swam down in the light of the scales all the way to where I remembered the doorway to be. The relief of seeing Rime in the doorway was indescribable. He sensed me and looked up. I reached my hand out to him. Rime smiled and shook his head as my hand touched his chest. A black surge of the ichor came through the portal and him. His body slumped and floated in the ichor.

I burned all the ichor from around us. Where the opening had been was nothing but a scar in the very structure of our world. The heavy plane was no more. Rime laid on the ground, hardly breathing. I turned him to his side. His eyes barely opened.

"Rime? Can you hear me?"

He nodded but couldn't speak. There was ichor running from the corner of his mouth and his ear.

"Why didn't you just wait for a moment longer? Just a moment."

"What good...would that...have done?" he asked, gasping for air.

"Well...I don't know."

"No...pain. Now."

"That's good. Please don't give up yet," I pleaded and tried to concentrate on him to burn the ichor from his channels. But there were no channels anymore. He was wholly made from the ichor. I could feel a certain amount of life force within him in this world, not enough for a soul, not by a long shot.

He was weakening with every breath. The power I felt seemed to concentrate on his heart. The odd nodule at the end of the little channel? That was it. It was his scar.

The joy of figuring it out washed away with the realization of what I would need to do. I placed my hand on Rime's cheek and stroked him with my thumb while conjuring a soft, reassuring smile on my face.

"Rime..." I began, but his name barely made it out. "I ran out of time. I'm sorry, I have to kill you. But only to try to save you. I want you to have the dream you told me about. Even if I'm not ever going to be there."

Rime's eyes opened a little more. It took a few moments before they focused on me.

"That's how...it ends," he said. "I...trust...you." His consciousness was faltering.

"I love you; I would have given the world for you." I pressed my forehead to his forehead and my hand over his heart. It was absolute agony to overcome the resistance within me to end his life. A pulse of blue flame destroyed his body in one breath. I gathered the life force he had carried and did my all to keep it intact, so it would not dissipate entirely from this world. It wrapped around my hand as I cradled it near my heart.

I felt around in the ashes until I found it—the nodule. I lifted it and blew the ashes of it. The attempt should be made in the chrysalis, as it was partly of both worlds.

"Tammaran!" I screamed.

As he stepped out by me, he froze, looking at the ashes and me.

"Is that...?" Tammaran asked as he went pale.

"What is left of his body. I have the remains of his life here. I need you to gather all who knew him. As many as you can and get them to where Arid sprouted."

"Rime's dead... I... He can't be."

"Tammaran, now! If you want him to have a chance at another life!"

Tammaran looked at me. I could feel his heart squeeze from the pain. He buried his face in his hands. It took a moment for my words to sink in, but when he realized the situation, he snapped back to his soldier mentality and wasted no time. He began gathering people as I hurried towards Arid.

Riestel helped me back into the chrysalis. He did not ask, and he did not question. Only once I sat with back against Arid's trunk did he break the silence.

"Let me help," Riestel offered. "I can share the burden with you."

"Keep him from dissipating here once I enter the lighter world."

"As you wish," Riestel agreed and began to feel out the boundaries of Rime's lingering essence. His serene demeanor and his power helped to contain Rime. It also helped to comfort and calm me so that I could think and act with more precision and intent.

As we waited, people from all walks of life started to show up to the tree. None dared to speak, so they all just gathered around us and sat down to wait in reverend silence. Each and every one focused their thoughts on their memories of Rime. Just as on his promotion evening years ago, the stories were varied with the common theme of him helping and making this city into something better.

The last to appear was Tammaran, with Samedi and Rime's dog, Ika, on their trail. I had not seen the jolly little mop for months. Rime had kept it at the barracks ever since moving to the Peak as he had wanted it to have more companionship and time than he could offer as the War Council.

"We should proceed. We can't hold his remains forever," Riestel said softly. "The energy always seeks to return to the lighter world, to carry on in the cycle."

"You are right," I said and faced the group of people.

"I presented your wish to them. They all agree to it," Tammaran explained. "We as well. Take as much as you need."

"Thank you. I had Tammaran gather you here to take a portion of your memories and your life force."

People seemed a little unnerved. Who wouldn't?

"It will not harm you permanently, but it will allow me to attempt to save the War Council from becoming nothing. It will allow me to attempt to create him a soul and reward him with a new life for all that he did for us. I will give a part of myself to this attempt as well. If any of you should not wish to partake in this, then leave now."

Not one single person moved. Then I heard a whimper.

"Oh, Ika." I sighed as the white dog leaned on my shin. "He's not here anymore, and he won't ever be here again."

Ika looked at me. It poked the nodule I still held.

"Ika, do you want to help your master, too?" I asked.

The dog tilted its head from side to side and then barked once.

"There is no way that fluffball can understand what you are asking it," Riestel said. His tone betrayed him, though. He respected the little animal.

"Ika, do you want to follow Rime?"

The dog touched the nodule again.

"Every bit counts. You are a very good little dog. Stay put if you want to help."

As Riestel held a cold shield in place that kept Rime's life force from escaping, I transferred my mind to the lighter world. I gathered the brightest, most powerful memories that connected the volunteers to Rime. I followed them all to their end and then yanked them loose from their owners. People muttered, gasped, and yelped as they felt a sudden sharp pain, but it only lasted a moment. I also took memories from myself to use. Giving them up felt like watching Rime die a second time.

Once I had enough, I focused on the nodule. It was hard to burn, but once it yielded, it revealed a deep green light. A small preserved piece of his soul tether. In the lighter world, I felt around for the scar's counterpart, and once I found it, I reopened the wound. The green light hovered over my hand, and what was left of Rime's life curled around it. His soul tether and natural connection to the lighter world gathered all the energy and then floated from my hand in the normal world to my hand in the lighter world. It had passed through the reopened scar that had formed in the lighter world where his connection had originally been cut when he had been made into an emptied soul.

I destroyed the memory strands into pure power and forced it to mix with the green light. It took days of unyielding concentration, but there it was. A soul that held all that had remained of him. It was hard to answer the question burning in everyone's mind. Was it Rime? The undestroyed memory strands that had previously just floated freely close to the scar were now fusing with it, recognizing it as the counterpart in those events. Maybe it wasn't purely him, but it carried an essence of him. Enough to say it was him.

After all these forced connections, the soul changed color from a deep green to a brighter green. It floated in the lighter world, close to me. I could see it connected to me. It sought my company. The relief was profound, but there was still one thing I needed to do for his future happiness.

"Come here," I requested, and the soul floated onto my palm. "I hope you will have the life you dreamed of. I will hold the memories I have left of you in my heart for all eternity. Go, now. Find your happiness with all the blessings a god can grant you."

I drew a small, secret sign on him for luck and protection to guard him and his line after him. The soul stayed on my hand. I shook my head and gently threw it upwards.

"It is time for you to seek out new adventures," I ordered Rime. The soul floated higher and further away. As it marveled at the choices before it, I took hold of all the remaining strands of memories, hopes, and dreams that united us and cut them from him.

"Why did you do that?" Riestel asked, having quietly observed everything. "Now, you will never know who or what he will become. And he will not recognize you should you cross each other's paths."

"That is how it should be. This life brought him nothing but tribulations and loss, a horrible decision after another. I am a part of those, and I wish nothing more for him than a fresh start. If I held onto this connection, I would be tempted to seek him out to see how he was. He will be better off without any connection to me. It would only draw us together someday, and I do not believe that the reunion would bring either nothing but sorrow in the end."

"Noble of you."

"And it is only fair to you as well. I will stay on our path as I promised. He will be a fond memory. You will be a loved reality."

XXXIX

The next sunrise and the cloudless horizon it brought with it felt surreal as I admired the scenery from the Needle's balcony amongst Arid's branches. It was all over. The resuscitation could be begun properly. I kept rubbing my left wrist to feel the bead-like burns. The idea of never seeing Rime again or talking to him did not feel real. The joy I felt having been able to save at least a little of him was thoroughly overshadowed by the longing to have him as a confidant.

Losing our romantic connection had been tolerable torture, but the pain I felt now was like phantom pain. Like I would have lost a part of myself. I had never realized how much I truly had depended on Rime. I kept thinking he'd come through the door at any moment and scold me for not taking care of my current duties. Hiding away like an irresponsible little annoyance.

The fact that I had severed ties to his soul made my heart spasm every time I thought about it. Yet, the feeling was the exact reason why I had done it. If I had not, I would now be tempted to find him in the lighter world, I would be tempted to seek him out in his next life, and the pain would just carry on through decades, like Riestel's agony with Istrata. If I sought him, I might ruin his chance to get his dream life that he had spoken about with such longing. A simple, good life. No rulers and gods trying to mess up everyone's day.

Avoiding everyone for a few days seemed to calm me. Being among the living, grieving, and celebrating was not something I was ready for. Only Riestel was allowed here for now.

"Do you want news, or are we completely ignoring the outer world?" he asked as he stepped into the Heart's version of the Needle. It was easier to hide here than in the human world.

"Tell me."

"The King is dead."

"Frazil died? When? Was it because of the heavier world collapsing?"

"I would wager so. Apparently, around the same time as his son. They are lighting his funeral pyre in a moment."

"Which one is it?"

"The biggest one, obviously."

"Right, silly question," I admonished myself. Finally, I understood Rime's adamant refusal to bring me to my other child. He had always known closing the heavier world would kill them all. Now, I only grieved the idea of having a child, but not the child itself. It was a kind cruelty, after all.

"Can I console you in any way?" Riestel asked and hugged me.

"Just being here is enough," I answered and closed my eyes. "I am healing."

"Good. Listen...Moras and his students began sampling the Peak and the city after the battles to find out how bad the corruption is. A lot of the ichor went into the very structures of this place."

"It is bad, is it not? I can feel it."

"Mostly unlivable for those who need food. We will have to find them new places to live. The city should be abandoned. And soon, before the winter sets in."

"Tell Samedi there is a map in Rime's office that has the locations for the last holy places of this world. They will need to travel to those to survive."

"They?"

"Yes. I will stay here to rid the place of all remains of people and the ichor."

Riestel went quiet and frowned. I knew he was torn between Elona and me.

"Do you not want to travel with them?" he asked.

"Want to? Of course, I want to. And yet, my duty will keep me here, in the Heart. I will cut the entire contaminated area off from the rest of the world so no one can reach it for as long as it is unsuitable for life. After that...who knows? I might travel the world a bit to see what has happened in the few lifetimes that will have passed."

"Alright. I certainly do not mind getting you all to myself. Right, Tammaran asked me to tell you that they will hold a memorial for Rime tonight if you wish to participate. The entire city is nothing but funeral pyres and rites to honor the dead... Still, it might do you good."

"I will attempt it."

Stepping out from the Heart of Creation felt strange. The normal world felt like a mirage, something not quite real. Yet the emotions and the destruction could hardly be avoided or claimed untrue. Samedi and Tammaran were now the only ones alive from Rime's guard. They had gathered all their gear for the pyre. As there were no bodies to burn, they would simply offer tokens of respect and gratitude to the flames.

Veitso's memorial pyre burned next to Merrie's a little to the side. Samedi was unnerved by the fact he had survived and not Veitso. He had never thought of that option. No one seemed to know when or how Veitso and Merrie had died, as their bodies were never found. That was the fate for many who had partaken in the battle. I could not bring myself to tell them the story. It would only add to our grief.

We all sat there until the next morning, greeting the cold ashes. For the next few days, the city was in a stupor. Everyone just rested and mourned. Then, people began to realize they had no King or War Council. Samedi and Tammaran were able to hold the reins, with Riestel backing them up in front of people. The worst problem, however, was the realization that the land here was damaged beyond suitable for a settlement to exist. The winter would be here in full force in three moons; a new place needed to be found before that.

Samedi took on the administrative responsibilities of everything. Tammaran saw to the execution. All horses and animals were gathered in the Harbor and the largest gate out of the city. Most remaining food stores and other necessities were packed and delivered there as well. Slowly, the Peak became empty and abandoned. At first, it was a blessing, as I needed the peace and quiet, but the more days passed, the less delighted I was.

"We are about to leave," Tammaran announced after he knocked on the Needle's door and came in with Arvida.

"Already? I guess that is for the best."

"Everything is packed for the road. We have the map you provided of the sanctuaries. We will begin from the closest and make our way until we find a place to settle," Tammaran explained.

"Are you sure you will not come with?" Arvida asked.

"I will not. I belong here for now. There is plenty of work to keep me busy here. It will be a few decades, at least, until this place is suitably recovering from the ichor spewed on it. I will miss you horribly."

"Come and visit, at least. You can do that, can you not?" Arvida pressed and gave me a big hug.

"Maybe. We will see. There is so much to heal here. Not even to heal. I need to destroy all the ichor before that can happen. The ichor resting on the surface is easy, but it has permeated the ground and all life here. It will take precision and time."

"Are you sure you do not want to keep some staff?" Tammaran checked.

"For what? Their fate here could be a slow, uncomfortable starvation. I will be fine."

"At least you will have Riestel to keep company." Arvida smiled. "Will you allow the temple's volunteers to stay? They have been pestering me for days about your answer. They want to serve you in any way you see fit. I would like to give them the answer before we go."

"They can stay. Just make sure they understand that I am not inviting them to stay. If they stay for their own reasons to support me, I will welcome them. But they will mostly be on their own. You should go now. Let's not drag this out. And please, watch out for Elona."

"We will raise her as if she was our own," Arvida promised. "She will not lack a family."

"Thank you."

We embraced once more, and then they left. Tammaran and Arvida would lead the people traveling by land to seek a new home. Samedi would take the ships that were still in working order and could accommodate enough supplies and people. Watching them stream out of the city and the ships growing ever smaller after they passed the bullhorn-like squeeze of the bay was bittersweet.

Riestel walked next to me on the balcony. His eyes were fixed on the wagons.

"You can go," I whispered.

"Go? What do you mean?"

"With Elona. Live this lifetime as a human still. Let her have her father."

Riestel turned to look at me, and his eyes welled up. There was no doubt in my mind that he would regret it always if he stayed now.

"You would allow that? After everything I put you through and everything you lost?"

"You love her."

"There is no less love in my heart for you than for her."

"Yes, but I can wait a lifetime. She cannot. Go. You will catch up with them easily still. And you can keep them safe better than anyone."

"I don't know how to say goodbye to you."

"You don't. You will simply promise to meet me here, where we were born, when she no longer needs you."

"I will return. You know I will."

"There is no doubt in my mind. One thing: do not dare to take a wife," I added. "If you do, I will burn her on your wedding night."

"Never. I will visit you when I can."

"Good."

"How can I leave you?" Riestel asked quietly and kissed me.

"In the night, while I sleep, if you are merciful. Otherwise, I will cry, and there will be no end to it."

"Then we must get you to bed," Riestel whispered. "A new dawn awaits."

EPILOGUE

Father always regaled me with his stories of her. My mother's copy. The mother I knew more than the one who gave birth to me. The last time I saw her, she was no longer one of us. She was all fire and spark with wings that could burn us all. And yet, she was the one to give us all hope.

There are those who praise her still, and those who already fear her. For ever since we travelled to this new home, the horizon has been ablaze with all the hues of fire. It did not cease for months as we travelled. I still remember it. Now, we are so far, we cannot see but a faint glimpse of it at night when the sun sleeps.

Father and aunt Arvida told me of the city often. I only retain a few memories of my time there. Our life is very different here. We work the little land that is left in tribes scattered across the vast world. But with each passing year, we see the earth revive a little more. The crops are more bountiful and the animals gain fat. We can spend more time building amenities and rebuild our culture.

The last time father went to visit her, she was resting for the first time. He told me she was surrounded by a guard of green. A group of fiercely loyal people who stayed to keep her temple alive and to rebuild it to serve her. A mix of humans and arochs. Father calls them brave idiots, but I think he is grateful to them for being there when he could not. I hear him talk to her when he is alone, when he thinks no one is looking or hears him. I hope she does somehow, because the things he says and promises to the evening wind are too beautiful to go to waste.

I feel a certain guilt, as he stayed all these years for me. But without him, we would not have these lands to sustain us as well as they do. After uncle

Tammaran and aunt Arvida died of old age, I took over with their sons. I have now served the people for three lifetimes as their council. My progeny is well equipped enough to take over, and as they are all blessed or cursed with this gift of an extended life, I hope they will prove steadfast and wise enough for the task.

Finally, I feel old age setting in, and I welcome it and the freedom it will bring my father. As he talks to her now, I will talk to him in prayer, if I am granted a new life. The world will heal, and I cannot wait to see it anew.

HI THERE!

Thank you for reading my book and making it all the way to end of the series! It means so much to me that you took a chance on someone unknown and their story.

Please consider leaving a review or a star rating if you liked the story. Reviews are the only way I can know if there are people out there who like my writing. If you can't leave a review, you can always say hi to me via my blog at https://strandsofexistence.blogspot.com/.

ACKNOWLEDGEMENT

Nicholas – for being kind enough to step in as the editor for the last part of the series and delivering very toughtfull comments.

STRANDS OF EXISTENCE

This series is a four-part fantasy series chronicling Istrae Elona's life and how she acts as a catalyst to bring about change and sometimes chaos. After this book, there will be one more. Island Girl First book in the series. Sea of Shadows Second book in the series.

Island Girl

Sea Of Shadows

King Of Nought

Cloudless Horizon

Printed in Great Britain
by Amazon

37069470R00169